blue
rider
press

G-MAN

ALSO BY STEPHEN HUNTER

Point of Impact

Black Light

Time to Hunt

The 47th Samurai

Night of Thunder

I, Sniper

Dead Zero

The Third Bullet

Sniper's Honor

Hot Springs

Pale Horse Coming

Havana

Dead Zero

Soft Target

The Master Sniper

The Second Saladin

Tapestry of Spies

The Day Before Midnight

Dirty White Boys

I, Ripper

G-MAN

A BOB LEE SWAGGER NOVEL

STEPHEN HUNTER

Blue Rider Press • New York

blue
rider
press

An imprint of Penguin Random House LLC
375 Hudson Street
New York, New York 10014

Library of Congress Cataloging-in-Publication Data

Names: Hunter, Stephen, 1946- author.
Title: G-man : a Bob Lee Swagger novel / Stephen Hunter.
Description: New York : Blue Rider Press, [2017] | Series: Bob Lee Swagger
Identifiers: LCCN 2016050117 (print) | LCCN 2016058089 (ebook) |
ISBN 9780399574603 (hardcover) | ISBN 9780399574627 (Ebook)
Subjects: LCSH: Swagger, Bob Lee (Fictitious character)—Fiction. | Family
secrets—Fiction. | Snipers—Fiction. | BISAC: FICTION / Suspense. |
FICTION / Thrillers. | FICTION / Mystery & Detective / Traditional
British. | GSAFD: Suspense fiction.
Classification: LCC PS3558.U494 G23 2017 (print) | LCC PS3558.U494 (ebook) |
DDC 813/.54—dc23
LC record available at https://lccn.loc.gov/2016050117

Printed in the United States of America
1   3   5   7   9   10   8   6   4   2

BOOK DESIGN BY LUCIA BERNARD

Thus speaketh the red judge: "Why did this criminal commit murder?
He meant to rob." I tell you, however,
that his soul wanted blood, not booty:
he thirsted for the happiness of the knife!

—Nietzsche, *Thus Spake Zarathustra*

Baby face
You've got the cutest little baby face
There's not another one could take your place
You baby face

—Popular song by Harry Akst and Benny Davis, 1926

For the late John Carroll
Great newspaperman, great guy

G-MAN

PRELUDE

EAST OF BLUE EYE, ARKANSAS

The present

THE BLADES OF THE GRADERS contoured the land to spec. They rounded hills, felled and flattened woods, scoured underbrush, crushed rocks, filled hollows, collapsed ravines. Nothing but raw earth remained. What had been complex became plain, according to the latest large-project construction principles. Streets had been staked out, while sewers and wiring and cable were planted in furrows. Then the houses would spring up, rows of them, all alike, but soon to be differentiated by their new owners. It was progress—or, at least, development—it was growth, it was capitalism, it was hope. It couldn't be stopped, so mourning was pointless.

This land had sustained one family for more than two centuries, first claimed in the late 1780s by a quiet couple from over the mountains, where the war was just finishing. They gave no account of themselves. They and theirs stayed for seven generations, and for that whole time they were steady, solid; they went to church, they gave to charity, they did their share in emergency or crisis. But more, it turned out they were a family of heroes. Their boys learned to shoot; they learned the hunter's patience, his stoicism, his courage, his mercy, his honor. They had a gift for the firearm, and more than a few of them took that gift off to war. Some made it back, some didn't. Some became officers of the law, for in those days that too called for the shooter's talent. They shot for blood many a time, and, again, some made it back and some didn't.

They were all gone now. The last of them had sold off the place for a substantial amount and fled, not wanting to see what was done to his home-stead and the homestead of his ancestors.

Now the contouring was all but finished. Only the old house remained, atop a hillock that dominated the spread, a comfortable, rambling joint that had been added to over the decades until it practically made no sense at all. The hill was too much for the graders and so the company brought in a big Cat excavator, the 326F L model, a machine classified medium by weight, and set it loose, under the guidance of a professional genius named Ralph.

From afar, it looked like some kind of Jurassic ritual. A yellow Tyran-nosaurus rex had downed a Bronto or a Stegosaurus and now fed on soft underbelly. The knuckle boom of Ralph's big Cat pierced and ripped and tore, its bucket armed with side cutters and teeth, taking down walls and floors swiftly, in a single day reducing what had been a large house to a large pile of rubble. The next day, using the bucket as an artist would a brush, Ralph cleared the shattered remnants of two centuries' worth of history, loading them into the trucks, which hauled them off to the landfill. Fi-nally, on the third day, only the foundation remained, and he directed the bucket to continue its feast of destruction, smashing the stones into smaller chunks, then scooping them up for disposal. It was all going according to plan—until it wasn't.

The managers saw him stop, pop the big machine out of gear, turn off its hydraulics, then leap from the yellow house, dash along the tread and swing down off the boom, pass under the knuckle, and reach the bucket, which was frozen in place on a particularly large chunk of foundation that would not shatter according to plan.

They approached and swiftly became an inspection committee.

"Something wrong, Ralph?"

"You didn't bust a pump or lose a piston?"

"Did you spring a hydraulic leak there, Ralph?"

Of course all this really meant but one thing: how much is this going to cost us?

But Ralph was on his knees, studying on the joinery between the bucket's teeth—those hard T. rex fangs—and earth.

"I felt something," he said. "You know, you get so you can read the vibrations. It wasn't stone, dirt, pipe—nothing like that."

He poked, prodded, messed around with a spade.

"What'd it feel like?" he was asked.

"Some kind of metal. I don't know, a sheet or a—"

He stopped, spotting something, leapt forward, examined more closely, inserted the shovel's blade, dug, pried, cleared, sought leverage, and finally, with a spray of dirt like an explosion, exposed something from the Great Beneath.

"Jesus," he said, now pulling the treasure free, "it's a strongbox of some kind."

It was, looking like the sort of thing carried by Wells Fargo and subject to larceny by men in dusters and hats, with bandannas across their faces and Winchesters in their hands.

The committee gathered around. Curiosity now overcame their need, if only for a bit, to stay on schedule.

"Maybe it's full of gold," somebody remarked.

Ralph, whose genius was practical, not speculative, smacked at the padlock a few times with his spade, expertly driving the corner tip of its blade under the locking hasp, and the hasp's old metal couldn't bear the spike in pressure and broke open on the third blow.

The committee gathered closer as he tossed the busted lock away and pulled the lid back on the strongbox's rusted hinges.

The contents were initially disappointing. A number of objects wrapped tightly in heavy canvas, loosely secured by disintegrating tape, their outlines muffled by the heavy swaddling. Ralph popped a Kershaw knife from the pocket of his jeans, where it had been clipped, cut the tape, and used the point of the blade to push through the mass of canvas. It gave way to an oily cloth wrapping, under which the thing, shed of its canvas raiments, assumed a familiar shape. At last, he got this final oily wrapping away from it and held it out, gleaming in the sun, for all to see.

"It's a damned pistol," he proclaimed.

"It's an old .45 automatic," someone who knew said.

"Old?" someone else said. "Hell, it looks brand-new!"

They were otherwise stunned into silence. Finally someone said, "Man, I bet that bad boy has a story to tell."

PART I

1

WASN'T MUCH. Wasn't a thing, really. Trees, an abundance of them, all green and dense, so thick you couldn't see the forest for them. And closer in, the road. Gravel, not important enough to wear so important a name as Highway 154. That sounded like, well, civilization, and out here, in the boondocks of the boondocks, wasn't civilization, just gravel and trees?

Charles anchored the line. Captain Frank put him there because he wanted boys he trusted at key spots. Frank wasn't the sort to leave much to chance, which is why, fifty-one men later, he was still alive (though he'd been hit seventeen times). So that is why Charles sat in full man-hunting stillness in the bush, twenty feet from the gravel. Next to him, though invisible, was the Dallas policeman Ted Hinton with a big Browning gun, and then some of the Louisiana boys (Charles hadn't caught their names), then Manny Gault, another trusted friend of the captain's, another Louisiana fellow, and finally, anchoring the other end, the captain himself. They all sat or crouched, aspiring to different styles of stillness and silence, clearly men on the stalk, though some were born to it and others merely pretending they knew what they were up to. A cough, a slap at a mosquito, a hawked gob of phlegm, a scratched itch, a shuffle, all muted, kept in close, all of them with hats at ears and brims nearly to eyes, after what most guessed and some knew was the gunman's style.

You'd have thought this posse was off on a raid in the Great War, so heavily armed it was, and Charles should know, having led many a raid in the Great War. Then, as now, he had a .45 Government Model in a shoulder holster, but not as then a Model 97 short-barreled Winchester riot gun leaning next to the tree and another of Mr. Browning's fine creations, a semi-auto Model 8 in .35 caliber, in his hands. It held five big rounds and could be fired quick, as the trigger went back on it, a skill that took some practice, though with Charles's gift for the firearm, not as much practice as with some others.

But Charles would have been fearsome without the hardware. He was a tall man, seemingly assembled from blades. He was forty-three, had a hard, long, angular blade of a body, a blade of a nose, two cheekbones that looked as if they could cut steel, and was long everywhere else, arms, fingers, legs, even toes. If you could meet his eyes—few could—they were black anthracite, and when they fixed and narrowed on something, that something was about to get a hole in it. Though it would be another hot, airless, dusty Louisiana day—a July day by Arkansas standards, an August day by Chicago or Washington standards—he wore a three-piece suit of thick gray wool herringbone, a black tie cinched tight, as it always was, a sheriff's star on his lapel, and a pair of brown high-top boots. A brown felt fedora was pulled low on his face, as if to shield the world from the force of his eyes. He looked like a funeral director, which was close, as he was really a funeral provider.

"See anything there, Sheriff?" came a softly phrased question through the bush. Hinton, who couldn't stay true to manhunt discipline and had squirmed and chattered the last few hours as if he were on the beach or at the bar.

"Not a goddamned thing," said Charles.

Another of Charles's freakish attributes was his vision, held by all to be unusually sharp. It was perhaps the key to his shooting, and it was another reason the captain wanted him farthest out. His job wasn't merely to shoot well but to see well; the captain counted on him to catch a whisper of dust from a long distance to announce that a car was coming, about to crest a low hill, under the guidance of a fast and skillful driver, which would mean the commencement of the day's work and the conclusion of a long and grueling ordeal.

Charles scanned for dust again, saw no disturbance in the atmosphere, and wondered if this one was going to go south like all the other ambushes. This pair of peckerwoods was hard to figure because they were such creatures of childish whimsy, going here and there as the mood took them. It was like hunting not sparrows but a particular pair of sparrows, trying to guess where they'd be when the sparrow brain was not advanced enough to encompass any notion of the future.

"Maybe we ought to pull tail. Could use me a nice iced tea. My mouth's full of dust 'n' grit."

"You just hold still," said Charles. "The captain gives the orders and we sit until he tells us we don't sit no more."

He scanned again. Trees, trees, trees. Across the gravel road, an old truck and an old man. But it was all ambush theater, a decoy to bring in the scrawny sparrows. The truck was on a jack and its tire lay in the middle of the gravel. The old man lounged on the running board. His name was Ivy and he was father to a boy who ran with the pip-squeaks. All this was happening by arrangement with and through him. In exchange for getting his boy Henry off on certain Texas charges, the old man had volunteered to keep the man hunters up on the ramblings of the outlaw pair and to act as tethered goat in the actual ambush if it came.

Charles was an Arkansawyer. He was hero of the Great War in two armies, one Canadian, one American. He was the winner of the famous First National of Blue Eye Gunfight in 1923, when he had killed three city boys with heavy guns who'd wanted to take a small-town bank for liquor money. He was the father of two boys, each one more of a mystery than the other. He was the sheriff of Polk County, Arkansas. He was here in secret at the captain's request because the captain felt gun time was near and he wanted men with him who'd done the work before and none were better at it than Sheriff Charles F. Swagger.

It was about then, getting on to 9 a.m., he saw it. Just a trace of drift against a far-off green wall of trees, nothing really there, but to his sharp vision, it was bold as a dancing girl.

"Car bearing this way, coming down fast."

"Yes sir," said Ted, with a slight tweak to his voice indicating a spurt of emotion, and he heard Ted turn and say, "Coming in. Coming in. Get yourselves ready."

For just a second it sounded like they were in a factory, not on the edge of the woods. That was because of clicks, clacks, whacks, cranks, and snaps— all gun business. Safeties came off, bolts were released, slides thrown, levers and pump actions jacked to lift .30-30s or twelve-gauge buck into chambers. There was probably also, if you listened close enough, the low hiss of breath, sucked hard into lungs for the enriching force of the oxygen, being now expelled as each man, seeing action on the come, tried to breathe his way toward control of the yips that coursed through hands and arms and the fear that suddenly lubricated each thought and breath. Lots of guns would be fired, lots of lead in the air, and no one could predict with any certainty what would happen yet.

"Ivy, get your goddamned old scrawny ass up and start dinking with the jack" came the captain's order to his tethered old goat, and the old man stood, his face suddenly acquiring the gravity of its own fear, and then hustled over to the jack and pretended to be making adjustments.

"You boys, now, you wait to my command while I check to see when Ivy breaks free of our line of fire," the captain explained casually, he and Charles the only two among them whose heartbeat hadn't increased a thump. "And then again, maybe it ain't them, only the Baptist minister up to say words over a dead Negro. We don't need no Mexican hat dance like them federals at Little Bohemia."

No one wanted that: the wrong people shot and killed or wounded, federal officers downed, and all gangsters gotten away into the cold Midwestern night. It was a famous fiasco, a warning for all who carried steel, lead, and a badge.

Sounds now of men squirming in the brush, acquiring a tension-engineered shooting position. Most chose to go to one knee, some tucking foot under ass. A slouchy feed bag like Frank probably didn't think too much of such a thing and just made himself comfortable. Charles went into an athlete's crouch, because he would be the only one breaking cover. His job, now that the early sighting was done, was to rotate around the vehicle to get shots in from the quarter angle, then close and finish the job with his Government Model if needed. If by some strange chance either bad one made it out of the car on this side, Charles would handle the last applications of rough justice, issuing quick dispatch. His long finger went to the safety lever of the Model 8, which was a gigantic thing (another reason your gun-savvy peace officers liked it, as it required no fumbling with a nubbin of a button when lead filled the air), and slid it smoothly down. He tucked the rifle under his shoulder and coiled the necessary muscles to break from cover, circle fast and low behind, and come up on the other side.

Now it was Ted Hinton's show. He was a car expert and always up on the latest Detroit issue. As soon as details became clear, Ted would know if it was a 1934 Cordoba-gray V-8 Ford 730 DeLuxe. That seemed to be the car—these folks traded up whenever it was possible as the fellow was, like Ted, a fan of Detroit's latest—which would be the final go-ahead. Then it fell to them to halt at Old Man Ivy's flat tire to give assistance that would put them flat in the beaten zone that the captain had laid out.

Charles watched it come. The car pulled a screen of dust behind it, for the boy behind the wheel knew what he was doing and was good at it, loving the roar of the engine, the buzz of the vibrations, the smell of the gasoline. The car was gray, all right, and as sleek as Mr. Ford could turn out, a blur as it unzipped the dust off the still gravel bed, now and then dipping out of sight but never able to escape the marker of its roiling signature.

"That's it, by god!" screamed Ted, way too loud, for a bubble of excitement in his lungs had pushed his voice up a register and he signified the end of his sentence with a loud, involuntary gulp as he swallowed excess spit and saliva.

"On my shot," the captain reminded, and at that, the car—its occupants having now seen Old Man Ivy and his tire-distress diorama—had gone to gentle brake and begun its slowdown as it drew near. It was a hundred feet, fifty feet, twenty-five, and then, as close as the end of his nose, it scooted by Charles, slow enough for him to see the slouch of the boy driving it. Lord God, he was smallish. Looked like Our Gang, scrawny, cowlicks pointing this way and that, but, wanting to be grown-ups, all dressed out in grown-up clothes, even to his cinched-tight Sunday-school tie.

As the car eased to a halt, Charles stepped out, low, to get to his duty position, hearing the boy yell through the window in a surprisingly mellow voice, "Say there, Dad Ivy, what's the problem?"

So Charles had his head cranked down the left side of the vehicle when all the shooting commenced. There was a first shot, but the second and third and fourth, out to the hundred fiftieth, came on so strong, like a blizzard wind, there was no sense of independence to the notes. Ted's Browning gun was closest to Charles, thus loudest, manufacturing hell in the form of noise, flash, and lead. Ted just dumped the mag, loosing all twenty .30-06s in about a second, and possibly even hit the target a time or so. Meanwhile, wincing, Charles had a glimpse as the other five all opened up, and he could see the lead in the air, not palpably as singular objects but as a kind of wavering disturbance, as it sped through and pushed the atmosphere aside in its hunger to strike flesh. The wind of lead blew straight from the cemetery into the vehicle and through it, and where the bullets struck—seemed to be everywhere at once—they lit into the car hard, banging it, causing it to wobble, ripping and twisting the metal to slivers and craters, powdering the glass into diamond spray, all the damage heaped on in what seemed but a fraction of the first second.

Charles continued his scuttle, came up just at the right rear fender and got a good look into the cab at the two kids. They lounged behind a smear of fracture that occluded the windshield, smoke rising from themselves but also from it seemed a dozen punctures in the car's dashboard, and they were festooned with metal shards torn from the Ford body, dusted with the atoms of glass where the windows were blown out and had the stillness of the death that already afflicted them. They had that rag-doll look that the dead find so comfortable, all akimbo and beyond caring, on the loll and only obedient to gravity.

But at that moment, by the rule of farce, a dead foot must have fallen from the brake pedal, and even as the men in the brush were slamming reloads into their now empty hot guns, the car began to creep ahead.

In a move that was pure gunman's instinct, Charles threw the rifle to his shoulder to find the front sight just where it should be—that is, sharp and clear against the fuzzier outline of the boy's head slumped back against the seat—and with an unconsciously perfect trigger pull, he fired a big .35 through the glass, hazing it to spiderweb for a dead-center hit, knocking bone fragments and brain spew everywhere; then, even coming off the stout recoil, he rotated and put a second one into the back of the seat on the other side, against which, dead or alive, the girl had to slump, and where it hit, it kicked up a big cloud of dust and debris, to add to the toxins afloat in the air.

By this time the deputies had gotten their pieces reloaded or picked up new ones, and as the car drifted slowly down the road, they came out of the brush, gun-crazed, and launched another but completely pointless fusillade, rocking and ripping the car still more. Only Captain Frank did not participate, for he knew the day's business was finished.

The car came to a rest on the left side of the road, pitched toward but not quite in a ditch. It looked like a piece of metallic lace, a Ford doily, so penetrated and violated by the firepower spent against it. Smoke still rose from the engine and some whispered from the interior, where the corpses, still warm to the touch, lay. Meanwhile, a fog of burned powder and carbon residue crept heavily about everything, bringing tears to eye and bitterness to tongue and dust to lips.

The boys approached and peered in at their handiwork, though Charles had little curiosity, as he'd seen much of such human ruination in his life of duty. A man shot through the center of the forehead looks the same, whether in a trench in France or a Ford V-8 motorcar in Louisiana.

"They ain't goin' nowhere," someone said.

"No siree. Them eggs is broke."

"Don't look so big now."

"Ain't nothing but kids. Little wet rats, or dogs. Chipmunks, maybe."

"Looks like we done killed little Spanky," said another. "Only thing left is the haircut."

"The boy ain't wearin' no shoes."

"Sure tore-up. Musta hit 'em a thousand times."

Charles knew it to be so: it was death for Bonnie and Clyde.

A FEW MINUTES HAD PASSED, as the men eased themselves into coolness from the heat of the shooting and the frenzy. Lassitude now came over them, and nobody felt like doing much though there was much to be done. Someone had to head back to Gibsland and make the phone calls. And get the circus rolling. Someone had to pull all the guns from the shattered car, and from a quick look-see, it had been confirmed the two bandits traveled ready to take on an army. But all that was still in the future.

"Make sure you boys all get a good look," said Captain Frank. "Go on, git close and memorize the details. See what we done here today. You don't want to think back in twenty years and realize you never got a look. And if you have any doubts about shooting first, take a gander at the two shotguns Clyde had next to his legs and the .45 on Bonnie's lap. Give 'em the chance and they'd have gone down hard and taken as many of us with 'em as they could point a muzzle at."

Then he came over to Charles and drew him aside.

"Sure you don't want to be part of this, Charles? It's going to be a famous gunfight in its time, even if it was just like hosing out a steel drum. You have a chance here to step into legend. Can't hurt none. The newspapers loved these two ever since they seen that picture of the gal with a cheroot."

"Nah," said Charles. "Thanks, Frank, but it ain't to my taste. Besides, the Arkansas people want their sheriff at home, doing his job, locking up drunks, not out on ambuscade with Frank Hamer."

"Okay, we'll keep your name out of the papers. You're steady through it all, Charles. As I said before, if there's going to be lead thrown, I want Charles Swagger on my side."

2

L ORD GOD, how did I last this long?

He was old, so old. He was seventy-one. Better off than most, but not so lucky as others, he did feel diminished in small ways. The nightmares were worse, even if sleep harder to come by and, in the morning, harder to shake. Seemed always cold too, dammit, after a life spent in largely hot places. Each joint had its own separate melody of pains, aches, squeaks, cracks, and pops. He'd had a hip replacement recently for the third time and it had healed up just fine, and was his strongest, smoothest-operating pulley now. It was like an old enemy becoming a new friend. Stiffness came and went, and when it decided to visit, it was a plague, gnawing him everywhere, like a tribe of rats. It turned his first few steps, infirm and crazed in balance, into a comedy of lurching and grunting to stay upright. That wasn't all: he dropped things too, all the time, but by the time he dropped them, he'd forgotten what he'd picked them up for in the first place. He fell, not a lot, but now and then. Hadn't broke anything yet, but in downtown Boise last year he went down hard on his left arm, and if the doc said it wasn't broken, it sure pretended to be for three months afterward.

The air still tasted good, though. He'd sometimes breathe in deep, suck as much down as possible, just glorying in the hard, cold rush against his lungs, feeling them inflate gloriously, and that was a pleasure and a half.

Other pleasure: old friends. A loyal wife who refused to take him too seriously or be shocked by what he said. Two kids flourishing as adults, and the youngest, his stepdaughter, off at some place in the East called Princeton. She was a smart one, that girl.

And the money. He'd gotten rich—rich, at least by non-oil standards—which meant warmth and provision against the cold and enough money left over for ammo. He had seven layup barns in four states, and affiliations with more than three dozen large-animal veterinarians across those states. Partly it was based on the rumor that he'd been a marine hero (true), but mainly it was because he never had any energy for chicanery, and told the truth in the simplest terms possible, and people out here seemed to like that. More, after resisting for years and years, he'd finally sold the hunk of land his people had lived on and off of in Arkansas for more than two centuries, since some fellow and his pregnant wife had come over the mountains at the tail end of the Revolutionary War. The land he'd acquired and added to over the years sure paid off for the seventh-removed grandson. Bob had never thought of it as an investment, just a hunk of his past of which he couldn't quite let go. But an investment it sure turned out to be: the money it brought in was substantial—more than substantial. It meant he could afford all sorts of cool things now, the only problem being that he didn't want them anymore.

So now there was only one question left and it was: what happens from now until?

So far, nothing.

Enough had happened, he supposed, and so nothing was just fine. Nothing meant a three-hour ride on land that was all his, another hour of horse care, then three or four hours in his shop working on this or that rifle project (this year: .375 CheyTac at over thirty-five hundred yards, and, damn, if he didn't own over thirty-five hundred yards' worth of Idaho on which to find out what it could do). Then on to the email thing, for conversations with old friends the world over, including reporters and retired sergeants, Russian gangsters, Japanese Self-Defense Forces NCOs, FBI agents, a thousand or so former marines, relatives of the too many dead he had loved and seen die, and such forth and so on. It was just fine. Except that it wasn't.

"You need something," his wife said. "You were never one for aimlessness. Give Swagger a mission and he's the best there is. Let him drift and he'll end up in the drunk tank."

"I have a mission," he said. "I mean to wear out the rockers on this damned chair."

He might just make it too. Day in, day out, the magic hour, five to six, he sat and rocked on the porch, watched the changes come to the prairie, the seasons change, the mountains in the distance acquire and shed their snow, the leaves swirl and disappear and then magically regenerate six months later. Sometimes there was ice and wind, sometimes mellow breezes and the smell of summer flowers. The wind was persistent, the deer and the antelope played, and the skies were cloudy most days, but in the good way of showing off towers of fanciful architecture, full of turrets and bridges and secret passageways, all lit to glowing by the sun as it settled toward the horizon. It was all good. Really, it was.

I don't need a thing, he told himself. My life is finished, my accomplishments accomplished, I am too old to do a damned thing but watch my children and my estate grow, even if none of the kids seemed yet to notice a considerable sum would come their way.

But she would not buy it.

"Not something dangerous, not with the guns or anything. You've been shot at a lot and mostly missed."

When she said "mostly," every one of the little squibs of scar tissue he wore like chain mail across his pelt perked up and issued a communiqué.

"But a goal, a thing to do, that would give you pleasure in the work and in the finishing, that would tie a bow on it, and so you could meet your father up there and him saying, 'You did me honor.'"

"I am too old and too tired to start anything new."

"You feel old and tired because you have nothing new to do, not in spite of it. Find the project and you will find the energy."

"I've seen enough of the world. Besides, the airports these days are like refugee camps."

"No travel. I think you should write a book."

"Oh, that's a good one. My grammar breaks down every ten minutes and I revert to mountain English and you want me to write a book?"

"Any man who can use 'revert' in a sentence can write a book."

"Nobody's interested in my stuff. If they's interested, they wouldn't believe it. If they believed it, they'd arrest me. I'm lucky as it is to be on this side of the iron bars with all my enemies dead and all my debts, money and justice, paid in full. It's time to settle back and read some books, not write one."

"I was thinking of what has given you the most pleasure over the past few years, apart from your children. And that is when you got back from Russia and you and Reilly had dug out the truth about that woman sniper and what a hero she was. That made you happy."

"Still does," he said, because it did. "She's a real hero, not a lucky phony like me, she deserves the glory. Now she's got her face on a Russian stamp, and she's the subject of Reilly's book. Yep, that one still feels good. But . . . You have to say, it was a stroke of luck Reilly finding her. Don't think I'm going to run into that one again."

"My idea: your father. He was a great man. You love him still. His story needs to be told. Sheriff's son in dirt-poor Arkansas, goes on to be a five-invasion marine and receive the Medal of Honor at Iwo Jima, has some other adventures you've only heard about as legend, then dies tragically young in a cornfield, shot down by a punk in a T-shirt and Elvis sideburns."

That wasn't quite the truth, but it would do.

"I don't think I could do that," he said.

"You have marine connections still so you'd have no problem getting that information. You have an Arkansas lawyer from old gentry in Jake Vincent, and he is very well connected. He could open those few doors that the Swagger name alone wouldn't. You could find old folks—"

"There are folks older than me?"

"—old folks, pick up rumors, memories, old photos. You could read. The libraries have dozens of historical manuscripts that no one has ever looked at. I think it would be fascinating. Plus, you're good at that. Pattern recognition, smart deductions, re-creating imaginatively what did happen, as opposed to what everyone believes happened. When you're done, or sort of done, maybe then Reilly would know an actual writer who'd put all the information into prose."

"It don't feel right, somehow. I mean, dammit, it doesn't feel right."

"You're scared. Swagger—scared of no man and no force on earth. But scared of this."

"That's right. Nothing back there but bad news. But it's not just my father, Earl. It's his father, Charles, the sheriff. He's the mystery. Another gunman. He's the scary one."

It was so true. The Swaggers, on back over the years, men with guns. And the men of the last three generations, Charles, his son Earl and his son Bob, they had it in spades and were, each of them, defined by war. Throw in Bob's son, Ray, now at the FBI, defined by the War on Terror in the world's brutal sandboxes. That made four straight. They all had it, that Swagger singularity that set them apart, curse or blessing, as circumstances dictated. Who knew where it came from, that odd gift to take a firearm, understand it, and make the first shot count—always.

But it was Charles, the grandfather of Bob, the father of Earl, who was the strangest of them all. He was a hero in the Great War, and came back to Polk and put his skill to work as a deputy and then became the sheriff of the county. But it seemed the man didn't want anyone knowing his business, anyone poking about. He was solitary, a figure of rectitude and distance, blazing good with the gun but otherwise not a chum, a pal, a buddy, a laugher, a storyteller. He just stood for pure force, and his reputation alone, especially after a 1923 shoot-out with three Little Rock hotshots called the Warrens (final score: the sheriff, 3; the Warren brothers, 0), kept most bad boys out of Polk. Death was too sure a thing at the speedy hand of the sheriff.

But—the stories were unclear, always blurry, ever-shifting—something persisted that carried the information that Charles had turned not just drunk and mean and surly but against the law he enforced. In 1940, there'd been a train robbery in Hot Springs, some real Mob professionals, and they'd simply vanished. Someone who knew the forests—Charles had hunted them his whole life—had to have gotten them out. Did someone have something on him? Was he compromised by criminal interests? It was like an inkblot, a smear, that warned all to stay away.

But if there were civic mysteries encapsulated by his public career, there were even more abiding ones on the family circuit. Why did Bob's father, Earl, never speak of the old man? Hate, fear, anger, unforgiveness?—it could be anything except indifference. Why'd Earl leave home at sixteen for the Corps? Then there was Bobbie Lee, Bob's own namesake. Earl's brother, Charles's second son, evidently some sort of damaged goods. He hung himself in 1940—almost simultaneously with the train robbery. Why? Was Charles abusing him or was he just so beyond the bend there was no helping him and he himself saw no further point. Why was all this shrouded in mystery? Any small town is a nest of scandal and shame, and this was one of Blue Eye's juiciest, and yet so powerful, it kept people away seventy-five years later. Was there a truth too terrible to bear?

Swagger decided to put it from his mind. But the past was like a big cat, a black panther, that, having slipped the cage, would not go away. Instead, it haunted the fringes of the property, leaving sign, howling in the night, possibly seen as a dark blur for a second or so when least expected, somehow ominous and waiting at the same time. Invisibly, it prowled, scuffled, left bloodied carcasses about. Bob knew it would come.

It attacked when Bob was riding the rim one morning. A bitter memory leapt from a tree and took him down hard and clawed the wound that never healed, the death of Earl Swagger in 1955. The wound opened, bled, puckered, and hurt like hell. It put in Bob's head the thing he hated the most: the memory of his father on that last day, pulling out of the farm in his black-and-white, waving at his only son.

How does such a man happen? How can a man contribute so much and demand so little? Where does pure moral strength come from? It doesn't come from nowhere. As Bob's character was formed in obedience to his ideal of his father, Bob now saw that Earl's was formed in a different smithy; he was formed to be the anti-father, the anti-Charles. He ran his life in such a way as he would never end up as that dark figure who haunted it, his father. So, yes, inescapably, everything his father became had to do with the man the sheriff already was.

It all had to do with the sheriff. Who was he? Why was he? He scared Bob.

THEN THAT SAME AFTERNOON—it had to be coincidence because he was too sane and too old to believe in any system running the universe but brute whimsy—Bob looked in his email and saw something unexpected. From: jvincent@smathersvincentnichols.com.

That was Jake Vincent, his Arkansas lawyer, one of Sam Vincent's boys, all grown up and made good and partnered up in a fancy law firm in Little Rock.

Jake had represented him on the sale of the land to a big corporation for residential development and he was a fine one for dotting all *t*'s and crossing all *i*'s. A small fortune had been spent on stamps to get the deal finally done and the money transferred into the Swagger accounts. Jake had done it all, as Bob had no other reason to conclude, superbly.

"Bob," the email read, "something small and odd has come up involving the property. I don't feel comfortable discussing it by email or even letter. Can you call me on my private cell tonight?" and he gave the number.

That night, Bob called.

"Jake, it's me."

"Ah, right on time. Thanks so much."

They palavered a bit about recent fortunes, the state of the estate, Arkansas politics, the Razorbacks' chances in football and basketball, the destinies of their children.

"So anyway, Bob, this odd thing has happened."

"Go ahead."

"As your lawyer, let me formally inform you—this is for your protection as well as mine—that some of the information I'm about to give you suggests commission of a federal crime, and if you don't report it, you could be subject to indictment yourself. It's probably a long shot, but I'm not earning my money if I'm not telling you that."

"What kind of law?"

"I'd guess receivership of stolen property."

God, had Earl been on the take and stowed away a quarter million that had just come to light? Bob wasn't sure he wanted to know.

"Lord," he said.

"The objects in question are two. One is a government-property Colt .45 ACP automatic, serial number 157345C. We tracked the number via the Colt Company and it was from a lot that was sold to the Department of the Post Office in 1928, the year of its manufacture. It wasn't an army gun but a commercial variant, purchased for use in certain law enforcement situations. Now—I don't know, but somehow it ended up in a tin strongbox that was hidden under the foundation of your old farmhouse. The clear implication is that it was illegally appropriated. It had been very carefully secreted away, God knows when, and after the house came down, the excavator was tearing out the foundation and the bucket caught on the corner of the box and pulled it out of the ground."

"I sure don't know nothing about that," said Bob. "I know my father brought a Thompson back from the war, but after he died, my mother turned it over to the State Police out of fear of legal entanglement. But if it'd been a gun my dad cropped from the Corps—it must have happened to a million .45s in the war—"

"At least. I think my dad had one too."

"—it would have had a government serial number and said 'Property of U.S. Government' on it, so it doesn't sound like a Marine Corps pistol. You say there was something else that could have been stolen?"

"Yes."

"I can't wait."

"A thousand dollars in cash."

"A thousand!"

"A fair amount of money now, a lot more then."

"Maybe my father confiscated it from some bust, maybe he— Well, he was no angel, hero or not, and that much money in 1955, unaccounted for, you know, maybe he just figured . . ." He let the words trail out.

"I don't think so. First off, it's only one bill. A thousand-dollar bill. On top of that, it appears new and uncirculated, which could mean many things. By serial number, it's a 1934-A type bill. We're consulting a numismatist to learn more, and possibly we'll try to trace it through the Treasury Department, but that takes time. Maybe months."

"So the 1934 serial number and the fact that it's uncirculated shows it can't have nothing to do with Earl Swagger. He was in the Marine Corps in China or Nicaragua then, didn't get back for two more years, no way he could have laid a finger on it. That's a relief. Anyhow, that money should be returned with the gun as soon as possible and this thing put right."

"Then another gun exhibit. Or we think it's related to a gun. It's a kind of machined cylinder—very high-quality metalwork—but weirdly gigantic, too big for any rifle or shotgun of the time. Maybe it's a machine-gun muzzle. Has slots milled into it. Heavy piece of work."

"I don't have no idea at all."

"There's a couple more oddities. The first is a map of some sort. Very crude, just the diagram of what I take to be an oddly laid-out wall with ten steps marked off to what could be a tree trunk, then another few steps to an X that marks the spot."

"Hmm."

"Bob, maybe that crisp bill was stolen from a bank or something. Maybe other money, more money, is under the X. But of course without knowing where or what the building was, the map is useless."

"Yeah, I see," he said, trying to mull it over in his mind.

"And there's one other thing. Was any of your family ever an FBI agent? I mean other than Ray of course."

"What?"

"Any FBI agents in the family tree? I think I would know, but I'm getting nothing."

"Well, Ray's the only one—" His son Ray was second in command at the FBI sniper school at Quantico.

"No, no, I don't mean that. I mean in the thirties."

Bob had nothing to say. But he realized his grandfather, Charles Fitzgerald Swagger, who had lately occupied his thoughts, the sheriff of Polk County and victor of the famous Blue Eye gunfight in 1923, war hero and mystery, would have been, what, forty-three in that year. Just the right age, and just the right profile, salty yet still spry, a gunfighter with much killing behind him and no fear in front of him.

"Because we found an FBI Special Agent's badge in the box too."

"You're kidding," said Bob.

"Not a bit. And there's more. It actually was a badge for the Justice Department's Division of Investigation, which they called the FBI for a single year."

"Oh?"

"That year was 1934. The year of all the gunfights."

3

I T WAS A TYPICAL DAY for the sheriff of Polk County.

He made sure his .45 Government was cocked and locked and slid it into the floral-engraved shoulder rig, made custom by a fellow in San Antonio, one of the few "nice" things he allowed himself, and the gun felt especially heavy. Then he pulled his fedora low over his sharp eyes and set out. He pulled out the long driveway, turned left, and headed into Blue Eye, the county seat, with its seven church spires, water tank, and two-funnel power company twelve miles to the west.

He had rounds: first to check with his one deputy in Niggertown, where he only wanted a general report, as it didn't do to look too carefully at how Jackson Johnson, his Negro deputy, ran the law-and-order business down here. Jackson kept the crime down, and made sure no one ever acted disrespectfully toward a white person, and so was otherwise left alone.

Then Charles checked on his two snitches among the subversives. There were basically two subversive groups in Blue Eye—Communists and Republicans—and Charles confirmed quickly enough that neither group had any revolutions planned. Then he dropped in at Tom Bode's to tell Tom that the bank was complaining to the judge about Tom's delinquency on his mortgage and he didn't want to have to do any foreclosing, as that was nasty business for everyone. Tom said he'd let a man go and they'd work triple overtime to get the okra in.

He rolled into the actual sheriff's office about 11. He usually found his clerk, Millie, and one of the three deputies on the day shift, the other two being out on patrol, driving slow, careful patterns around the county, ready for anything and reachable instantly by a primitive radio. At the transmitter, he ran a check on both, and all seemed okay, quiet and pleasant, meaning no labor agitators and no one using too much sugar at the doughnut shop. He went to his desk in his office off the squad room and went through his in-box, which contained the night's tickets and reports, expecting nothing, finding nothing. No real crime seemed to exist in Polk County, assuming you didn't count when a Willie thumped a Willie or some trashy transient farmworker broke a bottle over another's skull or the even rarer domestic disturbance among the town's quality, usually involving liquor, untoward accusations, and a fist or slap in anger that announced itself by loud crying and a call to the sheriff. It happened. People were people and it happened, all of it of no real significance. It just rolled on, well-oiled, self-sustaining, unseen, but trusted by nearly all.

But this day there was something unexpected.

"Sheriff, a Captain Hamer from Texas called you. Wants you to call him back. Shall I call him?"

"Yes, can you, Millie?"

It took a few seconds for Millie to put the call through, operator by operator, so that finally Blue Eye and Dallas were connected, by which time Charles had gotten into his office and closed the door.

"Hamer. That you, Charles?"

"It is, Captain." Frank Hamer was one of the few people in the world that Charles felt at home around.

"How're you feeling? See all the ink we got for steppin' on them two pip-squeaks?"

"Yes sir. You're a hero, Frank, but you always were a hero."

"You're just pulling an old man's leg, Charles. As I said, plenty of glory to go 'round. It ain't too late. You can magically appear in the accounts just like you magically disappeared."

"Not sure how the damned judge would take it, Frank. The job was its own reward. An out-of-season hunt, what could be better reward than that?"

"Well, I do agree. Clears the sinuses better than a shot of fine whiskey. Now, I have something for you, Charles, thought I'd best mention it."

"I'm all ears," said Charles.

"Seems the federals are recruiting gunfighters. That *cucaracha* dance in Little Bohemia, where all the gun boys just went through their ranks like shit through a goose? And the federals only bagged a few innocent townsmen? Mighty embarrassing. That's because they got no old salts, just wet-eared college boys. Fools and poofs, nobody righteous who'd stand and shoot it out."

"I see," said Charles.

"So a fellow comes to me yesterday, an Inspector Cowley out of Chicago. My reputation being so sterling and all, would the captain be interested in going up north, appointed a Special Agent in what they call the Division of Investigation, to be part of a unit that's going after all them famous bad boys—mainly, Mr. Johnny H. Dillinger—but the other big ones, the one they call Baby Face, the one they call Pretty Boy, then there's a Wilber, a Harry, an Alvin, even a old lady called Ma. The Division needs shooters, Charles, men who can shoot and take fire without panic. And this inspector wanted me to head it all up."

"Sounds like a fine opportunity, Frank," said Charles.

"Maybe for a younger man. But, Charles, the six weeks after Bonnie and Clyde done flattened me out. I mean to sleep and drink and hibernate until the fall at least. At my age, a fellow can't be running around and sleeping in cars no more."

"I feel the stiffness myself."

"You are ten years younger, Charles, and tough as a buzzard that feeds on coyote."

"Well, sir," said Charles, "I might have some tough left in me."

"I gave him your name, Charles. Told him about the war, about 1923, about all the frays since then, told him special how it was for duty, not glory, you put your grit to the use of the law. He liked that. He liked that part a lot."

"Thanks for the advertisement, Frank."

"So any day now he may show up. He may invite you to join the federals and their hat dance. Be a fine move, Charles. More money, a dose of fame, freedom from that damned judge, better opportunities in Chicago for your sick boy."

It had its appeal, no doubt about it. It's what Charles was born to do. It would fill his mind too, keep it from going other places, places it shouldn't want to go but, goddammit, did anyhow.

"I'm thanking you for the tip, Frank. I'll give it hard thought, and if the inspector shows, I'll be ready for him."

Inspector Cowley showed up two days later. He was a well-dressed, handsome thirty-five-year-old, who seemed much older and graver than his years, more Grandpop type than Pop type, and seemed immediately to Charles somewhat soft for the job he had. To face men with guns with your own guns took a certain steel. Men could master it under severe military discipline for a year or so—Charles had seen it in the war—but to make it a career took a certain harshness of spirit, a lack of care for the pain dealt to other men, an obsessional quality, a certain gimlet-eyed view of reality, quick reflexes, the talent to shoot well and fast, to say nothing of first, and finally a grit that would drive you forward even with—especially with—the possibility of your own death. That's what Frank Hamer had, which is why he became a legendary Texas Ranger, and Charles knew he himself had it, along with the cold heart, which was he had no trouble pulling the trigger on a fellow human being, making him go still forever. Some men deserved killing, you had to believe that.

But clearly such was not the case with Inspector Cowley, who admirably made no pretense that it was. He seemed instead like a sort of pastor. His was the kind of talent for quiet leadership and organization and inspiration, but he'd never be a barker, a shouter, a discipline monster, a man killer.

"Thank you for seeing me, Sheriff."

"We are in the same business, sir. I owe you courtesy and attention, and that's what you'll get from me completely."

"How wonderful. In some places, federals are not beloved at all, and on my trip I've run into a fair amount of acrimony."

"Not in the judge's Polk County, sir."

"I'll come to the point, Sheriff. You're too busy and important to waste time. You have of course heard of our unfortunate arrest attempt in Wisconsin in April? Little Bohemia?"

"I believe I have, sir. Not a happy day for police officers countrywide."

"No, a disgrace, to be sure. We lost a very fine young agent, we shot two innocent men, killing one, and our quarry, so neatly gathered in one spot as never before, scattered to the four winds."

"I have seen all the bulletins. You were up against some very nasty folks. Shooters all, and I have learned that too many in our business get squeamish when it comes to the gun."

"Our Director had a vision, Sheriff Swagger. He envisioned a scientific national police force, incorruptible, untainted by ego, vanity, and politics. Alas, as we have learned, that also meant untainted by experience, toughness, cunning, and marksmanship. Lawyers make poor gunfighters."

"Fighting's a technique, like anything. It's a skill to be learned, that's all."

"So our Director, and I agree with him of course, now sees the need for your kind of law enforcement. That is, heroes. Men of the gun. Our criminal class is too violent and too skilled to be arrested by lawyers. We need the likes of you, of Frank Hamer, of D. A. Parker, of Bill Tilghman, of Jelly Bryce, of men who've been hardened by battle, in war or arrest situations. Do you see what I am driving at?"

"I believe I do, sir."

But Charles saw something else. He saw his family up north, he saw his damaged boy in some sort of caring facility, where the other children wouldn't tease him and throw rocks at him, where his wife wasn't beaten to a frazzle by the ordeal of caring for such a boy, where he himself could look at the boy, whom he knew had been delivered to him by a stern God as punishment, and not feel a racing current of self-hatred.

And he saw one other thing. Certain developments were weakening Charles. Certain opportunities were available as never before. He felt the yearning, the needing, the hunger, but he could not give in. The punishment was eternity in hell. Thus, Chicago was escape. It solved an immediate problem. It saved Charles from his worst enemy, who was Charles. It was his getaway.

He knew in that second he would take the job.

"I was also impressed by your modesty. I have it on authority that you were part of the team that ended the careers of two famous bank robbers. Yet you chose to leave the scene early, you had no hunger for special attention, the adulation of the press, the advancement of your reputation. Most man killers are like baseball stars and they love to be at the center of things."

"I am a private man," said Charles.

"That is very impressive and entirely in accordance with the wishes of the Director, who believes it is the organization, not the man, who should get the credit. That ensures the survival of the organization, and believe me, Sheriff, as America fills and gets yet more and more sophisticated, so will its criminals, whether gangsters or Reds, and we will need the most sophisticated, most modern law enforcement organization in the world, if we are to keep up with them."

"I can't help you on modernization, sir. I can win fights for you and help your boys win fights, that's the extent of my talent."

"And that is what we need right now. Yes, I'm here to offer you a job. You would be appointed Special Agent, a rare privilege, as most men have to go through six months' training. You will work under me out of Chicago, and the pay is about twice what you are now making, eight thousand dollars a year. Needless to say, it will be a much better life for your wife and boy."

"I believe I would leave them here for now, sir. My wife has family here, my boy is set in school, and I don't want her obsessing about the danger."

"Certainly. You would know best. To continue, you would be in charge of firearms training, to try and get the fellows to shoot a little better and not lose their heads when they are being shot at. If we're thin, you'd have stakeout duties, which nobody enjoys, but it's part of the job. Even I do it. You might be asked to run security on crime scenes where our technicians have to work undisturbed. Interrogation is a special art, and possibly you have an old lawman's gift for it, but, if not, no problem. Interrogators are easier to find than gunfighters. You're familiar with the Thompson gun, the twelve-gauge riot gun, the Browning rifle, the Remington Model 8, and the Colt .45 automatic? It's said you're a superb shot."

"I have fired them all courtesy of our State Police, some more than others. We could have used that Thompson in France, let me tell you."

"A bit heavy for a lawyer like me, I have to say. Is there anything else?"

"Sir, I'm wondering if we could do this on the sly. No publicity, no newspapers, some way I don't have to resign this here job. I'm sure the judge will let me go, perhaps even encourage me, as he's a big Democrat and a true Roosevelt man, but here are my roots and I'd like to have something to come back to."

"It's an excellent idea," said Inspector Cowley. "I wish more of our men felt that commitment to the team."

"Then I think you've got yourself a man."

"I am gratified and will notify the Director immediately."

"If I get Johnny Dillinger in my sights, I will bag him for you or die trying."

"I know you will. But the newspapers have perhaps made too much of Dillinger. He's got a gift for publicity over and above his talents for larceny, and it seems he's not a key larcenist as we've been led to believe. In any event, it's not Public Enemy Number One I fear. It's a man called Lester. Now, that's a scary proposition. Only a Charles Swagger has the nerve to face Lester J. Gillis."

"Lester?" said Charles. "Never heard of him."

4

B OB, IN A SUIT THAT HIS FORMALITY DEMANDED, sat in the law offices of Smathers, Vincent and Nichols in a skyscraper in Little Rock and looked at the odd collection that Jake Vincent's assistant had gently removed from a much-battered and dirtied old box.

The pistol was at least knowable. It was a well-preserved Colt Government Model, greasy from the oil-soaked cloth that had been its shroud for eighty or so years underground. The firm thoughtfully provided Bob with rubber gloves, so he could pick it up.

His fingers knew it immediately. As a design, the thing was one of many masterpieces that had tumbled from the brain of John M. Browning before World War I, so perfect in conception and execution, such a chord of power and grace and genius of operation that even now, more than a century after its year of adaptation in 1911, it was the standard sidearm of many of the world's elite units. Nothing plastic, nothing sleek and streamlined, with a huge magazine of smaller cartridges, could really replace it for the trained man.

This one bore no rust, testament to the care with which it had been packed and the airtightness of the tin box, which, upon reflection, could not have been tin, as all had assumed, but welded steel. Again, that expressed care and savvy.

Bob eased back the slide, finding it smooth, until it locked, exposing through the ejection port the pistol's cockpit. He looked in, and though slick with oil, the pistol showed its perfection in the harmony between barrel and magazine follower and the firing-pin hole in the bolt face, with two other nubbins projecting slightly, the extractor and the ejector. Amazing that an eighty-year-old spring held so tight and true, locking the whole gun in powerful tension. He held it close to his eye to behold the workmanship of the old Colt Hartford plant in those days, the precision of the Colt lettering—COLTS PTS FA MFG CO/HARTFORD CT U.S.A.—along with the patent line, and, on the other side, COLT AUTOMATIC/CALIBRE .45, complete down to old-school spelling. The serial number was 157345C, meaning it left Hartford in 1928, and the Colt Company had cooperated swiftly, locating the bill of lading, which had sent a batch of fifteen pistols to the U.S. Postal Department. Evidently the Postals didn't like the heaviness and big, smacking kick of the big-bore, and the guns must have been shipped to the FBI in '34, where the high impact of the fat bullet was more meaningful to the operators than the size and weight of the piece. To an experienced man killer like Charles, the .45 would have been far preferable to the mousy .38 Special that most of the other agents carried, though some of them might have upgunned to a higher-powered .38 on a .44 frame. The .357 Magnum, which became synonymous with the Bureau, didn't arrive until '35.

He drew it closer to his eye. The fit of metal to metal was flawless, all the pieces locked in and held by precision machining, not pins or screws. In fact, the whole mechanism was united in solidity by a single pin that ran from the slide release through the body of the gun, and only by popping it out—it took a touch—could the gun be disassembled. The checkering on the hammer spur was a constellation of perfectly aligned pinpricks, the parallelism of the slide serrations was masterful. They knew how to build them in those days, when it was the machinist's skill and intuition that made it happen, not some computer algorithm. He popped the slide release and let that heavy part ease forward in capture, encompassing the barrel again, let the gun settle into his hand, and peered through the tiny sights that took someone with talent to get the most of.

No holster, as whoever squirreled it away knew that the leather, being organic, would disintegrate, moisture or not. He put it down and moved next to another relic of the firearms world of 1934. Unwrapped from a coil of oiled cloth, it revealed itself to be some kind of cylinder, obviously created at the lathe by a skilled machinist. It was a fine piece of work, a heavy chunk of sculpture cut from a single block of high-strength steel. It looked a little like a Japanese grenade or something, but it was hollow, and perforated at each end lengthwise by a hole that appeared to be roughly three-tenths of an inch wide. At one end, the width compressed into a cone that encircled what had to be the muzzle; at the other, the interior of the opening had been machined expertly with precise screw grooves, so it could be twirled on and tightened against the barrel of whatever weapon it assisted. It was cut by twelve grooves, each exactly parallel to the others, all angles squared perfectly to ninety degrees.

"Ever see such a thing?"

"Not exactly. Looks like some sort of automatic weapon accessory, a muzzle brake or something. The slots let hot gases escape upward, and their jet action keeps the muzzle down. Most automatic weapons have 'em. But this is so big and strange. Maybe from a Japanese or a French gun, a Belgian or Czech, something he brought back from the war, I'm thinking."

"What would it be doing here?"

"Hell if I know," said Bob.

Putting the cylinder down, he next considered the bill. It bore the picture of the stentorian Grover Cleveland, and its green was a lighter green. All the zeros after the 1 looked kind of goofy, particularly up at the corners, where they had to be curled around to fit. Some associate had wisely sealed it in a baggie so nothing of this century could tarnish it. Passed from teller to robber at gunpoint. What else could it be? Then, tossed somewhere, maybe as getaway money, in case someone had to move fast and didn't have time to pack. Or maybe it was swag that old Charles had picked up, a bill from a big gambler in Hot Springs he'd shaken down or found dead or money otherwise unaccounted for in the aftermath of a robbery that he presumed nobody would notice if missing. He put it away for the rainy day sure to come, knowing nobody would ever look for it. But its denomination had to make it something of a singularity that would make it easy to identify, easy to trace, less valuable than its face value, since it would have to be stepped on several times by brokers before a third of it returned as usable, untraceable cash. Unlikely that Charles would not know that. Unlikely also that he'd have the connections to get the job done and the time to wait for it to happen. And, finally, unlikely that it would be worth the effort, in 1934 terms, for a payoff coming in at two-thirds less than a grand.

So the getaway stash made the most sense. A bad guy on the run would need to finance his travel. The folks he dealt with would be far from law enforcement, would take the dough without question in small increments as he voyaged, and it would be months before any of it came to Treasury's attention and tracking efforts were started.

"A thousand?" said Bob to Jake, who sat across the conference room table from him. "How much is that worth in today's money?"

"A thousand in 1934 buys about three hundred dollars' worth of goods today," said Jake.

"Ain't getting rich on that," said Bob.

"Don't be so sure. It's not the value, it's the bill's rarity. That makes it worth something, perhaps a lot more worth than a thousand. The numismatist told us it was quite rare, an AC-1934-A out of San Francisco. He said it was Friedberg-2212-G, rated as 66EPQ, which is called Gem Uncirculated. It's pretty close to perfect. Worth about six or seven grand today, depending."

"But that's now. Then it was just flat 1934 one-grand value. After being walked through the cleaning process, it would go down to three hundred."

"That's right."

"So it hardly seemed like killing money, like a big chunk of swag that enters legend, and if located, would confer a life of luxury on its locator."

He put it down, picked up the map, or whatever it was. Well, *map* was too grand a word. It simply traced what appeared to be one wall of an irregular dwelling, with juts to sustain windows, and a diagonal of ten dashes leading off to the northeast quadrant, if the map was oriented with the north at the top, of which there was no indication. At the tenth step, in the same steady fountain-pen hand, a circle denoted what was certainly the trunk of a tree, and on the back side of the tree, from the wall of the house, if it was a house, was an X marking a spot.

"All of this stuff makes some sense if the year was 1940, the year of the big train robbery in Hot Springs, which rumor tied to Charles. But this was six full years earlier, and nothing happened down there in 1934. So we can discount the train business."

"Got it," said Jake.

"Why would he bury a treasure map under a house? He buries the map to buried treasure? Odd. Why wouldn't he just bury the treasure under the house?" Bob asked.

"Maybe the 'treasure' was too big. Maybe it was some sort of contraband, and if he was caught with it, it meant jail. So he wanted it off the property. Did he ever say anything?"

"He died four years before I was born. I don't know a thing about him."

"Did your dad say anything?"

"Not a thing. But my grandmother told my mother, who told me that he had the bottle disease. His pleasure was rye, lots of it, lots and lots toward the end. He started going to the Caddo Gap Baptist Prayer Camp for help with it, but the bottle beat down the Lord, because he drank hard till the day he died."

THE REAL MYSTERY was what happened in 1934 that prompted the gun to be hidden as well as the money, some kind of treasure buried in some unknowable place? And maybe sent him staggering down the Rye Highway toward a dissolution so deep, even the Baptists couldn't help.

And all of it had to revolve around the last of the objects in the reliquary. The badge. Both his forefathers had worn badges, had been lawmen, and so as a totem the attraction to such emblems of state power must run strong in the Swagger blood. And his own son now wore a badge. Yet Swagger himself was an outlier from his own DNA, in that it had never drawn him in. He had no police impulses. The Corps, with its top-down, to-the-death mandates of discipline, had been enough, and when it was over, it was also not a bad thing to be done with certain ceremonial requirements that a police career would have maintained. And like his grandfather ruined by the song of hooch, he had that same weakness. So he'd been too drunk after invaliding out to go into the State Police, and had never felt the call that his father and his grandfather, and who knows what Swagger before then, had felt? The bottle was far more interesting than the badge, and though he hadn't touched a bottle in years, it remained so.

When he picked it up, it meant nothing, delivered no charge. It was just a piece of—what?—an alloy of some sort, bronze, iron, maybe a salting of steel, crushed into a symbol of not merely justice but also authority and its facilitator, force. Had his grandfather worn this one? He looked carefully, and having no meaningful acquaintanceship with badges, only saw the random set of power emblems, as basically invented by the Roman Empire— that is, scrolls, raised lettering—*embossed*, that was the word—the whole thing a kind of mini shield that suggested a legionary's strength and probity, though some Knights of the Round Table shaping had crept in, as it was more elegantly designed than the legionaries' minimalist rectangle. It was heavy too, like a gun, much heavier and more substantial than it looked like from afar. In the dull but shadowless illumination of the overhead fluorescents of the law firm, it threw off glints of sparkle as you turned it, and the light caught or missed various heights and depths it wore on its uneven surface.

It didn't say FBI. It said, in an arch across the top, JUSTICE DEPARTMENT, and in a straight line under some kind of bas-relief of blindfolded Greek Lady Justice, DIVISION OF INVESTIGATION.

"They didn't become FBI officially till 1935," said Jake. "I'm an expert, I looked it up on Wikipedia."

"I should have done the same," said Bob, still rapt in the presence of the badge.

"It was only a division for that year. That's what they called it, the Division. Sounds kind of *1984*. The newspapers simply called it the Justice

Department, or Justice. They liked the pun, as in 'Justice fells Dillinger,' that sort of thing."

"I see," said Bob.

"So, what do you want to do with this stuff, Bob? Take it? Leave it? Report it?"

"Well, I guess the money should be turned in to Treasury. It's clearly a bank's, not mine, so let's get that one over with fast. Can you take care of it?"

"No problem."

"Then, I'd like to xerox the map, just in case, just in case of I don't know what. Maybe something will occur to me."

"Makes sense."

"As for the pistol, I think I'll take that, at least for a little while. I want to shoot it, see what I can learn from it. If it was his pistol, maybe it'll tell me something. Maybe we can communicate through the gun, since we both loved guns so much."

"I don't see any problems. Just don't sell it. You can destroy it or keep it, but if you destroy it, it might open you up to destroying government property. I have to look into the law here."

"Got it," said Bob.

"There must be an old briefcase around here. We'll put it in that."

"Great."

"And the 'cylinder'?"

"You keep it for now. I'll look in various books I've got, maybe I can come up with something."

"And the badge?"

"Can you keep it too? I won't know what to do with it until I figure out who and what he was. Let's keep it here for a bit. In the meantime, I have to look into my grandfather's life. I have a very good friend, Nick, recently retired from the Bureau, and maybe he can help me dig out old files. I can see if there was ever a Charles Fitzgerald Swagger on the payroll for a few months in 1934. Maybe that gun has some historical provenance and it should be returned to the Bureau, though they don't have no museum.

Maybe my grandfather's career has been expunged; he got drunk one night and shot up a whorehouse, something like that."

"You sure you want to dig into family secrets? Some things are best left underground. I could tell you a thing or two about Sam Vincent that would surprise you and that, even now that I have made peace with them, I wish I hadn't learned."

"I have had the same thoughts myself and it *does* scare me. But now I'm hooked. Charles invented Earl, Earl invented Bob. To understand Earl, I've got to work that line backwards in time. I have to answer the one question Charles didn't want asked: who was Charles F. Swagger?"

5

LITTLE BOHEMIA LODGE
MANITOWISH WATERS, WISCONSIN
April 22, 1934

L ES RAN THROUGH THE WOODS BLINDLY. He was not one to panic, but hearing what sounded like gunfire, he'd looked out the window of the cabin and suddenly the tree line had erupted in machine-gun fire, and even if he wasn't in its direct line, from the number of guns he knew the federals were here in force.

His first thought, Where was Helen? while the gunfire rose and rose, as if a whole battalion was on the attack. Then he realized she was in the main lodge with Tommy and Johnny and Homer and the boys, and there was nothing he could do except escape and survive and pray for the same outcome for her.

He had his .45 tucked in his shoulder holster, because he always did; he lived with that gun, trusted it, and kept it close for just this occasion. But from the sounds outside, he knew he needed more, and he opened the closet and there his Thompson gun leaned against the wall, as casually as if it were a golf club or something, with its bulbous and awkward drum of fifty rounds giving it weight and clumsiness. His enthusiasm for firearms filled him with energy, and the prospect of using one against human targets always made him happy—that is, if he weren't boiling with rage, which was his other mode of being. He was a contradiction, and no one could explain him, a handsome, dapper fellow, capable, a family man, the proud father of Ronald and Darlene, the loyal husband to one wife (he never messed around, and he never left Helen for long periods of time), and, to see him, you'd think he was one of life's little mechanics, solid, a churchgoer. But he did like to shoot things up, he liked adventure, he had an abnormal absence of fear, and killing wasn't a thing that lingered in his mind for long.

He grabbed the weapon, feeling its heaviness, which, far from being an irritation, was an attribute that helped keep it steady when fired at the quick march. He called it a machino, and it was one of the reasons he had entered this line of work, for the thrill it gave him when unleashed righteously against those who would do him harm was beyond ecstasy. And such a moment was now upon him, happily, like the reward of a drug rush to addict. Machino held all the answers, was a god that paid for fealty with victory. It pushed out all doubts and fears. He was happy, happy, happy.

He stepped out the front door of the cabin and found himself at an angle to the tree line, whose concealed gunners continued to lay their fusillade against the large log structure fifty yards immediately to their front, which itself was now adrift in smoke and vapor from all the bullet strikes and the dust they ripped free as they buried themselves in wood or plaster.

He was not stupid, and he was not without aesthetic impulse. At this moment, he took in the dramatic spectacle of what lay before him and knew that this was where he belonged, amid the smell of burned powder and the hammering of the guns, illuminated by flashes dancing out of muzzles, the whole thing livid and clear in the coldness of an early-spring evening in the northern latitudes. It didn't get much better.

HE ORIENTED THE GUN EASILY, and his finger went fast to the trigger, knowing that, against the chance of visitors, he kept the bolt cocked and the safety lever down, because if you needed it, the chances were you needed it that second. It seemed to melt into his body, so brilliantly engineered was it, and he hunched, braced, smiled, and fired.

Machino spoke. It lay a long strip of .45s against the tree line, and though he did not see the bullets strike, he saw dust kick, branches shudder, leaves disintegrate, trees vibrate, under the wondrous power of machino. The drama of the gun at full blast offered other pleasures too, the spray of spent shells ejecting like kernels of popped corn from the skillet, the building shudder of the vibration, the superspeed blur of the bolt as it rammed forward and back under the power of the firing cartridges, the flame squirting upward, almost over the gun, as the configuration of the gun's compensated nozzle aimed it upward in order to hold the muzzle down by counterforce, the glint of the fins on the barrel, the solidity of each grip in his strong, tight hands. So much to enjoy, such pleasures to behold! It filled his anarchistic heart with joy. Some men are born to destroy, and nothing satisfies them but that. Whatever you've got, they want to tear it apart, from architecture and bank vaults to order and society itself, anything, just to watch it twist, shred, and die.

Then the gun ran dry. He'd dumped the whole drum in a few seconds, sending fifty half-inch death warrants out into the night, and tough luck for anyone who got served by them. This, however, issued a problem, which was, where was another drum? And, second, how quickly could he get it in? For the drums, with all that ammo, were so heavy, the engineers had come up with a sliding rather than a clicking mechanism by which to attach them to gun, and slipping the lips of the drum into the slots that were milled into the frame was never easy. But even as he identified the problem, he solved it. He had another weapon, so unique it seemed to have been just planned for this situation.

THUS, he dashed back in the cabin while the federal gunners ducked, pulled back, tried to gauge this new stream of incoming fire, and he picked up something as yet unseen in the world. It was built for him—he had several and had even given one to Johnny as a gift, as an acolyte gives the cardinal a small token—by a gifted gunsmith in San Antonio. It was a true machine pistol, a Government .45, but with certain adjustments to its internals so that one pull of the trigger emptied all the rounds in a three-second blast. Because it fired so fast, it needed a lot of ammo, and the gunsmith, Lebman, had carefully welded several magazines together so that it held eighteen of the robin's-egg-sized .45 ACP cartridges. Because the longer the trigger was held down, the more the recoil built, it meant rounds ten through eighteen would have been hosepiped aimlessly across the sky, but Lebman had thought this one through as well. He had mounted both the Cutts compensator and the horizontal foregrip from a full-sized Tommy to the pistol, the comp to fight the muzzle's rise, the forestock to offer the second hand a sculpted wedge of wood with finger grooves by which it could be pulled against the same muzzle's rise. You could zip off a magazine, therefore, with a fair chance of staying on target through the whole of the transaction, all eighteen rounds' worth, as no force on earth or in engineering could halt the gun's hunger for ammo once the trigger had been jacked.

So he couldn't have been more perfectly prepared for what lay ahead. Nothing beats or satisfies like the perfect tool for the otherwise undoable job. He ducked back to the porch, cut left, and dashed down its short length. Bullets came his way, but were magically dissuaded from his flesh, or so he believed, by the charisma of his boldness and the size of his personality, and indeed a few struck nearby, tearing out splinters and debris and pulverized wood, but nothing struck him, and in a second he was off the porch and had deviated backwards, where the woods soon swallowed him.

Les was bold, but he was also lucky. He had no map, he had no particular sense of the terrain, indeed had never set foot into this part of Wisconsin until yesterday afternoon, driving up with Helen and Tommy Carroll, and even now the spurs of evergreens and as-yet-unleafed maple and elm sprigs cut at him but did not slow him down. He had no orientation, as woods skills were not among his talents, and the trees were too heavy, in any case, to make out any direction-suggesting stars. He just ran. He was young, twenty-six, full of a sense of fun, and sucking so powerfully on his badness and his glamour and yet another slick escape that no branch dared oppose him seriously, and the forest itself did not conspire against him by leading him off on twisty return trails so that he'd run like hell without advancing anywhere.

He ran, ran, ran. Behind him, the firing had stopped, and now and then he turned, swung around and looked for targets. But he could see no shadow pursuers, and when he managed to still his over-dramatic intake of oxygen, heard no crunching in the brush or thudding in the dust that might signify pursuit.

In time, the forest offered him a path carpeted with pine needles, and his night vision had adjusted to the low illumination, so the way was as sure as any of the Chicago alleys in which he'd grown up. He felt relaxed enough to steady up on his gait, sliding into something of a smooth jog, as opposed to the helter-skelter ragtime of insane escape speed. The shoulder holster held the .45 tight under his arm, as it was designed to do, and though the heft of the machine pistol grew in his hands (no holster could accommodate it because it was so big and ungainly), it rode in his hands, and he sometimes carried it lefty, sometimes righty, sometimes pointed up, sometimes pointed down, subtly shifting the point of balance and relieving his muscles. But it was too necessary to even think about jettisoning. If he fell in a lake, it would drown him, that's how much clinging to it meant.

He drifted on, hearing the silence of the night, his powerful eyes keenly locked ahead in case of ambush. But he was not the paranoid type and so no dread crushed against him. He did not see phantoms from the Division behind every tree, and the natural sounds of the forest—the hooting of owls, the scurrying of small mammals, the click and clack of branches moving against each other in the wind, the leaves propelled by the same force rubbing—did not grow in his imagination. He didn't have much imagination beyond guns, cars, his kids, and his wife. His whole world was feral, not planned, narrow, not broad, predatory, not nurturing, tough-guy proud, not afraid, and though not now, insane at times with rage. He needed anger management desperately but there was no anger management yet, nor were there antidepressants or other drugs that could have pulled him back to the normal range, but he'd been crazy for so long, and had enjoyed it so much, there was no getting him back.

How much time? An hour, not more than two. But at a certain point the fact that God himself is also crazy rewarded him, and he did not fall into a lake or a ditch and spare the world much pain, he came instead to a road, and in no time at all a Model A came chugging along. God was again taking care of Les.

"Goddammit," he yelled, pointing the strange little machine pistol at the two astonished occupants. "Get me out of here, goddammit!"

He scooted into the back.

Nothing happened. Both were frozen with fear. After all, imagine what an apparition he would have seemed, a dapper, rather handsome chap, well dressed in a suit, a thick head of hair, a sprig of movie-star mustache on his square pug face, yet armed with a weapon the likes of which they had never seen even if they recognized its deadly components, most notably the yawning .45-inch bore, and the fellow was acting fully insane, red-faced, swaddled in sweat, which flew off of him as he moved like a dervish toward them, eyes as wide as a rabid dog's. He looked like the picture-show comic boy Mickey McGuire with a real big gun, hopped up on tequila.

"Get this sonovabitch moving," commanded the man, and reluctantly, with shivering fingers and stunted movements, the driver eased her into gear and began to move.

But the tricks weren't done for the night, not by a long shot. The light beams filled the vault of trees curving over the road, and the car edged ahead, began to build speed, and Les had a glimpse of the perfect escape he so richly deserved. And then the lights went out.

"What the hell!" he screamed.

"Sir, I didn't do nothing, swear to God— Oh, Christ, I don't know—"

"I swear, sir, this here's an old buggy, wiring's all shot to hell, I could dicker with her under the hood, maybe get the shine on again—"

"Jesus H. Christ!" screamed Les. Yet he couldn't imagine these two bozos conspiring against him on the spur of the moment, and he knew if he killed them, the damned gun was done for the evening, as he had no other big mag. "Goddammit, get going, take her easy, don't pile us up, Grandpa, or I will have your ass for breakfast."

Slowly the car crept ahead, essentially feeling its way through the woods, stopping now and then when someone's eyes detected a problem with the road. At this rate, he'd be free and clear of Wisconsin well before Christmas.

"This ain't working, goddammit," he screamed at them.

"Sir, I am so sorry, I just—"

"Okay, okay. Shut up, now. See, isn't that a house up on the left?"

"It's Koerners'," said the other occupant, as if Les was going to answer, "Oh, that's where the Koerners live."

"Pull in," he commanded, and the rube slid the car off the road, up the driveway in front of a well-lit clapboard, back in the trees, off the road. They sat there while Les tried to figure out what to do next. Best thing: crash the house, see if they had a car, then take off in it, presumably lights running, and whiz through the night until he reached the Illinois or Iowa or Michigan state line, he didn't know or care which. That was the best idea, and he took a deep breath and began to compose himself to issue instructions, when, absurdly, another car pulled in, just behind them, and three men got out.

Jesus Christ, was this an escape in a Keystone comedy? People keep showing up exactly where they shouldn't be, and he's got hostages coming out the butt. What's he supposed to do with these hostages. Start a band?

He leapt from the car, leveled the machine pistol at the three, noting intently even in the dark that they lacked that cop deportment—he'd been studying it his whole life—which was equal parts size, steadiness, and seriousness, and screamed, "Get those paws up, you mooks, or I'll blast you to hell."

The three turned, hands flew up, but he knew instantly that whoever these mooks were, they knew there'd been action at Little Bohemia, and the night would be full of spooks, gangsters, feds, and machine-gun fire. They eyed him with fear, expecting difficulty, offering no resistance, as if obedience could buy off his craziness.

"Go on, goddammit, get in the house, you two"—meaning the two he'd already nabbed—and the five of them formed into a loose confederation of civilians, with hands high, controlled from the rear by a man with a nasty pistol.

This motley crew marched into the Koerners', and those folks looked equally stunned at the size of the menagerie that had just tromped into the living room, particularly the extremely agitated young fellow who was calling the shots, yelling orders, dancing this way and that, sweating like a boxer, his eyes racing over everything as he drank it in for information.

"All right, everybody, get on the goddamned floor if you don't want to be in a massacre. If I have to fire, you get famous, but you're dead, so no time to enjoy it."

The group eased awkwardly to their knees in front of a nice sofa-and-love-seat arrangement the Koerners had set up, near the switchboard, which was how Koerner made his living.

"Okay," he said, "sorry for the yelling, don't mean to hurt no civilians. But I have to get out of here and I want you down and quiet. Keep your mouth shut and maybe you'll live to tell your grandkids. You and you"—he pointed to the two men nearest the door, who happened to be in the party of three he'd just taken—"we're going out and get in your car and drive away, got that? Play ball and you should be okay, except for the extra trip. The rest of you, stay down, stay quiet, be calm. I don't even have time to rob you."

He eased them out of the house, off the porch, and over to the last car in the now crowded driveway.

"Now, get in the front, and— What the—"

Astonishingly, there was already someone in the backseat. Another band member! Now what? He was just making this up.

"You, outta the car. Jesus Christ, where do you people come from?"

This one, who seemed to have been sleeping, rousted himself and staggered out of the car, utterly befuddled, but wise enough to keep his hands up.

"Okay, you, lie down, go back to sleep, don't make a peep. You others, get in, start 'er up, and we'll get the hell out of here"—and, just like that, *another* car suddenly appeared out of nowhere, this one also carrying three men, and it pulled off the road right at the driveway.

What now? Les thought with exasperation. Next a bus, or maybe a plane will land or a ship will come sailing up the river?

He turned the muzzle on the three new passengers, dangerously near rage, screaming again.

"Get out, get out, goddammit," and he pulled open the rear door to discover himself staring into the maw of a Thompson submachine gun.

He was dead.

I'm dead, he thought.

But he was not dead, for though the federal's face broadcast effort and exasperation, no flash announced the release of a bullet stream that would, from this range, cut Les in half.

Les had no reaction, but, faster than a leaping rat, his finger saved his life by jerking hard on the trigger of Mr. Lebman's machine pistol and it emptied itself in three seconds, kicking out a spew of spent shells as the gun ate its magazine, as it had been designed to, in one gulp.

It felt like he had a rocket by the tail, all whoosh and burn and shudder, bucking and twisting, yet with both his fists locked around the grips, it did not deviate, and its freight hit and devastated the automobile and its passengers, hazing windows with webs, pulling out puffs of horsehair from the upholstery, spreading punctures in a general south-to-north pattern across the exposed metal that comprised the body of the car.

The G-Man never got his trigger pulled but instead reared backwards, dropping the weapon, hands flying to throat and the sudden jets of blood that were gushing his life away, staggered from the car, the Thompson spilling off his lap, and fell to earth. The others beat it too, hit or not, and Les didn't even see them go, as he was too absorbed in the drama of killing.

When he came back into his real head, he found himself standing alone by the car in a fog of gun smoke amid a pile of spent brass. All other humans had vanished from the earth, as hostages and targets alike had taken off like rabbits and managed to find cover in the dark.

Les jumped in the car, tossing the gun on the seat behind him. The driver hadn't even killed the engine, so he simply clutched it into gear, pulled onto the road, and sped away.

Ha! he thought. I made it.

Or did he?

After a few miles of forest road, well lit by his headlights, he came to a straightaway, and a quarter mile ahead, two other headlights came onto the same stretch of road, a sedan driven fast, so fast it had to be law people.

Fuck! he thought.

And then he thought, Fuck them!

And then he thought, You boys want to play tough. Let's see how tough you are.

He foot-stomped the gas pedal and he felt the engine surge in aggression, now swallowing gasoline at full hunger, and around him the forest, the road, the onrushing headlights of the enemy car, all went to blur.

We'll see who's got brass balls, Lester J. Gillis, known to press and cop as Baby Face Nelson, thought with a snort, a laugh, and a sudden injection of joy, as he aimed the car straight between the headlights and floored it.

6

BETWEEN FIRING RANGES, the differences hardly matter. This one was in a strip mall, contained a retail store of late-modern pistols, not so many hunting rifles as many might have, a fair sampling of assault rifles and shorter-barreled shotguns, and no doubles or over-and-unders. It was not paneled in knotty pine, and no deer heads gazed at eternity through marble eyeballs from its walls; instead, zombies and insane clowns were on display, as well as ana-tomically revealing silhouettes and competition cardboard. Clearly, its theme was self-defense for the burgeoning concealed-carry market, and at the recep-tion desk of the range proper, which lay in darkness behind thick plexiglass windows, the old Colt excited some comment.

"Wow," said the range officer, "that's a nice piece, sir. You sure you want to shoot it? It might have some collector value."

"I want to run a function-and-accuracy check," said Bob, "before I strip it down for detail cleaning and put it on the market. It hasn't been fired since 1934. I need a box of hardball."

"Yes sir, but, again, we do have 200-grain lead semi-wad reloads. A lot safer, a lot less kick."

"I reckon I can get through the hardball," said Bob. "If my granddad could, I could. It was built by Hartford to play the hardball game. That was the only game in town in '34, but you know that."

"If I did, I forgot," said the man, who had the face of a Roman legionary behind glasses that had last been fashionable in the '70s.

Bob accepted the white box of fifty generic Winchester 230-grain full metal jackets, the man-stopping load the government had issued for seventy-three years under the designation ".45 caliber ball," thus earning it the nickname hardball forever. Then he put on the mandatory safety glasses and earmuffs and pushed through the double doors. As he entered, the officer turned on the lights, illuminating a cavern with eight shooting booths, each with an electric pulley setup to run targets out to the twenty-five-yard line. Bob went to his assigned booth, put the briefcase on the shelf, and pinched an NRA bull's-eye target, a simple black circle on an otherwise blank sheet, into the clamp. He turned, found the toggle switch, which sent the target downrange twenty-five yards until it bumped the far wall.

Then, quickly and without ceremony, he removed the gun from its case, popped open the white box, poured the ammo onto the shelf, where it clicked and rolled with heavy authority, then locked the slide back and pressed the button to remove the mag.

He threaded seven in, for Charles Swagger would have carried it that way, or perhaps he cranked one into the chamber, put the safety on, removed the magazine, and inserted one more against the tightness of the compressed spring. An old gunfighter's trick, it would give him one more round in a fight where one round might be the difference.

Charles would have shot one-handed too, for in those days the concept called modern technique, which counsels a two-handed, bone-tightened isosceles grip in all applications, hadn't been invented, and wouldn't be till the late '50s. Everybody saw a pistol as a one-handed implement, as all the old pictures showed, which may be why they missed so much in those days.

But Bob hadn't practiced one-handed shooting in years, as it had all but vanished from the earth, and he knew if that was his theme today, he'd get nothing but disappointment. Instead, he bladed himself at forty-five degrees to the far target and commenced locking down, meaning right grip on pistol, locked down hard; left hand wrapped around right hand, locked down hard; right elbow, locked down hard; straight back; left arm, pulling right hand, locked back hard. The point was to go robotic, but when he found the sight, again he marveled at the skill of the first-generation 1911 shooters, for it was only a pinprick, and the embracing rear sights, whose ears were supposed to buttress that pinprick, were miniature too. But he got the front aligned in the rear, as narrow a margin as could be imagined, felt his trigger-finger pad lock flat on the curvature of the trigger, and slowly eased back.

When the pistol fired, it was a surprise break, coming sooner than he anticipated, kicking harder, administering a shot of pain to the webbing between his gripping thumb and index finger because he'd held way up high, as modern technique demanded when there was no oversize safety grip to cushion the shock, so the pistol discharged its energy right smack into the tender spot.

He looked, could see no sign of a hit, thought, Damn, I missed the whole thing, and went through the drill six more times, holding to the same six-o'clock position on the target. There wasn't much smoke, but in the little room only eight lanes wide, it collected and drifted back, and would have brought a lifetime of memories to him—hard places, lost men, desperate nights, fear everywhere—if he'd let it. He didn't.

Glancing toward the target, he saw he'd missed clean.

Out of practice, he thought. So out of practice.

But when he reeled the target in, he was surprised to find a cluster of four in the black, just bisecting the 10 ring, and three more punctures close at hand, the farthest out splitting the 6 and 4 rings.

He reexamined the shooting experience, trying to find nuance against the harshness of the recoil and the pain it had injected into the webbing in his hand. He realized then how smooth the trigger pull had been, smooth with-out grit or little micropatches of resistance, not a hair trigger but certainly a useful one. Peering intently at the weapon, he noted as well that its front sight was slightly bent to the right by the expert application of a padded hammer, a testament to this particular weapon's insistence on throwing shots to the left, and its caretaker—his grandfather or some other gentleman?—had made a hairsbreadth adjustment to stay in the black.

He quickly ran through the remaining forty-three rounds, and found that at twenty-five feet, for example, he could stay within an inch without hardly trying, even after adjusting his grip so that flesh wasn't jabbed by the fulcrum of the safety grip. He shook it, heard no rattles, signifying that the gun was tighter by far than most government-issue .45s, which were built loose so that even clogged up with Flanders's mud, Iwo's ash, or Da Nang's grit, they'd function long, hard, and hot.

When he was done and reentered the shop through the double doors, the range officer said, "Say, I watched you, I'd say you done a peck of shooting before. Most people here can't hold in the black at twenty-five yards. That's why they shoot at zombies."

"I shot a lot of practical many years ago," he said. "Is there any chance you could take it to your gun-cleaning station and break it down so we'd get a good look at the parts? I need to get a sense of what's been done to it."

"Sure, be damned interesting," said the officer, who was turning out to be one of those immediately likable men who was probably half the reason this place stayed open in a bad economy.

They went to the bench that was mounted against a wall where rental guns were cleaned when too much crud jammed them up. The range officer took the pistol and broke it down expertly.

"You've done that a few times, I'd say," said Bob.

"Army. 'Nam. 'Sixty-nine, 'seventy. Did twenty years, got out with eight stripes."

Bob laughed.

"You beat me, Top," the universal term for a first sergeant, "I only managed six before they kicked me out."

"Army?"

"Marines. 'Nam too. Pretty interesting."

"Wasn't it, though?" said the sergeant. "Anyhow, let's see what we got here."

The two men took turns closely examining the thirty-seven parts that Colt Commercial Model, serial number 157345C, disassembled to.

"Clearly," said the Top, "someone who knew what he was doing did a once-over. Look how all the sharp edges of the trigger surfaces have been filed with a very soft hand, just to break the ninety-degree angles a bit, and smooth up the trigger, without cutting out any loops of the spring."

Bob squinted, eyes not what they once were.

"Yeah," he said.

"I also notice he took a ball-peen hammer to the slide rails, very carefully tattooed them, very skillfully widened them just a hair, so they hold the slide much more tightly. Then he polished both surfaces, both the top of the rail and the groove in the slide. Nice tight, smooth fit, sure helps accuracy."

"I see that," said Bob, who'd noticed—and felt—the same.

"He's also polished the feed ramp and broken the ninety-degree angle there where it fits against the frame. The cartridges will never hang up, just extra reliability insurance. With hardball, these things hardly ever jam, but that wasn't good enough for him, he had to change 'hardly ever' to 'never, ever.'"

"Good catch," said Bob. "I missed that."

"Basically, he's given a sloppy combat gun all kinds of accuracy and reliability enhancements. He knew what he was doing."

"Finally," said Bob, pointing to a subtle linear variation in the pistol's black sheen that ran around the front of the grip just under the trigger guard, "you got any idea what this is?"

"Never seen that before," said the Top. "Looked at a lot of .45s, that one's new to me."

"You didn't look in the right place, which would be the Texas Ranger Museum in Waco. The Rangers used to tie a rawhide strip around the grip to hold the grip safety in—that is, off. In case they had to go to gun fast, and I guess a lot of them did, they didn't want to miss the grip safety in their hurry and come up with a click instead of a bang. So this one had rawhide tying down the grip safety, and over the months it rubbed a strip of finish off. That's what you're seeing. Some of 'em were so sure they'd have to go to gun quick-time, they milled off the trigger guard. Have to be plenty serious kind of situation before I'd do anything like that."

"If I tried to holster a 1911 with no trigger guard and the grip safety tied down, I know I'd blow my own knee off by the third day."

Bob laughed.

"But seriously," said the Top, "if you could prove Texas Ranger provenance, you'd double, maybe triple, the value for certain collectors. Lots of Texas Ranger fans out there."

"I bet the owner of this gun knew Texas Rangers, had seen how they operated, and picked up a few tricks from them. I don't know that he was a Ranger himself."

"But if he was going to some kind of war, he'd give himself every advantage," said the Top. "It figures."

"This has been a great help," Bob said. "Can I pay you for your expertise?"

"If you did 'Nam, brother, no payment at all. You already paid up in full."

AT THE HOTEL, he found a FedEx envelope on the floor of his room, slipped under the door, and he knew exactly what it was. He called his wife.

"Hi, it came, thanks."

"I hope it helps," she said.

"Well, you never know, I might pick something up, even if the chance is small."

"How much longer in Little Rock?"

"I'm done now. Heading to Blue Eye tomorrow, Andy Vincent is going to meet me. I told him I want to keep it discreet, no conquering-hero-returns-home kind of thing, and, again, I doubt if much is left of the old man. Hell, there wasn't much left of my father, I don't expect anything from a generation earlier."

"All right."

"And then to D.C. to see if Nick's fished anything out of the files. I should be home in three or four days."

"I've heard that before," she said.

At last he turned to the envelope. He opened it and took out a single four-by-six-inch sheet of ancient paper and, turning it over, looked into the harsh face and unforgiving eyes of Charles Fitzpatrick Swagger, snapped

one fine spring day in 1926. It had been his own father Earl's only acknowledgment that he had a father, and it had been in a tattered old Buster Brown
shoe box with other Earl documents and souvenirs that he'd last looked at
twenty years ago. He'd noted the photo but not checked it at all.

Now he stared at the murky sepia, turning it back over to read the inscription, "Daddy 1926," in what had to be his grandmother's flowery fountain-
pen script.

Charles had a man-killer face, all right, if you believed in such things, and
Bob could see both his own and his father's bone structure in the thinness
and length, the prominence of cheekbones and hollowness of scraped-clean
cheeks, the severe and unyielding prows of nose. The mouth looked geneti-
cally incapable of cracking a smile; its hard dash might have been rectitude
or moral authority or self-belief or just plain cop-tough.

The man leaned against a rural fence on a sunny day and posed for his
wife's Brownie box camera. He was into a cowboy kind of look in 1926,
with a lot of hat covering up his hairline, a white Stetson twelve-galloner,
with prim, flat brim circling under the bullet-blunt crown. He wore a dark
three-piece suit with the insouciance of someone who wore a dark three-
piece suit every day of his life and would not think of stepping off the porch
without such. The shirt was white, with a round, stiff collar held tight by a
collar bar, above which a black tie sprung, which hung down his chest and
was swallowed by the tightness of his dark vest. A star-in-circle badge dominated the left lapel, and no one could miss it. Around his waist he'd cinched
tight a much-tooled gun belt, its loops displaying a healthy number of .45
Colt big boys, making the statement that no matter how hot and heavy it
got, he would not be running low on ammo. On his right hip, revealed by a
suit coat dramatically tucked back by a seemingly casual hand in pocket, he
displayed from the forward angle the familiar plow curve of the 1873 Model
Colt, the Peacemaker, that had decorated every Western or Southern lawman's belt for close to fifty years, as well as appearing in enough cowboy
movies to win its own Oscar. It was probably a ceremonial gun, its lines
proclaiming the heritage of the Western lawman, but for real work he'd use

the Government .45, which he'd used so well in the trenches. Only the hammer and curve of the butt strap of the Peacemaker and the ivory of its grips were visible above the embrace of the holster, but Bob looked and saw strong, large gunman's hands that would have been adept at the draw and could probably put lead in any antagonist out to forty yards or so in less than a second, even with a single-action antique—so obsolete in 1926!—like this one.

Bob looked at the face. Born in 1891, Charles would have been thirty-five at the time, Earl would have been nine, Bobbie Lee, Bob's namesake, not yet conceived. Perhaps little Earl clowned just out of the frame in this frozen moment of long-ago life, and Daddy was going to take him for an Eskimo Pie at the general store in a few minutes. Or perhaps he'd beaten him raw for some infraction of a code only he knew yet enforced with the rigor of a prison guard, and the child languished in a locked cellar room, sore everywhere, but mostly in the mind.

You couldn't tell. Not a bit. It was just a picture of a mid-'20s American lawman, proud of self and devotion to duty and social rectitude, incorruptible, brave, willing to shoot it out with anybody for the safety of the citizen. It was almost a poster for a movie called *I, Lawman* that only got made in its country's mind, and like all symbols, it did not yield its secrets easily.

PART II

7

THE BANKERS BUILDING
CHICAGO
June 1934

H E SQUARED IT WITH THE JUDGE, who agreed it should be kept quiet, as Charles's absence might lure criminals. He told no one else except his deputies and his secretary where he was going and what he was doing, and them as little as possible. He packed his two suits and six white shirts and one black tie in his one suitcase, along with a pair of Sunday go-to-church brown oxford long wings, a pair of dungarees for rough work, and underwear and handkerchiefs. And his elaborately engraved .45 shoulder holster, though he left his own gun at home. He also took five hundred in cash, in small bills, from a squirrel fund he'd started on his own behalf, unknown to anybody.

His wife drove him to the station, not even in Little Rock but a full day's drive away, across a flat and bleak landscape littered with broken-down trucks, past sad Hoovervilles rotting in the middle of nowhere, past fallow fields ruined by drought, and parched forests and dry riverbeds. The destination was Central Station in Memphis, where no one would see him by accident.

Bobby Lee had the backseat. He was handsome enough, a towhead, long and lithe at eight, who should have been the leader of the gang. But his hair was always a thorny mess, his mouth full of drool that spilled onto and encrusted his lips, and his tongue never seemed quite right, the way it probed and rolled like a mollusk of its own accord. He couldn't sit still either, and was always twisted up as if his own limbs were rope, ensnaring him, and he squirmed and bumped against them.

"Da go bye," he said.

"Yes, Bobby," said Charles. "For a time, Da go bye. You be good and take care of Mommy."

"Da go bye," Bobby said again, for answering wasn't his forte.

She finally said, "Where will you stay?"

"Well, guess I'll rent a studio somewhere. One room, foldout bed. Can't have roommates, my nightmares'd wake them up."

"You should get help, Charles."

"Some doctor asking me questions about my secrets? It's just war things, no way to get rid of them. I'll just sweat them out. Nobody needs to know my business."

"You don't share much with me. You're so locked up."

"You knew that. It ain't like I pulled it on you."

"I thought you'd soften. But that war just hardened you. You'll never soften."

"Da go bye," said Bobby from the rear, and in the mirror Charles saw that his boy's nose had leaked a gobbet of snot and, leaving a glistening trail, it had lodged in the corner of his mouth.

He caught Illinois Central 244 to Chicago. It was a rum-dum old thing, its black steam engine a manifesto of industrial purpose, in the colors of grime and grease, spewing cumulus roils of smoke as it went out into the world in general, and its own nine cars in particular, so that no window was clear, the smell of carbon lurked everywhere, and tears came to the eyes. The caravan behind it was all pre–Great War stock, with the smell of must and mold in the cars, to say nothing of sweat, vomit, and blood. A lot of living, and even some dying, had been done in those old cars. At least the government had sprung for a sleeping berth in the Pullman car and he didn't have to ride sitting up with all the poor Negroes headed north in hope of better times. The meal in the dining car, served by waiters in jackets that may have once been white but were no more, was certainly edible, but well beneath the mythical standard of the fabulous Panama Ltd., one of the most luxurious trains in America, which had regularly run this up from New Orleans route until two years ago, but as the Depression wore on and times got harder, no matter what Mr. Roosevelt promised, the big money went away, and luxury services like gilded vacation trains with it.

THE BANKERS BUILDING, 105 West Adams, upon whose nineteenth of forty-one floors nested the Chicago Office of the Justice Department, Division of Investigation, was a brawny structure; its gigantic profile would block the sun for miles if it weren't for all the other equally brawny structures on the same mission. Charles had seen Chicago and was not impressed, as he had seen London and Paris and Miami and not been impressed either. The size and breadth of the Bankers Building meant nothing to him, nor did its immense stairway design, steps for a giant to reach heaven, all in brick, with friezes of Greek ideals of the foundation of civilization standing ceremonial guard over the glorious, shiny brass and mahogany of the Adams Street entrance.

To Charles, buildings hardly registered, nor did the thousands of Chicagoans who filled the street of the nation's second-largest city. You couldn't fathom a Depression here, as the suited-and-hatted citizens ran this way and that, dodging the heavy traffic, wincing at the smell of the thousands of cars, telling themselves to ignore the insane clamor of urban life at its full intensity, while, like circling Indians, the elevated trains roared around them in the circular conceit called the Loop. Charles wasted no time gawking, swallowing, and Wow!-ing. He was too old. He was too salty. He had killed too many men. Besides, there was something that had to be handled. Its name was Melvin Purvis.

"You'll like Mel," Cowley had said, after having lassoed Charles into the job. "He is a decent man, an intelligent man, a brave man, and an honorable man."

"Yes sir. May I ask, what is his problem?"

"He is one of those men cursed by beauty."

Charles had nodded. As an analyst of human strength and weakness, he knew that the handsome ones could be tricky. It's something an infantry officer and a cop pick up on fast.

They get used to being the center of attention. They expect things to go their way. They don't like to take orders, especially from the many less attractive than they are. They move at their own pace. Sometimes they seem not to hear what is said to them. They are very stubborn, not out of commitment to a certain line of logic but to the idea that their beauty confers on them certain divine rights. The moving pictures and the fancy magazines have only exacerbated these problems, for on-screen the handsomest man is always the best, the champion of the show, the lure of all the gals, the hero of all the guys, and your real-life pretty fellow too often comes to assume the same of himself, except he has yet to do a thing to earn that reputation. So problems—little, knotty difficulties, little spats, grudges, pissing contests, garbled communications, slights too slight to mention but annoying to suffer, a sense of self-importance—all make every transaction with the handsome man more bother than it should be.

Charles's strategy in all things was aggression, which is why he wanted to get himself set up with this handsome man early on, and before even glancing across the crowded squad room that dominated the floor, he went straight to Purvis's office, told the secretary who he was and hoped the office chief had a few minutes for him.

Or was he the office chief? That was the issue here. The Director sometimes liked things a little blurry so that the after-action reports could be adjusted most favorably, and who exactly was in charge of this group of Division investigators was unclear. Purvis got all the attention and, called the Clark Gable of the outfit, was the face the public knew, for better, for worse. He was learning that with fame went criticism, always. Sam basically ran the place as an investigative entity, and he was a wheeler-dealer, an organizer, an insanely hard worker, with his own line to the Director, and he talked with the august personality many times a day, while Purvis was more or less out of the inner circle.

"And you will do me a favor, if you can," Sam had said. "To all outward purposes, please treat Mel as if he's in charge of the office. The men will become restless if they know there's confusion at the top. All details should reach me through Mel. I don't want him feeling bypassed. Is that all right?"

"I think I can handle that," said Charles. He knew from the army and county politics that organizations were seldom as straightforward in life as they were on paper. You had to play to the real, not the ideal.

"And then there's Clegg," Sam had said. He went on to explain that Clegg, another inspector who was supposedly the tactics genius, was technically in charge at Little Bohemia, and if the public didn't know his name, the men of the Division did. Thus, he took most of the unofficial blame. But he was old Division, actually predated the Director's appointment, and so no official approbation could be affixed to him. And he was the sort quite happy to pass the blame along and act as if nothing had happened. His career would not be affected. But he had been delicately "adjusted" out of the tactics-and-training job and now was almost purely an administrator.

That left the tactics part of the job open, and Charles had a pretty good idea who'd get it, first because he knew a thing or two about such matters, having led more than fifty raids in the Great War, and also because as an outsider without a constituency he could be easily sacrificed if things got balled up again. He sensed that going in, and had no problem with it, as he planned to let nothing get balled up.

Purvis turned out to be quite a nice fellow—if anything, even softer than Sam Cowley had seemed. As Sam had said, he was remarkably handsome, maybe thirty, with movie-star blond hair smoothed back, as was the Hollywood style, an aquiline profile, and white even teeth. He dressed impeccably, also like a movie star, his shirt starched, his tie, held rigid by collar bar, of the latest foulard plumage in deep red, his suit a three-piece example of top-of-the-line tailoring, glen plaid in the style made fashionable by the Duke of Windsor, everybody's candidate for best-dressed man in the world, and he put out a handful of manicured fingers and said, "Call me Mel, Sheriff. Glad to have you aboard."

As he stood and reached, Charles noted another unfortunate reality. Purvis was short. Handsome and short: tricky combination.

"Very pleased to be here, sir."

"Please sit down. Light up, if you care to. I'm going to have a cigar myself, care for one?"

"No thank you, sir. I'm an old country boy, committed to rolling my own."

Purvis took out, trimmed, and lit up a stogie as big as a torpedo, enjoying each step in the ritual to full sensual potential, and also using it to forestall his little lecture, as if even now he hadn't planned on what to say. Charles noted the stall while he rolled a tailor-made to perfection—a small skill God gives those with gifted hands—and lit and enjoyed his own smoke break. He picked a fleck of loose tobacco off his lip, then turned to face his new semi-demi-quasi-partial-who-knew-what boss.

Purvis started with flattery, not realizing Charles was invulnerable to it, even if he appreciated the energy.

"You may be country, but you're no hick, not if the records are any indication. All those raids in the war. Victory in seven gunfights, including the famous Blue Eye First National affair, you against three city boys, heavily armed, and you polished them off."

"Luck had something to do with it."

"Luck and marksmanship and guts, I'd say. Anyhow, right now my name is mud around here—around everywhere, as a matter of fact—because of that mess in Wisconsin. If I believed the rumors, I'd be packed and have my tickets back to South Carolina in my pocket. You know that?"

"I am aware, sir. Don't know the details."

"Here are the details. We screwed up. No one is interested in any excuses, they just want results. Clegg screwed up, I screwed up, our people with the guns screwed up. Too much shooting, none of it to any purpose. The wrong people hurt. An agent lost. My standing with the Director is mud too. So if you can nab me Dillinger, not only are you doing your country a great favor, you're helping Melvin Purvis of Florence, South Carolina, quite a bit too."

"Yes sir."

"We want you running a marksmanship-and-tactics class, maybe at the Chicago police firing range, twice a week. That'll be a tricky sell, but our boys need to learn to shoot. They're good fellas, smart too, but they joined to be professors of crime, not Western gunfighters. We have to get them up to the level of the men they'll be fighting, and the truth is, these gangsters seem to be good shots and very bold in action. They should never be taken lightly. They are a formidable opponent. It is said that the one called, however improbably, Baby Face is the best marksman in the country with a Thompson gun, and Homer Van Meter and Red Hamilton aren't far behind."

"I will happily run a shooting-and-tactics course. The best tactic is: shoot first."

"Excellent. Unfortunately, we fired first in Wisconsin and hit three innocent boys and alerted the gangsters."

"Bad intelligence."

"I'll say. Okay, a few rules. First off, no talking to the press boys."

"Got that."

"Second, no glory. The Division gets the glory, not the agents, and the Director *is* the Division. I made a mistake early on and let myself become known. I talk too much, I can't seem to make myself shut up. That's why I'm in hot water. But I don't know how to get out of it, because all the newspaper boys expect me to make a statement, and if I don't, they'll think something's wrong. So the more I do my job, the worse off I am. Don't make that mistake, Sheriff."

"I won't, sir."

"Coat and tie, trimmed hair, clean-shaved, every day. I don't need to tell you that."

"Not a problem."

"All communications and co-operations with other agencies, federal or local, through this office or Mr. Cowley's."

"Yes sir."

"No shared intelligence with other entities, federal or local, without permission from myself or Cowley."

"Check."

"The Director wants his fellows to be clean livers. That means if you're a drinking man, keep it quiet. If you need to cohabit, keep it quiet. No muss, no fuss. Got a car?"

"After I'm settled, I may bring mine up here."

"We'll issue you one until then. Mileage is half a cent per. No per diem unless you're sent somewhere temporarily or it's overtime. Incidentally, no overtime per se, not even in the form of a thank-you, and there will be plenty of twenty-four-hour days. Also, I'll get you a list of Chicago joints where we'd not like to see you, gin joints, clubs, brothels of course, other known gang spots."

"Yes sir."

"Certain practices you have to get used to. This is a Mob town. We're not interested in them, that's for Treasury. They got Capone, not us. The Director has made Dillinger and the other bank boys our main focus. So you may have to show a blind eye to certain activities you run into that put money in the banks of fellows with Italian names, like Nitti."

"I can handle that."

"If you develop snitches, you have to share the intelligence with myself or Special Agent Cowley. We can't have, and the Director will not abide, lone wolves, glory hounds, solo artists."

"I understand."

"Finally, I'd be delighted to see your new training ideas on paper. Can you do that?"

"If you don't mind a misspelling or two."

"I can live with that. I'll have Clegg show you around. He's tricky, very sour on his situation, but I know you can handle him."

"Yes sir."

"You'll draw a weapon from the arms room. Most of the boys carry a .38 Colt revolver. There are some .45 automatics we got from Postal. Plus, of course, ten Thompson guns, five of the big Browning rifles, and five more of the Remington Model 11 riot guns. As for the handgun, you get to choose."

"I'm a .45 fellow. The army taught me how and now I've got the taste."

"Suit yourself. And this."

He opened his drawer and took out a badge, a chunk of oval bronze, well-worked, dull, and heavy.

"This makes it official. The younger boys like a swearing-in ceremony, but I'm guessing you're a little grown up for that."

"I don't need no ceremony. Pinning it on is ceremony enough."

Purvis pushed it over, Charles took it up.

"It is a war," Purvis said. "Young, inexperienced troops against professionals of long standing and great tactics and courage. This is a great opportunity for you, but it's also very dangerous. You'll be point man on all engagements, you will get shot at a lot, you will have to shoot to kill, maybe a lot. Any day can be your last, and you won't have Frank Hamer backing you up but Dink Stover instead, fresh out of Yale."

"I wouldn't have it any other way, Mr. Purvis," said Charles.

CLEGG WOULD BE TROUBLE. He wore dark attitude on his face and knew, unofficially at least, that Charles was his successor as tactics boss and he didn't like it. He was heavyset, out-of-shape, shifty-eyed, well-dressed, and was called, as Charles would soon learn, Troutmouth by the boys, for his small but prehensile and overactive set of lips, always atwitch or aflutter or puckered up in sourness. His whole performance was smile-free, charmless, condescending, and self-important. Charles wouldn't take this from any man, normally, but first day on the job had its own rules, so he wouldn't be bracing Troutmouth for some time. But he looked forward to it.

"I doubt you've ever seen a squad room so big," said Clegg, gesturing to the pen before him that filled almost half the nineteenth floor. Actually, Charles had, as Dallas, Atlanta, and Kansas City all had big, busy detective departments, and he'd been welcomed in them all.

Charles simply gazed at the large room, filled with grim government furniture, stacks of paper on desks, the typewriters that justified such a spread, telephone lines, wanted posters on the wall, the whole cop squalor and messiness that was universal from Scotland Yard to the NKVD to the Tokyo Municipal Police. In this room, men scurried, talked on the phone, worked paper, consulted and kibitzed. None of them had caught on yet to who Charles was, so nobody paid him any attention.

"Suit coats on, that's how the Director likes it. Ties up, no rolled-up sleeves. No feet on desk. No loud talking or laughing. Business first, last, and always. Shined shoes, trimmed, clean fingernails. You have to present well around here as well as work hard, pay attention, don't crack off to any superior, and return all your phone calls. Suits only. No sport coats."

"I don't own no sport coats," said Charles.

"Wonderful," said Clegg. "You're already ahead of the game." It was doubtful he meant it as a compliment, for it carried the heavy weight of irony with each word. Clegg, also Southern, had a "high" aspect to him; coming from a fine family, he was a little too good for a fellow such as Charles, who fractured grammar, had big, strong, splayed hands and a bony, raw vitality, which he would consider red-dirt hillbilly compared to his own manner and tastes. He deserved better, he seemed to be saying.

"Now, this way, let me show you the arms room."

"Yes sir."

He took Charles out of the big room and down an interior corridor lined with doors to smaller rooms, ticking off their purposes languidly.

"Teletype. Interrogation, interrogation, interrogation, with one-way mirror and observation room available, Mr. Cowley's office—"

"He's back here?"

"It's his preference. No name on the door, no receptionist's office, no secretary. He's in there by himself, and he types his own memos. Most days, you won't see him, as he's going over reports, on the phone with Washington or other field offices, talking to various law enforcement entities, that sort of thing. He makes assignments, keeps track of case progress, looks to cut down on duplicated effort or step in if communication breaks down somewhere. But every morning there's a fresh memo on the bulletin board, and if you're mentioned in it, it's a good sign."

"He seemed like the no-bull sort, didn't need much attention."

"That would describe him perfectly. Even though he was a minister for two years, saving heathen souls in Hawaii, he's a technical. Everything by the book, then recorded in the book, the book then sent to Washington for the Director's pleasure. Here we are."

Clegg led him into a large room, clearly a rough or wet room, meant for gunwork. A bench stood against the wall, with gunsmith's tools, and jars of Hoppe's No. 9 and Rem Oil, the pungent stench of the Hoppe's clouding the air almost visibly.

"Is there an armorer?"

"We have a young agent named Ed Hollis who has recently inherited this room as one of his administrative duties. He's more of a glorified clerk than an actual armorer, much less a gunsmith. He keeps track of ammo, records the guns coming in and going out, fills out a report if anything is damaged in a fight, ships guns to D.C. for lab work—really, it's a hard, crummy, filthy job. But he earned it. He was at Little Bohemia and did not distinguish himself, so I thought it better to take him out of the lineup, so to speak, for a bit."

It was your plan, thought Charles.

"He also runs the motor pool now, and maybe he's tending to that. But on a day-by-day if you've got the possibility of a serious engagement and you need to check out a bigger weapon, you file with me and I'll approve it and unlock the vault." He gestured to the large steel door in the wall. "We store them in there. When you return, you bring your chit back to me for filing. That way, we always know what's out, what's not. The last thing we want to do is misplace a Thompson. The newspapers would fry us."

Troutmouth added, "The reason the gun room is here is because that"— he pointed—"was already there."

It was a grating, behind which, in squalid splendor, rough-walled, dirty, its paint peeling, lit by a single bulb, was a freight elevator. "We had it re-wired so it only stops here on nineteen and in the lower-level garage, where our cars are. If we load for bear, that's how we get to our vehicles. Don't want to be storming through the lobby with machine guns and Browning rifles, looking like one of those army raiding parties."

Charles nodded.

"Any questions?" asked Clegg.

"I'll have much business for Hollis later today. Does he, by the way, know anything about guns?"

"I don't know if he can take them apart or not, but I do know he has no idea when to shoot them."

Charles realized that it was, therefore, Hollis who had fired first on the three civilians getting into their car after dinner at the Little Bohemia Lodge. What was he supposed to do? Let them escape? Why wasn't there an alternative plan, or a fallback against just this situation? Why hadn't it been anticipated, as, after all, the agents had had time to fly up to northern Wisconsin, rent cars, and move to the lodge two hours from the Eagle River Airport? So this wasn't an operational mistake, it was a tactical one: poor planning by Clegg here, and it's Hollis who gets hung out to dry. He'd seen it all over the army.

"Now, one last thing," said Clegg. "This way, please, Sheriff."

He took Charles back to the squad room, and when they entered—and this time, word having gotten around—all the typing stopped, as did the chatting, the writing, the paper-shuffling. Charles felt eyes upon him but did not acknowledge them.

Clegg led him to a big wall and upon it were the faces of the men they were hunting.

"You'd best get to know these faces like your own children's," said Clegg, annoying Charles because of course he already did.

Clegg rattled off the names. "Homer Van Meter, Harry Pierpont, Pretty Boy Floyd, the little pug is Les Gillis, known as Baby Face Nelson, a name he's said to hate. And that one there, that's the big dog, John Dillinger himself, Public Enemy Number One."

Dillinger didn't look like much more than a potato-faced fertilizer salesman in a small Indiana town, which is how he might have ended up had he not been sentenced to twenty-five years for a rather minor crime when he was nineteen. In prison, he learned a trade, and like any trained man, when he got out he looked for a way to make a living practicing that trade.

"He's no genius, believe me, and possibly not even the leader of the gang. He doesn't make plans or anything, he doesn't scheme and plot, and there's no record of him having a particular need to hurt or kill. He wasn't a tough guy in the joint. In fact, they once found him snuggled in bed with another guy, so who knows what's going on. This one is the psychopath."

Clegg's elegant, polished finger came to rest on the square face of a guy who could have been in the Our Gang comedies, for he resembled the little picture-show boy Mickey McGuire more than anybody else, with a square, uptilted nose that spread his nostrils, a tumble of lengthy, pomaded hair full of blond highlights, a pair of small but not menacing eyes, and a blur of matinee-idol, make-believe mustache.

"Don't know what makes him tick," said Clegg. "But he's a monster, that's for sure, and poor Carter Baum found out the hard way at Little Bohemia. Baby Face killed Carter in one second. If you see Baby Face any other way than over a gunsight, he's probably going to kill you."

8

NOBODY WAS IN A GOOD MOOD, except for that idiot Homer. But Les was in the worst mood of all. Tommy Carroll's death hit him the hardest. He'd driven into Little Bohemia with Tommy sitting next to him, Helen in the back, and as old friends and colleagues who'd been on the wrong end of enough cop gunfire to know and trust one another well, the trip had been fun. Helen liked Tommy too; he was a big, handsome lug from Montana whose jaw had been busted in his boxing days and never set right, so that at its new angle, it looked like a lantern, making him look stupid, but of course he was not stupid.

But the way Tommy Carroll had died had been stupid. Not on a job, not in a police ambush, not in a betrayal or a plot, but just by the dumb-bunny roll of the dice.

He makes it out of Little Bohemia, the federals blazing away with choppers and filling the air with a blizzard of hardball and not a one comes near Tommy. And he gets downed by two hick detectives in a town called Waterloo, Iowa. The coppers probably didn't even know who he was.

"When your time is up, your time is up," said Johnny. "That's our business. That's the risk."

Johnny would know. "Johnny" to his pals, he was John Dillinger, the most famous bank robber in the world. He had a gift for publicity, a vivid personality, a terrible beauty, and a sublimely cool aspect that enchanted everyone, friend or foe. Plus, a genius for escape, over and above his criminal skills. Twice he'd wriggled out of tough joints, once with pals and once on his own genius with three cents' worth of scrap wood and shoe polish. He was a great criminal.

"Some license plates in his backseat," said Les. "Can you believe that? Some kid, some junior G-Man, notices 'em and that's it, buster, you've been ventilated." It seemed so unfair.

"Arf, arf," said Homer. "Me sad puppy."

Homer: his name was Homer Van Meter; he was as Indiana as Indianapolis, a string bean with a thick gush of hair and a long, bony Grant Wood face. He had a marksman's gift for gunwork and a sense of humor that could be likened to the sound of sheet metal being ripped by insane dogs. In his life—he was twenty-five—he had told ten thousand jokes, of which at least nine, or possibly even ten, had been funny. He kept trying, however. He was a very good bank robber.

"He didn't even have a gun," said Charlie in his Oklahoma twang. "As he's running away, the cops shoot him down. They don't even know who he is. The great Tommy Carroll."

Charlie—Charles "Pretty Boy" Floyd—was out of the Cookson Hills and mean as a splinter in your ass. He was a good shot; too stupid to know the meaning of fear, either as a word or as a concept; big, strong, sullen, bitter. And that was sober. Drunk, look out. No one would ever accuse him of genius, and he couldn't be trusted to plan his next bowel movement, but he was solid, steady, a good man with a gun, and so obsessed with bringing financial relief to his people back in the Oklahoma hills, just about unbudgeable in determination.

"He did good at Brainerd," said Johnny. "And he was a good man to be on the run with. No complaints, no whining, no 'Why me?' bullshit. He was a pro. He was there when we put Red in the ground." Red Hamilton was another recent departee, having caught a slug at a roadblock he and Johnny had busted through on the way out of Wisconsin. They'd all been there. There were obligations, even in this little tribe of outlaws. You didn't forget somebody just because he caught a cold from a bullet. You put him away, right and proper, or if you couldn't, you drank a beer to him and said words. "He was an ace."

That was as good an epitaph as Tommy was likely to get, and of course Johnny, who always had a view toward the bigger picture, was the one to give it.

And Les himself: he hated the moniker Baby Face, hung on him accidentally and not remotely accurate—he was a lithe, quick, fully developed male of a reasonable height, by the standards of the time, and had no physical oddities that compelled the name. His psychology was hammered into place by a drunken father, who hammered other things as well, namely, Les's mother and Les himself. At some point Lester Gillis, of the West Side of Chicago, Illinois, with a hideous Windy City accent that turned all his vowels into the shrieks of geese as they were fed into a meat grinder tail first, just decided to hammer back at the world for giving him a childhood comprised mainly of getting the shit beat out of him, which didn't bother him, but seeing his mother get the shit beat out of her, which did bother him. Smart, feral, without moral compass beyond the immediate tribe, devoted to his hot little bundle of wife and his two kids, though somewhat undone by a hair-trigger temper and an inability to conceive of getting hurt that expressed itself in a recklessness that was also sheer bravery, he was another professional, with great ambition, skill, and dedication. He wanted to be a great bank robber.

The last man here was Les's pal Jack Perkins, no genius and way overmatched by the all-star talents in the room, but at least he could be counted on to do what he was told, and he always had a smile on his face. The only thing demanded of him was that he learn his lines and not bump into the furniture.

The chamber itself was the back room of a tavern that was, guaranteed Homer, part of the big thing the Italians had going. That is, it was connected up and therefore part of a web of activities and plots, all against the law, all nefarious, and so it could be trusted to play host to, and give suffrage and rest to, various on-the-lammers, various would-be torpedoes, even the odd actual torpedo headed to Cleveland or Chicago. It was about twelve miles out of South Bend, and all were here at the insistence of Homer, who was no Jimmy Murray when it came to spotting, planning, and pulling off jobs.

Jimmy was a master; he'd run the biggest heist in history a few years ago in Illinois and that one had been a triumph, start to finish. Money, money, money for everybody and nobody dead. Now Homer was thinking he could come up in weight class, become a Jimmy Murray–class setup guy and thus grab a double share.

"Why did the duck cross the road?" he asked.

Nobody had an answer. Each had beer before him, except for Les, who never drank and kept a clear head. The air roiled with cigarette smoke, and from the bar in the front room the music of somebody's Chicagoland band beat on, tinnily and slightly out of sync. "It Might as Well Be Spring."

"To get to the quackers on the other side, quack, quack," said Homer, blowing up in laughter. Johnny laughed, though it was phony, and Homer's cheap dame Mickey Conforti laughed, showing her horse teeth, and always polite Jack laughed, but Charlie, sour as cow piss, said, "Get on with it, god-dammit, this ain't no radio hour."

It was the only thing Charlie and Les would ever agree on.

"Hey, a joke a day keeps Mr. Frowny Face away," said Homer. Homer, a good man with the Winchester .351 he carried around in a billiards case, and he'd somehow glommed onto this hideous, loud skank of woman who was known to pass out sexual favors to any and all when she got a little buzzed.

"All right," said Homer. "Merchants National, South Bend, twelve miles north of here, sis-boom-bah, home of Notre Dame, and we are the Five Horsemen, not the Four, so we can't miss. It's a tidy little joint, the coppers are amateurs, but it's got all that money these Indiana farmers rack in for growing peas in pods and corn in husks and chickens with goobery red beaks. Plus, every Saturday at eleven, two postal inspectors mosey down from the Post Office with a big bag or two of cash they've pulled in all week selling the folks stamps. That stamp money adds up!"

"What's the take?" Charlie asked.

"Figure fifty, easy. More than Brainerd, more than Sioux City, a good haul with minimum risk, with the stamp money boosting it. Y'all are going to thank me when you're in Miami, going to the track every day."

"I ain't no track tout," snarled Charlie. "I got family to take care of. There's a Depression on, and nobody in Oklahoma is working—that is, them parts of it that ain't blowed away in the wind."

"Yes sir," said Homer, trying to oblige. "Well, we'll get you paid up good. Now, I see this as an in-out car job, never no split-up, so we don't need to set a meet-up, one car for all of us, the South Bend coppers ain't set up with radio nets, to any degree. Mr. Charlie, you'll be the ringmaster, run the show; you got the deep voice, and you're as scary as you are pretty."

"I ain't pretty a bit," said the sour Oklahoman. What a dick he could be!

"You guys are big enough to have nicknames. Les's Baby Face, Johnny's Johnny D, and you're Pretty Boy. I'm just And Others. It ain't fair."

"When every cop in America knows it and your face, you won't be so crazy about a nickname," said Charlie.

"I got a name for you," said Les. "You're Mr. Talks Too Much, Don't Say Nothing."

"Les," said Johnny, "calm down and stick to robbing banks. Comedy ain't your talent."

"The feds I ran off the road in Wisconsin while you guys was shivering and shitting in the forest thought I was pretty funny."

"Anyhow, Mr. Jack," said Homer, trying to get back on the program, "I know you're new to this line of work, so you're the early bird. You just set up and make sure no coppers are around and the postal clerks have brought the stamp money along, and if it's clear, you give us the high sign, we park, we pile out and take it. Jack, you just hang outside as the sentry. Then we all pile in, and we're gone in three minutes flat, while the cops are still sitting in the doughnut shop talking Notre Dame football."

"It's never that easy," said Les. "Johnny, you know that. You got to have backup plans, meet-ups set, maps in and out, alternatives, the whole she-bang. You can't just waltz in, waltz out. Jimmy Murray always—"

"Is that your nose or are you eating a banana?" said Homer. "Jimmy ain't here, in case you hadn't noticed."

"Oh, I noticed when I felt the breeze blowing through your left ear and out your right," said Les, riling up.

He riled up too easy, too fast, and he knew it. It was always a problem. He would just sail away on a sea of anger and nothing else mattered. Only Helen could calm him down.

"What did Helen say when she looked into a box of Cheerios? Oh, look, doughnut seeds."

"You're an idiot," said Les. "Johnny, are you going to let this clown call the shots? His head is full of mothballs, and I'm afraid I'll get the clap just looking at his broad. Hey, Mickey. Sooey!"

"Baby, he can't talk to me that way."

But he could. Though Les was average height, he was not weak, fright-ened, or unable to fight. If you messed with him—win, lose, or draw—you had an enemy for life.

"Hey, little man, you leave Mickey out of it, quack, quack. You got no cause to beat up on her."

"The Twelfth Army's got no cause to beat up on her. They all remember the night—"

"Okay, Les," said Johnny, "you can lay off the girl. She ain't a part of this."

"Yeah, go home to your little woman, but be sure to bring a tomcat to sniff out the fishy stink," added Homer.

The next thing he knew, hands were pulling him off Homer, whose face and eye were puffed up from Les's blows, one hard, one glancing. Les him-self had no memory of flying around the table and launching fists, then himself, at the hayseed, the two of them tumbling, chairs flying, beers spill-ing, the girl screaming, Charlie bitching, Jack pulling back, and somehow, some way, Johnny getting them apart.

"Save it for the Division," Johnny said. "Goddammit, Les, calm down. He didn't mean nothing, he just likes to tell a joke now and then."

"Don't you ever say nothing about my Helen again!" said Les. The screwball intensity of his expression would have melted a statue.

"Okay, okay," said Homer, "I didn't mean nothing by it. It was a joke, I'm funny—ha-ha—quack, quack—that's me. Sorry for Tommy, sorry for Red, but now we need to get back to work, and I got us a good one. No need to get so steamed. Just because when you took her to the top of the Empire State Building and planes attacked, that ain't my fault."

"You knock it off too, Homer. Sometimes I don't know which is worse, your dumb jokes or Les's firecracker personality."

But Les decided at this moment he would kill Homer. He would put a fat .45 into his gut and watch him bleed out in the gutter. He'd beg for Mama, he'd ask for a priest or a doctor, he'd tell Les he was sorry, he didn't mean anything about Helen, but Les would just watch, studiously, as the life bubbled out of the man, forming a delta of red rivers on the pavement.

So when Johnny got them back to the table, yelled to Vince to bring more beer and a Coca-Cola for Les, and got the meeting back to a semblance of order, it wasn't quite the victory he assumed it would be. It was because having sentenced Homer, Les felt an immediate calm come across him. Suddenly he felt all right. No fury, no seething in his gut, just the pleasing image of Homer afloat in a lake of blood on some raw and windy corner. That's how it was with him; it blew in, it blew out.

"Okay," said Homer, "I will do some more scouting. Maybe Les's right, we need more dope before we jump. We'll come back here and split the grab and go our separate ways until we need to fill our pockets again. But that'll push it back a week, maybe two. I'm thinking June thirtieth. Meet-up here June twenty-eighth, the twenty-ninth I'll take you through it, and on the thirtieth we go. Agreed?"

"I'd like this one to go real smooth," said Johnny. "Those Division assholes think we're on the run, all scattered and scared and hiding under the blankets, after Wisconsin. I'd like to pull off a nice, clean big job just to show them bastards."

"See, I don't want to show nobody nothing," said Les. "I just want to kill some of the suckers, and that's the way we teach them who we are."

"Quack, quack," said Homer.

LES DROVE TO the Happy Hoosier Tourist Camp & Cabins site seventeen miles away, pulling in to the space in front of the little log home labeled No. 14, and saw his two kids playing in the front yard. That always filled him with a kind of bliss nothing else on earth did. Kids! They were his! He had made them, he and Helen, and they were going to be something much better than their old man!

"How're my little cowpokes? Oh, Daddy loves his cowpokes so much!"

He grabbed Darlene and flung her skyward so that her legs flew parallel to the ground as he whirled her around. The child giggled with pleasure.

"Me, Daddy, me!" shouted Ronnie, the boy. "Oh, please, Daddy!"

He set Darlene down, where, giggling and dizzy, she sat with a bump in the grass, and picked up Ronnie to do the same. The boy squealed in mock fear as he was pulled in circles, also in defiance of gravity, by his dad.

"'Round and 'round we go," shouted Les. "Where we end up, nobody knows."

Finally, he slowed and then stopped, freeing Ronnie to fall dizzily, giggling.

He sat on the running board of his car, a stolen Hudson with plates from another stolen car.

"Whoa!" he said. "You guys wore me out! I'm too old for this sort of thing! Pick on somebody your own size!"

"Daddy, Daddy, can we go to a zoo tomorrow?"

"Hmm," said Les, "maybe." He thought Indianapolis might not be too far and there'd probably be a good zoo there. "If not tomorrow, the next day. Depending on where we go."

"I want to see the lions," said Darlene.

"Roarrrrrrrr!" said Ronnie, snarling up his face and turning his little hands into claws.

"Roarrrrrrrrrrrrrrrr!" said Les. "Yep, that's what they do, all right. You don't want to get too close, I'll tell you that."

Helen stepped out of the cabin. She was a pretty girl, in that down-home Chicago way, blue-eyed and trim, and, best of all, she was solid. She was all Les ever wanted. The other fellows with their whore girlfriends, it made Les sick. What did you get out of that except maybe a dose? With Helen, it was every time he wanted it, always good, and to have her there, to depend on, to take care of little things, to look after stuff—all that—it was so good. He never wanted anything more. Who could ask for something more, like gambling on horses—stupid—or going out to fancy places every night—stupid.

And, better yet, she was loyal. Picked up at Little Bohemia, she spent a week as a guest of the state of Wisconsin and didn't say a thing, even if the Division boys put the pressure on her hard. She clammed up, and nothing they threatened her with got her to budge. She could be a stubborn little mule when she wanted to.

"Hi, sweetie, they run you ragged?" he asked.

"They can be a handful, but it's not so bad I can't handle it."

"What's for dinner tonight?"

"I got a nice slice of ham at the A&P and some potatoes and fresh green beans. Pineapple upside-down cake for dessert."

Who could ask for more, especially with people starving or going on the dole all over the place.

"I can't wait." And it was true. He couldn't. It sounded so good.

"How did it go?"

"Oh, you know. Johnny's fine, he's a good man, the others ain't bad. That damned Homer, though, can't abide him or his girlfriend. I don't trust her any further than I could throw her. She'd talk her head off first chance she'd get." In his mind, he ran a quick comparison between the slut Mickey

Conforti and Helen's decency, kindness, sweet temper, and loyalty. He'd really won that one!

"This one isn't going to be rough, is it? You said it would be easy."

"I said it *should* be easy. You can't never predict these things. Look at how poor Tommy checked out. One minute as happy as a pig in clover, the next he's riding the handcart to hell because of a coupla Iowa hicks. I won't lie about that, sweetie, never have, never will. It can be a dangerous game. But nobody's been born yet can get the drop on me. I should come out of it flush, and that'll give us a stake for the next year, we can move somewhere nice and put the kids in a good school."

"Oh, Les, that would be so swell."

"Quack, quack," said Les, because he was so happy.

9

BLUE EYE, ARKANSAS

The present

THERE WASN'T MUCH CHARLES LEFT IN BLUE EYE. There wasn't even much Earl left. In fact, there wasn't much Blue Eye left in Blue Eye.

Bob ordered himself not to mark the changes out loud. It could turn the afternoon into an ordeal. Remember when Nickerson's Five-and-Dime stood here, now it's a Mexican laundromat. Oh, and over there, that was a Winn-Dixie, at least until Mr. Sam built out by the Interstate and closed it down. And Fred's, where all the farmers had breakfast between 4 and 6 every morning, that's long gone. Now there's a Sonic. What the hell is a Sonic?

No, he wouldn't be that guy. He just reacted numbly to the undeniable reality that what had once been a little town out of which a sheriff named Andy Griffith could have operated was now mostly shuttered and bleak, and all the action seemed to be in fast-food restaurants set up on the bypass. It wasn't all that much different, he supposed, from Cascade, Idaho, a similar spot of highway blight he called home.

It wasn't quite dead, though. Andy Vincent, Sam's grandson, Jake's nephew, ran the Allstate Insurance agency, and was doing well enough to afford a tribe of kids who called Swagger Mr. Bob, and still had reputation enough to open doors in the town. That's because he was also the mayor.

For example, when they went to the *Blue Eye Star-Clarion*, though it was owned by an out-of-state newspaper chain, the receptionist went and got a managing editor who was most decent, and once they'd explained why they were there, had told them that the old papers—then it was just the *Clarion*,

"Western Arkansas's Democratic Voice for a New South"—no longer existed anywhere except on microfiche, but they could be accessed in the library, and he'd make a call over there to ensure Bob was well taken care of, not fobbed off on some seventeen-year-old intern.

"That's very kind of you," said Bob. "It's much appreciated."

"Is there a story in your returning?" the newspaperman asked. "It seems like you haven't been around in a long time." And, true enough, as it had been a while.

"No sir. It's just family business, is all. My grandfather. Realized I didn't know a thing about him and it was time to learn a little something."

"Got it," said the journalist. "A trip to your own past. It should be private, then, and it will be private."

At the library, a nice young lady set Bob up on a microfiche reader, and it took him a bit of time to get used to the mirror-backwards manipulations necessary to bring the pages under the magnifier, but he got the hang of it quick enough.

"We went to this just before the whole cyberspace thing broke," said Ms. Daniels, as plain as a pie but small-town friendly and helpful in every way, God bless her sweet soul, "and I guess we thought it would make us so modern. And we were obsolete two weeks after we got it set up."

"Ms. Daniels, to me indoor plumbing seems like a miracle, so this is just fine by my standards. I hate the computers anyhow. I do know left from right, so I should be all right."

Mayor Andy went to sell a policy or run a council meeting or something, leaving Bob alone in the pages of the *Clarion*, January through December 1934.

It was so very long ago. Everything was different, but everything was the same. The cars were beasts, but in their humps and gropes toward smooth, you could see lines that would eventually permutate into today's Big Mac–mobiles. All were black too, or a shade of gunmetal gray, maybe navy, maybe green. Men wore coats and ties and hats in those days, everywhere, all the time, frequently with vests, always with cigarettes, pipes, or cigars. Pipes!

Hadn't seen a pipe in years. No sunglasses. Ties never loosened except at a ball game or when going bowling. The hats were fedoras mostly, and the fashion that year demanded a circular, downward slope to the brim, no snappy little uptick to the rear like a duck's ass. Some wore theirs atilt, rakishly, but most just pulled it down to the eyebrows, to keep the sun or the snow out, and forgot all about it. No "sport clothes"; casual clothes were merely last year's suit pants and beat-up, worn-down work shoes. The women all wore stockings, all wore girdles (he supposed) and almost always wore hats, usually little feathery constructions that curled around and were nested in their carefully tended hair. Veils were rolled about the hats, and the dresses were big-shouldered, also flowery in both material and corsage, waists trim but not cinched in to wasp dimensions. Nobody was trying to look sexy; they left that to movie stars. And they looked like they did their vacuuming in heels and pearls. Also: no feet. The foot was taboo. Toes even more so, none glimpsed in the pages of the *Clarion*, January 1, 1934, through December 31, same year. Farmers wore dungarees and had open shirt collars but the same fedoras. A few straw boaters revealed themselves in the newspaper pages, standing out like bright coins in the universe of gray-black dots that was printing in those days. Lots of shots of trains, the dominant mode of transportation, and many civic ceremonies seemed to take place at the station, in front of some gigantic locomotive leaking steam and grease from a dozen portals. No airplanes, except now and then a War Department–released shot of "Our New Pursuit Ship," a biplane with a clear plastic hood over the cockpit and a long telescopic-tube gunsight along the fuselage just fore of the windscreen, where the pilot could convert to sniper and put the crosshairs on—who? Hun? Jap? Red? They had no idea of the hurricane of violence that lurked a few years ahead and would consume so many of these happy, content, tie- and girdle-wearing citizens.

A figure known as "The Sheriff" was occasionally seen, though he faded into the background of photographs and usually looked away from the camera at the moment of the snap. Who was this man? His star, always in focus;

his face, never. Was he hiding something? There was something about him that seemed not to want to be pinned down, held to account.

SHERIFF ARRESTS TWO WITH ILLEGAL STILL
SHERIFF TO CLOSE DOWN ON SPEEDERS
SHERIFF SAYS NO THREAT FROM MIGRANT WORKERS
VIOLENT CRIME DROPS, SAYS SHERIFF
SHERIFF, DEPUTIES WIN STATE SHOOTING TOURNEY
SHERIFF NABS GAS STATION ROBBER

He was everywhere, even as he was nowhere, a blur, a phantom, an image of rectitude on the move. Bob tried to get a fix on him, bringing the magnification of the machine up as high as it would go, but at a certain point the image separated into dots and only the dots were visible.

Who are you, Charles Swagger? What's your action, your ken, your mission, your passion? For a hero, you're quite vague, scattered, separated. You never sit still long enough for anyone to pin you down. What are you hiding?

It occurred to him to mark his grandfather's appearances in the *Clarion* and so he started at the beginning and began the laborious process of examining every page for every day, every month, through the entire year.

"Hard at work?" said Andy Vincent, returning in late afternoon from his obligations.

"Trying to get a fix on what he was up to in that year," said Bob.

"Learn anything?"

"Well . . . yes. He's in the paper, photoed either at an emergency or a crime scene or at some stupid ceremony or other, about three times a week, from January through June. That's what you'd expect from a small-town sheriff who's part of the administration, is elected on the party ticket, is wired into the establishment, so to speak. But then, mysteriously, he sort of disappears halfway through June. No announcement, no discussion, no reference to illness or whatever, he's just gone. Some deputy named Cyril Judd becomes the main man for law enforcement. 'According to Deputy Cyril Judd'—you must have seen that in the paper a hundred times. But then, in December, he's back again, same as always. 'Sheriff Swagger said today that the county raised over $900 in speeding fines over the fiscal year,' et cetera, et cetera. He just went there, he did what he did, he came back, and nobody speculated. If he was missed, it never reached the level of official scrutiny and went unnoticed in the *Clarion*. I'd guess Judge Tyne, who seemed to be the boss of the county in those days, had a hand in telling the paper what it could publish or not. It ain't a cover-up so much as an agreement between consenting adults."

"I wish I could tell them what to cover and what not to," said Andy, with a kind of scoff in his voice.

"It sure was different in them days," said Bob.

AND FINALLY, the grave.

"Did you want some privacy?" asked Andy.

A breeze rushed through the cemetery. It was for veterans, and you could work up a tear or two by looking to the long ranks of white stones rolling off toward the ridge, against the green of the grass and the here-and-there plumage of tree or bush. But Bob ordered his emotions to shut down because he was here on some sort of business that didn't have a thing to do with young boys shot down before they even got fucked, for a cruel bitch that old and withered men had dressed up under the phony name Duty, to make them go without complaining. He'd been mourning them since he came out of his coma in the Subic Bay Naval Hospital.

"Nah," he said. "I don't have no feelings toward him, and won't be feeling much. This is just an obligation of some kind."

"Duty?" said Andy.

"Yep," said Bob.

They walked the pathways through the garden of stone until at last they came to the site that had been registered to Charles Swagger.

"I guess as a town celeb, he got more than a stone."

"Would that make him a success?"

"In the way they figured in those days, I suppose," said Andy.

Still, it wasn't much to show for a man's life, a war hero and public servant, or so the official record insisted.

"Bob, Dad's not far from here. I think I'll go over there and pay a visit while I'm here."

"Your dad deserves a visit," remembered Swagger, and Andy trotted off.

That left Swagger alone with a chunk of marble inscribed with the six-pointed star of the official law enforcer, over the inscription

CHARLES F. SWAGGER
1891–1942
MAJOR, A.E.F.
TOWN SHERIFF
DUTY FIRST

As to the last line, Bob thought, maybe so, maybe not. We're sure going to try and find out.

But there was another revelation and it carried an echo. His grandfather had been an officer. In a short war he'd made major. Which was odd, not because it confirmed Charles's combat effectiveness and leadership ability but because his own father, Earl, had been so committed to remaining an NCO, something that had seemed DNA-level deep in the Swagger men, as Bob, despite offers, and in some cases pleas, had also chosen to so remain, and Bob's son, Ray, who hadn't even been raised by Swaggers but by his original Philippine adoptive family, also went the sniper's way, and also stayed an NCO despite blandishments, and Ray was really smart, smarter than most generals.

Bob tried to think this through. Why would such a thing be? One possibility had to do with the Swagger freakish shooting talent, way beyond the norm and way off the charts. Most Swagger men were shooters. That gift stood them well especially in war or gunfights in civilian society, but it meant that knowing that about themselves and taking pride in such a talent, they'd be drawn to ways to use it most productively. Thus, sniping, machine-gun-nest destroying, and highway patrolling, gangster hunting. So the Swagger preference would be to stay close to the gun, and a commissioned officer's role would take him away from the gun and the man he was to a man who he would have to pretend to be.

But another reason might be that Earl was decreeing his distance from Charles. If his father had risen beyond his shooting talents into the officers' ranks, he would not. He was declaring himself to be not the same man. I will not my father be, Earl was saying. And thus Bob's dynamic, a generation later and haunted by the death of the man he still considered the greatest he ever knew, is: I *will* my father be.

Which brought Swagger back to Charles F. Swagger, moldering in the grave under an eroding chunk of marble, unvisited, unremembered, possibly unloved. But he died with the reputation for Duty, so he must have—sometime, somewhere, somehow—impressed someone.

His phone buzzed and—it was never a sure bet—he heard it. He looked, saw the caller was Nick Memphis from Virginia.

"Nick?"

"How are you today, Doctor?"

"My feet hit the ground before my nose, so that's a good sign."

"Very promising. Look, I've got some stuff here. I can't mail it down, but the old records show some definite possibilities that your grandfather was in the Bureau. And then—er, how can I say this?—out of the Bureau. Rather suddenly, rather dramatically."

"I'm betting he was a sonovabitch on wheels," said Bob.

"On wheels?" said Nick. "He may have been the first one through the sonovabitch sound barrier!"

10

THE BANKERS BUILDING, 19TH FLOOR
CHICAGO
June 1934

"Look, Hollis," said Charles, "I know you're in everybody's doghouse because of Little Bohemia. But that was before my time, so it don't cut no ice with me. You work hard, play square, give me two honest days' labor for every one on the calendar, and you'll do all right by me."

"Yes sir," said Hollis, who proved to be an earnest stalk of boy out of Iowa by way of law school.

"I won't hold your education against you, fair enough? Too many well-educated fools 'round this place, not enough sheriffs or cops."

"Yes sir."

And Hollis did work hard, even if, by casual oral transmission, his account soon provided the field office's staff with its nom de guerre for Charles, which was of course "The Sheriff."

The younger men adored him. Rumors of his proficiency and victories filled the air. Someone dug out an account of his famous 1923 bank shootout in Blue Eye, someone used a connection to get his service record out of the War Department and learned from that that not only had he served eighteen months in our army, emerging as a highly decorated major, but before he'd spent two years in the Canadian army in the trenches, and, besides, a chestful of medals won a battlefield commission there too; suddenly he was the warrior king that all these young men knew they would never be. And the fact that he didn't woo them made him all the more alluring; and that he didn't recognize or pay heed to his reputation and never mentioned it himself, added to his mystique, as did his severe appearance, in his dark three-piece and low-brimmed brown fedora and the new .45 he carried in his shoulder rig, where all the others had chosen the lighter, less recoil-intense .38.

"If it don't start with a 4, I ain't interested," he said—much quoted in office lore—when choosing a weapon, and picking the one he did after diddling with all of them, testing for trigger pull, tightness of slide to frame, and some indefinable something he called feel—how could manufactured items such as pistol frames have different feels? they wondered—all these un-self-conscious signifiers conferred upon him a status he had not sought and did not welcome.

First order of business: his long memo to Purvis, carbon to Cowley, on law enforcement firearm training, which argued persuasively, as opposed to successfully, for the elimination of the box concept of the shooting range in favor of a more fluid setup that would emphasize moving in and among targets, shooting on the move and from different angles and positions, snap-shooting against a clock to gauge time, caliber selection (the famous 4 again, as in .45 ACP or .44 Special or .45 Long Colt), reload and clearance drills (mandatory!), dry-fire, dry-fire, dry-fire, and basic first-echelon maintenance skills, not for gunsmithing but for field-expedient emergency clearances. He preached total flexibility, in other words, after the model of a real gunfight as fought by a real gunfighter. Then there was the issue of sighted fire, which he believed in, versus the Division mantra, "the crouch," which mandated that the agents dip into a position where they were bent forward, the pistol itself thrust forward and down, then tipped up. The Division relied on muscle memory to get the gun on target, and Charles knew that some men have much better muscle memory than others—his own was superb—whereas all had eyes to align sights.

This document was greeted with enthusiasm by Purvis, praised, and a copy put on the bulletin board. It was bucked to Washington, where at least two, and possibly as many as three, people read it to conclusion, but one of them was not the Director and so as an enterprise it was doomed from the start.

Then he spent a long Saturday with Hollis in the arms room, examining each of the office's weapons, looking for signs of wear, poor maintenance, bent or damaged sights, loose or stripped screws, burrs, over-lubrication or under-lubrication. He showed Hollis how to break each piece down, finding him an eager acolyte with some mechanical aptitude, and once he overcame his fear of the intricate, a skill equal to the cuckoo-clock guts of the Colt .38 revolver.

He worked the long guns too and discovered why young Hollis had been point man on the Little Bohemia debacle. It was that he had a natural feel for the Thompson and had clearly spent much time with it, knowing how to break it down already, how to sight it, what the proper firing position was, and was adroit at fast reloads, a crucial battle skill. Charles guessed that he shot it quite well. Thus, Clegg had placed him in the vanguard of the assault, even though he'd never been in a gunfight before, and thus it was him that had to make the half-second decision in the pitch dark whether to fire on three men getting into a car. His head charged with nonsense about the importance of the raid, the evil of the bandits, the one-in-a-million op-portunity in front of the agents, what choice did he have but to fire? He'd fired, the whole thing had gone south, and, given the nature of large orga-nizations, what rolls downhill rolled downhill on Hollis, while Purvis and Clegg stepped as far from the rolling as possible, not that they didn't get splashed. But in all this, nobody seemed to notice only Hollis had hit his targets while everyone else had shot the holy bejesus out of the lodge and cabins and accomplished nothing but too many holes for tourists to gawk at for the next hundred years.

The issue of the shooting range came up sooner rather than later because Charles forced it. The only range in the city was in the basement of the new Chicago Police Headquarters, on South State at 11th, not a few blocks away, but access to it was a tricky political issue. Trainees for CPF had it every fifth week, full-time, as they ran through their cycles. At all other times it was supposedly open for voluntary fire by all local and federal law enforce-ment personnel, though few took advantage of the facility. However, that did not stop the officer in charge, a Sergeant O'Malley, from going all Lord of the Manor on it, and turning it into a sort of boys club for fellows out of County Cork, who hung around, kibitzed, and clucked and gossiped but didn't do much else except use it as a treehouse.

"It's the Chicago way," said Purvis. "Those that have, keep. Those that don't have, cooperate. Meaning: the Irish have, nobody else gets. O'Malley holds the cards, because he knows we're the new boys, he hasn't felt us out yet, he's not sure if we'll be around awhile or we're just a flash in the pan. I could write letter after letter to Commissioner Allman, but they'd all get lost, and if I complained, my complaints would get lost. It's a tough situation. And let me be frank, Sheriff: to prevail, I'd have to use a lot of juice, and I don't have much juice since Little Bohemia. I'm sure Sam Cowley would tell you the same."

"I ain't one for going from boss to boss," said Charles, earning a smile from Purvis. "Would you mind if I took a crack at this O'Malley on my own? Unofficial-like?"

"I don't know what you have planned, Sheriff, and I'm not sure I want to. But go ahead. Just don't get caught."

So Charles looked into it, then ambled over one afternoon all by his lonesome with a couple boxes of government-issue hardball in his suit pockets. It was a pleasant summer day in Chicago, with a cooling wind blowing in off the lake, and the eight-block walk took him straight down State, past the big department stores, under the roar of the elevated trains that formed the south side of the Loop, past a couple of burly houses, and finally to the new building, which looked like a brick set on its end. It was thirteen stories of rectitude, with a couple stories of fraudulent frill plastered on the bottom two stories to disguise the grim utility of the place. He came into the lobby and took an elevator down one story.

Nothing new here. Just a shooting range behind a sign-in desk, the thumps and bangs of cops on remedial missions echoing beyond the soundproof walls. He showed his badge, was assigned a lane, stuffed his ears with cotton—a few others did so, but it was not required—and stepped into familiar damp cement darkness, the smell of burned powder, the litter of spent casings on the floor, and the long hallway of booths. He went to his assigned booth, fetched a target, and reeled it out to twenty-five yards, which was the range's ultimate challenge. He set his pistol down, removed the three loaded magazines he carried on his belt, placed the two GI boxes on the shelf before him. It was one of those absurd silhouettes where the guy just stands there, all in black to show up better in the raw light of the range, in a kind of rigid please-kill-me posture. It had nothing to do with gunfights.

This was his first time with the new Colt Commercial he had signed out of the inventory. It felt like all the other Colts he'd fired, and it was nice and tight, with no wobble to the slide as they sometimes had, with a dull shine slightly incandescent in the bright light. He fired one-handed, off the ninety-degree orientation to the target that was the consensus style of police gun-work, because he didn't want to showboat.

In short order he had blown the black centers out of the silhouettes. The pistol shot well enough, though when he had time, he'd like to take a file to it, knowing all manner of little tricks that could be applied to Mr. Browning's geometry within the frame to make a good pistol into a superb one. He left twenty-nine rounds in the second box and carefully threaded seven apiece into his three carry mags and the mag that went in the pistol. That one he placed in the pistol, jacked a round into the chamber, applied the safety, removed the magazine and replaced the round with the one left over, and slammed it into the gun, for an eight-round combat load on the first draw-and-shoot. He slid the cocked and locked pistol back in its elaborately carved holster tight under his left arm, turned and discovered that his shooting had drawn an audience. At least ten cops stood well back, clearly astonished at the marksmanship, the likes of which had been rarely seen down here.

"Gents," he said, nodding as he eased through the crowd, and they parted easily to let him through.

Outside, the patrolman clerk told him the sarge would like to see him and gestured him toward a nubby little office off to one side.

"Pretty good shooting, I hear," said O'Malley, whose face appeared evolved from a large shoulder of beef, and his body from other large aspects of the bovine species. His blue tunic was tight and all the brass gizmos well shined. Hair parted in the middle and well brilliantined, he was a dapper addition to the world, looking every square inch—and there were many of them—the proper Irish cop. "Word's got around, we have a real serious marksman on the range. You'll always be welcome here, federal man." He gestured for Charles to sit.

"Thanks, Sergeant. I have fired a pistol a time or two in my time."

"I hear some man killing was involved."

"The war of course. Seemed such a waste of life, even German, but you have to hit them before they hit you. Then, on duty, had to face some armed boys, and my skill at marksmanship got me through the day. The truth is—and I'd only admit this to a man in blue—I sort of like it."

"We all do, Sheriff. Though I'd admit that only to a man with a badge himself. Anyhow, I wanted to say hello, welcome to the gunman, and make it clear you're always welcome here. Maybe my own fellas can pick something up from him?"

"I'd be happy if that happened," said Charles. "But now that we're here alone, Sergeant O'Malley, I'd like to be square with you on another issue. Do you mind?"

"Not at all," said O'Malley.

"I'm hoping to bring my boys over in a nice orderly fashion," said Charles, "and see if I can't lick some sense into them so the kind of nonsense that took place at Little Bohemia won't never happen again. I want the best gunfighters in the city."

"Ah, now," said O'Malley, "isn't that commendable? Pass on the knowledge, get all those lawyers and accountants up to snuff on the shoot-to-kill issues their fine and proper educations may have not offered them."

"That's it," said Charles.

"Oh. But, see, there'd be a problem. We don't like to commit the range to no outsiders on a regular basis. If Commissioner Allman is showing his various official visitors the department, he likes to let me know in advance and I scare up some boys in blue so that when the commissioner comes down, all the lanes are full and everybody's banging away. We even dig out some Tommies, so it looks like our own are always on it, the very model of modern police training. It makes the commissioner happy. And if the commissioner's happy, I'm happy."

"So I can't get no two afternoons a week out of it? Only individuals can come over here and shoot?"

"The sheriff can shoot anytime he wants, as his reputation as righteous officer of the law is well known and to be respected. The others, I'm afraid it ain't possible. They can come, and if we have the room, it's onto the range they go. But that's all. That's just the way it is around here, Sheriff, sorry to say."

"I suppose I could make a donation to some Hibernian Lodge of your specification and that might ease the crowding issue?"

"Why, ain't that a nice thing to say! I do like a man with a charitable inclination. It certainly might help your cause. You do catch on fast."

"Don't let the drawl fool you. I might actually know a thing or two."

"I like a man who understands without being told."

"The problem is, we are low-budget and don't have the petty cash to put into the party fund of St. Mary's FOP District 1."

"Well, Sheriff, see the thing is, much as I am liking and respecting you, I'd have to advise you that's your problem, it ain't mine."

"Would you consider this one of your problems: a certain Italian gentleman named Lucente Barrio, also known as Lucky Bananas, was seen visiting the offices of FOP District 1 last Tuesday, where it's rumored he makes a weekly contribution. However, since FOP District 1 is a public entity, under federal license as a charity, its financial records are on file. I done looked at 'em. Your outfit claims donations of under fifteen thousand dollars a year. Now, if Treasury were to pick up Lucky Bananas and he were offered ten years in prison against testifying how much he actually contributed, and if that money went unreported—not taxed, mind you, as a charity is not required to pay taxes on contributions, but it sure as hell has to report 'em—Treasury could close FOP District 1 down in a week. Under federal, not Illinois, statute. Treasury is hot these days because of putting Big Al away. That would be a problem for you, wouldn't it, Sergeant O'Malley? And that house you're building in Petoskey, where the fishing is fine and the water clear, maybe there wouldn't be enough left in the kitty to pay off that mortgage."

"You bastard," said O'Malley.

"Ain't no bastard at all," said Charles. "Just introducing my friends in the Chicago PD to the Arkansas way."

"**E**VER HEAR OF THE MEMORY HOLE?**"** Nick asked.

"Uh, from somewhere, yeah."

"It's from *1984* by George Orwell. The hero's job is to rewrite the past. It's a dictatorship, and the state motto is 'Who controls the past controls the future; who controls the present controls the past.' So this guy goes back into the London *Times* files and erases people who are now considered traitors. He rewrites the news articles without them, then drops the original in a 'memory hole,' where it's incinerated. See, the memory hole is really the anti-memory hole."

"Okay, I'm getting it."

They were sitting in Nick's den, near his glory wall displaying artifacts of what had been a stellar FBI career, his collection of John Wayne DVDs, his CDs of Shostakovich symphonies, and his library of American history books. The house was a big Colonial on a tree-shaded cul-de-sac in this D.C. bedroom community, his wife was off somewhere prosecuting someone, it was afternoon, and the two friends felt such comfort in each other's presence, it was like old whiskey, which in fact Nick was drinking, if Bob was not.

"Look here," said Nick, gesturing to his worktable.

Stacks and stacks of Xeroxes lay across it in piles, each with a yellow Post-it marking contents—John Dillinger, Baby Face Nelson, Homer Van Meter, and on and on.

"Now," said Nick, "I have gone through them very carefully. No mention of your grandfather. No Charles Swagger. He didn't exist. He's the man who never was, officially."

"I'm with you," said Bob. "But still—"

"Yes, there is a 'But still,' a giant 'But still.'"

Bob took a sip on his warm Diet Coke; the ice had melted, degrading the taste significantly. It was like caramel cut by deer urine.

"Boy, I wish I could join you," Nick said, hoisting a glass of Buffalo Trace on the rocks. "But, you know, doctor's orders. What can I do?" He took a sip, enjoyed the smoothness all the way down.

"Damn, that stuff smells good," said Bob.

"Brother, you should see how it tastes! Anyhow, back to the memory hole concept. Your grandfather, certain evidence suggests, was dumped into the memory hole and disappeared."

"You have my attention," said Bob.

Nick picked up his first exhibit, a page out of the Dillinger file. Bob could see that a few words had been magic-markered in translucent yellow. He looked hard at one, seeing a common word.

"Most of the typing in the Chicago Field Office was done by a very capable woman named Elaine Donovan, Purvis's secretary," Nick said. "She was an excellent, strong typist, no doubt about it, and a very hard worker, absolutely first-class. You see her initials *EPD* all over the place, on the other side of slash marks identifying the author, *MP* or *HC* or *SC*—Purvis, Clegg, or Cowley—the three kings of Orient. But about every fourth page in several of the files was typed by someone else. Same typewriter, same office, different typist. If you look carefully, you see that Mrs. Donovan's left hand was very strong, and she really hit the *Q, W, E* keys hard. But whoever typed the odd pages wasn't a lefty, and his *Q, W,* and *E* strikes are much weaker. Don't get me wrong, he's good, he doesn't make mistakes, he's a virtuoso on the board, but he lacks a certain strength in one of the strands of muscle in his left hand."

Bob looked at the yellowed word and saw that it was so, the *E*'s especially, since there were so many of them, giving the game away. These *E*'s were at least a magnitude fainter, sometimes not being struck hard enough for the entire letter to print.

"And these were inserted in—"

"Yes, yes," said Nick, "we're not talking about extra pages added at the start or finish but contiguous pages—that is, in the body of the work, that read naturally from the page before to the page after. What I'm saying is, someone retyped those pages alone, threw out the originals, and slid the new ones in. What do the new pages have in common? Good question. Too bad you didn't ask it."

"What do the new pages have in common?" asked Bob.

"They're all pages where an agent named Stephen T. Wharlis is cited."

Bob looked at the document again, this time noting that this agent's name was highlighted in red.

"All right," said Bob, "never heard of him, but that doesn't mean anything."

"Nobody has ever heard of him. That *does* mean something. He's in no memoirs, he's not listed by the Bureau, or by the retired agents' association, or in the index of any of the histories of the 1934 campaign against the gangsters."

"He's a fraud?"

"Not just a fraud, a very specific fraud, a designer fraud. The name Stephen T. Wharlis has seven letters, a one-point-five-space middle initial, and seven more letters to the surname. The Christian and surnames have the same typeface space value as Charles F. Swagger, meaning that if the documents were retyped, the spacing would remain the same and not be thrown off. You could just retype the pages with Wharlis's name and not have to retype the whole file."

Bob let it sink in. Someone, not Elaine Donovan, had gone to a great deal of trouble to replace the pages with Charles's name in them with pages where a fictitious agent was named. That is, if Charles's name were in fact on the original pages.

"Why on earth would someone do that?"

"It means also the pay records were removed, the evaluation reports, all paper traces of Charles's term with the Division. Or I should say it *could* mean that, as it's not ipso facto evidentiary. But it could also hardly mean anything else. The chances of someone coming up with a name exactly the numeric space value by Underwood Office Typemaster Model 11-7B are highly unlikely."

"I get the picture. He got very powerful people mad at him."

"Madder than hell," said Nick. "And he ended up in the memory hole."

12

SOUTH BEND, INDIANA
June 30, 1934

J ACK LOOKED NERVOUS. He lounged near the Merchants National's prosaic entrance—it was no Deco/Egyptian temple to money but instead a
mid-block storefront on Michigan Street under a jutting clock, between a
jewelry store and a pawnshop. He smoked a cigar, his lips drawn, his face
pale. He wore no overcoat because he carried no long gun.

But he gave them the nod, signifying that on schedule a postal inspector
had arrived with all the loot from the Post Office. Though, indicating by
finger, only one, not two.

"Okay," said Johnny. "Money come in."

"That boy's going to shit up his pants like a drunk hobo locked in a box-
car," said Homer, trying as always for the chuckle. None of the others in the
boxy Hudson said a thing as Homer cruised along the street. They were
nervous too, as no matter how professional you got, how much experience
came into play, when the guns came out, when force was applied, when lead
flew, it was a dangerous time.

Instead, harsh breathing, a kind of obsessive fondling and checking of
the guns, a kind of willed relaxation meant to calm the heebie-jeebies that
flew through the car like insects, threatening to land anywhere at any time.
Only Johnny was completely relaxed.

"He's fine, he's fine," he said after a bit. Then he added, "No parking yet.
Go around the block again, will you, Homer?"

"Cock-a-doodle-I-will-do," said Homer, driving, his eyes darting this
way and that for signs of cop.

Meanwhile, Les, Thompson drum-charged with forty-nine .45s under his three-sizes-too-big suit coat (it hung down past his fingers, making him look childish, and the hat, too large, pulled too low, didn't help: Mickey McGuire with machine gun), was thinking about killing Homer as a way of keeping his mind off the thirty pounds of steel bulletproof vest he wore under his shirt and the little ants of sweat tracking down his body.

"We're in the money," sang Homer.

"Clamp it, vaudeville," said Charlie Floyd. "Save them jokes for the showers when the niggers get you."

It was like a family. Nobody liked anybody except all liked Johnny. He was the big brother.

Silently, Homer navigated the big Hudson, turning off Michigan to Wayne, then turning off Wayne to Main, Homer driving carefully because things could go wrong off a little bumper scrape or a cop seeing a stop sign or a yellow-light run. This block of small Indiana city on a sunny Saturday morning rotated past the right-side windows as Homer circled, yielding visions of American life that had no meaning to the car's occupants for they had conspicuously chosen to live outside its neatness, its primness, its orderliness, its optimism, its regularity and consensus. What drove them collectively was not merely greed to have what wasn't theirs but the need to be the outlaw, that figure who played by no rules, who was big by his own definition, who dared to flamboyantly grab, and though knowing doom was sure, would revel in reputation and respect until the last cop bullet found its mark and dumped each into the gutter to bleed out, waiting for an ambulance that nobody remembered to call.

The car turned right again on Jefferson, then eased around the last corner and back onto Michigan Street, and since nobody had bothered to pull out, Homer came to a halt in the traffic lane and double-parked. And why not? It was going to be a quick in-out against rubes and hicks.

"Gee," said Homer, "we might get a parking ticket."

He left the car running, set the parking brake, and pressed his .351

Winchester tight against the denim leg of his sloppy overalls, as he had dressed country so they didn't look like a team.

A last check with Jack, who fed them another nod, this to indicate no cops inside, none on the street, nobody suspicious hanging around.

It was time to go to work.

"We're in the money," said Homer, tracing the idiot rhythm of the picture-show song, "we're in the money."

AS DESIGNATED BARKER, it was Charlie's call. He hit the double doors hard, stepped up into a not-as-fancy-as-some-banks-he'd-seen interior, and let Johnny slide to the gate that led to the tellers' cages from behind, and then pulled his big, brutish Thompson out, waved it dramatically like in a picture show, and shouted, "Everybody on the floor!"

Nobody went to the floor. Nobody even noticed. The place was crowded with customers, all, it seemed, with urgent financial issues and all, therefore, bent over their little account books with rapt concentration, or standing next to the ornate high tables and diddling with checkbook mechanics, because of course none trusted the banks, these being Midwesterners, and so they would calculate their interest to the penny, in fountain pen.

Charlie had a moment not of panic but utter frustration. What was wrong with these idiots? He shot a look to Johnny, whose hand had slipped inside his jacket to rip out his .45. As bagman, he couldn't have a long gun.

Johnny shot him a what-the-hell look and a nod, and Charlie raised the muzzle of the unnoticed Thompson to the ceiling, thumbing the safety lever down, making it hot, continued to raise it, and when it was adequately skyward, he pressed the trigger.

LES NEVER ENTERED. His job was to slide down the block and station himself at the corner of Michigan and Wayne, since any big cop action would come hauling ass down Main and it was his job to persuade them to seek other objectives with a few T-gun bursts that would send them crashing onto curbs or into parked cars. He sort of hoped it would happen. There was nothing he loved more than the hydraulic surge of the gun's recoil, the spew of spent shells, spurting gases, a radiance like a sustained photo flash from his muzzle, and above that wonderful drama, a vision of the world gone to chaos and anarchy, as his bursts ripped anything they touched.

Then he heard the burst from inside the bank.

Oh, boy, he thought, this is going to be fun.

Then he heard a shot from the bank entrance, where Homer patrolled with his long rifle.

HOMER SAW THE COP before the cop saw him. Homer had no joke for the cop, since all humorous impulses had left him and now he was down to business, to his own personality, which consisted of little other than the willingness to use force and the hunger to succeed as a bank robber. The money wasn't even the important part. His bad jokes hid an ambition to be good at his job. It got him nice clothes, late-model cars, and hot women like Mickey Conforti who knew stuff he didn't even realize existed.

But even though images of Mickey's creamy thighs were never far from his mind, when he heard the Thompson burst from inside, knew it was loud enough to rattle teacups and window frames and policemen, he knew instantly that everything had changed, that what was to be a quick in-out would now be a crazed gun battle, and if you didn't push the attack, you ended up caught in an alley.

At the same time, he immediately found the cop, who had been directing traffic in an intersection, approaching with caution, a kind of low infantry-man's jog, unsure, wary, but his revolver in his hand. Homer didn't wait a second. The .351 went smoothly to shoulder exactly as the finger found the trigger and the muscles locked the gun tight against the body and the dominant eye found the bead sight, brought it into focus, while behind it the blue tunic of the officer seventy-five yards out was fuzzy. His finger, educated in trigger craft, pressed nicely and the rifle fired, much of its recoil absorbed by the mechanics of the automatic function, ejecting an empty, admitting a new round to chamber, locking it in, resetting the trigger. The cop seemed to elongate under the impact of the center-chest hit, then lost all energy, tried to keep upright with compensatory leg action but instead twisted, turned, and went hard to street, where he lay, flattened and splayed. But then there was nothing else to shoot at, as it seemed the crowds on the street had panicked and people were racing crazily to get out of the fire zone. Homer hunted for targets in blue.

WITH THE SHOT, Les abandoned all pretext of being man hiding machine gun and became man holding machine gun. It came out from under, and he felt a surge of love for the big thing, true beauty in his eyes, feeling his fingers clutch hard into the front grip, clutch hard into the pistol grip (no need for safety switch off, because he didn't believe in safeties and went everywhere with his guns hot), buttstock wedged between his arm and pressing ribs.

The image alone—gangster man, heavily armed, pivoting and swinging the muzzle of the Thompson, face grim and merciless, jaw clenched, fedora low, from half a hundred picture shows—drove the masses at his end of the street into panic, and he watched—it was almost funny, people dropping their bags, moms snatching up babies, dads putting themselves between the gunman and their kids—as all seemed to go into spasms and lurches, all thoughts of dignity gone, running wildly, some tripping, sprawling, picking themselves up. They looked like clowns! This was fun!

Then he got shot.

PLASTER FELL from the ceiling where Charlie's shots had torn it up. As expected, all customers went into paralysis, then, on Charlie's second order, fell to the ground in sloppy, demeaning fear. Johnny busted through the gate, holding his .45 and yelling, "Tellers, hands up, don't be no hero, the bank don't care."

Fast and professionally, Johnny scooted down the aisle, pulling out a clutch of flour bags tucked into his pants under his coat and flipping one to each teller.

"You throw the big bills in, take as many of the small ones as you can get into your pockets, cinch up the bag, and hold it out for me. That means you too, sister," putting the .45 close to the head of an older woman, who had momentarily frozen.

She swallowed and unfroze.

"Attagirl," he said, "knew you wouldn't let me down." He threw her a wink.

He moved down the aisle until he'd passed out six bags, moved back, picked each one up, felt each heavy with wads of cash. But that wasn't the big money. With the six bags looped over his left arm, he kicked in the door to the administrative office, where men in suits stood, gray-faced, in a nest of desks and adding machines.

"I am John Dillinger," he said, "and you know why I am here. Where's the postal money? You, pops, you look important, where is it?"

He had chosen wisely. The old man had no need to defy him, no urge for heroics, no desire for trouble or pain, and weakly gestured to the two canvas sacks, secured by padlocks, on the desk, U.S. MAIL, in official typeface, emblazoned hugely on the outside.

"That's what we came for, pops, you're a peach!" Johnny said, and as a strong fellow had no trouble scooping up the two bags in his left hand while keeping the .45 in motion, sweeping the rigid managers and vice presidents.

"Nice doing business with you folks," he said, smiling in his charming way, then turning to join Charlie, and as they turned to leave, at that moment it seemed that the Great War had come back to the earth again and landed square on Michigan Street, U.S.A.

IT OCCURRED TO LES he wasn't going to die, though it felt like someone had kicked him in the center of the chest. He fogged a second, then remembered: bulletproof vest! What a smart move that had been. But in the next instant rage flashed hot and white and spastically, and he turned, seeing no shooter, and decided, what the hell, this'll get their heads down.

He squeezed off a long burst in the general direction of everywhere, and his bullets danced everywhere, and everywhere they shattered storefront windows in cascades of sleet, pulled hurricanes of debris up from the street, or whanged hard with thrumming vibration as they drilled half-inch blisters into fenders and hoods of abandoned cars.

That was so much fun.

And then—what is it with these people, first he gets shot, then this!—some monkey lit on his back and began smacking at his arms, as if he was trying to get him to drop the gun.

You sonovabitch, thought Les, and he drove himself hard backwards against the wall, felt the man on his back flatten with the impact, wriggled an arm free from the pinioning arms engulfing him, and managed to drive three or four hard elbows into the monkey's rib cage. Then he rammed the cargo against the wall again, heard the creature grunt in pain, all the while Les twisting energetically to break the grip.

It had all gone away. No bank robbery, no Tommy gun, no goddamned South Bend, just this sonovabitch riding him, holding on hard for life, as if Les were some kind of bucking animal, and at last Les felt his grip loosen, so again he smashed backwards and this time, groaning in pain, the hero slipped off.

Les spun to confront him, discovering a teenager under a mop of disheveled hair, stepped back as the boy raised his hands in fear, as if to ward off what fate had in store for him, so Les drove gun butt into face, feeling a wet, satisfying thud on impact, driving the kid back into plate glass, which surrendered, and the boy went down in a waterfall of sparkles and lay, covered by diamonds and shards and splinters, in a jewelry-store window frame.

"Asshole," cried Les at the boy, then killed him, raking the fallen boy with a splatter of .45s that brutalized yet more vapor and debris into the air. He turned back, and still aflame with rage at the world for denying him the dignity and grace he required of it, unleashed another long burst in the general direction of everywhere, and with his superb marksmanship, hit that target squarely.

His moment of kingly conquest, however, vanished when, too damned close, a car window atomized as someone had rushed a twelve-gauge blast at him, missing and blowing out the window instead, and he turned to answer, seeing no shooter, so he just finished the drum into the city. It took a few seconds to unsnap it, pull it out, then toss it, grab the second one, which had been wedged through all this in his pants at the small of his back and had not come loose, and rolled away and slid the heavy thing into place—you had to thread the metal lip into slots milled into the receiver on each side for tight locking. Then he rammed back the bolt atop the beauty and, presto, he was back in the fight.

"OOPS, FOLKS, AIN'T DONE WITH YOU YET!" yelled Johnny, gesturing with his .45 at the bank officers in the office. "Get your asses out here and earn your cut."

The three men exchanged worried glances, but Johnny's big Colt was the more convincing argument, and so they obeyed, even as outside someone was refighting the Somme.

"Make a little circle around us, fellows," said Johnny. "And relax, your friends ain't gonna shoot you. Who'd foreclose on 'em then?"

The three took positions around Johnny and Charlie, and together the five began an awkward shuffle-dance to the door and out, where the police—many had arrived to take up positions behind abandoned cars—instantly opened fire.

HOMER HUNTED FOR TARGETS, taking a shot at a cop with a shotgun who'd just blown a hole in a car window next to Les, aiming low, not to kill but to send the fellow running. It seemed like there were cops everywhere—who knew they had so many in this shithole?—and he went after them, but always put the bullet near, but not into, the cop, forcing him to spin and duck away. But if he was missing them, they were missing him, and the lead filling the air like ice pellets was generally useless.

He looked over at Jack on the other side of the entrance, saw him to be frozen, and yelled, "Goddammit, open up! Drive 'em back, don't just stand there!"

Jack nodded, swallowed behind his cigar, and came out with a revolver of some sort, which he proceeded to fire to no purpose other than noise and maybe a fractured window here and there.

At that moment the bank doors blew open and a mob emerged, revealing itself to be Johnny and Charlie and three hostages. If the cops paused, it was for less than a second, because immediately they opened up, and some jackrabbit in blue had worked over to the left with a pump gun and he blasted at the group twice, though low, and the hostages went down as Charlie whirled in pain, then regained his composure and sent a fleet of hardball slugs off to punish the shooter.

"Let's get out of here!" screamed Johnny. "I got the swag."

"Yeah, yeah, let's go," yelled Homer in reply, grabbing Charlie to point him, though his leg trailed blood from the charge of twelve, toward the car.

Homer, jokester and vaudeville fool, was magnificent. After launching Charlie, he stood upright, clicked in another magazine of .351s, and went into the statue mode, calm, strong, without tremor or doubt, providing aimed fire near, but not into, the cops, while the three others staggered to the car, like the drummer, the fifer, and the flag bearer of Yankee Doodle Dandy legend. They got in, and Homer screamed at Les, just coming up from a reload, to join them.

Les nodded, rose, and ran, covering himself with one-handed shooting, yielding much noise but little consequence, while Homer, again heroic beyond reproach, stood, firing calmly, driving the cops back with well-aimed marksman's rounds that instructed the recipient to keep his head down if he cared to survive.

When at last Les had made it, Homer raced his own self to the car, careful to weave around the front and thereby not expose himself to Charlie's fusillade as it poured from the rear window, another careful example of shooting at everything and hitting nothing, except putting a bullet mustache on the face of a movie poster on the air-conditioned picture-show palace across the street. Charlie, in his rush, may have thought Gable was a cop.

Homer threw in his now empty .351, slid into driver's seat, and then it felt like he caught a Dempsey haymaker in the side of the head, saw a flash in which he and his brothers threw apples at Billy Dawes and his brothers in a war they had fought in 1912, and then went to sleep.

NO DIGNITY! None! He ran like a comedy hobo, with his pants on fire and a mob after him with a rope, as clouds of spray and grit flailed him. All the cops in the world were shooting at him!

Les turned slightly, raising the Thompson with one arm, and squeezed, sending a crowd of missiles a half inch wide into space. It was as much for his own morale as it was to drive the cops back, though indeed it did seem to quiet the less aggressive police shooters.

"Come on, goddammit!" yelled Homer, who stood like a monument, dishing out his rifle rounds, stopping to reload in a dazzling blur, while simultaneously the small knot of robbers reached the idling Hudson and—no dignity here, either—piled in.

SOMEHOW, Les made it to a safe zone behind the fender only to feel Homer's strong farm-boy hand on his arm, pulling him toward the rear door, still open for him.

"Cock-a-doodle, don't get tagged," yelled Homer, really shoving him face-first into the melee that was already two men deep, with Charlie trying to squirt up to get gun to window to fire, and poor Jack, scared witless, trying to untangle himself from Charlie. When he landed, Les felt a blow to his nose, which was issued by Jack's plunging knee, bellowed, "OW!" and slid to the floor like a child, as Jack sort of segued over him with, of all things, a bag in his hands. Then the roar of Charlie's Thompson, as he finally got it into play and began hosing down Michigan Street.

LES GOT HIMSELF UP but couldn't get close enough to the window to get his hose-gun muzzle out and he didn't want to fire inside, as the recoil could bounce it around the car cab.

The driver's-side door opened, Homer tossed in his rifle, slid in, and put foot to pedal, one hand to wheel and the other hand to brake—then suddenly snapped, elongating to full length, as he was hit in the head. Les could almost feel the vibration as the bullet blew into Homer's thick, slicked-down hair and threw blood spots across the upholstered ceiling of the car.

PURVIS CAME RUSHING OUT of his office, climbed on a desk, and began to bellow.

"All right, the bastards have shot the hell out of South Bend, nobody knows how many dead. We have good preliminary IDs on Dillinger and Pretty Boy, and you can bet the other whiz kids are there too. Mr. Cowley is on the phone with Washington, we're trying to get a Tri-Motor ginned up at Metropolitan. Mr. Cowley will stay here and coordinate with Washington, the Director, and the various agencies involved, and there are a lot of them. Clegg, you and your people stay here with him and give Mr. Cowley your total support. If I hear— Well, let's just put it this way: any order from Mr. Cowley is to be viewed as an order from me. If we have to move fast and I'm not available, he may call directly on field agents, and you jump too if that happens. Any questions?"

"Do we have time to pack?"

"Nope. You can wash out your drawers in the sink, and we'll go in together on razor blades and shave cream and toothpaste. Sam will rent us some rooms in the town. He'll have that by the time we land, but we won't be sleeping, except on the plane, until tomorrow night. I want to get there while the scene is hot. We'll see if you science geniuses can come up with an actual clue or something."

"Mel, what about logistics?"

"I will have Mrs. Donovan along, not right away but tomorrow by train, to handle typing up reports and keeping us up with anything from the Director that doesn't come to Sam or me directly. Anything more?"

That seemed to be it. The guys were young, bunked together in apartments, five to the joint, or just married and had prepped their wives for this sort of action. But Mel covered that too.

"The rest of you call wives, or whatever, and tell 'em, tell them you're on the road until further notice. Hollis, you get the Thompsons issued, and plenty of .45 and .38."

"BARs?" asked Hollis. The big .30 caliber guns were so penetrative, they were seldom issued.

"No, not this time. If we think we'll need 'em, we'll send for 'em. Sheriff, you're on the South Bend team, we want you looking hard at the shooting aspects. Big gun battle, tell us what happened and how. Jesus Christ, it's still smoking. Okay, people, why are you still here? Let's go!"

"CHRIST!" yelled Johnny, and in a flash had yanked Homer's corpse under while going over, and again though it was without dignity, it was not without proficiency. Johnny was fast in action, and everything he did was right and smart and not driven by the panic that Les could sense riding in the desperate muscles of both Charlie and Jack on either side. He cracked a grin. Johnny! The best! Always!

Johnny clutch-pumped into gear, veered into the street, found a path through the obstacle course of shot-up cars on the road ahead, took the car through several sharp and squealy turns, riding two tires as it cranked around the corner, while Charlie emptied his drum into the sky, the bag in Jack's hands turning out to be full of carpet tacks, which he seeded the road with behind them. There was nothing for Les to do except hope that Johnny could outdrive the law.

Soon enough, Johnny found a stretch of empty, straight highway out of town and hammered it. Like a beast, the great Hudson in-line eight delivered its full-throttle roar, spewing exhaust as it ate the pavement.

The world turned to blur, and Johnny held at eighty, gracefully passing slower cars ahead of him, driving oncomers into ditches with his bravado, and the car sailed along toward the empty Indiana horizon, soon into fields of corn and wheat and roads so straight that it seemed they had entered fantasy.

"We're in the money," came a voice from somewhere, and, damn, if Homer, blood sopping the left side of his face, didn't pull himself up with a grin.

13

"TWENTY-EIGHT GRAND!" Les shouted at Homer. "We went through the battle of Verdun for a lousy twenty-eight grand! I got shot for twenty-eight lousy grand!"

Homer didn't really respond to him. He was glassy-eyed, tending to drift into and out of reality, and had a killer headache.

"He ain't right," said Johnny. "The bullet didn't go through, but you take a bash like that and your brains are scrambled. It'll be a couple weeks before he's back to himself."

Mickey Conforti had wiped the blood off his face and improvised a kind of bandage from a dishrag. She'd soaked another one in cold water and curled it over his brow. He lay on a beat-up sofa in the back room of the Green Cat Tavern, where the gang had gone for refuge after meeting another confederate in another Hudson, dumping the original, and picking their way back here over back roads. All that remained was the split-up and the trip home, wherever that might be.

"So let's get it over, goddammit," said Les. "I got to raise some cash for the winter months. I got kids to feed, I got a wife who needs a new coat."

"When she molts, you can trade that in for some new scales and rattles," said Homer from the sofa.

"See, he ain't hurt. He's just hiding down there so he doesn't have to say, 'Hey, I screwed up, there wasn't any stamp money to speak of, why don't you boys take my share to make up for my mistake.'"

"Calm down, Les," said Johnny. "He earned his share. Twenty-eight isn't a bad day's take."

"Less than six apiece, Johnny. Chicken feed! When Jimmy Murray set a job up for us, he never put us in a place where we took out less than fifty. And we didn't have to shoot our way out. Those cops were just about to call in the artillery."

"Okay, guys," said Charlie Floyd, "I got my take, I'm hitting the road. Time to get scarce. I won't say it's been a pleasure because it ain't, but now's the time to find a hole, preferably a broad's hole—"

"Charlie!" said Johnny, "there's a lady here."

"It's all right, Johnny," said Mickey. "I heard worse."

"Anyhow, anybody got any good-byes or hugs for me? No, I didn't think so. Then I'm gone."

With that, his Thompson disassembled already and packed in a suitcase, his fifty-six hundred dollars crumpled into the same suitcase, he gave a nod and headed out.

Les's verdict: "Dumb cluck'll hit a trooper roadblock and get himself killed or captured, and if he's captured, he'll rat us out in a second."

"Charlie's okay," said Johnny. "Les, you have to calm down."

"Easy for you to say, Johnny. You didn't get clipped in the gut, then jumped by some hick trying to be a picture hero. I feel like Dempsey teed off into my chest. You just walked in and walked out."

"Someone had to keep his head," said Johnny.

"I didn't lose my head. I needed to keep the cops down and away and that's what I did. If I didn't empty two drums into your home state, we'd be looking at life-plus-forever at Crownsville. And, this time, no wood gun will get us out. You only get to use that trick once."

"Les, there's no quieting you when you get a rage on like this. Chase, can't you take him to Helen and she can talk some sense to him?"

"We'll go after dark," said Chase, who'd driven the new Hudson down to pick them up at the old Hudson.

Chase was a tall, angular man, by no means unattractive, by no means an exemplar of the gangster charisma and lifestyle, who always dressed neat and who, for some reason or other, had been infatuated with Les ever since they met performing mysterious errands in Reno a few years earlier. Who knew the chemistry of the connection, and who could even understand it? He was one of a series of minor-league hitters in orbit around Les. John Paul Chase would always be there for Les, and if you wanted to work with Les, John Paul was the price you paid, though it wasn't a high price since the guy was pretty solid in his own right.

And Chase was one of the few who could talk sense into Les, control him, get him settled down and halfway rational again. That was half his value right there.

"But, Les," he now consoled, "Johnny's right. No sense staying all het up about it. You got out clean, nobody's dead, nobody's bleeding out, nobody's hooked, you copped some good dough, times being what they are, and Helen'll give you a nice back rub when you get back to the cottage."

"Did you call her? I'm worried all the radio reports will have her worried."

"I did. She's swell. Making spaghetti for dinner."

"Okay," said Les.

"You got room in that big tub for Homer?" asked Johnny.

"Cock-a-doodle, no," said Les. "It ain't up to me to get him and his nun girlfriend back to St. Paul. I got John Paul, Jack, my two kids and Helen."

"Thanks for the compliment, Les," said Mickey from the sofa, where Homer was resting his head on her lap.

"That wasn't very nice, Les, you should know better than that," said Johnny.

"She knows it was a joke. Mr. Laugh-a-Second, that's me."

"All right, Homer," said Johnny, "get ready to move in a couple hours. Looks like I'm the guy who'll drive you back to St. Paul."

"You're a prince, Johnny," said Mickey. "Always count on Johnny for being a good guy. He never lets anyone down. Unlike some other guys who ain't so noble."

"I don't have room for that mook," said Les. "And I ain't no chauffeur."

Things settled down, as each fellow decompressed from the shoot-out in different ways, Homer by aching and moaning; Johnny by smoking cigars and sipping Pikesville rye in shirtsleeves on the porch, watching the sun set over Indiana's green fields; Jack by being innocuous and, secretly aware he didn't belong, swearing to never do this kind of work again; and Les by slowly cooking off his rage and hatred at the world for again denying him the dignity he felt he had earned.

By nightfall, he had settled into a kind of dull spell and didn't feel like much fun at all. He was like a reptile, all heated up and feisty in the hot weather, dolorous and numb in the cold. John Paul had to take the initiative.

"Okay, I'm going to get him back to Helen now, and then to Chicago."

"Don't forget his cut. He'll go nuts again if he thinks he's been cheated out of his cut."

"Got it," said Les. He patted his suit pocket where his near six grand had been wadded into a big roll. The Thompson had been broken down, butt-stock separated from the receiver, the drums laid flat, the whole thing wrapped in canvas and stored in a large suitcase. Les still had a .45 aboard, and his .45 full-auto pistol between the seats, if it came to shooting, though with kids in the car, he knew he could never blast it out with the cops.

On the drive back to the cottage, as flat, dark Indiana slipped by, Les said to John Paul, "When we get back—first thing, we got to look for some new jobs or opportunities. Put out the word we're looking for action, any action. Last time I'll let Homer set anything up. He ain't got the brains of a squirrel."

"And with a bullet squashed against his skull," said John Paul, "that would be a dumb squirrel."

14

AFTER THREE TWENTY-HOUR DAYS, they were pretty much done. Every witness had given a deposition, every bullet hole marked and charted, every surface read for fingerprints (none), every spent shell located, every square inch of the rather large crime scene examined, and examined in depth, then examined again. It was scientific crime fighting at its best, with pix of the suspect sent out by wire nationally, all small-town sheriffs and police chiefs notified: "These men are heavily armed and dangerous. Do not approach. Contact Justice Department, Division of Investigation, Washington, D.C."

Now a last meeting, in the grand ballroom of the South Bend Excelsior, where the fifteen tired agents gathered, with shorthand notes taken and transcript typed by Mrs. Donovan, as all conclusions were hashed out and formalized.

Finally, Purvis got around to Charles.

"Sheriff, you looked at the shooting aspects of the event. I saw you on your knees most days, taking close notes over spent casings, so I'm betting you have something for us."

"Well, Mr. Purvis, I don't think I come up with anything you and all these bright young fellas don't already know. I do have some observations."

"Please, go ahead."

"Here's what I got, not IDs so much as personalities. Maybe some help when we get close and have to figure how to arrest. What I see is two cool hands, one dumb ox, one nothing, and one nutcase.

"Johnny and Homer are the cool hands. They make this robbery work, and, in a funny way, they keep the casualty numbers down. First, look at Johnny. Never fires a shot, or at least I could find no .45 shells on the floor inside the bank that, under the magnifying glass, didn't have the little ejector-nick characteristic of Pretty Boy Floyd's Thompson. So Johnny doesn't shoot, and he even jokes with the folks he's robbing, that's how calm he is, but, at the same time, he knows it puts them at their ease, so they don't panic and bust for the door, which would mean Pretty Boy would hose them down. We owe Johnny on that one. It stays a robbery and doesn't become a massacre because of Johnny's coolheadedness. Meanwhile, outside, Homer and his .351 are holding off the cops. He plugged one dead—Officer Wagner, God rest his soul—but after that he shoots accurately, driving cop after cop back, and I have to believe that as good a shot as he is, he could have killed cop after cop. But he knows that America sort of loves its bank robbers and that makes him feel good, that's part of what he's after, to be a ballplayer figure as much as an armed robber, and he knows if he kills ten small-town cops, it'll be a different game. He won't be no hero but instead a rabid mutt to be shot on sight. He needs that wide sense of public celebration to operate and he skillfully preserves it while taking fire. Also, while he's up there taking fire, he's letting all the others get to the car. Maybe he's dead now, as several witnesses say they saw him take one in the head, and that's a hit you don't come back from too often. Anyway, he's the hero of the bank crew, give it to him.

"Then there's the dumb ox. That's Pretty Boy. He's really the fool that turned the whole thing into a gun battle. He makes a stupid decision when nobody obeys him and fires a thirteen-shot burst into the ceiling, walking the gun all over the place. It was a dumb move, the dumbest. He could have got their attention with one shot. And on the outside, what's one loud noise? Could be a backfire, a bucket of paint falling off a ladder, one tenderfoot ramming another tenderfoot's Model A, a door slamming, the baker hitting his wife, anything. Folks'd wonder, but that's all. A good man on a Thompson don't even have to move the lever to semi-auto, he's got a light touch and can feather off a single. Ed Hollis over there can fire singles on full auto all day long, I've seen him do it. Not Pretty Boy, and once the sub gun goes rat-a-tat-tat, the jig's up. And from then on he don't do much except spray, pray, and take up space. Didn't hit anybody, could only come up with a few bullet holes in windows, which means he was mostly hitting sky. Oh, he did manage to hit Clark Gable in the head on the movie poster across the street.

"That leaves two. The least interesting is the lookout. No long gun because he had to stand outside so long trying to be invisible, no spent shells, which means he never reloaded his wheel gun. I guess he was their tip-off man, but other than a nod, he didn't do much. Again, I couldn't find anything he hit, but if you get around to digging all the bullets out of all the walls, you might find a few was .38s, and that'd be his contribution. The names I hear are John Paul Chase, Jack Perkins, Fatso Negri, all Baby Face cronies. Maybe it's one of them, maybe he's a Johnny fan or even, God help us, another Oklahoma sodbuster. Don't know.

"Finally, Nelson. This punk has a firecracker where his brain ought to be. He's a hophead who don't need no hops. Don't know what makes him tick, but he don't have no trouble spraying a city street full of moms and kids with his Tommy gun, and if he didn't hit nothing, it wasn't for lack of trying. God must have had his eye on South Bend that day. I counted, all told, seventy-seven spent .45 casings with the mark of his Thompson extractor on them, meaning he ripped off one full drum, reloaded, and ripped off half of another. Then he stood over that hero kid, Joe Pawlowski, and put rounds into him, though by the grace of God and Nelson's excitability, he managed to miss everything but the boy's hand."

"Sheriff, is he the most dangerous?"

"Yes sir. By far. He'd be shoot-on-sight, in my opinion. Tricky, nasty, crazy sonovabitch. You see him, put him down hard, that's my advice, and if I get a chance, that's what I'll do without a second thought. He's too dangerous to take alive."

"And the others?"

"Charlie will do something stupid to get himself killed. He won't think nothing out. Mr. X is a pussycat, he'll go into the cuffs without a fuss. He knows he ain't got the constitution for Thompson gunwork. Johnny and Homer could go either way. Both are smart and disciplined. I don't quite see them as shoot-on-sight, but you got to hit them with maximum manpower so that they see no escape is possible from the get-go. Cornered, they'll give up. Johnny's escaped already twice, and he believes he can get out of any jug. Probably the same with Homer, so it's in them that tomorrow is another day, and on that day they'll pull a wood-gun trick and go free. Plus, they ain't haters. They're in this for the money and the glory, not to burn the world down. They really ain't trying to hurt nobody, whereas Baby Face likes to hurt folks and gets his laughs thinking about all the tears been shed."

"Mrs. Donovan, did you get all that?"

"I did."

"Great, Sheriff. One more question: since you know so much, how many banks have you robbed?"

There was a lot of laughter, and even Charles rewarded Purvis with a rare-enough smile, enough to insert him further into legend, but then he said, "None that I can tell you Yankees about," and more laughter busted out.

When it had died down, Purvis addressed them all.

"Please mark that if you get yourselves into an arrest situation, Nelson gets a slug in the face; the others, depending. Fair enough? Okay, anything else?"

A few minor questions about per diems came up, another big laugh— say, wasn't this turning into vaudeville?—and Purvis fielded them gracefully enough, and then said, "Okay, fellas, good work, y'all did well, you have an hour to pack, and Mr. Cowley already has our Tri-Motor on the runway. Sleep late tomorrow, but the duty day will start at one p.m., and I expect to see you in the office. Sheriff, got a sec?"

"Sure," said Charles.

When the room was empty, Purvis said, "As I said, I think that's good work. We don't get that kind of thinking. But you have to understand—and think this through—you can't just crash ahead. That's what we did wrong at Little Bohemia."

"Just trying to apply common sense," said Charles.

"Gunfighter's common sense, hard-won. Anyhow, this is personal, I didn't want to say anything in front of the men, but your wife called the Chicago Office and she needs to talk to you. They said she sounded kind of upset. If you come to need a weekend off, just let me know and it can be easily arranged."

Charles had a sinking feeling. Had Bobbie Lee wandered off into the woods again and this time nobody could find him? Or maybe he'd been hit by a car. The weight of the damaged child was never far from Charles's shoulders.

"Yes sir."

"I'm going to get some lunch. Go to my room and call from that phone. Don't worry about the cost. I'll see you in a bit."

Charles thanked his supervisor, acknowledging the thoughtfulness of the offer, took the key, and went upstairs.

He found himself in the Excelsior's best room—no surprise—as befits the celebrity that Purvis had become, and the maid had already come through, so it was immaculate and impersonal. But it had probably stayed that way, as Purvis's personal neatness was already a legend.

He picked up the phone, got the hotel operator, and after the connections were made, heard his own phone ringing, the operator asking her if she wanted to take the call, and finally he was on the line with the woman he married, the mother of his sons.

"Hello," she said, her voice crackily over the long-distance wires as they hopped from connection to connection.

"It's me. They said you called. Anything the matter? Is Bobbie Lee—"

"He's fine."

"You have to watch that fool kid. He'll end up facedown in a pond or eaten by bears."

"Charles, he's fine, he's been quiet. He stays in his room and draws rocket airplanes. Every once in a while, he says, 'Where Dada?' That's the only thing."

"You know I don't believe that. He don't even know who I am."

"He loves you very much, Charles, if you'd let him. Anyway, got a letter from Earl. He made corporal. He likes the field, he says he hasn't been in a fight yet, but his mind is all set for it if it happens."

"He'll do well. He's got sand, even if he's no booster of his mean old father. You're getting the money okay? They said it would take a while for the paperwork to go through."

"We're fine, Charles. Better off than most. You provided for your family, Charles, when so many weren't able to."

"So what's this about?"

"Charles, the judge came by yesterday."

"What?"

This was unprecedented. The judge rarely left the courthouse. It meant something significant.

"Yes. He said he had a message from some folks in Hot Springs. He said—and I wrote it down—he said that you should go to the World's Fair Saturday at four p.m. and sit on a bench across from an exhibit called Midget Village. They have a whole town there of little midget people."

"Ain't that something?" said Charles. The sarcasm was lost on her, however.

"Go there, sit there, have an ice-cream cone. A man will come and talk to you. Do you know what this is about?"

"No idea," he said. But he had an idea. If this came out of Hot Springs, it meant someone from the Italians was reaching out, because the Italians had connections and influence everywhere.

"Anyhow, anything else?"

"No, Charles."

"Okay," said Charles, and hung up.

15

B OB HAD COME TO Nick's under urgent entreaty. Nick had something. Good old Nick.

"I can't wait to hear this," said Bob. "I ain't got nothing but the Underwood stuff."

"Well, this is substantive, but it's not empirical. As I said before, not ipso facto evidentiary. But it is solidly circumstantial.

"I've read these reports over and over again," he continued, "and after a while you learn the tone and the way of thinking behind them. Mostly, they're assembled by lawyers, and they seem to be very thorough legal documents. They proceed logically, they conform to format and outline, they're put together in such a way as to yield their information quickly—for prosecutors, that is, other lawyers. It's like you're reading internal memoranda from a law firm. If I remember, I went to law school three thousand years ago and even passed somebody's bar, so I think I know what I'm talking about."

"Makes sense."

"So I've read all the Dillinger reports and all the Nelson reports, going back to Itasca, Illinois, October 3, 1930. Lots of others. Plainfield; Hillside; Peoples Savings of Grand Haven, Michigan; First National of Brainerd, Minnesota; Security National in Sioux Falls, South Dakota; First National in Mason City, Iowa; and, finally, South Bend."

He gestured at the stacks of Xeroxes of '30s-style typing, with the odd diagonal designations of CLASSIFIED or FOR INTERNAL USE ONLY randomly stamped across them. They lay on the worktable in Nick's office/den.

"They're all the same, and, frankly, they'd put a sugared-up child to sleep. But finally, in South Bend, I get— Well, you read it yourself. I've marked it in yellow."

Bob took the page, put on his reading glasses, and stared at the Xerox, typed up so long ago by the ubiquitous and efficient EPD, and read:

"Noted that robbery team consisted of five different individuals whose shooting actions revealed personality traits. Two, thought to be Dillinger and Van Meter, were cool, collected, and professional. The third, possibly Floyd, exhibited poor decision making and then slow reactions . . ."

And so on, culminating in a set of recommendations of arrest strategies.

"Thus, Nelson demands instant-shooting action without warning (this should be cleared by legal), while great care must be exercised to take only Dillinger and Van Meter, under controlled circumstances, far from public access, and finally Floyd may be counted on to make a bad decision. The unknown suspect is thought to have little criminal experience, and less initiative, and will probably yield to arrest quickly."

Nick said, "I'd recognize that voice anywhere, though clearly it's been slightly edited by EPD. That's pure Swaggerspeak. That's someone who's thought hard about this sort of thing, learned lessons, has insightful observations no one else in the office is capable of making. That's Charles through a screen of bureaucratspeak."

"I think you're right," said Bob. "But what's this?"

Someone had scrawled *Very good! Disseminate!* in fountain pen in the margin of the document.

"If you'd ever been in the Bureau, you'd recognize the author of the comment," said Nick. "Even today, you'd recognize it. It's that hallowed."

"God himself?"

"God himself. And that's tantamount to an offer of lifetime service, with a guaranteed high finish. It's the original FBI ticket to ride."

"Wow," said Bob. "Charles must have really screwed up to go from there to oblivion in so few months!"

16

CHARLES WAS EVEN LESS IMPRESSED with the future than he was with the present. The future, according to the genius architects of the World's Fair, was a soaring white boulevard made up of cheesy buildings out of some screwball Hollywood picture show with rocket airplanes in it, like the machines Bobbie Lee so tirelessly drew as his brain decomposed further into nothingness. Charles saw lots of flags, pennants, things to blow and flap in Lake Michigan's stout offshore breeze, all white and tall, but shaky. Towers, triangles, trapezoids, all the features of geometry, turned to stucco in imitation of stronger engineering substances meant to last a while, then go down under the steam-shovel's grind without much trouble. Get a good blow in and the whole damned contraption-city would end up in the lagoon, and that included the giant zeppelin that hovered overhead, said to be the future of travel but looking to Charles like a bag of gas ready to dissolve in flame. He'd seen a few smaller varieties shot down on the Western Front, and nobody wanted to be near that much hydrogen lighting up.

He walked down the broad cavalcade that transected the peninsula jutting off the Chicago shore and passed by the grand exhibits from the big boys, like GM and Chrysler and Sears, Roebuck, then "Halls" of various things, such as Religion, Science, Electricity, and the U.S. Government. Mock Greyhounds transported folks on the ground, or through the air on something termed a Skyway, a big gizmo that hauled little cars of people through the blue ether on wires, tower to tower. Or you could just walk, which Charles did, noting it all with a dyspeptic heart and an abiding cynicism hard acquired through acquaintance with the century's charnel houses and hellholes. He passed the French village, where beyond a gate and behind fencing a fraud Frog street was visible, and he wondered if you got the bonus dose of clap that was a part of every GI's Paris experience in '18. Other displays to the art of counterfeit included complexes from Belgium, Germany, China, and little Japan.

After a bit the grandeur wore itself thin, and the fair became the Midway, full of honky-tonks, Cracker Jacks, and Sally Rand (not showing her ass till nightfall), where hucksters of various disciplines plied their gaudy trade. He bought himself an Eskimo Pie and sat on the designated bench across from the hutch of buildings claiming to be the famous Midget Village, where all kinds of tiny delights were promised, though Charles could see nothing amusing in that prospect.

He sat but couldn't relax. The sun was still high, but the shadows had begun to lengthen, and the lake, its blue immensity visible here and there between gaps in the busy landscape and structure of the exhibits to the far side of the Midway, provided a famous Chicago windy bluster to keep things cool and the mosquitoes from forming mobs around human flesh. He had switched, it being a hot day, to informal clothes; that is, a khaki suit, his black tie, and a new-bought indulgence, a tan fedora, brim low, shielding his eyes. He sat alert, conspicuously aware of the Government Model .45 nesting in floral-carved leather under his left shoulder, and the two full magazines of hardball wedged into a leather keeper of his own design over his right kidney. He ate the chocolate-covered frozen treat, not noticing it much because his eyes were so busy noticing other things, such as the thin crowd of humanity that trickled by, mostly adults with squads of beat-to-hell kids, all messy in melted ice cream or clingy puffs of cotton candy, as well armed with pennants, little-kid horns, all sorts of crap meant to soak the rubes' nickels and dimes.

He couldn't really feel at ease. If the judge his own self had come all the way out from town to deliver a message, it meant that somebody very high up in the as-yet-nameless organization had given the order, and the judge, a king in a little fiefdom, had popped to like a PFC. The judge's involvement, instead of a mere phone call, carried its own weight in communication; it said to Charles that a decision had been reached, that plans were afoot, and he was to be a part of them, no matter what his own inclinations were.

It wasn't long before a gent came over—he seemed to arrive from nowhere—and sat next to Charles. A well-turned-out character too, in a double-breasted blue pinstripe, shiny black shoes, and a straw Panama up top, very sporting. He was olive-skinned but quite handsome, in a picture-show kind of way, and had a whiff of cologne to him, and a white carnation bright on his lapel. It certainly wasn't an outfit you wore to a fair, not even a World's Fair.

He carried a newspaper with him, and paid no attention to Charles, but when he flipped the paper open, Charles saw that it was six days old, last Sunday's *Tribune*, and it wore the vivid eight-column headline DILLINGER GANG STRIKES SOUTH BEND. A batch of photos darkened the center of the page, and Charles didn't have to look to know that Mel Purvis was prominent, plus dramatic shots of bullet holes in glass, with Joe ("Heroic Teenager") Pawlowski and detectives bending to examine spent shell casings.

The fellow seemed to notice Charles's interest, and said, "Say, isn't that the limit? These hoodlums go in and shoot the hell out of a nice little town like that, kill a cop, wound four, use machine guns on Main Street. What a shame!"

Charles nodded glumly.

"I hate that stuff," the man continued. "Men with guns, shooting the hell out of everything, messing everything up. Know what we need? Strong law enforcement, men who can go gun to gun with these bandits, who can shoot better, faster, straighter. But I guess men like that are hard to find."

"Wouldn't know about that," Charles said guardedly.

"I think you would, Sheriff," said the man, turning to face him, displaying a taut, intelligent face, exquisitely shaven, though a blue-steel blur of shadow highlighted his dark eyes, set off by a white inch of scar across the knobby cheekbone. His personality was like his wardrobe: spotless, perfectly fitted, regal, yet fluid and creamy. "I hear you're the best shot in the Division, and they brought you in from the South to go gun to gun with Johnny and his pals. I think I spot a suspicious bulge under your jacket. Heavy iron, *serious* iron."

"Okay, I'm here. This is the meet. What's the play? Who are you?"

"No names. But you're no hick. You know how it works and who's doing what. You know that in most circumstances, you and the people I represent work on opposite sides of the street."

"I get that."

"But our interests momentarily converge. What you want, what we want. This crap has to end, for everybody's sake, so we look at the options and we chose you as our vessel. You come highly recommended, because I know you're not so rigid, you can't deal with reality in an adult manner. Not like most of these kids in the Division, all full of Ohio State boola-boola, who don't really get how it can work and want to throw everybody in the hoosegow."

Charles finished his last bit of Eskimo Pie, wiped his lips and fingers with a napkin, and got out his makings and began to assemble a tailor-made. Getting it together deftly, he put it to his lips and fired it up with a Zippo he carried, snapped the lighter shut with a power-thumbed clack, and looked across the boulevard choked with humanity parading by.

"I'm here to listen, so you'd best make your pitch."

"Good man, all business. Okay, here it is. I am here to talk about Johnny, Homer, Pretty Boy, and that king of all screwballs, Baby Face Nelson. You know who Roger Touhy is?"

"May have heard the name."

"West Chicago. Tough guy, bootlegger, all-around bad citizen. Here's the joke: Baby Face Nelson was such a nutcake that Roger Touhy kicked him out of his outfit! He was too crazy for Roger Touhy, who's as crazy as a burning duck!"

"If I get him in my sights, I will finish that issue for good," said Charles.

"I want to put him in your sights. That's what this is about. We hear things. We get information from cribs, brothels, clubs, truckers, safe houses, people on jobs or on the grift. We knew two days early about South Bend, from the guy who owns the tavern they worked out of. So here's the deal. When I have something, someone will call your office and tell you Uncle Phil wants to talk. You go across the street to a phone booth, right down on State, outside of the Maurice Rothschild main entrance. Pretend to talk on the phone, but hold the cradle lever down. When it rings, let the lever up and I'll give you the latest."

"Not so fast. You guys can be slippery. How do I know this isn't some kind of deal to screw us up so bad, the Division gets closed down? I need assurances, guarantees. I'm not just rushing in with twenty agents and machine guns because some guy with whorehouse cologne tells me to."

"Fair enough. You have to be protected. Okay, I'm going to give you info on a meet Baby Face has set up next week in Mount Prospect, in the northwestern suburbs. He needs to get going on something quick because he didn't make the score he thought he'd make in South Bend and he needs the dough to get through the winter. He's meeting with some pals late on a country road. Off the main stretch. You'll get a map tomorrow. You check it out. You'll see I'm dealing aces."

"Okay, next question: why? What's in it for you? These guys take a lot of heat, but nobody notices or talks about you. You're not interesting compared to machine guns on Main Street."

"Hey, Sheriff, none of your beeswax. It's been decided, that's all you need to know. The breeze is blowing your way. Fly your kite or go away and shut up forever."

WOLF ROAD
CHICAGO
July 15, 1934

"Baby, can't we stop, spend the night in a cabin?" said Helen.

"No, sweetie, I know it's tough, but we're almost there. I got to make this meet."

Les pushed the Hudson through the steamy night. It had been over 100 all day, suffocating hot, but he roared through the heat like he rolled through everything, hard and remorselessly, fueled by his surging anger at everything that was not Helen. Ahead, at last, the glow of Chicago's bright lights blurred the horizon. It had been a hell of a grind from Sausalito, almost the breadth of the continent away, where he and Helen and J.P. had headed straight off the South Bend job. Distance was safety, they all knew.

But now it was time to get to work.

"You want me to drive a while, Les?" asked J.P. from the backseat.

"No, pal," said Les. It was a quirk of his. He liked to do the driving. He could put himself behind the wheel as the hours turned into days with few ill effects. And now, so close to the meet, he didn't want to relinquish control—heat or not, fatigue or not. He wanted to get there, get something set up, get something started. As a professional, he had a great work ethic.

"Couldn't we go to a club, Les?" said Helen. "I could use a Coca-Cola. You know, the Rainbow or the Crystal Room?"

"Cops are watching 'em all. You forget how famous I am now. I'm bigger than Gable!" He laughed.

"You ought to go to Hollywood, Les," said J.P. "You're handsome enough to be a star."

"Aw, they put makeup on you, like a dame. Not for Les, no sir."

Illinois rolled past, the Hudson's engine devouring the pavement. When they were within twenty miles of city limits, Les looked for a solid north–south route, found it, and turned north. Here the lights were sparser, the roadhouse opportunities less available, mostly everything was closed down. But that also meant little traffic, and that meant few cops, and he motored on, gliding through the night.

He hit the far reaches of Touhy Avenue at about 1, right on schedule. He'd planned it perfectly. Turning east on Touhy, he took that road in, just north of Chicago, until at last he hit Wolf Road, another through and through, and turned north again. Closer in, more stuff, but most of it silent, the roadway empty—he still obeyed the occasional traffic light, just in case—and headed toward Mount Prospect, his actual destination just north of it, a little road to nowhere where he and the boys had rendezvoused before and knew well.

He hoped Jack Perkins had come up with the soup, as they called the volatile liquid explosive nitroglycerine. You'd have to blow the safe on his next objective, which wasn't a bank but a mail car on a streamliner, meant to be intercepted just out of Chicago. Mr. Murray, who had a long record of setting up jobs going all the way back to the Newton boys, had scouted out this one and said the take would be six figures. Mr. Murray should know, as he'd set up the Newtons' biggest robbery, at Rondout, downstate, fifteen years ago. He was a solid, reliable guy who planned carefully and knew all the tricks.

So Jack would be there to report on his nitroglycerine quest, and so would longtime pal Fatso Negri, and Carey Lieder, a mechanic with aspirations of joining the big boys who had in fact fronted Les the big chunk of luxury automobile he now drove.

Beyond Mount Prospect, he slowed. Country here, few lights, it wouldn't get bright for another few miles, when they skirted Wheeling, which is why it was such a great spot for a meet.

"I think it's pretty soon," said J.P.

"Hard to find the goddamned road," said Les. "No road markers out here or anything. No lights. Just prairie and trees. What a boring place!"

"But you don't want no action, do you, Les?"

"You're right. And I'm not sightseeing neither. I ain't no tourist."

They rolled onward, Les checking his watch—1:45 a.m.—and in a bit hit the mark.

Miller was a nondescript farm road that ran west, unpaved, designated only by a billboard on the northeast corner for Standard Oil, showing a happy family packed in the car on a vacation trip: *The Open Road—It's the American Way!* it said.

"Okay, folks, we made it. Helen, honey, an hour here, read a magazine or something, and then we'll check in someplace and you can take a shower and get some sleep."

"It sounds so great. I'd kill for twenty-four hours of uninterrupted rest."

"You don't need to kill nobody, honey. That's Daddy's job."

They turned left, onto Miller, and drove about a quarter of a mile, over a rise in the road, then downhill into a dip. The big Hudson tossed dust as it progressed, and then Les slid off the road and parked.

They sat quiet as the dust settled and the big car cooled down, occasionally offering a mysterious click or snap or crunch. Les patted the wheel.

"Nice doggie," he said. "You relax now too while Les takes care of business. You okay, Helen?"

"Yeah, babe. I'm fine. I have the new *Modern Screen*."

"So who do I look more like? Gable or Fredric March?"

"You remind me more of the New York guy, Cagney."

"He's too Hell's Kitchen."

"No, Les, she's right," said J.P. "You've got his pep, his quick moves, his guts."

"Yeah, yeah, I see it now. Hey, good thing there's no grapefruit around."

"You better not, Les," squealed Helen, laughing. "I'll smack you right back!"

"I know you would, sweetie." Les laughed, getting out of the car. He lounged against the fender, enjoying the night sky, the lower temperature after a July scorcher cramped in the car. The breeze fell gentle against his face, the crickets buzzed, occasionally a shooting star left an incandescent blur across the black vastness up top. Up there, far away, pinwheels and comets blazed, but it meant nothing to him other than display. He just saw fireworks. He glanced at his watch, whose radium dial told him it was 1:50, and just at that second headlight beams swung his direction as one car, then another, both Fords, turned off Wolf and down Miller, raising their own mild spumes of dust as they approached. He waved.

The two cars pulled off and parked not far from his, and he felt a surge of warmth as his guys piled out. Fatso and Jack were in the first car, Carey Lieder in the second.

"There they are," said Les. "The Hardy Boys and Tom Swift and his electric corncob."

All three laughed, and J.P. got out of the backseat of Les's Hudson and joined in the group hug and hand-slapping-hand, hand-shaking-hand, arm-pumping, backslapping greeting scrum. It looked like Notre Dame had just beat Navy 28–3.

"Man, you guys look good."

"Glad you're back, Les," said Fatso.

"Now we can get stuff rolling," said Jack. "And this time we'll do it right." He bent, waved, yelled, "Hi, Helen, how's the girl?" and Les's wife smiled, waved back.

The five of them moved over to a space between the cars and lounged on fenders and bumpers, enjoying one another's company, lighting up, Jack the same brand cigar he'd smoked in South Bend, J.P. and Fatso firing up cigarettes.

"How'd she run?" asked Carey, pointing to the Hudson, wanting to make sure he got credit for his only tangible contribution to this confab of authentic big guys.

"Like a top," said Les. "That Hudson builds some kind of machine. Hey, Jack can tell you, if the Hudson doesn't move like a bat out of hell when

Johnny punches it, we're pinched in South Bend and looking at ten-to-twenty at Crown Point."

"Yeah, and old Homer's got a date with a certain big chair for clipping that cop!"

"Damn, that's the only thing we did wrong," said Les. "Should have left Homer at the curb!"

More laughter, though Jack's was forced, for he remembered it was Homer who'd covered them all and kept the cops back when the battle was at its most pitched.

Then Les had his scoop.

"I got something big for you," he said. "Johnny wants in on this one. He's shacking up with a whore on the North Side, but this deal is so sweet and easy, he wants a piece of it. Having the big guy along will make it easy. I got a meet set up with him."

"What about Homer?" Fatso wondered. "Did that slug in the head knock any of those corny jokes out of him?"

"Mickey got him back to St. Paul. He's okay. It'll take a while, but he'll be back full steam. I don't want him, we don't need him, it shrinks the cut, so there's a lot of reasons to keep him out. No Charlie Floyd, either, that dumb ox. He's probably in the basement of some Anadarko whorehouse drinking up the last of his seven grand . . . Okay, let's get down to it."

"I got a line on soup," said Jack. "It wasn't easy, that stuff is hard to come by. But I know a guy whose brother is a mine foreman in Kentucky, and I drove down last weekend to see if he could put us on to it. It won't be cheap, but he's going to drive it up and handle it for us. He says otherwise we'll blow ourselves up. It's tricky."

"Is he a solid guy?" asked Les. "Our work is tricky too."

"For five grand, he'll be Alvin friggin' York. Yeah, he's solid. Miner. That's the hardest, most dangerous work there is. Have to be a hero to even think about making a living a thousand feet down for a buck an hour!"

"Okay, good. Five grand seems okay."

"That's good," said Jack. "That'll make him happy."

The reports went on. Carey had two cars lined up, purchased cheap from a downstate car-theft ring operating out of Cairo, on the Mississippi. He said he'd get 'em in in a week, work 'em over, make sure they did eighty on the straightaway, were lively on the pedal, and had heavy-duty shocks for any hairpins that came along.

"I hope we don't need 'em," said Les. "I want this one to go easy, no gun-fights in downtown anywhere, no high-speed escapes."

"Amen to that," came the chorus.

"Have you picked a site yet, Les?"

"Nah. I want to drive the whole Illinois section and see what's best. Also, now that I'm thinking of it, Carey, you head down there too and find a school bus you can boost. We park that baby on the track and you watch how fast that train comes to a halt."

"Hey, that's good, Les."

"Damned right," said Les.

Fatso reported on the train itself. It was Illinois Central 909, originating in Iowa City. At six of its thirteen Friday stops it picked up money sacks from federal banks, all headed to the Chicago Federal Reserve Bank. As Jimmy Murray had estimated, it could easily go over two hundred and fifty thousand dollars, and even stepped on five times—now six with Johnny, with the soup guy, cut in—that worked out to forty-one grand apiece, not bad for a night's work.

"So by the time we get all this shit done and our soup up here, it's going to be at least another month. You guys okay on dough?"

The chorus all jabbered in the affirmative.

"Great," said Les. "Now, let's—"

At that moment a wash of headlights rotated by and crossed them, re-vealing them, as another car turned down Miller.

"Shit," said J.P.

"It's a goddamned cop car," said Fatso, as for a brief second the black-and-white color scheme of the vehicle stood out against the glow of Chicago to the east as it headed down the road before it disappeared momentarily behind the rise.

"Get down," said Les. "And watch this."

He went to his car, opened the back door, and from a briefcase on the floor removed his machine pistol and a few twenty-two-round magazines welded by Mr. Lebman.

"Helen, slip out low and get behind the wheel well."

"Les, I—"

"It's nothing. Got it covered," he said, snapping in the magazines, heavy with fat .45s, and throwing the slide.

CHARLES GOT IN to see Purvis near 6, just as His Elegance was freshening up, tightening and aligning his tie, gargling with mouthwash, and combing his hair, at a mirror and sink specially affixed to the wall in his big, well-lit office, where the ceiling fan sliced the air into cooling motion.

"Yes, Charles, hello, sit down, I just have to priss up, my wife is dragging me to the Opera tonight."

"Yes sir."

"What's up?" said Purvis, working intently on the part, running to the left side of his handsome head.

"I have a tip, I'm sure it's nothing, but someone said he overheard someone say that some 'big boys' were meeting on a country road out in far north Cook at two a.m. tonight. Anyhow, this info went to a cop and he called me. Chicago Gang Squad said, forget it, it's nothing, and I'm sure it isn't, since there's no names attached, but I thought I'd go out there and park and take a look-see."

"Did you run it by Sam?"

"He left early. It just came in."

"You sure you don't want to take a couple of these kids and some Thompsons?"

"Mr. Purvis, these kids have been working like dogs, and it's 100 out. I hate to put 'em on a double shift in this heat for something so unlikely."

"Yeah, you're probably right. What are your plans if the one-in-a-million plays out and you strike something?"

"Follow from way, way back, get an address, then we'll set up surveillance, and if it's a go, we'll set up a real good raid, off of recon intelligence, just like we did in France."

"Good thought, Charles. Very thoroughly worked out."

"I have a car chit, sir. You need to sign for Hollis to release a car to me."

"Oh, yeah," said Purvis, taking the chit and dashing out his signature on the appropriate line. "Sure you don't want to log out a Thompson now since I'm signing stuff?"

"I'll be fine. No action tonight, I guarantee it. I just want to get the drive mostly done while it's light out so I'm not stumbling around in the dark."

"Good. Okay, Charles, good luck. And let me know how it works out."

"You'll be the first to know, Mr. Purvis."

"Call me Mel in here, Charles. You're smarter than I am, more experienced than I am, braver than I am, whatever the ranks say, so in here, please, it's Mel, Mel, Mel."

"Got it, Mel."

Charles took the chit, went to find Hollis, and found him in the arms room cleaning a Thompson.

"You clean 'em whether they've been fired or not, huh?" he said.

"Sheriff, if we need 'em, we may need 'em fast, so I want to keep them sparkling."

"Good work, Ed. Here, I have the chit, I need a car."

"Sure. Big date tonight?"

"Ain't been on a date but once in my life and that was my wedding date. Maybe someday I'll go on a real date, but I doubt it. Anyhow, no, I got a tip to run out. Help me figure out how to get out there."

With that, the two went out to the main squad room, where a bank of rolled-up city and state maps hung on the wall. They unspooled Greater Cook County and spent several minutes locating the site, as indicated by the map Charles had just received from Uncle Phil, and the best way out there, considering the play of traffic.

"You want me to come, Sheriff? No problem. I'll call Jean."

"Nah, go home, take some time off. I'm sure this'll turn out to be nothing but farmers sitting on the fence, talking pennant race, the kind of thing farmers talk about when they ain't complaining about the weather."

"Okay, Sheriff, whatever you say."

The best route appeared to be a run out Michigan until he hit the Outer Drive at Oak Street, stay on that a few miles north of downtown, then head west on either North or Belmont.

"I'm guessing Belmont would be little lighter, though you do go by Riverview, the big amusement park. Maybe traffic will back up."

"Nah, not in this weather, unless they figure out how to air-condition fun houses."

"After the park, you run through River Grove, Franklin Park, and Bensenville. Belmont T-bones into Wolf. You go right on Wolf and, according to this map here, it's about five or six more miles to this Miller."

"He said there was a sign, a big Standard Oil billboard, on the corner. I'll park there and mosey on down with binoculars and see what's up."

"You sure you don't want me along?"

"Nah, it'll be nothing, I'm almost certain."

"I've got six cars left. The number thirteen Hudson is the best."

"Let's do number thirteen, then."

All the paperwork taken care of, Charles took the freight elevator down to the underground lot and found number 13 by license plate number, and it started right up.

He exited onto Adams Street, hit State left, fought the Loop traffic for a bit, then took a right, which took him out of the Loop, passing under the looming fortress of the El station, then turned left on Michigan, heading out of town, finally hitting open highway on the Outer Drive, as they called it, which let him speed along the lakefront until it was time to turn west on Belmont.

The two-hour drive went pretty much as planned. The intersection of Miller and Wolf, set in farmland halfway to hell, or Wisconsin, whichever came first, was prosaic, and without the billboard, you'd never notice it. He scanned the field and saw that it was fallow, not plowed, and would be easy to traverse. He'd arrive, lights off, park, go diagonally across the field, hit Miller and ease down it, seeing if he could get close enough for a look, or even to overhear any chatter, assuming anybody showed up.

His plans made, he got back to his car and drove down Wolf, and ten miles farther on in Mount Prospect found a restaurant and had a meat-and-potatoes dinner. He read the papers while he waited for the food, forced himself to eat slowly, had coffee and rolled a cigarette to burn time. But time wouldn't be burned, not readily.

He got back in his car, found a service station, and refueled, making sure to save the receipt for expenses. Then he drove stupidly around Mount Prospect in the dark, seeing nothing, until at last he came upon a movie theater on the outskirts of a town called Wheeling. He hated the pictures, but, what the hell, it would kill some time.

The only thing playing was a drama called *Manhattan Melodrama*, a Gable picture, and he paid his nickel and watched the thing. It was actually pretty good, if a little dopey, but who didn't love Gable, with his commanding air, his self-deprecating humor, his easy way with the ladies, the sparkle of brains behind his eyes and a smile that would melt hubcaps even as it showed spade-like teeth, all polished and shiny. It was about two kid pals grown up to be a big gangster and the governor. The plot was full of stuff, but it came down to the governor, William Powell, another mustache guy, having the power to commute gangster Gable's chair date, but Gable wouldn't let him do it. "Let me have the death I've earned," he said. That was fine with Charles.

He got out at midnight, found another diner, had a cuppa and a piece of pie, being the only customer, a real nighthawk sitting alone with nothing to look at but a brutal slab of dark through the window amid hard, dark angles. Soon enough, a couple came in, all lovey-dovey, and they had burgers and Cokes and paid him no attention, and neither did the counterman, who was too busy cleaning the intricate coffee machine to notice much.

Finally, it was moving on toward the appointed hour, so he paid his bill, went to his car—still hot, but maybe not as much—and started back down Wolf Road.

It was a twenty-minute drive, with no traffic oncoming or trailing, and with hypnotic regularity the darkened outposts of civilization passed on either side. His headlights illuminated the dash-dash-dash painted line at highway's center dividing it into north and south lanes. A mile out from the Miller intersection, he turned his lights off, confident that no cars were headed his direction on the long straightaway ahead, and eased along at about thirty, orienting on the painted line but peering up every few seconds to look for the big Standard Oil billboard.

He saw it, and in the light of the half-moon, saw the intersection, saw the silver band of road running off to the right, slowed to stop, and then heard the unmistakable spasm of a burst of machine-gun fire.

THE CAR HALTED just short of Carey's vehicle, the last in the line. Crouching behind Carey's rear fender, sure that he was invisible even in the moonglow, Les saw the marking ILLINOIS STATE POLICE on the car's white door. He could make out motion inside, identifying two shapes moving without urgency or suspicion in the dark containment of the front seat. The driver rolled down the window, switched on a searchlight mounted on the fender, and guided it to the three cars.

"Everything all right, folks?" came the cry.

Les stepped from behind the car.

"It's just fine, Officers," he said, and then fired.

The gun of course fought him, being small and light against the force of twenty-two hardballs spitting out of it jackrabbit fast, and its flash was a genie emerging from a bottle, leaping crazily into the sky above the muzzle in a slithering, flickering undulation, the superfast thrust and recoil of the slide pulling the muzzle up and to the right as the gun ate its ammunition, the hot spray of ejected empties flying to the right like a squad of pursuit planes climbing to apogee, then diving to attack. But his left hand, locked solid onto the Thompson front grip Mr. Lebman had welded on the dust-cover, kept the fire stream steady into the police cruiser. The fleet of slugs all found glass to pierce, web, and atomize, and the two silhouettes yanked and twisted and shuddered as the bullets tore into them.

Then it was over. The machine pistol had gobbled its magazine in less than a second. The sweet smell of gun smoke drifted to Les's nose and he sucked at it through his nostrils like an aphrodisiac. He had to have more. It smelled so good. He felt so slick, man-with-a-smoking-automatic-gun triumphant, this was the moment he so loved, he lived for, it was so GREAT! Coolly, he thumbed the mag-release catch, felt the empty slide out and caught it with his off hand, as he didn't have too many of them, welded up so skillfully to take three times the normal number of cartridges, and couldn't afford to discard it. Pocketing it, he fished another one out, slid it into the grip, where it disappeared with oily slickness until the mag catch snapped, locking it in. Then he pulled back on the locked-back slide, un-locking it, and it shot forward with a determined metal-on-metal clack, signifying the machine pistol was fully loaded and ready to go again.

He started to walk around the car. Had to finish them off. A burst in each body, no doubt about it, and they were food for vultures, and his war against those symbols of authority whom he had hated and feared his whole life had claimed two more definite kills. He circled around back of the car, aware that while one of the cops slumped over the wheel, the other had col-lapsed in his seat but had enough left in him to open the door, spill out, and begin a bloody crawl to the ditch.

Too bad for you, Mr. State Policeman, with your saddle-shoe cruiser, with your black uniform and tie, all spic-and-span, too bad for you but I'm going to saw you in half.

Suddenly a puff of dirt erupted at his feet, and in the same split second the crack of a heavy pistol reached his ears. He turned, and on the crest a hundred yards away, silhouetted against the glow of the city, isolated and stoic, erect and unflinching, stood a man with a gun, the last thing Les expected. The man fired again.

CHARLES STEPPED ON IT, the Ford spurting ahead, squealed through the right turn onto Miller, chewed up a ton of dust as his tires fought the surface of the country road for traction, and went like a dart to the crest of the hill.

He braked and spilled out. Maybe there were ten mobsters with Thompsons down there, and he didn't want to drive into that kind of a mess. Instead, he stood on the crest, and since his eyes were already accustomed to the darkness, he had no trouble seeing what lay perhaps a hundred fifty yards beyond him, which was three cars pulled off to the side of the road, a black-and-white State cruiser, and a fellow hunched and bent with a gun walking around the back of the car with, by his posture, a depraved heart. The .45 came to Charles's hand with raw speed, and he locked knees, hips, torso, elbows, shoulders, hands, after snicking off the safety, for an impossibly long shot.

He held off and high to the moving figure, and when his internal machinery told him he was on, it also fired the pistol. The crack, the flash, the jump of recoil, the trajectory of spent shell, and back on target, before time in flight had ended for the bullet. He saw the dust kick up maybe five yards this side of the mark, and a man ahead, and so quickly calculated adjustments, but by this time the man had stopped moving, considered, and bent in to his weapon. He and Charles fired at the same time, but where Charles fired once, Mr. Gangster fired ten times in half a second, the flash rising off the gun muzzle a gigantic blot of white heat.

Dust floated into the air as the burst dashed against the ground, erupted, and released the debris in rows of geysers, all neat and pretty unless it hit you. Charles didn't care; he was shooting, and the only thing in the universe was the front sight, now adjusted a third time—two and a quarter men high and half a man forward—and he fired, seeing a splinter of a second later the man take a ragged step back as if hit.

THE GUN CAME TO Les naturally, and without thinking he jacked off half a magazine. His good instincts at flash shooting rained lead on the statue-like figure assaulting him from afar. He saw the dust kick, and expected in the next second to see a lurch, a spin, at the least a sprint, to cover. Instead, he saw a flash and felt the sting of dust way too close for comfort.

Knows what he's doing came to his mind, even as a wave of astonishment hit him. The guy hadn't buckled and run, hadn't sought cover, but stayed hard and straight, calculating without fear the way to a hit.

He fired: flash, crack, the bullet hit the brim of Les's hat, twisting it on his head, shredding the knitted straw.

Les pressed off another burst, emptying his piece into lock-back, and again, off his sound instinct for hip-shooting, the rounds seemed to straddle the guy even as they struck, and again they yanked dust into the air in spumes of grit, and again the fellow didn't—wouldn't? couldn't?—move.

That was enough. Les launched himself, before a fourth round, perfectly adjusted for range and wind, would have caved in his skull, and sprinted back to his car. It seemed his pals had already departed the scene; J.P. was behind the wheel of the Hudson, Helen hiding on the backseat floor, and Les all but flew through the open window, at the last moment opening the door and diving in.

"Go! Go! GO!" he shouted, but J.P. had already put the pedal to the floor, and the great vehicle roared from the battleground, distributing tons of dust behind it as it hit highest velocity in a matter of seconds, and plunged into the already gushing dust the first car had ripped up in its own flight. Six fast shots erupted from the side of the road, where one of the Highway Patrol men had wildly emptied his revolver, but to no effect. Les looked back.

"What was that?"

"One of the cops. It's nothing."

"Is that sonovabitch coming?" J.P. said.

"I don't see lights. He must have stopped to help the cops."

"Jesus Christ, who was he?"

"I don't know, but that guy could shoot. You see how close he came? One more and I'm whacked cold at a hundred fifty yards by the Lone Ranger."

"Sonovabitch!" said J.P.

"You okay, Helen?"

"Just scared."

"It's okay. No damage."

"I'm so scared, Les."

"It's okay, baby," he said, and reached over the seat. Her hand came into his, and both squeezed to feel the firmness of flesh and to commemorate the joy of survival.

But Les's mind was elsewhere.

Man, that guy had some balls.

CHARLES DROVE DOWN the road to the cruiser, where the one officer had gotten out of the ditch and now leaned into his vehicle and was working on his more severely hit partner.

"You okay, Officer?" Charles asked.

"I'm not hit bad," said the cop, not looking up. "Fred's shot up pretty bad, though. Man, what kind of gun was that?"

"Some kind of jazzed-up pistol. You got radio?"

"No. Maybe we could pull him over a little, and I'll take off for the nearest hospital."

"That's a good idea. I'll follow to make sure."

The two men eased the slumped Fred over into the other seat, finding him sodden with his own fluid but breathing and conscious.

"Jesus," he said, "I hurt everywhere."

"Fred, I don't see anything bleeding hard or spurting. I think he missed your arteries."

"Just get me to the hospital."

"Next stop," he said, getting Fred set up for the drive.

He pulled back.

"You sure you're okay to drive?" asked Charles.

"I'm fine, nothing seriously damaged. Say, who are you? Where'd you learn to shoot like that? You sure saved our asses. He was coming 'round to finish us."

Charles turned his lapel to show his badge.

"Justice Department, Division of Investigation."

"Man, you must be made of guts, the way you stood there while that sonovabitch unloaded on you."

"Too stupid to know better, too old to care much," said Charles.

The cop got behind the wheel and gunned the car through a tight U-turn and lit out up the road. Charles duplicated the turn and followed.

IT TOOK A WHILE for the scene to develop at the hospital. First it was just Charles sitting in the lobby, smoking, berating himself silently for wrong decisions. If he'd had that Thompson, he might have been able to bring down the shooter and take the others. With a couple of the better kids along, law school or not, the advantage would have been with them.

On the other hand, he knew if the shooter had had a Thompson, he would have been able to bring down Charles.

Charles also realized it had to be Nelson, with that small-scale machine pistol. Its short barrel and powerful kick made it hard to shoot well at anything except within contact distance. It had to be the gun he used on Carter

Baum because the surviving witnesses had remarked on the excessive flash, which was the signature of the weapon. But he also decided to keep that fact from everybody until he'd cleared it with Division. It was a nice piece of intelligence, and he might need it, because he knew he could be harshly judged for his mistakes tonight.

Calming himself with the ritual of assembling the makings, he lit another cigarette. Meanwhile, two, then three, then six more State Troopers arrived, then an older fellow in a raincoat over a bathrobe to whom all deferred and Charles presumed was the superintendent or commanding officer.

Several of the State boys came over to shake Charles's hand and tell him how much they appreciated his work. People kept arriving, in hastily thrown-on civilian clothes, perhaps other executives, detectives, maybe the dedicated State Police surgeon, Mount Prospect patrolmen and supervisors, someone from the State Attorney's Office, and soon the waiting room was jammed, and outside more and more cars were cramming into the parking lot.

After a bit, the disheveled older man came over.

"I'm Claude Bevens, Superintendent of the Illinois State Police," he said, extending a hand.

Charles rose to shake it.

"Swagger, Justice Department. Are your officers all right?"

"Both will survive, I'm told. Cross was only nicked; he'll be back on duty in a week. Fred McAllister was all shot up, hit six times. But because he was low in the car and didn't catch one in head or throat, they think he'll be okay too, in time."

"Glad to hear that."

"My boys say you saved their lives. Say you shot it out with whoever that bastard was and damned near clipped him. You didn't duck, flinch, drop, move, or anything, all those bullets from that crazy little gun bouncing all around you. I don't know what stuff you're made of, Special Agent, but I wish I had a little of the same."

"Sir, I was in the war. I've been shot at before. A lot."

"Most men run and hide."

"Didn't think about it. Too busy trying to drop that fellow."

"Well, our detectives would like to take a deposition. I know you want to get back downtown and write this up for Mr. Purvis. Can you give us a few more minutes?"

"Sure."

"I'm going to schedule a press conference for four p.m. today. Maybe you could be there for that? I'd like to get Mr. Purvis out here for it too. You deserve recognition for what you did. He should know, you should get some kind of medal."

"Sir, if you could do me a favor, it would be to leave my name out of it. Our Director is very particular about individual agents getting special credit. Between you and me, he's a little fed up with Purvis for getting so big in the papers, and the rumors say Purvis's position is shaky. I'd be happy to talk to your detectives, and feel free to communicate with Purvis or Mr. Cowley, but putting me behind microphones in front of cameras won't do me no good at all."

"You sure? These are times when we all need heroes to believe in."

"It's my best move."

"Okay, Justice. It's your call."

18

"NOTHING," he said to Jen over the phone from his hotel room. "I am out of leads and real low on hope."

"Well," she said, "you are not known as a quitter, so I know you'll break this one open just like you did with that Russian woman sniper."

"But I had leads with Mily Petrova. Plus, I liked Mily. This old man's an undertaker with an attitude. What's his problem, anyhow? He won't let anybody near."

"He doesn't care for fools. Sound familiar?"

"The old buzzard left nothing behind him, and there's nothing in the records. The hints are all circumstantial, and while they suggest, you couldn't go to the bank with 'em."

"I know that—"

"Well, wait," he said. "To be fair, the Historical Society let me go through the photos again, and I did fetch one from December of 1934, when he was back on the job, and no mention had been made of his five-month absence. Silly picture, 'Sheriff Swagger awards the 1934 Crossing Guard of the Year with a gold plaque.' Small-town-newspaper stuff not important to anyone except the little girl who was in the picture. So—"

He paused. Time passed, the universe began to move again.

"There you go," she said.

"She'd be ninety-four, if she was still alive. The chances are small that her mind is clear. And even smaller still that she'd remember having her picture taken with a sheriff in early December eighty-three years ago."

"But you do have her name."

"The newspaper gives her name as a Mary Sue Bridgewater."

"There's your lead," Jen said.

So the next morning he called Jake Vincent in Little Rock, asked Jake to recommend a good private detective, got an outfit the firm had worked with many times, and via Jake soon found himself talking with an investigator, and he laid the specifics before him.

"It is a long shot, Mr. Swagger," said the professional detective. "But we have document specialists who will go through census records, tax records, newspaper obits, property deeds, anything on paper, and if ninety-four-year-old Mary Sue Bridgewater is still breathing somewhere in the continental U.S., we'll find her for you."

"Thank you, I appreciate it."

But that left him with but one task that he could do himself and it was as foolish a fool's errand as any fool had ever thought up.

He had the Xerox of the strange "map" from the strongbox, where the badge, the gun cylinder—or was it from a car, an airplane, a refrigerator, a locomotive, or a popcorn popper?—the Colt pistol, and the thousand-dollar bill had been found. It was an aerial scheme of what appeared to be a wall, presumably some structure's external wall. It sported two window wells, or that's what he assumed the indentations in the wall had to be, and from the second one, on a northeastern angle—again assuming the map was oriented with north at the top—ten dashes stood for ten steps to a circle, which Bob assumed was a tree, and on the other side of the trunk were three more dashes leading to an X. X marks the spot. X the unknown. The X factor. Mr. X. X!

Bob realized it could be no dwelling on the Swagger property, because at no place in the house he grew up in, and Earl before him, and even Charles before that, had there ever been two windows as close together as these seemed to be, assuming they were windows, assuming this was a map and not a doodle, assuming this, assuming that.

It's so thin, he thought. Everything about this old bastard was thin. He sure as hell didn't want anybody poking into his business, and he'd either left no tracks or carefully erased his own.

At any rate, Swagger's solution to this problem was short on insight, long on labor. Out of the same Historical Society, he'd come up with a telephone directory, fortunately quite brief. He guessed that his grandfather's acquaintance circle would have mostly been prominent civic types. He was "The Sheriff," after all. So Swagger found the town municipal guide, wrote down the names of all of 1934's county officials—there were twenty-one—and then looked them up in the phone directory, yielding twenty-one 1934 addresses, most in what had been the "quality" section of town in those days. Then he added doctors and lawyers. So after much listing and recording, he finished up with thirty-nine addresses.

Thus, he spent the next two days visiting each one, peering from afar, as he compared windows and wall variations and tree occurrences with the map, and if he noted a possibility, he knocked, introduced himself, and was allowed to circle the house perimeter—assuming the house had been built before 1934—and of the thirty-nine addresses, thirty-three remained, him searching for that magical arrangement of windows and a single tree, along a wall that itself was oriented to the north.

The result: nothing.

Nights, he went through old Vincent family scrapbooks, just hoping, but the result was the same. The Vincents knew other old Blue Eye families, and he had access to a batch of other albums, and were he writing a book on the agrarian aristocracy of Polk County in the '30s, he'd have been all set, for he saw lots of men in three-piece suits, ties tight, with fedoras low, at backyard parties with women in tea dresses of flowery, flimsy material, all of them prosperous and well pleased with their place in time and society. But of the man-killing sheriff and war hero, not a thing. Had the sheriff exiled himself or did he prefer people lower in the order, or, even more likely, he preferred nobody, nothing. He was a loner on his family farm, working his guns, doing his hunting, and maybe as an alpha he had some low-grade gofers around happy to do his bidding in exchange for the presence of the genuinely heroic. But if this even happened, it left no record.

At the end of his two days of labor in Blue Eye, he had learned exactly nothing.

19

CHICAGO

July 16, 1934

W HEN HE FINALLY LEFT THE HOSPITAL, Charles drove straight downtown, arriving at the office at 7 a.m. He went up to nineteen and sat
down at his typewriter and clacked out a bare-bones report of last night's
incident over two carbons, including the info that he'd prevailed on the
State cops to keep his name out of the papers, then put the original on Sam's
desk, the first carbon on Purvis's, and the third on Hugh Clegg's.

Then he went downstairs, went to the nearest Toddle House, and had
himself a breakfast of eggs and bacon. And a pot of coffee. He figured it was
better to work straight through the day than to go home, nap, and come in
by 2 p.m.

When he got in, he went straight to his desk. His schedule was to work
through a pile of reported "sightings" of the bad boys, most of which could
be checked out by phone. If he was dissatisfied with that conversation, he'd
put in for a car and put it on his list of face-to-face interviews. Then at 1
there was a meeting of the Dillinger Squad with the Gang Intelligence
Squad—the police's Dillinger Squad—at Central, to share information and
coordinate strategy, though Charles thought it was mostly silliness and fantasy. From 4 to 5, he was to be at that same installation's firing range, where
he was going to run three newly arrived agents through his course of fire,
evaluate them, see who had the gift and who'd best be kept behind the lines.
Looking at the files, he saw one had served in the Michigan State Police for
seven years, and he assumed that fellow would already know a thing or two.

But of course the incident of the night before had to be processed, and who knew how long that would take, so the schedule was pretty much up in the air. He worked steadily through the morning at his desk, on the phone, and at around 11 a call came; it was Purvis's secretary, Mrs. Donovan, saying that Mel would like to see him. He rose and walked through the office, which was suddenly uncannily silent. When he got to the hallway that led to the offices, he turned, curious, and saw every agent in the place staring at him. And then they stood. And then they clapped.

"Swell, Charles," said Purvis a few seconds later in his office. "As you can see, word has gotten around. Cops talk to other cops, and some of those other cops even talk to us."

"Yes sir," said Charles. He sat at a table across from Purvis and Clegg. Sam sat off a little, not exactly at the table, content not to face him or dominate the chat.

"You are to be congratulated," said Purvis. "I had a call from the State Police Superintendent by seven a.m., and he told me one of my agents had saved two of his officers' lives, and had shot it out with at least four or five heavily armed men—men with automatic guns, in fact—and had driven them away. That makes you an official hero, and, as you know, we haven't had many heroes around here lately."

"Thank you, Mr. Purvis."

"We've all read the report by now," said Clegg, who technically had no authority over Charles but whom Purvis had included almost as an invitation to take a swing at him and see if he could land one, as Clegg was not in the Purvis camp and therefore not in the Swagger camp. "But perhaps you'd take us through it orally."

"Yes sir," said Charles, and proceeded to narrate the events of the evening.

"When I left," he concluded, "I was assured both troopers McAllister and Cross would make it and be back on duty fairly quickly."

"Charles," said Purvis, "after a gunfight, many men need a day off, to get rid of the shakes, to refuel emotionally those feelings which were spent in the rush under fire, to consider, to gather, to relax. Do you need that?"

"I've been shot at before," said Charles, "and it ain't fun, but I'm okay. No shakes, no nightmares, no cold sweats."

"Agent Swagger," said Clegg, "no one here is questioning your heroism, but it has occurred to me that certain of your judgments leading to that heroism might need further explanation."

"That's what I'm here for," said Charles.

"I know you were an expedient—*expeditious*—hire and didn't attend the academy, or even the one-month special crash training program that some of our recent agents have been through, and your grasp of our regulations could well be shaky. But that can't be an excuse. So we have to look at your decisions and our regulations anyhow. Those regulations specifically preclude you acquiring sources but refusing to disclose them."

"He did inform me of a source, let the record show," said Purvis somewhat testily. "There was no formal 'refusal to disclose.' I never asked."

"It seems rather sketchy to me," said Clegg. "And I'm sure Washington will conclude the same."

"I had no reason to place any faith in this source," said Charles. "I had no idea if he was square or not. It could have been an ambush too. Or some kind of double cross. Or some prank or stunt the Chicago cops decided to play on us. So, yes, my decision, no one else's, and against the advice of Mr. Purvis, I decided to go out alone, that's all. If someone was going to get shot, I preferred it to be me and not anyone else."

"Yes, but if you'd run it by all of us instead of just mentioning it on the fly late in the afternoon, we might have insisted on a full effort and you'd have been out there with ten men and ten Thompsons. Then you wouldn't have just 'driven them away' but killed or arrested them."

"I understand that. While you're at it, I made another bad decision. Inspector Purvis tried to get me to take a Thompson. With one Thompson, I believe I could have closed them down, never mind ten. That was bad judgment on my part. I couldn't do much but make noise with a handgun."

"State Police investigators found a straw Panama in the gully whose brim had been shredded by a .45," said Purvis. "That had to be your shot. With a handgun. From one hundred and fifty measured yards."

"That was the hold. Another shot without a breeze and I'd have nailed that little peckerwood between the eyes."

"But your superb marksmanship shouldn't deflect from questionable judgment," said Clegg, not looking at Purvis.

"Mr. Clegg, more men don't necessarily mean better outcome. Little Bohemia, for example. But also the war, where I led many a raid and saw them go wrong all the time and boys killed out of stupidity. Operating with a team at night takes a lot of experience, a lot of planning, a lot of communication. I didn't have time for none of those things, so I made a judgment it was better handled by one man. I didn't want these kids, many of whom have never shot for blood or been under fire, running around in the dark with Thompsons and Browning rifles. Night battle ain't twice as hard as day battle, it's ten times as hard. We ain't ready for it. Nobody is ever ready for it, but these young fellows, no matter how brave and enthusiastic, really ain't ready for it."

"Well said, and duly noted," said Purvis.

"Well, let's go to the issue of the Thompson, then. Or the Browning rifle. If you would have had them—hell, if you'd had the Model 94 my dad hunted deer with in the Mississippi woods, with your formidable marksmanship skills, you might have tagged Nelson and two or three of his pals."

"It could have happened that way. But you can't make that presumption. I rolled out of my car into a shooting position with the Colt in about one second flat, and it was that first shot that stopped the gunman from closing on and finishing the two troopers. If I'm running back to the trunk, pulling a big gun, inserting the drum, running the bolt, then heading to the crest, maybe those cops are dead. Then maybe I bring 'em down with the Browning or the Thompson or maybe I don't. I get one, say, and by that time they've got three or four Thompsons on me. Sir, believe me, it's tough to stand against three Thompsons. Two cops and an agent dead, maybe Nelson is only wounded, and all of the outlaws make it out. That's another risk that has to be considered. It would sort of fit in with the Little Bohemia thing."

Sam spoke for the first time.

"You're positive it was Nelson?"

"Now I am. But the source just said 'big boys,' whatever that means, another reason Chicago Gang Intelligence wasn't interested in it. But I could tell he was shooting that machine-pistol thing, short-barreled, with no shoulder stock to brace it, and a whole lot of muzzle flash, more flash than a Thompson. That's why I'm alive. If he'd have had a Thompson himself—and I'll bet there were several in them cars—he'd have planted it on his shoulder, aimed carefully over long sights, and I'd be goose crap now. So the fact I ain't dead is proof that it was Nelson, because according to our findings, he's the only one with that custom machine pistol. Agent Baum learned that the hard way at Little Bohemia."

"I wonder if we haven't gotten enough out of Agent Swagger," said Purvis. "I think he's made good account of all decisions, and while it could have had a better outcome, it also could have had a worse outcome. Much worse. We ought to consider this event closed, report to Washington, move on."

"One last question," said Clegg. "Your source: I think it's time for you to formally identify him so that we can vet and approve. I don't like being led by the nose by someone we don't know a thing about."

"It's not even really a source. It's a cop who I knew in Hot Springs and did a favor for. He got his big-city job here, and he's worked his way up to the new headquarters, where he hears things. Anyhow, he heard that Chicago Gang Intelligence was sitting on this rumor of something someone overheard in some chatter in a known Italian joint and he went to me with it. It's not a thing we can count on. Now, maybe this cop is just telling us a story and he does have a source and we will get more out of it. But I can't say. But if I roust him, if we ruffle Chicago for his records, if I haul him up here or set up a meet with you fellows, it could all go off the tracks. It's the sort of thing where patience is better than action. It happens that way sometimes."

Like most police officers, Charles lied easily and without tremor, swallow, gulp, or shifty eyes, and he had no reason to believe anyone was on to him.

"I think that'll have to do it for you, Hugh," said Purvis. "We'll let it rest. Maybe if we're in a jam, we'll press Charles to press Officer X, but right now let's just enjoy a minor triumph, his good judgment in keeping his own name and the Division out of the papers, and, as I said, let's share this provisional success with our friends in Washington."

So that was it. But Purvis indicated with a nod that he wanted Charles to stay.

"Don't worry about Clegg, Charles. He's just a bitter blowhard. By rights, he shouldn't even have been there."

"Thank you, Mr. Purvis."

"*Mel.* Anyhow, you must be beat. Want to take the rest of the day off?"

"Got lots of stuff set this afternoon."

"Fair enough. Tomorrow."

"Same. I'm fine."

"Okay, Charles."

He clapped Charles on the shoulder and Charles left. He got back to his desk, and as he half suspected it would be, there was a note from the agent on his phone.

"Charles . . . Your Uncle Phil called. Wants you to get back to him right away."

20

NORTHWEST COOK COUNTY, ILLINOIS

July 1934

A NOTHER COUNTRY ROAD, another hot night.

The discussion: the last country road, the last hot night.

Les was morose. It was one thing for two State Troopers to show up, and the papers said they made a habit of taking back roads home at the end of the duty day to look for people in trouble off the main roads. Their appearance was simple luck of the draw, unpredictable. It represented nothing in the cosmic scheme of things.

It was the guy—a federal, Les was convinced—who got there just in time to save the troopers' hash and almost put one through Les's face. What the hell was he doing there? That had to be more than coincidence, even if the papers said nothing about his arrival. In fact, that alone convinced Les he was federal, and he saw him as a sort of night-riding phantom, a man of mystery, who had magical ways of knowing, and always, just like on the radio or at the picture shows, got there in the nick of time.

"You didn't say anything?" he queried his pals. "I mean, how could he know?"

With J.P., it was about his girl in Sausalito, Sally.

"You didn't say a thing?"

"Why would I? She thinks I'm a tractor salesman."

"Could she have eavesdropped or gone through your pockets, sniffed a reward, and come up with the tip."

"Sally's not that kind of girl. She's pretty, and like a lot of the pretty girls, she don't get it. She isn't a noticer, a rememberer. She just thinks I'm a handsome guy, a salesman on the road, lots of fun, knows stuff, and that's it. She never heard of any big-gangster crap. She doesn't read the papers or listen to anything but music on the radio."

Les always had a thing about women. He didn't trust them. He felt the same about Mickey Conforti, Homer's honeybee. But he could get no satisfaction out of J.P., so he moved on.

"It couldn't be wiretap," said Fatso. "Les, we're on to that. You can always hear the click when they come on to listen. There were no clicks. It's impossible."

"Think! Think! Think! Did anyone overhear you? Did you talk in public? How could they get inside if—"

"Les, if it had been federals, they would have had a whole outfit out there, with machinos and Browning rifles and the works. It would have been the Fourth of July. It was one guy. He was driving by, remember, he wasn't there at the start. He wasn't hiding by the road. He heard your fire, turned, raced to the top of the hill, piled out, and opened fire on you. If he was planning anything, it wouldn't have been shooting at you from a hundred fifty yards out with a pistol. He couldn't have known. It's just coincidence."

"One coincidence, I get," said Les. "First the cops just happen to show up, then this fed shows up. That's two, one on top of the other, back-to-back. That don't make no sense. The world don't work like that."

Nobody was interested in arguing how the world did or didn't work with Les, whose ideas were pretty much etched in stone, unchallengeable, unchangeable. He might go off if you pressed him too hard with your system of logic against his. Fatso backed off fast, as did Jack, when his turn came, and finally Carey.

"You haven't noticed anything odd at the garage?" said Les. "You got the only fixed address in the bunch. Maybe they're on to you? Maybe they followed you?"

"Les, I swear, I'm being careful. I double-check every move, every day. I come and go by different routes. I don't conduct any of our business over this phone. I keep that part of my life completely separate. I got a nose for guys fishing around or peeping. I don't have a record, except for juvie shit no one cares about. I'm perfect for you! I'm good at this! That's why I want to be with you guys, I have a talent. I don't want to spend my life changing oil in cars I can't afford for people who treat me like a monkey. Man, if they knew I was in with Baby Face Nelson, they'd shit a brick."

For once Les didn't explode when he heard the name the papers had pinned on him, which always slapped him raw since he didn't have a baby face, he wasn't a half-pint or a squirt, but pretty much average-sized, and good-looking, as everybody said, and he always turned out well in suits and ties. But Carey's sheer bliss at being this close to Baby Face Nelson was enough to keep Les from throwing punches, as he'd been known to do.

"All right," Les said. "You're still on with the cars? And you can boost that bus?"

"Yes sir," said Carey.

"Good kid," said Les.

He returned to the tourist cabin he'd rented just outside of Glenview for Helen, not far from Curtiss Airport, though the planes were an annoyance. Wasn't much to do. She shopped every day and bought the *Tribune* or the *Herald-Examiner*, going out again at night for the *Daily News*. He read, he listened to the radio, and every once in a while they snuck out to the movies. One night they went to *Manhattan Melodrama* in Mount Prospect, surprised that it was still hanging around, since it had come out two months earlier, in May. But he liked it, and it really felt good to leave his troubles in the old kit bag while he watched Gable act it up as a gangster, unlike any gangster Les had ever known, and he'd known them for years, going back to his teenage days as an errand boy for the Capone and then the Touhy mobs. Gable was too likable, too charming. Your real gangster was a man of extreme toughness, and no matter how old and how much dignity he had, he would go to fists or knives or *pistolas* at the drop of a hat where matters of honor or business were concerned. Edward G. got that, and Cagney, but as handsome a palooka as Gable was, he wasn't any gangster. He wasn't tough enough. He was big, not tough, and there's a difference, as Les's whole life had proven. That's why he liked the gangsters so much: they took shit from no man and gave shit when and where it pleased them, never looking back, always having the best dames, cars, clothes, and pals. He fashioned himself on that image, if his stronger ethic was to Helen, whom he loved almost as deeply as he loved being the gangster, and she had never, ever once told him to quit his ways. How great was that?

Their only contact was J.P., who came by every day to see if anything needed doing. He had liberty and flexibility because he wasn't famous like Les was after South Bend and he could still live a normal life. One day he and Les drove west and tracked by map the Des Moines train as it came in around 5 p.m., as per Jimmy Murray's scouting report. They were looking for a spot to heist it and had found a good enough place just outside of Wheaton, a long straightaway with a road that led quickly enough into a forested area with lots of crossroads. They could stash a car there, hit the train, disappear back into the woods, change cars, and get out with nothing showing to give them away. Following wider circles in the farming community, they came across a lady dropping off kids in a big yellow school bus. They followed her and, sure enough, she kept it at home, outside. It would be easy for Carey to jump it that day and lay it across the tracks to get the train halted, and then the guns would come out.

"If Johnny comes in," said Les, "it should work fine. We need a gun to hold the engineers, we need four guns to take the mail car and blow the safe and conk the crew out—and no telling how many are in a mail car. I don't count Carey—nice guy and all—because he ain't been in this neighborhood and I don't know which way he jumps if it goes hot. Four guys with guns should get 'em quieted down fast, and then we're out of there. I figure no more than five minutes flat."

"I wouldn't mind another gun," said J.P., and Les always listened to his sagacious advice.

"Homer?" queried J.P.

"That piece of crap," said Les. "He said rude stuff about Helen. I was going to kill him."

"Les, he was cool as air-conditioning in South Bend, I hear. Some are saying none of you would have gotten out of South Bend if he hadn't plugged a cop and kept the others back."

"Hey, I was out there too," said Les. "Talking about cool, I took one in the chest and didn't bat an eyelash. Now, that's cool."

"No doubt. But you don't want to work with Charlie Floyd, do you? I mean, if your choice is Charlie or Homer, who do you pick?"

"Got a point," said Les. "It don't make me happy, but it is a good point. We do need another gun, and as long as Homer ain't spongy from that shot in the head, maybe if he swore to keep his yap shut, we could take him aboard. Only, I'm doing the planning. This one, I'm running. He has to get that."

"He'll get it. I'm going to see if we can't get Johnny up for another meeting real soon. I can reach him through that lawyer. He's in contact with Homer, he can bring him."

"Say, the twenty-first?"

"That should be enough time."

"We'll meet at the Matty's Wayfarer Inn, on Waukegan, in the back room. It should be clean now."

"Got it. I'll make it happen."

That was pretty much it. Radio ate the time: the Cubs or Sox games devoured afternoons, and the bands on the networks nights. Neither of the ball teams would win a pennant, but the boys played hard, and Les liked to lose himself in their fortunes. In time, as the meet-up with Johnny approached, his spirits lifted some.

"Well," said Helen, "someone is out of the dumps."

"I'm feeling better, sweetie. Things are going along smoothly."

"You're not scared?"

"Sure, a little. That damned federal spooked me. Another couple inches and I'm wearing a bullet hole where my forehead used to be. I sure heard that one when it whizzed by and took my hat off. I hope that was the one with my name on it."

"Did it get you to thinking?"

"Sure, and I know this is no good with our kids at your pop's place. I want to raise my kids, I don't want Pop doing it. I miss 'em bad. We haven't seen 'em for three weeks, since just after South Bend. But I can't get out without a big score, so we can go someplace, live nice, buy a little business, and be regular people. You need a bankroll to finance a move like that. You can't start cold." He wasn't sure if he meant it. He said it frequently, sometimes meaning it, sometimes not.

"I love it when you talk this way."

"Helen, I know how hard this has been on you. You've been great. You're my girl, always there for me. You're the heroine of this picture show. I love you so much, I think I'll die from it, if the cops don't get me. I am the luckiest man in the world."

There followed some private between-couple baby goo-goo talk and then some private between-couple fucking, both great fun.

21

"**A**ND WHAT DO YOU DO, YOUNG LADY?" asked Mrs. Tisdale.

"I'm a news producer for Fox News in Washington," Nikki said.

"I hate Fox News," said Mrs. Tisdale.

"I hear that a lot."

"Well, I shall try not to hold it against you, dear. People have to take what's available. Anyway, who's this fellow? Does he talk?"

"He's my father. When I was late getting home from dates in high school, he sure talked. Not so much now. I think he sort of dried up."

Mrs. Tisdale turned and fixed hard eyes on Swagger. He felt under-dressed, even if he was wearing a suit and tie.

"You're the hero? The letter said you were highly decorated military."

"He doesn't consider himself a hero," Nikki said. "He considers himself lucky. He says all the heroes were killed. But he did do three tours in Viet-nam, though one was cut short by wounds. On the other hand, one was extended."

"Can you say something, please, sir?"

Mrs. Tisdale's room labored at cheer, but the gloom of death hung every-where. It was all yellow with artificial flowers and pictures of lambs and brooks and meadows. But it also boasted about a million dollars' worth of equipment, most of it gleaming, with gauges and tubes and knobs every-where, to keep people who were supposed to be dead alive for another few seconds. Some of the equipment was electric, some just mysteriously inert. Every few seconds, something beeped. Bob, as one might expect, did not care for hospitals or anything that reminded him of waking up in the Philippines with his hip shattered and his spotter, Donnie Fen, football hero and all-around good kid who had already finished his tour, gone forever.

"Hello," said Bob. "Thank you for seeing us on such short notice."

"Short is the only kind of notice I have."

The detective firm had quite expensively located ninety-four-year-old Mrs. Tisdale, née Mary S. Bridgewater, in this place, where, having outlived or gotten bored with all her tribe, not that she seemed to notice, she lay abed in a cheerful yellow gown that spoke of lively memories. She was a look-forward-to, not a look-back-at—that was clear from the proud jut of her chin, even though tethered to an oxygen tank by nose nozzle and tube, and monitored by a dozen robot contrivances, so that she looked like a creation of Frankenstein's lightning. *She's alive!*

"I'm grateful," Bob said.

She turned back to Nikki.

"Why are you here and not in D.C. making up lies?"

"I only make them up on Tuesdays. This is Thursday."

"Excellent riposte," said Mrs. Tisdale. "I enjoy a girl with some snap, crackle, and pop."

"I'm really here because I'm cute and likable and an experienced interviewer. My father is none of those things. So he asked me to come up and sort of, you know, make it go more smoothly—that's how he put it."

"Well, you've succeeded. You must be something, Mr. Hero, to raise such a lovely, smart daughter. When does she move to CNN?"

"They've offered. She's too stubborn to budge. Hardheaded girl. Can't tell her a thing."

"Well, if I like her, I suppose I have to like you. Now . . . you said Blue Eye. Lord's mercy, I left Blue Eye in 1941 when I was seventeen. And my father—Daddy was an engineer, but during the Depression the only job he could get was as a draftsman—you know, got a job working for Martin Aviation, just outside Baltimore. I've been here ever since, lived nicely in the valley through two husbands, six children, and I'm not sure how many grandchildren, whose names I can't seem to remember either. As you can see, my brain is a large piece of ancient Swiss cheese, and I fear that the part that contained Blue Eye memories is one big empty bubble. May I ask, what is this in support of? If the letter said, I've forgotten."

"The letter was vague," said Bob, "nothing in it to remember. I can't explain it too well even now. See, my father, Earl Swagger, was a great man. He was awarded the Medal of Honor for something he did on Iwo Jima in 1945, and he also took part in five island invasions in the war. He came back and was a State Trooper, and was killed in the line of duty in 1955 when I was nine. But his father is a mystery. His name was Charles Swagger, and he was a hero in World War I, in two armies, the Canadian and the American. He was the sheriff of Polk County from 1923 until his death, also in the line of duty, in 1942, just before my father was sent to Guadalcanal. I realized when some of his relics came my way that I knew nothing about this man, and it seems he wished nothing to be known. He may have even covered his tracks. But he shaped my father into something special and my father shaped me."

"Into something special—like father, like son."

"No, my father was a real hero, I'm just a lucky imitator. Anyhow, I have taken it upon myself to learn something about my grandfather and see what lies at the root of his mysteries. I have called homes for the elderly all throughout Arkansas, taken out ads in elder publications, dug through the photo albums of old families in Blue Eye, finally hiring a sophisticated detective agency to try to find someone who was alive and remembers when my grandfather was alive. After all that, I've found only one such person: you. That's all."

"I'm afraid I must disappoint you, then, Mr. Swagger . . . *Colonel* Swagger?"

"*Gunnery Sergeant* Swagger."

"Sergeant Swagger, I have no memories of your grandfather."

"I brought some pictures. I thought it might help. These are from the Blue Eye Historical Society."

"All right," she said, "I'm game. Abracadabra, bibbity-bobbity-boo, let's see if some magic happens."

He handed over a batch of glossies from his briefcase and the old beauty took them, scanned them, now and then stopping to meditate, or at least go into search function, and commented as she navigated.

"The trees—I *do* remember the trees. Elms, hundreds of them, and in the fall the whole world blazed with their coloration."

"Yes, ma'am," said Bob.

"They burned leaves in those days, and from August through early November the stink of burning leaves and a fog of smoke hung everywhere. Is that right?"

"It is," said Bob.

"Is it me or were the colors really different then? I seem to remember nothing was as hard a color as it is now. It was more pastel somehow, thinner. There was more light in the air. There wasn't so much insistence on being noticed."

Bob sort of got what she meant, but no words came to him.

"Not big on colors, are we, Sergeant Swagger?"

"He was too busy ducking to notice colors," said Nikki.

"Point well taken," said Mrs. Tisdale. "Your life has been too full of meaningful action to put up with ironic jibes from a rich old lady, Sergeant Swagger."

"None of it had much meaning, ma'am. I take no offense."

"Anyhow, of course homes were bigger, but hotter, no air-conditioning. I remember big black boat-cars. Everybody smoked, everybody wore hats, everybody drank. Yes, there was a Depression, but I was among people who seemed untouched by it. I remember tennis, but I think that was later, more toward the war. My father played golf and was in the country club. The black people were very subservient, and invisible, even if they were in your home . . . Oh, I do remember this home, I believe Billy Marlowe lived there. I think he kissed me in 1941, when I was seventeen, right before we left for Baltimore. I think I heard he died in a plane over Germany. The shoes are so funny. I don't remember them, though I do remember saddle shoes, though maybe that was later. I think I have the 'thirties and the 'forties and half the 'fifties lumped together. I'm afraid next I'm going to remember going to the movies to see Lewis and Martin."

"What about Shirley Temple?"

"I remember seeing those movies, I remember the theater, and my friends Frannie and Thelma, but it's in space, just floating, not connected with anything. Sorry, I can't help. Anything else, Mr. Swagger?"

"Finally, this one."

"My god," said Mrs. Tisdale. She looked at the photo, considering it carefully. In time, she squinched up her eyes so that she was regarding it like a sniper peering through a scope, only through her dominant eye.

"Here's how it appeared in the paper, ma'am." He handed over the cellophane-wrapped clipping from the December 11, 1934, *Clarion*. "Sheriff Awards 'Crossing Guard of Year' Medal."

"The actual glossy has more detail," he said. "The printed version gets all fuzzy with those dots."

She continued to stare intently. Then at last—it seemed an hour had passed, but it couldn't have been more than a few seconds—she said, "Yes, now that I see this, it does in fact conjure some memories. I cannot believe I still am capable of such."

"Please, go ahead."

"Ah, suppose I tell you something about this man that you won't like?"

"I would be surprised if you didn't. What information I've come up with suggests he'd just done something that resulted in some kind of scandal and returned to Polk County in shame. And I assume since it was the custom, that as part of the apparatus that ran Polk County in those days, he was party to all matter of graft, grift, and bribe."

"Perhaps . . . I wouldn't know any of that. But I did notice that he smelled like Daddy, which was my code for whiskey on his breath. I remember too that he had the sort of over-friendliness, over-politeness, over-precision that attends someone in a state of alcoholic blur who is pretending to be sober."

"He seems to have had a drinking problem. I'm guessing it started in 1934."

"What happened to him in 1934?"

"That's the mystery I'm trying to solve. I know that later it got so bad that he started going to a Baptist Prayer Camp for help. But the Lord was otherwise occupied."

"The Baptists talk to God, you know, so if they couldn't help him, he was beyond redemption. Are you sure you want to know?"

"No. But I am sworn to try my damnedest."

"Fair enough. All right, he was, as I said, slightly drunk. Nobody said a thing, but I could smell it. He must have favored rye, as my father did. There were other things manifest now that I remember. He was treated by all with great respect. It was clear many viewed him with awe and considered themselves lucky to be in his presence. Perhaps it was all those medals he won in his two armies."

"He had also shot it out with some very bad fellows from Little Rock, and when the smoke cleared, he was still standing and they were not. Actually, that happened several times with various fellows, and he was always the one left standing in the end."

"Yes, that was the aura. He was the gunfighter. But at the same time, even as I sensed that, I can remember not fearing him. He didn't make you uneasy. He seemed a good man, to a ten-year-old girl. I remember that plaid jumper I wore on special occasions. Each of the crossing guards got a medal, but because I had never been late or missed a day, I was considered the best. I was rather proud of that medal; it remains the only prize I ever won. It also was the first time I ever succeeded at anything, and I had been considered a dull girl. But having a big important man like The Sheriff give me that medal, and hold my hand, and telling me I should be proud, that was one of my favorite moments."

"I'm glad he was part of that for you."

"I am too. Maybe he wasn't the bastard you think."

"We'll have to see."

"Now I am getting a memory. It's gurgling out of my unconscious. Is it real or is it a figment? No, I think it's real."

They waited. The old lady closed her eyes, as if waiting for the séance to begin, then laughed.

"Oh, yes: the ear."

"The ear?"

"You can't see it here. His head is turned slightly. It was his right ear. The top half of it was bandaged. It could not have been a major wound. I mean, an ear. The top of an ear! But it wore some gauze wrapping and adhesive tape. Yes, definitely. Had he been in a minor accident?"

"I don't know. I'll go back to the newspaper and see if there's any mention."

He sat back, looked at Nikki, who nodded.

"I can't tell you how much you've helped me. You've given me something I didn't have before: an ear."

After some farewell ceremony, they left the old woman, found a place to eat, and then headed back to D.C. He would drop Nikki off at her apartment, then head out to Nick's, where he was bunking, to see if Nick had come up with anything.

As he dropped her off, she said, "By the way, are you aware that you're being followed?"

22

CHARLES TOOK THE FREIGHT ELEVATOR DOWN, stepped into the Chicago heat—it hit him like a hammer—and walked the few blocks to State. Chicago's main stem was thronged. It was the season of the straw hat, that flat-brimmed pancake head cover that had always seemed ridiculous to Charles. These big-city folks, how did they think they looked? But everywhere, the disk-like things bobbed and swayed and jiggled, their wearers seeming to believe in their magic cooling powers, though faces ashine with sweat in the harsh sun seemed to belie that faith.

Charles himself, even in cotton khaki, sweated badly as he moved the two blocks to the huge hulk of the Maurice Rothschild department store and found the central phone booth outside the main entrance. Fortunately, it was empty, and wiping his brow with a handkerchief, Charles entered and slid the door shut—even hotter!—took the phone off its cradle and pressed the lever down, putting the phone to ear. He wasn't much for pretending, but he made a halfhearted attempt to play the game, and Uncle Phil's spies must have been efficient, for in a few seconds the phone rang.

"Swagger."

"Well, aren't you the hero." It was the creamy voice of the man on the park bench, assured, vaguely New York, smoother than it ought to be.

"So what is this?"

"Your lucky day."

"Okay."

"No names. But there's a cop in the East Chicago police force so crooked, he can't find a bed to lie flat in."

Uncle Phil waited for his laugh, but Charles wasn't a laugher.

"Anyhow, he's trying to sell out Johnny D."

"All right," said Charles, "I am impressed."

"He knows a gal—this is the only name: Anna—she's an ex-madam, was in the whore trade since before you were born. Her mess is, she's some kind of European, she's in trouble with Immigration, and they want to ship her back to her country, to which she's in no hurry to go."

"Got it," said Charles, thinking, Get to the point!

"She runs a North Side rooming house, on the outskirts of respectability. It seems her newest roomer is a tall bub with a way about him. Lots of cash, flashy dresser, the dames got all their skivvies wet for him."

"This guy would be Johnny?"

"You're on it. So the deal is, Anna's willing to give up Johnny in exchange for help with Immigration. That's why the deal is coming to you, federal government, instead of local palookas, who can't do a thing for her."

"Give up how?"

"You'd have to discuss that with her."

"What's the timing look like?"

"She wants to move fast so she doesn't end up back in Sylvania or Pennsylvania or Transylvania or wherever it is. You could have him inside of a week."

Charles took a deep breath.

"This cop, will he be trouble?"

"No. He'll get a message from certain folks I know to back off on this one. He'll handle arrangements, put it together. He wants to be in on the pinch, or shoot—whichever—but he's not a worry. He'll either play ball or go for a swim in the lake with a refrigerator."

"You guys play rough."

"It's the only way."

THE MOON WAS A SLIVER, the lake a sheet of motionless gray, though here and there reflections winked. Behind them, the well-lit skyline of Chicago declared itself in dazzling illumination, the irregularity of the lights communicating the complexity of the architecture. Each vertical spurt of brightness stood for a building, too many of them to count, and between the buildings Charles could see more buildings, an infinity of buildings. Every two minutes the pulse of light from the Lindbergh Beacon atop the Palmolive Building swept over them, and when its brightness temporarily vanished, the glow of a metropolis going full blast rose in a great pink-orange crown over the skyline. The water lapped lazily against the concrete blocks of the revetment, and out there on the lake, a few lights disclosed vessels, whether yachts or barges being unknown.

There were two black Division Fords parked on this deserted stretch of shoreline a few miles north of the World's Fair of 1933, now 1934, on new landfill extending the lakefront east, claiming it from the big waters. Someday it would be parkland, but now it looked like a bleak battlefield.

In the first Ford, Mel Purvis sat, elegant as usual, and behind him, in the backseat, Ed Hollis and Clarence Hurt sat with Thompsons, fully loaded with big fifty-round drums, bolts locked back, safety levers down, ready to pour out streams of fire in case of ambush of some sort. Both the young agents had taken their jackets off, wore bulletproof vests over their shirts, but still had their ties cinched tight, their collars starched and pinned, and hats—those straw boaters—atop. You never could tell when the Director was watching.

In the second car, Charles sat behind the wheel and Sam Cowley was in the backseat. Both were armed with handguns, and a Thompson and a Model 97 riot gun rested in the trunk, Charles was smoking, and the air felt heavier than saturated cotton.

"Are they late, Sheriff?" asked Sam.

"Still two minutes to go," said Charles after checking his Bulova. "I hope they show. I hope this one don't blow away like all the others."

"But you think this Zarkovich seemed solid?"

"He knows the game. That's not saying he's some Angel of Virtue, but he knows the rules and doesn't want us pissed at him because he knows how much heat the Division can stoke."

"One of the advantages of working for the biggest boys on the block," said Sam. "I hope I don't have to shoot a Tommy gun tonight. I've never touched one in my life."

"I'll teach you. When I'm done, you'll be able to shoot ducks with the goddamned thing."

"Ha! Now, that's optimism."

At that point, a car turned off the Outer Drive onto this gravelly wasteland, dimmed its lights, and proceeded slowly toward the two government vehicles. It arrived, pulled off the road nearby, and went dark.

"Okay," said Sam. "You're on, Charles."

Charles said nothing. He exited the car, tossed his half-smoked tailormade away, and lounged against the fender, enjoying a bit of offshore breeze, as a figure emerged from the newly arrived car.

"Swagger?" said Detective Zarkovich.

"Yep," said Swagger, and the man, heavyset, with a rather pouchy, glum Serbian face, came over. Blue double-breasted, Panama. Cigar.

"Is she here?" Charles asked.

"Yeah, but she's a little fragile. Was crying all the way over. Doesn't want to do this, but she don't want a one-way to Bucharest either. What's a gal going to do? I guess what she needs to do."

"It's a tough life if you're a whore," said Charles.

"I've noticed. Anyway, you've got your big man?"

"The biggest. Purvis is in the other car, the real power belongs to Cowley. He's here to make a deal."

"Nobody in that other car's going to go nuts or anything?"

"They're trained men. The best."

"Okay, and it's accepted, my stuff? I get to be in on the bust, I get credit. Someone tells my chief what a hero I am. I get the reward."

"Not sure about the reward, and never said I was. The other stuff is all right."

"Okay, I'll get her."

He watched the man return to his vehicle, knock on the rear window until it was rolled down. After a conference, the door opened and a leggy broad in a bucket cap and chemise stepped out, elegant in both dress and comportment, but a little shaky in the legs, as if one of her heels was loose. Even from afar, Charles could see the way her large eyes were spotlighted by the artful cosmetics around them. She looked like a silent-screen star.

Holding her arm, Zarkovich escorted her to the car. Charles tipped his hat, said, "Ma'am," and opened the door. She slid in gracefully.

On instruction, Charles went behind the driver's seat. Sam wanted a witness.

"Please, make yourself comfortable, Mrs. Sage," said Sam confidently. "This is a conversation, not an interrogation. Smoke, if you care to."

"Thank you."

"Now, for us to help you, you have to tell us how you can help us. You understand that?"

"Of course."

"So please proceed."

She told the story in her vaguely foreign-shaded language, *th*'s becoming *v*'s, vowels elongating, the strange rhythms of Eastern Europe like a gravy over her words. She ran a rooming house, and had done some things in her past that made it clear that she wasn't the sort to cry to the cops. Various folks in town found that useful, and she became used to extremely virile types overpaying for two nights and disappearing without a trace. It was known as a place where you could go to earth. A few weeks ago, a big slugger had come to rent. Handsome, well-dressed, wonderful personality, catnip to women, lots of cash. She too was attracted, even if he'd quickly taken up with one of her roomers, Polly Hamilton ("Ze noize from ze room. Mattress springs—*bonk, bonk, bonk*—all night long!"). Finally, she figured out who he had to be, and he read it in her eyes, and they had a friendly chat. He didn't seem too concerned. He thought he was invulnerable. In fact, they frequently went places as a threesome, the stud and two very attractive gals. Nobody ever really noticed, it was so amazing! It was because he was so relaxed all the time, so happy and outgoing, and people were drawn to him. They'd even gone to the police station a few times!

Sam nodded, taking this in without comment.

But the situation had changed radically last Wednesday: an earlier conviction had finally caught up to her, and a letter from Immigration ordered her deported as an undesirable alien, even proclaiming a date by which she must be gone from the United States, under penalty of arrest and imprisonment. She began to weep.

"I cannot go back. There is nothing there for me, and war will come, mark my words. I have nobody in the world, and what I've built here is more than I've ever had. I cannot lose."

"All right," said Sam evenly, reaching out to put a calming hand on her shoulder, "let's see what can be done. I can offer no guarantees. But if you figure significantly in the apprehension of John Dillinger, I will write a strong letter on your behalf to the Director of Immigration. Moreover, our Division has considerable influence in Washington and that influence will be deployed to the maximum. I can have a lawyer draw this up as a formal agreement or I can ask you to trust me. I'd prefer the latter, because it's faster and less complicated, and more confidential."

"I understand. You seem trustworthy."

"Excellent."

"So first I offer you this. He has had surgery to change his face. A man cut him or scraped him, he says he almost died. Polly and I nursed him. He was in bandages for a week and now he's taken them off, obviously. I have to say, it didn't do much good. It's the same Johnny, only now he's what one would call droopy or melted. But the same face, the same bright eyes, the same crooked smile and hearty laugh. To me, it was a lot of pain and anguish he suffered for nothing."

"Good to know," said Sam. "I'll alert my men."

There was a pause, as if neither could think of a ploy, Sam not wanting to seem too greedy and forceful, Anna Sage not wanting to give up Johnny without at least some Theater of Regret.

"Mrs. Sage," Sam finally said, "I think you know where we are. This doesn't work unless you can put Johnny in our hands."

"You won't hurt him?"

"We never shoot first. But . . . these situations can be tricky, tough to handle, even with the most experienced of men. When the guns come out, what happens next is sometimes hard to control. So I will say that it is not our intention to shoot him. I have specific instructions, to that end, from Washington and my Director."

"I just fear some trigger-happy child with a gun."

"Mrs. Sage, the agent in the front seat will be the arresting officer. He has much experience in these matters and is noted for his calm disposition. Why don't you ask him?"

She turned and fixed Charles in her strangely huge and mesmerizing eyes. It was like being seduced by Gloria Swanson.

"Ma'am," he said, "I will make no promises neither. But I can say that I have no desire, no need, no hunger to kill nobody. I'm too old and salty to give a damn about reputation or fame. I don't need the ruckus, the attention, the paperwork. I just want to get those cuffs locked, put him in the paddy, and then go out and fall off the wagon for the first time in five years."

She actually smiled.

"All right," she said.

The Marbro Theatre. On Halsted. For the air-conditioning and the beauty of the movie palace itself, not the movie, which only the girls wanted to see, *Little Miss Marker*, with that annoying little tot Charles could not abide. Tomorrow night, probably the 7:30 show. She'd call if it changed.

23

GLENVIEW, ILLINOIS

July 21, 1934

T HE JOINT WAS OLD; it was two farmhouses joined together on a nice
piece of land just east of Curtiss Field—the roar of the engines arrived
with regularity—and it had been a roadhouse for what seemed like centuries, one of those quiet places that nobody notices and yet is somehow always there, a reliable second choice for hooch or food. It had green-shuttered
windows, gables, a riot of vegetation curling up its walls, and stood in a
grove of trees. In the night, it sent shafts of light into the trees, which pitched
shadows of leaves and branches everywhere in a kind of curlicue of light-
dark, very pleasant to the eye.

Les got there first, with Fatso and Jack, and chose a dark booth at the
back of the bar and settled in. A waitress came by; he ordered a Coca-Cola
and the others took Hamm's on draft. Then Jimmy Murray showed, a legend in the business, who, out of deference, was always called Mr. Murray.
He'd put together the biggest train job in history, in Rondout, Illinois, back
in '24 for the Newton Gang. Nobody died, a lot of dough changed hands,
and it entered outlaw history as the near-perfect job, if later Jimmy was
nabbed for it and did a few years.

They talked shop for a bit, spending time, until Johnny and Homer arrived, Mr. Murray more or less running the show, making sure everything
had been arranged according to the specifications of his plan. He also reported on his latest intelligence on the train, due in on Friday, August 10,
from Des Moines, the train among all the August trains that would

probably carry the most swag, as he had found that, quite often, the smaller federal depositories moved cash only once a month, usually on the second Friday. The damned safe would be busting with cash, and he hoped they had a good guy with the soup, as that stuff was tricky, you didn't want to get too fancy with it since you could blow up the goods along with the steel, as well as blow your arms off.

"He's good. Uses it underground, a miner. He knows how it is planted and detonated," said Jack. "He did a demo for me downstate. He was good enough to blow the hinges off a car trunk without damaging the spare inside."

Then a shadow fell across the table, and they looked up and saw that it was Johnny, the star himself, almost as if he'd arranged his own backlighting, Hollywood-style; he looked fine, as usual, in a sharp double-breasted, a striped tie pinned tight in a round starchy collar, and a straw boater low over his eyes. He looked more like Gable than a gangster. He'd grown a little mustache, and he had the twinkle in his eye that just drew everybody in.

"Is this the Our Gang comedy cast?" he asked, heartily. "Where's Spanky?"

That drew a laugh, and he squeezed in, gestured to the barkeep for something on tap, and looked at them all with some benevolence showing on his big face.

"So nice to be together again. The best guys I ever worked with! Les, a pleasure. Helen's okay, I hope. And the great Mr. Murray, genius and master planner. And you other palookas, soldier boys in our war on the banks. You guys are the best!"

Handshakes and backslaps commenced all around, as with any bunch of men getting together to get lubed up a bit, smoke, and talk business. And if Johnny was the star, he didn't play it up as much as he could have but was generous in attentions to his fellow pros. But Les, sober, had to start off on a sour note.

"Where is he?"

"Homer?" asked Johnny, struggling to get one of Fatso's stogies lit off

Fatso's match. "Oh, you know Homer, he comes and goes. He said he'd be here, but no sign of him."

"That sonovabitch. We need another gun on this job," said Les.

"Maybe that slug softened his head," said Johnny. "That was a hard conk. He said he had a headache for a month."

"Christ!" said Les. "If he isn't making bum jokes, he's not showing up."

"Les," said Jack, "he was sure there covering for you and Johnny and me when we were getting back to the car at South Bend."

"The one thing you can count on with that guy," said Les, "is that you can't count on a goddamned thing."

"Les, just relax," soothed Johnny, big brother of them all. "Maybe he'll show, maybe he won't. That's Homer. He's still a solid man when the lead is whistling. And anyhow, I'm sure we can run this with five guns instead of six. Don't you think we can, Mr. Murray?"

Jimmy Murray said, "Well, Johnny, six would be better, but five will work. Depends on how much fuss these Post Office boys care to put up. And I have to say, one less split, let's not forget that. Drink to one less split!"

He raised his drink, and all came up in unison, even Les's glass of Coke, if a bit late and without much energy.

"Okay, Les, you're the boss, brief me on the play and tell me what I've got to do to keep my new girlfriend in mink and diamonds, and cover the miserable nags that I have such a gift for picking."

Les pretty much reiterated the Murray plan, and Mr. Murray chipped in now and then with clarifications or amendments. Even the guys who'd heard it a dozen times ate it up, and Johnny was with it in an instant.

"I've never worked nitro before," he said. "I'm a little shaky there. You guys sure it's safe?"

"Yeah," said Jack, "this guy's a genius with it. The best deal with nitro is, you don't need a lot. You don't need wires, batteries, a plunger, that kind of stuff. And you can control it very precisely, which is why it's so helpful in coal mining. You can kind of chisel a vein out, if you need. You carry it in a box packed with excelsior. Then you put it in locks or hinges, or whatever you're going to blow, with an eyedropper. A little dab'll do ya."

"How does he blow?"

"You just use a regular fused blasting cap. Drop in the soup, cram in the cap—see, I'm talking about a lock here—maybe tape it to the lock. Then just light the fuse, three seconds later the fuse pops the ignition mix— little bang—and that produces enough shock to light the soup—big bang. Very concentrated blast area, cleans out the guts of the lock or blows the hinge free."

"Just don't forget to bring the matches," said Johnny, and everyone laughed.

It was a happy time. The waitress kept bringing brews from Augie, behind the bar, as well as on-the-house plates of onion rings, pork rinds, pickles, little sausages on the ends of toothpicks, even some raw oysters. It was fun being a bank robber if you got to hang out with Johnny D. Maps came out, routes were examined, Fatso updated the group on Carey's progress with the cars, and the guys had a nice night out, as, in time, the conversation drifted to baseball—Johnny was a big Cubs guy and had been to a batch of games since South Bend. And of course, finally, broads, and everyone gave Johnny the floor, for he had a gift at picking up lookers and going all the way around the track with them. But he was a gentleman about it, not one of these so-then-she-sucked-my-cock guys, and managed to communicate the sophistication of exchange he had achieved with new gal Polly without resorting to Anglo-Saxon.

Then track tips, hot ponies being named; then Mob gossip, what was Nitti up to, who would run the South Side for him now that Alberto Mappa was in the hospital with the gout—some said syph!—and on to where were the rackets going, what was the future of armed robbery in a land where all cops were in instant communication via radio, how big would the Division get, and wasn't this little punk Purvis a pain in the ass with his yip-yap for the papers every day? Fatso had heard that even the Director was getting sick of it!

Then, close to midnight, the new assignments were set—Jack would find a tourist cabin and a safe joint to stage from, and Fatso would put together a cache of a thousand rounds of .45 for the Thompsons, Les would scout alternative getaway routes, while Mr. Murray would monitor his Rock Island sources for any changes in the schedule, track route, train makeup, whatever. Johnny, the hottest man in America, would just stay put.

Then it was time to go, the tab was paid, and the boys filtered out, sadly giving up the comforting swish of the four-bladed ceiling fans that pushed the Wayfarer Inn's atmosphere into motion and kept everyone cool, if not quite to air-conditioning standards. They wandered into the parking lot, now empty except for their cars, where shadows of vegetation cut intricate silhouettes into the lights from the gabled windows, the air was tropical thick with humidity and bug life, and a whisper of moon occasionally slithered free of the low clouds. "Stormy Weather" on the radio somewhere. The banshee howl of big-piston jobs turning over at Curtiss arrived and departed regularly.

Les pulled Johnny away, into the shadows.

"Really, Les," Johnny said, misunderstanding Les's need for a private tête-à-tête, "don't worry about Homer. That's just him, nothing personal. He's a kind of a flighty guy, and this Conforti gal is teaching him stuff he didn't know existed."

"It's not that, Johnny. Listen, I didn't want to run this in front of the guys because maybe there's some stuff you don't want getting out."

"Okay, kid, shoot. Out with it. What is it? Tell Father O'Malley."

"It ain't nothing like that. Johnny, I'm worried."

He told him the story of the strange guy showing up on the crest, the marksman who almost nailed him on the button from a hundred fifty out with a .45 auto.

"Good shooting," Johnny had to admit.

"Yeah, the shooting was terrific. They say the Division is bringing in Western gunfighters—you know, cowboy experts who've got notches on their *pistolas*—to take us on. No more Mickey Mouse lawyers who get scared if they have to shoot and don't like guns because they're so loud. Experts, cool hands, old Texas Rangers and cow-town marshals, you know the type. Gun buzzards."

"Maybe so. As yet, haven't met a guy who could outdraw or outshoot me. But it's changing, that I grant you. As this radio stuff spreads, it could be that—"

"It's not that, Johnny. It's not how good the guy was; it's that he was there at all. What, he just shows up? How could that happen? Not a one-in-a-million chance, when the bank has already gone tilt five seconds earlier when the two State cops show. It's like two double snake eyes, one after the other. It never happens that way."

"Well . . . of course it can, and I bet it has. The dice don't know what number is up. They just end up where they end up."

"That's what everybody keeps saying. But I say no. Not in this universe anyhow."

"Okay, what are you getting at?"

"There's a leak," said Les.

"What?"

"Somebody's talking."

"How would they know? They've got nothing to leak. Kid, I'm just an Indiana farm boy, but who could put a picture together on us? We're all over the place, we're here, we're there, we're everywhere, we're nowhere."

"Only one outfit. You know, the Eye-ties and the Jews."

"I'm not getting it. What the hell do they care?"

"I've got some ideas, but figure them later. Just think about it from a feasibility point of view. We sort of live with, and off, the big outfit. They control all the joints we visit, the taverns, the whore cribs, the clubs; even this joint here, they have a piece of it. If someone high up wanted to put the picture together on us, he could. Wouldn't be easy, would require lots of calling, lots of figuring, information gathering, and organizing, this, that. Finding out what eyes are seeing and ears are hearing all over the place, then sitting down with all of it and putting it together like a jigsaw. It could be done, if for some reason Nitti wanted it done. He'd have a guy high up, probably his slickest, smartest guy, not a machino guy or an enforcer but a thinker, he'd have him put it together."

"Just because it's possible," said Johnny, thinking it over, "don't make it probable. It seems like a lot of trouble. What's the point? We all know it's going to be finished sooner or later, once they get the radios in all the cars and do away with the state-line or county-line bullshit and make the fast guns illegal. I know the big-score days are ending, just as you do, and, just as you do, I want one big one, one more perfect hit, and then I want to buy land and a house overlooking the Pacific in Tijuana, with you and Helen and the kids on the left and Homer and Mickey, and maybe their kids, on the right. I'll be with Polly, and when Billie gets clear, I'll send for her, and she and Polly can work it out, maybe Anna will sort of keep it straight, and everybody will live happily ever after."

"That's what I want too, Johnny, except without the Homer-and-Mickey part. But, yeah, Mexico, warm skies, sun, palms, forever. My kids would be so happy there."

"Then we'll make it happen. Forget about the Italians. They got other things to worry about, like where the dough's going to come from now that Prohibition has gone away, and then there's income taxes, as Capone found out, and which goombah wants to take over which territory and which goombah he has to torpedo in order to do that. They hate each other as much as they hate us, maybe more, and they hate each other more than they even hate the cops, and they don't give a damn about the Division, which hasn't even noticed them. It's not in their interests to conspire against us."

"Well . . ." said Les. Being a trifle emotional, he couldn't keep the anguish out of his face.

"Go on, spit it out."

"It's not in their interests up front, that I agree with. But those guys have been at this stuff for a thousand years and they're always thinking ahead, seeing the future. They knew Prohibition was ending and they were ready for it; they're moving in Hollywood, they're trying to set up a national wire so they can control gambling everywhere, they're looking for a city to own, a gambling town, like Hot Springs, which they'll take over hard one of these days—I've heard, they're even looking at Cuba—it goes on and on. Plus, they're unifying—Chicago, New York, Cleveland—it's not one outfit per town but a single organization coast to coast."

"We're farm boys scratching for chicken feed in towns meatball never heard of, like South Bend and Sioux City," said Johnny. "And next month, Wheaton. Do you think meatball gives a crap about Wheaton? It's too much trouble to step on us, I guarantee it. Les, you get so wrought up sometimes. You got to stay calm for this kind of work. Listen to me, kid, I love you, but you got to find a way to put this screwball shit out of your head. You could spook the boys, and you do not want to be on a job with spooked boys. No room for mistakes in our line of work."

"Okay, Johnny. Maybe you're right."

"You should be writing for the movies. You got that kind of mind."

"Ha-ha—wouldn't that be something? Me writing for Cagney and Robinson."

"Crazier stuff has happened. How crazy is this? Speaking of movies, the girls are dragging me to see that little kid I can't stand, you know, 'On the Good Ship Lollipop'"—and he jumped around like a moppet on a string, prancing it up for comic effect, and Les had to laugh hard, the big guy, broad shoulders, handsome as Gable, imitating a dancing child.

"Still, it's a way to beat the heat," Johnny said when he'd stopped dancing. "And I love that big house, the Marbro. It's like a palace or something."

"You ought to see this *Manhattan Melodrama*," said Les. "It's still around. Helen and I saw it a few nights ago. Gable is the gangster—Blackie, I think—and it's pretty good. He's not like any gangster I ever saw, but, still, he just makes you go with him all the way."

"Would the girls like it? I guess they would, if it's got Gable—they like Gable. Hell, I like Gable."

"He should play you, Johnny. What a picture that would be. *Chicago Melodrama*, with Gable as Dillinger! It would make a million bucks!"

"Nah," said Johnny, "they make you die at the end of pictures. It's the law now."

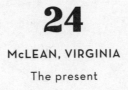

24

S WAGGER PULLED AWAY from her apartment building, drove three blocks and took a random turn down a residential street, flicked off his lights and waited.

Nothing. No car turned down the thoroughfare on his tail.

Followed? Who the hell would follow me?

But, then, Nikki was unusually sensitive to being watched or followed. Maybe it was a Swagger thing, as he himself had it; that is, the weird, hackles-rising shiver when a predator's eyes crossed over you. It had saved his life a time or two, and he knew enough at his age to trust it. Yet he hadn't felt it, she had.

On the other hand, his mind was all knitted up over 1934 and his grandfather. He'd been talking a blue streak on the subject, no doubt boring her to death. So he had been distracted, his mind occupied with theoretical prospects, the animal part of him even further away than it was normally. She, on the other hand, had probably stopped listening and was gazing off dully into space when her deep brain heard it, the whisper of the ax, the trill of the wolf, the snap of the hammer cocking. She'd gotten it, he hadn't.

He was puzzled. He waited a few more minutes, alone on a dark street full of beautiful old houses under elms, since he was in the northwest quadrant of D.C., and he knew enough to realize that was where "quality" lived. But no one came, there was no further traffic, and his internal radar system picked up nothing.

He started again, drove a few blocks and wound his way back to the main drag—Wisconsin—and turned left, aiming to head down to George-town, take the Key Bridge to Virginia, then the parkway to the Beltway to Nick's big house near McLean. He drove, checking mirrors for headlights that didn't waver in their pace or distance from him, and saw nothing. At a busy intersection, he looked around, committing to memory the cars be-hind him, and then pulled into a street parking space to let them slide by. He waited, he waited, he waited, and then resumed his journey. At the next stoplight, he made the same quick check to see if any of the cars were from the first batch. Nope, nothing.

He drove on back to McLean, again monitoring for pace and distance behind him, saw nothing. He finally arrived at the road off of which Nick's cul-de-sac was sited and, a street before, turned off, parked, went dark. No car followed along the road for some time, much less pulled into his street. He felt secure now, so he completed the journey to Nick's, waiting in the driveway for any action. There was none.

He went in the house with his key, found no one awake, reset the alarm code, and went straight to the guest room to go to bed. But first, he called his wife and had a nice old-marriage chat, and then said, "Look, this is silly, but you haven't seen anybody around, have you?"

"Around? What could that possibly mean?"

"You know, lurking, following, peeking."

"Lord, Bob, you promised on this one, no adventures."

"I can't see that this is an adventure. It's only my sordid old past. It shouldn't be of interest to anybody, it makes no sense, but I just had a feel-ing I was being followed." He edited Nikki out of the sequence to keep it simple.

"Maybe it's just paranoia. You have many reasons to be paranoid, and I don't know why you never are."

The answer: his enemies tended to be dead, not in the shadows.

"Okay," he said, "maybe it's just that," and signed off.

The next morning—he lingered in bed to avoid Nick's wife, Sally, who had never been a big Bob Lee fan—he put the question to Nick over coffee.

"No," said Nick. "Nothing."

"No strange parked cars, no weird sensations of being observed through glass, no odd coincidence like the stranger turning up over and over again."

"I haven't been paying attention. But I'd like to think I'd notice."

Bob told him of last night's oddness.

"She wouldn't feel something or see something if something weren't there."

"I'll bump my head up to Condition Yellow for a few days," said Nick.

"Appreciate that. See, what bothers me is not the possibility that she's wrong but that she's right. Because if she is, these guys were really good and when she picked them up they disengaged. How would they know their cover was blown?"

"Isn't that an interesting question."

"They're so good, in fact, either *a.* they don't exist or *b.* they're high-skill operators and that kind of talent doesn't come cheap, so whoever—again, if he exists—is behind this is investing big money in the op."

"So it would seem," said Nick.

"Now, let me ask you: you know everything I know about my grandfather, you know everything I've learned, maybe you know more because you've read the files a lot more carefully than I have, can you see any reason in any of it for anybody else to be interested?"

"Anybody else? Do you have an idea?"

"I have nothing. But, after all, I'm known to the Agency, I'm known to your folks, I'm known to various alphabet agencies that don't exist, and it's not impossible that one of them has opened a new file on me."

"Maybe it's the IRS. Have you paid your taxes?"

"Always over-generously."

"No alimony, no back payments, no debts, no angry husbands, croupiers, environmental impact agencies, nothing from your big land deal?"

"I don't think so. Nothing I can see."

"Well, maybe the Agency or Homeland Security have you tabbed as an antiterror consultant, subject sniping, and they're discreetly checking you out before they make an offer, because if you're up to something nasty, they don't want to go down with you."

"I suppose. But I've done nothing for months but sit on the porch like a lump and, all of a sudden, I go off on this little crusade to learn about a man who's been dead since 1942 and suddenly, somewhere, there seems to be a stirring."

"Any organized crime irons in the fire?"

"Nothing I've turned up. Maybe the old bastard's downfall at the Bureau involved organized crime somehow, but, really, that was over eighty years ago. Who would care now?"

"Well," said Nick, "if you're still thinking conspiracy, it's my experience that, more often than not, if any kind of conspiracy, even potential conspiracy, exists, it'd for one reason: not intelligence, not revenge, not justice, not anger, it's dough, it's bucks."

"That's a very good point, and I agree that the profit motive is the motive in just about everything."

"So . . . where's the lost fortune? Under the X in that Boy Scout map Granddad drew? Where's the treasure? Are you likely to turn up the lost John Dillinger millions? Did Baby Face steal an Old Master? Did any of the boys steal diamonds, stock certificates that later became Xerox, land deeds, gold-mine maps?"

This was the stumper.

"That thousand uncirculated I found in the strongbox. Maybe they think there's more, but I can't believe there was, as the sums those days were so much smaller. Dillinger stole about a hundred fifty thousand over all his robberies, and Baby Face was way behind him. So even if there's a hundred fifty grand under the X in that map, that's not so much by today's standards."

"No, it's not."

"And even if there were, uncirculated money from 1934 would be damned hard to reintegrate for profit without lots of attention."

"That's true," said Nick. "So thinking about units of wealth disproportionate to their small size that could be hidden in that final X-marks-the-spot, diamonds would seem to be one of the possibles, because you could get a couple of millions' worth of stones into a briefcase. Big uncut stones, unregistered. That might be worth mounting some kind of operation."

"I don't see anything about diamonds in this. All those other things, nothing either. These farm boys were strictly in a cash-and-carry business—as in, they carried a lot of cash out the door. I just don't see any kind of hidden wealth in play here."

"Many questions, no answers."

"Maybe it's just my imagination, but then there's one other thing."

"What's that?"

"I don't have no imagination."

PART III

25

LINCOLN AVENUE
CHICAGO

July 22, 1934

THERE WAS HUBBUB everywhere on the nineteenth floor. Young agents couldn't settle down to work, though it was Saturday, and drifted about, forming and reforming knots, full of ball-game excitement and not a little apprehension. Everybody smoked, and the heavy overheads pushed the fog out the open windows into the superheated Chicago air. It would break 100 again today, not that the young men were in any state to notice it. The bathroom was overused, nobody ate a thing, nobody could sit still. Some guys went all chattery, some went all solemn, some just wandered, dreamy looks on their faces.

Only in one room could serenity be found. That was the arms room. Since the apprehension was slated to take place in a public area, the Marbro Theatre, an ornate palace of exhibition, and it was certain to be crowded on a hot night where its air-conditioning offered some surcease from the hammer of the heat and the anvil of the humidity, Sam had declared no long guns. The Thompsons, the Browning rifles, the Model 11 riot guns sat in their rack in the vault, the vault door sealed, no chits out, no guns unaccounted for by Ed Hollis's careful reckoning.

Charles sat alone at the table. He was in shirtsleeves, but the hand-tooled, tied-down shoulder holster harnessed his shoulders in leather belting, holding the holster firmly below his left shoulder; a further strap ran from the toe of the holster to his belt, looped it, then returned to snap tight. He smoked Camels as he worked, as he didn't want any of the boys to see a tremor in his hand as he worked his fixings.

Before him, in fifty-two separate parts, sat his Colt Government Model, 1928 Commercial Variation, 157345C. Each of the fifty-two had been inspected for wear, oiled lightly, and dried off. Now he worked with a fine-grain needle file, doing the little things that could be done to turn the pistol into as smooth an operator as possible. He took just a few grains of steel off the ninety-degree angle at the cusp of the frame, where the cartridge rode from magazine to chamber under the propulsion of the slide's forward motion. He wanted to break the sharpness of degree a tiny bit so that no burr from a cartridge—they had already been inspected, of course, twenty-one government-issue .45 hardballs from the Springfield Armory, Springfield, Massachusetts, already fit into three likewise inspected magazines—could catch during the firing transaction. It took a while, and a great deal of judgment, because too much made the passage tricky. When he was satisfied, he moved on to work the sharp edge of the sear, where the disconnector pivoted under the trigger pull to remove it from its nook and thereby drop the hammer. Again, the harshness of the angle was just a bit too much and he gently softened it into a blur, which reduced the trigger pull from six pounds to two and a half, though still leaving enough metal to guarantee the hold's security.

"Charles, what're you doing?" asked Ed Hollis, who, though a competent armorer, had never seen the inside of the frame before.

"If I have to draw and shoot fast for blood," Charles said, "I want the one-in-a-million chance the gun will hang up on me reduced to one-in-a-billion."

"Can you do it to my Super .38?"

"Not today. Sometime in the future."

"Got it," said Ed.

After an hour of careful work, everything wiped clean, and wiped clean again, Charles swiftly reassembled 157345C, making sure all pins were centered, all screws were tightened up to the max, and that function was perfect. Then he reached into a paper cup and withdrew a six-inch piece of rawhide from its soak in the water.

Again, carefully and with much dexterity, he looped it around the pistol grip, including the grip safety, a shoulder of metal that emerged from the curve under the sweep of the hammer well and had to be depressed by a proper placement of hand to gun for the weapon to go *bang*. It was one of three safety systems John M. had designed into the piece. He pulled the loop tight, flattening the grip safety in the off position, tied a knot, then called Ed over.

"Not your finger, but hold this knot tight with a screwdriver or something."

Ed did as told, and Charles doubled the knot over the first knot, pulling it tight with his long, strong fingers. Then with his pocketknife he trimmed the extra lengths of rawhide down to the knot, which he adjusted till it was under the trigger guard.

"Old Texas Ranger trick. I want the safety grip pinned so that if my draw is a little off and I don't get square on the gun, it's still going to fire. I'd hate to have to provide my own bang while Johnny's filling me full of pills."

"Nothing to chance."

"Not where this damned character is concerned. Now, as the rawhide dries, it'll pull even tighter. Trick is, don't let it soak too long or it gets brittle. Then what have you got except a vaudeville that can turn ugly in a split second."

With that, he slipped a magazine in, threw the slide to hoist a cartridge into the chamber, and pushed the safety lock up into position, freezing the gun in pre-volatility. He slipped it into the holster, then slid the two additional magazines into the leather keeper on his belt behind his right hip, praying that if there were a fight, it wouldn't last long enough to require a reload.

"Sheriff Swagger?" It was Mrs. Donovan at the door.

"Mr. Cowley wants you. Big powwow in Mr. Purvis's office."

IT WAS LIKE SOMETHING out of *Arabian Nights*, a pleasure palace decreed into existence in 1927 by two genies named Marx, then sold to two other genies named Balaban and Katz in 1930. The Marbro even had what could have been a minaret outside it, piercing the sky. It was a vast, domed structure, covered with fretwork, pale in the vanishing sun, on Madison Street, the 4400 block.

Charles had infiltrated a few minutes early, from a staging point a couple blocks away. Sam, wisely, didn't want a mob of agents showing up at once so played them in at odd intervals so that at no particular moment it seemed unusually hectic. The traffic was heavy, the octane fumes intense, the theater buzzing with desperate souls ready to spend a few hours in the adorable company of a dancing tot in order to escape their dull lives as well as the crushing heat.

Charles had no such luck. He and his new pal Zarkovich tried to appear indifferent to their situation, which required milling in front of a women's haberdashery in the steamy heat just across the street from the Marbro while waiting to see Johnny appear. He would be with two gals: Mrs. Sage and another one, Polly something. Mrs. Sage would be dressed in orange. Johnny would be wearing a straw hat, a white shirt, and tan slacks over white suedes. That meant if he had a gun, it would have to be a small one, concealable in a pant pocket. No .45 auto was coming out, and he wouldn't have six more mags stashed in a jacket pocket. It also meant he wasn't wearing steel, so a torso shot would bring him down if that's how it broke.

All along the street, agents and East Chicago detectives—but not Chicago cops, for they had been exiled from the plan, out over worries about leaks and too big an assemblage to maneuver quickly—lay about with similar supposed lack of interest. The plan was fluid, depending on the whimsy of the actuality.

Sam originally wanted two teams of agents to thread down the aisles from each side of Johnny's seats, squeeze their way in, and go to guns immediately upon closing, presenting him with such an array of muzzles, he would see the idiocy of resisting. But Charles didn't like it.

"Sir," he'd said, "all those men, all those guns, all those people, all in the dark with a thirty-foot-high four-year-old dancing on-screen, plus music and picture talk blasting away, it could get away from us real easy, and nobody wants a shoot-out under those circumstances. Lots of people could get hit, our target hard to see and track, chaos everywhere."

"Duly noted, Charles. But my thought is, take him as early as possible, because the longer he's free, the bigger the chance of him seeing something and bolting. I've been on the phone with the Director all day and, believe me, the pressure's on this one. We can't let it fall apart."

Clegg was big on the inside arrest, which in itself was an argument against it. Purvis was agnostic.

"If you wait till he leaves," Clegg said, "you've got him in a flow of people and you don't know how they're going to react and mess things up. If they're seated and we do it fast, I think it's actually safer. They won't even figure out what happens."

"Moving in from the aisles on him seems tricky," said Charles. "He's too salty a boy. He'd see it coming and he might draw. Then you've got your shoot-out among three thousand suckers."

"Probably won't be a full house," sniffed Clegg.

"Charles?" asked Sam.

"There's an old hunting saying that might figure in here," Charles said. "Hunters say, 'Get as close as you can, then a little closer.' So that's what I'd do, outside the theater, still plenty of street light, no suspicions about him. I'd move a small team in from behind, get almost within contact distance, then, guns drawn, call him down. Hands go up or triggers are pulled. So close in, we won't hit nobody else, unless it's a through and through, but it probably won't be with handgun velocities. So what everyone else has to commit to is discipline. If you see him, don't draw and shoot, don't jump for him or move aggressively. He's as touchy as a jackrabbit. Let the arrest team move in quietly until they're almost in his pocket. Even if he's fast, he can't beat a drawn gun."

Sam's decision was more political than practical.

"When he's in and seated and the show is on, Mel will wander in and see if he can be located. If he's near an aisle and there's some maneuver room, then we'll go that way. If he's not, then we'll wait."

So now they stood, smoking, trying to keep their feet from falling asleep, handkerchiefs out to wipe the accumulated sweat from the brow. Zarkovich kept up a steady chatter, mostly about what he was going to do with the reward money, what kind of big car he'd get, maybe one of the new auto transmissions where there was no clutch, you just pushed a button or pulled a lever. He also thought maybe not black. Cars weren't all black anymore. You could get any color you wanted, any color of the rainbow. Why not a nice yellow car?

But at that point—it was about 8:45 p.m.—it was a black car that pulled up, a government Ford. Clegg was behind the open window on the passenger side.

"Cowley just got a call from the Sage woman. They're not coming here. They're going to another one, the Biograph, on Lincoln. Get in, we'll hop over."

"Where's the Biograph?" said Charles.

"A couple miles away. On Lincoln. Come on."

Of course that meant all the plans were atomized. No one had seen, much less mapped, diagrammed, thought critically about, the Biograph. It means the whole thing would have to be made up on the fly.

"We'll leave a few here, just in case, and in the meantime try and drop fellows over at the Biograph in ones and twos. I don't know how much time we have."

"Fewer might just be better," said Charles.

"I'm dropping you a half block away. Sam's in Brewer's Menswear, the back room, with his people. You check in with him, see how he wants to play it."

"Where's Purvis?"

"He's already there. He's seen Sage, so he's a key. He can make her out and get the ball rolling, one way or the other."

Charles didn't say: I saw her too. I smelled her.

"How about Hollis and Hurt?"

"I haven't got them yet."

"Get them next. I want them close by," said Charles, and as a conse-quence got a sharp look from Clegg, who didn't like his tone, his assump-tion of command, his closeness to Sam, and, presumably, Charles himself, and his taciturn sheriff ways.

Clegg left them off on Lincoln, and like Madison, it was a jam-up on Saturday night, in the dead summertime, with traffic clogged, lots of pe-destrian action, a batch of bars all busy and smoky, and the marquee of the Biograph—*Manhattan Melodrama*, Charles noted—blaring brightly, fill-ing the night with its brightness. COOL INSIDE, it said on a banner hanging from the front of the marquee.

The whole scene had an odd not-Chicago feeling to it. The buildings on both sides of the street were but two stories tall—all manner of bars, retail, honky-tonks—all aswarm, but there was nothing of that looming-city sense of tall towers closing out the sky. It could have been Saturday night in a Texas cattle town, with all the cowboys in for a night of hard drinking and, if lucky, soft rubbing. People milled and jostled, smoked, bumped, smiled, tried to find space at a new bar, celebrated the death of Prohibition by acquiring a happy, drifting buzz no matter the heat. Cow town all the way, with cars instead of horses, octane instead of methane.

Charles and the momentarily quiet Zarkovich slipped into the menswear place, walked between aisles of coats and piles of shirts, and slipped in the back, where they found Purvis and Sam, five or six others, gathered around a blackboard on which an awkward map of the theater had been inscribed.

"Okay," said Sam, "glad you made it."

"Ready to get this done," said Charles.

"We've got a real solid ID, with a girl and Mrs. Sage buying tickets for the eight-thirty show. I saw them from the car," said Purvis. "He was big as life. He looks a little, uh, different. The face is sort of blurred, but it's still him, you'd have to be drunk not to see it."

Charles nodded.

"What time does the show end?"

"Ten-thirty."

All checked watches, saw that the movie had little more than an hour to run.

"Mel, what about taking him inside?" asked Cowley.

"I walked in and didn't spot him. I can't say where he's sitting. I could go in again and get an exact location."

"No sir," said Charles, out of order but sound enough. "Too much hunt in that dog. He'd spook easy and then we lose our surprise and the whole thing goes into the crapper."

"I think Charles is right," said Sam. He paused, to think on it a bit, as the gathered agents—a few more had come in—waited. Finally Hurt and Hollis showed and moved toward Charles.

"Best thing," Sam said, having worked it out, "is to take him on the street when the show lets out. I see it like this, but please improve on it if you can. Mel, you are up near the box office, maybe a little to the left. You're eyeballing the crowd. When you spot him, you light up a stogie, and we'll see that and from that we can locate him. With two women, one young, one middling, him being in straw hat, white shirt, tan slacks, white suedes, we should have no trouble. I'm guessing he turns left and begins to amble down Lincoln. Charles, I want you to the immediate left of the theater with Hurt. Is Hurt here yet?"

"I'm here, sir," Hurt said.

"Okay, you move in on him from the rear. I'll put Hollis there too, and he can join the two of you as you get in close for the collar. Guns away, please. I'm afraid someone will see the gun too early and scream and it'll go bad. So the guns don't come into play until the very last second."

"If he sees us, he might draw. I'll have to draw against him," said Charles.

"Is that a worry? Are you fast enough?"

"Charles is so fast, it seems to be over before it starts," Hollis said, and there was some laughter.

"Fine," said Sam. "Good to have the gunfighter on our side, for a change. Anyhow, I'll be across the street with Detective Zarkovich and reinforcements en masse. I'll put two men in the alley about forty yards down from the theater, but I want them alert, and when they see your little parade approaching, they break cover and start moving against the crowd toward Johnny. When you converge, you call him out, Charles, and hopefully his hands go up and all of you can get him cuffed before he gets anything out of that pocket."

He paused, still thinking.

"My one worry is the Chicago guys. They don't know we're here, and if anyone notices a lot of us, they might show up. So you cannot get into it with them. If they show, you have to play it cool. And refer them to me, if necessary. We don't need five hundred uniforms with shotguns showing up in the middle of our arrest. Anybody got any questions?"

Nobody did.

IT WAS NOW AROUND 10. In ones and twos, the agents deployed themselves at the designated spots along the street, in the alleys and doorways, across from the Biograph and in parked cars along the busy road. The heat hadn't broken, but it had fallen off its perch a bit and, at 97, it now seemed cool. Above, no moon, but clear black sky, ribbons of dim stars bleached out by the hot lights of Lincoln and its spangled array of nighttime action.

Charles and Hurt found their spot. In a few minutes, they saw Hollis move into place, just across the sidewalk and up a bit, angled against a car with a slight bend, as if he were talking to a friend sitting in it.

"Hurt, mosey over there and grab Hollis. I want to talk to you birds."

Hurt nodded, ambled with exaggerated casualness to Hollis, passed the word, and each went through a bit of pantomime before they arrived back at Charles's spot.

"Okay, y'all recall the briefing?"

"Yes sir."

"Good. Now forget it."

"Ah, Sheriff, what do—"

"I said forget it. Too busy, too many moving parts, too much coordination, too much depending on stuff that can't be controlled. So you don't look for Purvis's cigar. You don't look for a lady in orange. You don't look for a fellow without a jacket in a straw hat. Got that?"

"Sheriff—"

"You look at me and only at me. I'll spot Mrs. Sage. In the first place, Purvis is short, he may not see Johnny. In the second place, Purvis is short, you and our other chums may not see Purvis. That's how it turns to crap, with nobody knowing, everybody trying to see stuff that can't be seen."

"Yes sir."

"Ed Hollis, I didn't hear a 'Yes sir.'"

"Yes sir," said Hollis over a gulp of air.

"I will move behind him, slide through the crowd. Hurt, you're on my left. Hollis, you wait until we're past. Also, neither of you fellows are to look directly at him. You'll see him clearly enough when we close, but these big-time bad men with lots of gun experience, they can feel eyes on 'em—some sort of snake instinct, I think. If you're staring at him, he will feel it, I guarantee it. Got it?"

"Yes sir."

"After we pass, Hollis, that's when you break from your position and come onto us. You're to the left of Hurt. We're three abreast, just behind him. Okay?"

Nods.

"Next thing. The two boys converging from the alley? Forget 'em. You got enough to worry about without trying to time it right so that they're where they're supposed to be. They don't matter. Nothing matters, because once we get in contact distance of Johnny, we go. You both have your .38s holstered on your belt?"

"Yes sir" came the replies.

"You can put your hand on the grips under your jackets. That way, you aren't disobeying no orders. But if Johnny wants to go hard, you will have to draw and shoot fast, making sure you see both the gun and him as you squeeze. You will find the point of aim naturally, but only if your eyes are driving the action. You don't shoot until the gun is low in your vision and the barrel is pointed right at him, right at that white shirt, which ain't gonna be but two feet ahead of you, then you fire. Got that?"

Again: "Yes sir."

"As I reach him, I'll skip ahead a step, so I'm at a kind of forty-five-degree angle to him. I will call him out. 'Johnny,' is all I need to say. And, believe me, he will know it's him I'm talking to. That's the key moment. He may draw, he may reach for the sky. It's his call. If he reaches, you two break him down, wrap his arms around backwards, knock his knees out, and get him in cuffs. I will have him covered. Now, if he decides to go, and if it turns out he's faster or he has a sleeve gun or maybe a crossdraw under his shirt, or if he even goes for a gun in the pocket, he will turn on me, and maybe he's faster, maybe I'm faster. In any event, if he gets a shot off, it'll be into me. Y'all will have clear shots, but keep moving into him and, as he goes down, be sure to track him and adjust your own hold to keep your slugs in him and not Joe Blow three feet ahead."

"Sheriff, if we come around him from the left and he cottons to it, draws, and gets a shot off, it could go our way instead of toward you—"

"No, this is the game I signed up to play and I will play it full out. I will initiate. Got it?"

The two younger men looked at each other and could think of nothing to say.

"Got it?" Charles repeated.

"Yes sir."

"Since I'm set, my drawstroke should be faster than his, unless he's John Wesley Hardin, and I believe John Wesley Hardin is dead. So in that situation, I'll draw and fire. I don't believe in shooting a man once. It's against my religion. If he's worth shooting, he has to be shot a lot. I'll put three or four into him. And that should be that. And you don't tell nobody about this little chat. As far as you're concerned, you followed Sam's plan perfectly, Sam had it all figured out. And if it goes wrong, it was because I got it screwed up. You don't blame Sam or Melvin or even Clegg. Any mess is on me. Got it?"

"Yes sir."

Charles glanced at his watch: 10:16.

"Okay," he said, "let's do this."

IT WAS HAPPENING, though somehow time slowed down so it all poked along at five miles an hour. Charles saw the tallish woman he recognized from the severe profile as Sage, slid his eyes to the man next to her, and beheld John Dillinger.

Johnny seemed to have melted a bit, or perhaps *wilted* would be the right word, for his clearly recognizable features were subtly softer, as if the bloom that drove the bush had finished and everything had lost its precision and begun the fall to earth. He'd added a mustache too, not Gable's full swagger of Fuller Brush but a more sophisticated, more dapper little pencil line just above the lip. He sparkled. Whatever you could say about the man, he had "it," which nobody could quite define, but it made him the one you noticed. Perhaps it was his comfort with himself, perhaps it was a number one's sense of entitlement and belief in his own self-achieved placement high in human aristocracy, or maybe it was just sheer animal testosterone, pure rampant, wanton masculinity radiating from every pore. Even now, the man wore his sloppy grin and wide-eyed apprehension of all things large and small with perfect grace. He actually looked good in a straw boater. The hat was tilted rakishly, he held hands with Polly, and the two were in lovers' syncopation as they walked the walk. His shirt billowed slightly—he was one of those men who wore his clothes well and turned every off-the-rack suit into a London tailor's masterpiece.

At that point, Charles slid his .45 from its holster, keeping his finger off the trigger, feeling the rawhide strip tight against and disabling the grip safety, snicked off the frame safety with his thumb, and inserted the weapon deftly into his waistband, just to the left of the belt buckle. Then he eased ahead, with his left hand quietly pushing his suit coat a little unnaturally to the right to cover the automatic's big grip. He felt Hurt beside him, heard the Oklahoma detective take a brief breath and mimic Charles's easy glide through the crowd. The two tried to slip, and not push, as they moved a little faster with each step, oriented on the silhouette of Johnny's straw boater, which was twenty-five feet ahead, then twenty, then fifteen.

Charles felt as if he was sliding, as he kept cranking a little to left or right to get between folks ahead of him without touching or forcing, turning sideways to get a shoulder between and ooze or wiggle through. If he was breathing hard, he didn't feel it at all, he just watched as Johnny grew nearer and bigger. Somewhere in here, he felt Hollis coming from the right, and he was aware that the young agent had gotten around Hurt and they now formed a line of three abreast. And if this last little knot of happy movie-goers could just be penetrated and passed, they'd be there and it would be time.

Charles broke from the two, edged his way with perhaps too much energy between a man and woman talking about the great Gable, and suddenly came free so that nobody was between him and Johnny and his two gals.

It went from slow to fast. It went from clear to blur. It went from five miles an hour to five hundred miles an hour. Without checking on, but with complete faith in, the loyalty and technique of Clarence Hurt and Ed Hollis, he skipped a pace and came around Johnny's right, shouldering Sage aside, with his left hand tugged his coat back to free the Colt's grip from its hiding place, and went to gun. At that precise moment, Johnny himself bucked a fast step beyond Polly. He knew.

Don't know how, don't know why, maybe just the animal in him sensing the approach of pure threat, some primordial feeling welling up from wher-ever that animal slept deep in the brain, but Johnny snatched for something in his pocket as he launched forward. He was drawing.

Johnny was fast. Charles was faster.

Mind to arm, arm to hand, hand to trigger, trigger to hammer, hammer to cartridge, cartridge to powder, powder to bullet, the need to act and the act itself were almost simultaneous. Charles felt energy and purpose coursing through his veins, liberated at last from the long discipline, and instantly alchemized into pure gunfighter's hunger to win. 157345C, all its safeties carefully disabled, streaked from where it was to where it had to be without thought or motive but only instinct, and Charles fired three times so fast, he seemed to have pulled a Thompson gun from his pants. His finger was a jackhammer against the trigger, firing before the recoil impulse could distract the gun muzzle, itself locked in a grid of hand, wrist, and forearm muscle crushing so tight it could have rendered the steel into pure diamond. He did not shoot well, but he did shoot fast. The first bullet grazed Johnny on the right side, the second went in behind the shoulder, and the third, the killer, off the gun's inevitable rise, hit Johnny square in the back of the neck, blowing a blister the size of a quarter into that stretch of flesh, continuing through the low brain on a slight upward angle, then exiting rather tidily from just beneath the right eye.

EONS LATER, it seemed, but in the same second, Hollis fired once, Hurt twice, each of the three a lethal but not immediately effective body shot, each of the three moot. Dillinger was done after Charles's third bullet had eviscerated most of his right-skull gray stuff.

His knees went, and like a sack of potatoes tossed off a truck, he hit the ground with a thud that could be heard in the instant of silence decreed by the thunderclaps of the six shots delivered in so small a fraction of time. He pitched forward onto the bricks of the alley, and Charles was surprised to see they'd progressed that far along Lincoln, but there the man lay, a pool of red spreading like a flood from his perforations, collecting in a lake of blood next to his head. The hat had fallen away and his feet were oddly pigeon-toed.

Charles knelt by the fallen man, who still breathed out of reflex, and when he saw the now gray lips muttering, bent close to hear the last words.

"I'm not dressed for company," Johnny said, and if there was a passing then, Charles missed it, as the eternal stillness of the dead just seemed to fall from nowhere and drape the body, no trespassers allowed.

With his left forefinger Charles touched the carotid, that river of blood that united brain and heart running shallowly through the neck, and could feel no pulsations.

"He's gone," he said to Hurt, who now leaned close to him, staring at the downed man, the blood, all of it bright, all of it shiny, in the power of the streetlights.

When they rose, they rose into a new world, one without Public Enemy No. 1 in it. It took a second, or possibly two, for this electric news to dazzle the crowd. And then—chaos.

Charles, with Hurt and Hollis as fellow centurions, stood mute above the ruined man, while some kind of crazed energy radiated from the crowd. The magic of the name turned into sheer electricity.

"It's Dillinger!"

"Jesus Christ, they got Dillinger!"

"Just shot him down, you know, *bang, bang.*"

"I don't believe it!"

"Look at him. Big Public Enemy Number One, flat-faced, in an alley."

"Ever see so much blood?"

"Did they have a machine gun?"

"That tall cop, he's the one. Man, did he shoot fast."

"Never gave the poor guy a chance."

And then it was Purvis stepping into the light—the limelight, actually—and taking over.

"Folks, folks, you have to move back and give us room! Anybody hurt, anybody else shot?"

"This lady here is slightly wounded."

"Okay, ma'am, just relax, we have medical on the way."

Other agents flooded in, chasing a few ghouls from Johnny's body, where they had knelt to dab their handkerchiefs, hat brims, even the tip of a tie, into his blood. The reinforcements formed a cordon, driving against the crowd's need to see, to be close, to participate in something called history. Sirens rose as the Chicago police, called by half a dozen, poured into the scene en masse.

Zarkovich seemed to have battled his way to Charles.

"You really blasted the sonovabitch. Man, great shooting."

Then it was Purvis.

"Charles, congratulations. I don't have to tell you what this means. You're the best."

Charles nodded, turned to indicate Hollis and Hurt. "These fellows were in on it too. It's them as much as me."

"I'll make sure the Director knows."

Someone suggested that Charles and his cohort move away from the body, to a Division car, and there relax and wait for Sam to arrive. Meanwhile, reporters—was it the smell of blood in the air that drew them?—arrived, along with photographers, who angled in for shots, each flashbulb a miniburst of illumination that blanched color from what it touched and created shadow and design and drama and artistic unity where there had been nothing but randomness. The hollowed-out pops of the bulbs firing became the preeminent sound and visual signature of the event as it imploded from reality into journalism.

"Smoke 'em if you got 'em," said Charles to Hurt and Hollis, and he pinched a Camel out of its half-empty pack, slipped it between his lips, and fired it up over his Zippo. The smoke felt great as it rushed into and inflated his lungs, bringing with it just the slightest softening toward blur. He was surprised how weak he felt. The comforting curve of the Ford fender supported him, and he tried to relax, to shake the heebie-jeebies, to eliminate the images of the automatic ripping to life as he pumped the three faster than a burning jackrabbit into Johnny. You don't want to treasure the killing part, only the shooting. It was good combat shooting—that was a compliment he allowed himself.

He watched as an ambulance nosed its way down the jammed Lincoln to pull up to the scene at the alleyway. Two attendants got out, opening the rear door, but the crowd was too thick and too intense to be penetrated by a gurney, so finally six agents just formed an ad hoc funeral squad and lifted Johnny, still facedown, and lugged him to the ambulance. An arm spilled out loosely, the hand, a big athlete's hand, now utterly relaxed. The guys got him into the ambulance without much in the way of ceremony or dignity and laid him on the floor. They turned him, awkwardly, so that his empty eyes peered upward. Charles could see vivid stains spattering the white shirt where Johnny's life fluid had arrived after he'd been deposited on the alley surface. Someone had put the straw hat on his chest, as if at a country funeral.

"You two," he said to Hollis and Hurt, "go take a last look so you remember it good and will always have a sense of what you done here tonight and take proper pride in it."

The two slipped off for that rite, just as Sam Cowley emerged from the death site, pushed his way through the crowd, and got to Charles.

"Charles, please, shake my hand. Outstanding."

"I heard we hit two gals."

"It's nothing. Grazed them. They don't even have to go to the hospital. They're already bandaged and giving our folks statements."

"That's good."

"Charles, I know you must be exhausted, both physically and mentally. I want you to get away from this circus, go to the office, file your report, then go home and take the next couple days off. See a ball game, have a drink or two, ride the roller coaster at Riverview or the zeppelin at the World's Fair, go to the big science museum. Or just sleep. I don't want to see you until Wednesday."

"Yes sir."

"And I don't mind telling you, the Director is immensely pleased. I was on the phone with him when the shooting occurred. We could hear the shots. It was a tense few minutes until the news arrived. I shouldn't have worried. As I said, this time we had the gunfighter."

"Just want to know: was he armed? I fired before I saw a gun, but he sure as hell wasn't reaching to itch a mosquito bite."

"Colt .380 Pocket Model, loaded and cocked. Another half second and he could have shot you or some poor lady in rhapsody over Gable."

"Good. Good to know. Sometimes it happens, but I don't cotton to shooting the unarmed."

"Don't you worry, Charles. You saved a batch of lives here tonight—your own, Hurt's and Hollis's, people in the crowd, and all the people he may have killed on down the line. And you may have saved the Justice Department's Division of Investigation."

26

GLENVIEW, ILLINOIS

July 23, 1934

IT WAS A GOOD DREAM. Les was in the Forest Preserve on a beautiful fall afternoon, with Helen and Ronnie and Darlene. J.P. was there, and so were Fatso and Jimmy Murray and the others. Then Johnny came along, on a bicycle, with his gal, Billie Frechette, waving and rushing to join them. The sun was bright but not hot, the waters sparkling, the pines filling the air with that spruce perfume, and everybody was happy. Even goofy Homer showed up, with that whore gal nobody liked, but Homer was on his best behavior and, for once, his jokes were actually funny.

Then it dissolved. Someone was shaking him. He forced his eyes open to see Helen's grave face just above him and knew from her drawn and pinched look that something bad had happened.

"Uh—" He struggled to find some clarity of mind and vision. The bed was so warm, he wanted to curl deeper into it, sink into its safety and protection. He didn't want to be awake. He didn't want to hear what she had to say and to deal with it. But there was no escape.

"Les! Les, they killed Johnny last night. They shot him outside some movie show downtown. It's in all the papers and all over the radio."

"Oh, Christ," said Les.

"Federals. They shot him down like a dog. He didn't even get his gun out!"

Les cranked upright, putting his bare feet on the cold floor, hoping to shock some electricity into himself. Oddly, he felt no grief, only the arrival of a large bundle of confusion. What did this mean? What else was happening? Who talked? Were the detectives outside even now? How much time did he have? He was going to see his kids tonight, was that off? Would his mother assume he had been killed too? That's the way her mind worked these days. Where were Fatso and J.P.? What about the big Rock Island train job? What would—

But then the grief struck.

It struck hard, heavy, and hurtful. It amazed him how much pain he felt. Johnny, gone! How could that be? He'd just met with the big guy a day ago. Johnny: bigger than life, with a lopsided smile for everybody, a glad hand, a twenty-spot for every loser, cool when lead was flying, smart where the planning was needed, able to hold everything altogether on force of personality. It was as if a huge hole had been ripped in the sky and was sucking stuff out into nothingness, and he felt inadequate to patch it, to save what remained.

"I told him to be careful. But the big dope thought everybody loved him so much, nobody would ever rat him out. If they were waiting, he was ratted. The idiot. He had to live like a king ballplayer instead of a guy on the run, which is what he was. Some clerk notices him going in and calls the Division, and they show up and hose him down."

Helen hugged him to make the pain stop hurting. It didn't work much, but he appreciated the softness and looseness of her breasts against him, the warmth of her body, the sensation that she would give him everything she could and never let him down, and that she, and a few others, stood for what was worth preserving in the world.

Of course next to arrive, as if by on-schedule railroad, was the rage.

The Division! Those bastards. They were so new at this stuff, how'd they get so good so fast when at Little Bohemia they'd been clowns and fools, tripping on their own size 14s. In his mind, he saw them standing over poor Johnny and pumping bullet after bullet into him, maybe with a big Thompson gun, laughing and hooting. In fact, he knew it had to be that lanky champion who'd stood still as a sculpture on Wolf Road while Les's squirts raised the dust all around him and he just coolly returned fire, even clipping Les's brim! That guy! That guy!

"Les, are you all right?"

"I am, I am. Just shook-up a little. Honey, put a pot of coffee on, I need it to get my brain working straight. I'm going to hop in the shower. Where's J.P.? Does he know?"

"He hasn't showed yet."

"Okay, after the coffee, we have to pack. We've got to make tracks until this settles down and—"

"But the kids!"

"I know, honey, I'm disappointed too. But I'm telling you, we've got to scram. We'll go somewhere else, to a town that ain't so hot, I'll get a big score set up, and then we'll be out of the life. It'll all work out, you'll see."

LES WAS OUT OF THE SHOWER by 7:20 and into his glen plaid double-breasted over fresh white shirt with red foulard tie by 7:30. Always had to look sharp! What was the point of gangstering if you didn't look the part?

At 7:35, J.P. showed with the car. Les poured him a cup of joe.

"You heard about Johnny?"

"Just a few minutes back, Les. Jesus Christ, we just were drinking with him a night or so ago."

"Shows how fast it can happen. Anybody on you?"

"Nah. Empty streets all the way over. None of those black Fords with two guys in 'em. We're clear."

"For now."

"What's our move?"

"Our move is, out of town, fast and far. Like . . . by eight."

"Jesus, you ain't messing around."

"J.P., we don't know one damned thing about this yet, and I ain't hanging around for further developments. Maybe the Italians ratted out Johnny and—"

"The latest—I just heard this on the radio, it's not in the papers yet—is some bimbo he was renting a room from blew the whistle. She made him and then used him to leverage a beef with Immigration. Some foreign dame, they want to ship her out. She tipped off the Division boys, and wore a red dress so they could spot her at that movie. They're calling her the Lady in Red. She's the one who—"

"I ain't buying that. They always put out some cover story to make it sound like it was nothing but dumb luck. That way, they cover up what's really going on, and who they're really talking to, and until we know what's really going on, we have to make ourselves scarce. Are you ready for a long drive?"

"Sure, Les. I'm with you, you know that. I always am. What about Fatso and Carey and Jimmy Murray?"

"Right now, it's every man for himself. But they're small fry, no way the Division is going to waste manpower on them."

"Should we call Homer or Charlie Floyd? They've got names, they're famous. Along with you, they'll be next on the Division squash list."

"I don't have a number for them, and if I stop to make inquiries on the subject, that's just what Mr. Melvin Asshole—excuse me, Helen—Purvis wants."

"You can't talk that way around the kids!" called Helen.

"The swearing really ticks her off," Les confided.

"Dames got rules. All of 'em. Anyway, you're right on the getaway, Les," said J.P.

"That's why I've lasted so long in this business. Hell, I'm almost twenty-six!"

Both laughed for the first time that day. They were young, beautiful, deadly gangsters after all. The world knew, loved, feared, and, best of all, respected them. The business involved a lot of fast moves as part of the craft, and if you couldn't do that, you didn't belong, as they both knew. Both knew they could lock themselves in a car and put hundreds of miles behind them in a day, rough roads or smooth, paved or dirt, grinding the American highways and state lines to powder behind them. That was part of the craft too.

"I got over fifty-five hundred dollars from South Bend still left," Les said.

"That'll get us a long way. Maybe somewhere in Oklahoma or Arkansas we can pick up some more dough, some little country bank or something."

"Got it. Oklahoma? We're not headed to L.A. or Reno? They're friendly towns."

"And the Division knows that! No sir. We're going to Texas. I got my eye on something Mr. Lebman has in San Antonio, and it can't be any hotter there than it is here."

"Is Helen okay with this?"

"I am fine," said Helen from the bedroom. "Les always figures the right move."

"Boy, did you get a peach!" said J.P.

"Ain't that the truth. Now, let's get the machinos in the trunk. The ammo too, though we could use a lot more. I want to be on the road before eight."

"**ARE WE GETTING ANYWHERE?**" asked Bob. He sat in the easy chair in Nick's den.

"Well . . . sort of. Let's take a look. Evidence the old goat wasn't an FBI agent—no mention in files, no official acknowledgment, no mention in any history of the period."

"Doesn't sound to me like we've made a dent in it."

"The best thing is the retyped report pages, with what could have been Charles's name replaced by a name of the exact same length as his own."

"That one is pretty solid," said Bob. "The others, not so much."

"Voice in memo analyzing South Bend robbery, shooting, typical Swagger in understanding the dynamics of shooting situation. Then there's the culture of the Director's Bureau, where his word was absolute and the ability to erase dissenters from memory was just like Stalin's. It certainly wasn't beyond him to do it. If your grandfather was disappeared, I'll bet others have been too."

"Plausibility is not evidence."

"Your granddad's possession of a Colt .45 automatic, known to be assigned to the Division, from the Postal Department. The way it was worked over to increase speed shooting, as in arrests, again knowledge of a higher form probably appropriate to a gunfighter like Charles."

"Maybe, maybe not. Certainly not convincing."

"The badge."

"Could have been picked up in a pawnshop."

"But it's been there since 1934. They would have been much harder to come by in 1934. Next, verified absence from Blue Eye and Polk County from June through December 1934."

"He could have been on an epic drunk and off whoring in New Orleans."

"A good Presbyterian like Charles?"

"Especially a good Presbyterian like Charles."

"The fact that you think you're being followed suggestive of . . . well, of exterior interest, shall we say, suggesting further there's some mystery here we haven't yet figured on."

"Yeah, maybe."

"The fact that he started his heavy drinking in late 1934, as per Mrs. Tisdale. It just gets worse and worse, until he's finally going to the Baptists for help. Drink to forget? Drink to ease guilt? To make the blues go away? Whatever . . . Drinking."

"Not evidentiary."

"Finally the other contents in the strongbox and the map. This goofy thing. I had Jake send it."

He pulled a tissue-wrapped object from his pocket and unrolled it—the cylinder of some mechanical provenance, sleek, bulbous, blued, slotted, produced by highly refined machinework, all angles square and sharp, all dimensions symmetrical, about twelve ounces of pure mystery.

"I guess I gotta go into the gun books on this one. Ugh. Or the car books or the airplane books or . . ."

The hopelessness of identifying a piece of oddly shaped metal out of the world's inventory of oddly shaped metal across all applications daunted him.

"You haven't gotten anywhere on the map, have you?"

"Nope, and that includes looking at every 1934-or-earlier house in Blue Eye for a similar configuration as what I take to be a wall. I suppose I could start on outlying homes and structures."

"That's an act of desperation."

"I *am* desperate. Come on, you're a detective. Detect something."

"I detect that I need a drink."

"Excellent. Wish I could join you."

Nick rose, went to the bar in his study, poured himself a finger of Maker's. It was twilight, midweek, moderate out, the sun through the window leaving streaks in the clouds. Nick disappeared, came back, having prepped the tumbler with a very large ice cube.

"Cheers," said Nick, taking a sip. Then he asked, "Coke, soda, coffee, tea, dancing girls?"

"I'm fine. Oh, wait."

Something was buzzing at his chest, either his heart announcing that it was about to quit or his iPhone signaling the arrival of an email. It was the latter, and he pulled out the iPhone to examine: it was from Jen.

"Just checking," she wrote. "Remember you have that speech for Bill Tillotson next Tuesday. Thought you might forget."

Ach. Bill Tillotson—Dr. Bill Tillotson—was head of the Idaho Veterinarians' Association and a former marine officer, and he'd been after Bob for years to address a joint meet of the Vets' group and the Marine Corps League. Finally, Bob had relented when it was so far in the future he didn't have to think of it. Now it was on him and couldn't be gotten out of. It meant he had to fly to Boise, though he'd given what he thought of as The Speech enough times, it was no difficulty and low-anxiety. It irked him, but maybe the removal from his quest for Charles might clear up his thinking.

"Trouble?" asked Nick.

"Nah. I just have to go home for a few days next week, that's all."

He was putting the phone back in his jacket pocket when it buzzed again.

"Ain't I the popular one," he remarked as he called up his emails on the device.

It was from Jake Vincent, at his law firm in Little Rock.

"Call me," it said.

He dialed the number.

Jake answered right away.

"Great. How's it going?" Jake asked.

"Out of leads," said Bob.

"Well, something just came in. Sort of nuts, may scramble things more, but kind of interesting."

"Please, shoot."

"You remember the thousand-dollar bill, unissued and still wrapped, we found in the strongbox?"

"Yeah. We were just talking about it."

"We returned it to Treasury and they tracked it for us—finally."

"Please, tell me it was taken at South Bend, June seventeenth, 1934."

"Wish I could," said Jake. "But it was taken in a robbery, all right. On July twenty-fifth, 1934. A small town called Mavis, Arkansas, on the Texas–Arkansas border. Six thousand nine hundred fifty-five dollars was taken in loose cash . . . and a specially ordered money pack of five thousand, in five thousand-dollar bills, from the San Francisco Mint, ordered for a peculiar landowner who didn't trust checks and paid in cash."

Bob thought perhaps Charles had been dispatched to the small town to investigate, see if there was any connection to the big-boy robbers. Maybe he tracked the robbers down, disposed of them, and plucked the dough from their cold, dead hands and reported it as an unsolved case. He spent the other money, just had the one crisp thousand left and dumped it in the ground. But still, that wasn't squaring with the Charles he was uncovering, not really. And he didn't want to believe it.

"Any suspects?"

"Oh, of course. They were widely identified. It was in the papers."

"Baby Face Nelson?" he said with a burst of hope.

"This is where it goes screwball. No, not Baby Face Nelson. Bonnie and Clyde."

28

MAVIS, ARKANSAS

July 24–25, 1934

"I'VE SEEN BIGGER," said Les.

"It sure ain't no Sioux City or South Bend," said J.P.

They sat in the Hudson parked across from the First National Bank of Mavis, on the shady, single street that Mavis offered, and amid its few retail outlets, a mom-and-pop grocery, and, farther back, a nest of dwellings, hazy in the shadows of the trees.

The bank sat on the northwest corner of Main and Southern streets, a single-story chunk of masonry, with a double-doored entrance set at an oblique to the right angle of the corner, the Southern Street façade displaying a double window, the longer façade on Main three single widows. It was all-white brick, as plain as a Dutchman's dream, distinguished only by the towering tree that stood above it, shielding it somewhat from the hot Texarkana sun.

"The money inside is probably as green as anybody's," said Helen.

"You do have a point, sweetie," said Les. With that, he put the car into gear, eased back into the sparse traffic, and headed out of town. He didn't want to risk suspicions of a stranger staring at the bank from a stranger's car for too long. In towns where nobody noticed a thing, everybody noticed strangers. In a few miles, he came to a bend in Highway 45, where it crooked south and plunged across a stout wooden bridge over the Red River into Texas. Other than which side of the river they occupied, there appeared to be no difference between the two states, each offering the same rolling prairie, broken here and there by stands of timber, with lots of fallow fields, lots of rotting but a few healthy farmhouses, old barns painted with chew advertising, fences fencing nothing in and nothing out, just Dust Bowl Americana at its dustiest.

"So this is where we got to git," said Les. "Get across this bridge and no Arkansas lawman will follow. He's not going to get shot in Texas. The Texans probably don't give a damn about crimes committed in Arkansas because they consider themselves so superior to the slobs in Arkansas."

"I don't see it as a problem," said J.P. "There can't be much in the way of guards or local law enforcement. It doesn't seem a bird has landed in that town in thirty years. They probably haven't heard of radio, much less electricity. Any town with nothing but outhouses isn't in modern times yet."

"But I bet their guns go *bang* just like yours," said Helen.

"That's why I go in hard with machino," said Les. "They see that big gangster gun and they start thinking Saint Valentine's Day, and seven men on the floor, and it tends to discourage heroism. I hate heroism. The last thing I want to run into is a hero. I've had my fill of heroes."

"Helen, honey," said J.P., "I love you like you were mine, but Les has the right idea."

"Sure, I don't like it," said Les. "There's guns in there, and there's heroes everywhere down here—ask the Indians—but I don't see we have no choice as we could use a refill in the purse tank, sweetie. Don't you see?"

"I see," said Helen. "Of course I see."

Then she said, "That gas station over there, in Texas? Let's cross and get a nice cold cola."

"I thought you were an orange gal," said J.P.

"I wonder if Orange Crush has reached Texas yet?" said Helen.

Les took the Hudson over the bridge and pulled in next to the station. J.P. went in for the drinks and Helen and Les walked to a picnic table set in a glade of trees. In a bit, J.P. came out with two Coca-Colas and an Orange Crush.

"See how sophisticated they are in Texas, Helen?" he said, holding up the Orange Crush, and they all laughed. Helen sat on the table's bench while

J.P. and Les sat on the tabletop. They enjoyed the cold jolt of the beverages, and the shade of the willow trees so close to the great brown rush of the river.

"Now, I don't know a thing about your business," she said, "but it seems to me that if you go in with that big gangster machine gun and shoot holes in the ceiling and blow out windows all up and down Main Street, the first thing that's going to happen is that everybody is going to say, 'Why, what's Baby Face Nelson doing in a little Arkansas town?' The second thing is, every Texas Ranger between here and Tijuana is going to head up to this very spot. And the third thing is, every Division boy in Chicago takes the Ford Tri-Motor to Dallas and joins the Rangers at the roadblocks. And you re-member what happened to Bonnie and Clyde at the roadblock?"

"Wasn't a roadblock, as I heard the story," said Les. "And it was only one Ranger and a bunch of cowboys and sheriffs."

"The point remains the same: anything that draws attention to the great Mr. Baby Face out of his Midwest stomping ground is big news. It's what they call man bites dog; it's so different, it makes itself noticed. It makes things hard. So if you and J.P. go blasting into that bank, you alert them all. 'Come get Baby Face,' you say, 'and get famous fast.'"

"Helen has a point," said J.P.

"Sure she does," said Les, "but can you take the bank all by your lone-some? That's the real point. You alone? Good a criminal as you are, it's no easy thing, you're looking one way and the farmer pulls the .47 caliber Dra-goon revolver out of his pants and blasts you. Banks are, minimum, two-man jobs. This gas station, that would work for one man. But, what, maybe seven dollars and change?"

"I am not saying he does it alone," said Helen.

"What *are* you saying?" said Les.

"I am saying, you wait here in the trees, three miles away, drinking a Coca-Cola," said Helen, "and J.P. and I will rob the bank."

After they were done laughing, it occurred to both Les and J.P. that Helen hadn't told a joke, she had laid out a possibility.

"Honey, it's very dangerous work. I can't risk you for a few dollars."

"I'm risking me, sweetie, you aren't. And if it's the difference between another tourist cabin, with J.P. snoring on the couch, and separate rooms in a first-class hotel, plus fine meals among the gentry in the dining room and a bath every single day, for two minutes of danger I can do it."

"Les, she's not far off, if at all," said J.P. "Two people aren't twice as good as one for a bank, they're twenty times as good."

"Here's another thing," said Helen.

"You have thought hard on this," said Les.

"I have indeed."

"So this one will be rich, I bet," he said.

"Very rich indeed, Mr. Gillis. I will get a cheroot and clench it in my teeth. I will wear a bucket hat. I will put on some black hose. I will call J.P. Clyde and he will call me Bonnie."

"Bonnie and that dumb buckra Clyde are dead, sweetie. As you mentioned, they ran into a Ranger with a Browning rifle and that was that."

"Dead in body but not in spirit. To these folks, they were heroes. They still talk and dream about them. So if they think it's Bonnie and Clyde, that's all they'll talk about, and no matter how the Division detectives hammer on them, it'll always be Bonnie and Clyde. It's like spreading a fog over it all, so much Bonnie and Clyde stuff, there won't be a soul who connects it with the great and famous Chicago gangster Baby Face Nelson."

"She has a point there, Les," said J.P.

And even Les had to admit, she has a point there.

"Besides," said Helen, "this'll be fun."

As it turned out, Les, who was very brave in a gunfight, was not very good sitting in a grove of trees while his wife robbed a bank. It was the next day. They had stayed the night in Texas, sleeping in the car, driven back across the bridge, and J.P. and Helen had each moseyed into the bank, saw it had a standard layout, with two tellers' cages, a small administrative area, a corner office for Mr. Big, and a vault in the rear, opened sharply at 10 a.m.

and closed at 4 p.m. The money in the tellers' cages did in fact appear to be quite green, even if there wasn't much of it, and the few customers were sad old farmers, mostly coming in to pay off loans or explain why they couldn't.

"It'll be easy," Helen trilled on the ride back.

"It should be easy," said Les glumly. "This sort of thing can go haywire on the tiniest screwup. A customer walks in at the wrong time. An old lady screams. The cop decides to take his coffee break an hour early. It can't be predicted. That's why you got to be ready to improvise on a moment's notice and hope you can do it right. Why, I remember—"

"Okay, honey, we will be on our toes, won't we, John Paul?"

"Yes, ma'am, Miss Bonnie Parker," said J.P., and they both laughed. But Les didn't.

They figured mid-afternoon, guessing the sheriff's deputies would mostly be out in the country on patrol, while the old man himself snoozed off too much lunch in his corner office, and if there was a sheriff around, he'd most likely be snoozing too, in one of his own cells.

They dropped Les at the station at 2 and he went in and bought a chicken salad sandwich the owner's wife sold, wrapped in waxed paper, a nice cold Coca-Cola out of a machine that suspended various soft drinks in a tub of very cold water, and a newspaper, the *Dallas Times Herald*, and sat at the picnic table as his wife and friend disappeared.

The time dragged. He forced himself to eat slow, to make the sandwich last, but no matter how long he dragged it out, it was gone, as was the Coca-Cola, by 2:30. Agh, now what? How many times can you read a sports page? How much further can the Cubs fall behind? How many more stupid picture shows can come in? How long can the Division crow about getting Dillinger? All these dramas were revisited in the pages of the Dallas newspaper, and after he'd read all the stories he wanted to, and all that he sort of wanted to, and even a few that he didn't want to read at all, there was no sign of anybody. But, at the same time, it wasn't as if Texas cops had raced to the bridge to seal it off, knowing a robbery had taken place.

He checked his watch and saw that it was now well after 3, getting on to

3:30, and now and then a car, more likely a truck, once even a tractor, ambled along and crossed over into the Lone Star State. He could feel his stomach knotting up, clouds of heartburn gas rising through his gorge, inflaming that which they touched, and his mouth and nose were dry, so that the air felt raw and harsh as it went into or out of these orifices.

Where were they?

What the hell was happening?

He bought another drink, but because of the stern architecture of the soda-pop bin, couldn't get a Coca-Cola out, as other brands blocked them in the racks. He had to settle for a cherry pop, which was way too acidic and only made his various pipes burn more fiercely. He'd sweated through his collar and his Panama hat band, and it occurred to him to loosen his tie, but there were some things he just could not do. Meanwhile, the .45 lolling in leather under his sweaty armpit seemed to grow heavier and heavier.

The geezer who owned the station came out and they chatted a bit, Les claiming to be a haberdashery salesman breaking in a new man on his route before moving himself to a bigger route, and the old fellow listened with no interest in his old gray eyes. His name was McIvens, he was from downstate, his people had always been cow people, but up here you hardly ever saw a cow, it mostly being just small-plot farming. Without the highway here, the whole county would dry up and blow away. Everybody had a story, the story was always sad, but it was the Depression.

Then Les caught a flash of motion as another car emerged from the woods and headed at a brisk pace to the bridge.

In another second, it revealed itself to be a State Police car.

THE FIRST PROBLEM was the sheriff. He decided not to take his nap in a cell but to park across from the bank, enjoy a pipeful, and perhaps think of better days. Like most country folk, he was content to just be. He sat there motionless, not particularly observant but not asleep either.

"He sure isn't waiting for a robbery," said J.P. "He'd have his shotgun out and there'd be boys all up and down the street. It's just this one old fella waiting for the clock to move but in no particular rush."

"We can't just sit here," said Helen. "Let's take a drive or something."

So off they went, a half hour back into Arkansas, then the same half hour back to Mavis. There was the sheriff, still sitting.

"Maybe he's counting crows," said J.P.

"Well, then, how about some ice cream?"

"Sounds good to me."

So they walked back along Main Street and found the drugstore, and it turned out that Helen didn't feel like ice cream, so she got a Green River at the soda counter and J.P. got a chocolate phosphate. They sat next to the big Coca-Cola dispenser, all red, with the white script of trademark big across it.

"I feel like a traitor to Coca-Cola," Helen said.

"I do too, but I've had so many in my time, I don't think the Coca-Cola people will hold it against me."

"They may be keeping track," Helen said. "They're everywhere."

At that point, the sheriff's car, visible through the window, pulled out of town.

"Well," said J.P., "looks like we're up to bat."

"Let's go, Mr. Barrow."

They ambled across Main Street, waiting to let a farmer, with two colored men riding in the back of his truck, pass by. He waved at them, as did the two colored men, showing off fine American hospitality, and J.P. touched his hat brim in response.

The two entered the bank, and Helen pulled her Bonnie-like bucket hat low across her forehead, then inserted a cheroot between her pretty lips. She sure wasn't going to smoke the awful thing, just as she knew Bonnie hadn't in the famous picture, but it made her feel all the more Bonnie-like. With the black stockings added to the hat and the cheroot, she thought she looked the role. Looking up, now fully Bonnie Parker, she saw that one of the tellers' cages was closed and that three people waited in line for the other.

"Okay," said J.P., slipping his hand inside his suit coat to remove his .45, "let me do the talking. You just—"

"HANDS UP!" screamed Helen, pulling a large .45 Colt revolver from her purse. "This here is a robbery!"

It was amazing! Helen, so quiet and cute her whole life, was suddenly transformed into a demon of energy and command by the liberating surge she felt in stepping beyond the wall.

"Ladies, hands up, dump those purses. Teller, you reach for the sky or I'll shoot you between the lenses of your glasses. Everybody else, freeze, reach, and pray I don't lose my temper."

J.P. did a double take, even as, for emphasis, Helen used her left thumb to ease back the hammer on the big revolver in her right hand, the ominous click of its new position filling the stunned, silent air.

"Clyde, get the cash, and fast!"

"Yes, Miss Bonnie," said J.P., remembering the Bonnie and Clyde gag, and he dipped beyond the counter, went to the teller's cage as he unfurled a flour bag from his pocket. He quickly dumped the bills in the bag, then turned to a fellow in a three-piece suit sitting deskbound, hands up.

"You, sir, you lead me into the vault and point out the cash drawers. No need to be a hero. Come on, now, git!" He gestured with his handgun. But he was good at this, and had not forgotten the president's office, so instead of following the clerk into the vault, he stationed himself just beside the door to the office, figuring it would have required just this much time for the president to win the debate with himself over the requirements of Duty, and just as he emerged with a double-barreled gun, J.P. clunked him hard on the head, but at nowhere near killing power, and the gentleman went down, dropped the gun, and curled up in a fetal position, his hands flying to the gash in his head.

"Bet many's the time you've wanted to do that," J.P. said to the clerk, who'd obligingly pulled open a drawer with tens and twenties stacked within. "Now, fill it up!"

The clerk filled the bag.

"That too," said J.P., pointing to an unsealed stack of clearly fresh-from-the-mint bills.

"Won't do you no good," said the clerk. "Them numbers is recorded. Use 'em and you get arrested."

"Granddad, 'preciate the help, but you let me worry about the technical questions."

"Hurry up there, Clyde," yelled Bonnie. "These ladies can't stand around much longer, they've got a tea to attend."

She smiled, but the flinty Arkansas gals had no smiles for robbers and instead sniffed their noses imperiously. Snobs everywhere, even in Mavis!

Then Helen noticed through the window: that damned sheriff was back, right across the street.

LES STUDIED ON IT. If the State boys were laying a trap for Helen and J.P., it occurred to him he had to act now. He saw it in a second: he could ease across the bridge, nice and smiley, waving, get up close, ask them something about the road to Dallas or somewhere, and then go to his gun fast. Close in, hardball, that should do it. Two pops a man, so close it would all be head shooting. Then he'd . . .

Then he'd what?

Wait for J.P. and Helen to show? Yeah, sit there waiting, lounging on the fender of a car, with two dead cops. Good idea. Meanwhile, what if Helen and J.P. didn't show? What if, just as he fired, six more cop cars came around the bend? What if . . . A trickle of sweat jiggled down his forehead from under his hatband.

He did not like this at all. With action, it was all about now. This second, this instant. You were lucky or you weren't. The bullet whacked you or it missed and hit the mom pushing the buggy. Too bad for her, but that's the way it went.

This sitting, waiting stuff was for the birds. He found himself doing unmanly things, like a dame or a nancy, sitting there with a boob's look on his mug, trying to guess how cops would act, trying to figure where he could run to, hoping he was lucky instead of making his own luck. But . . . he was no good at that stuff, never had been. He was the guy you want with the Thompson in hand, not bluffing and charming his way through touchy situations on savvy and intuition.

He found himself breathing hard, his focus scattered, the gases in his stomach really scorching and wasting his pipes, the sick, weak need to take a crap. It was as if his whole personality was falling apart—him, the famous, the legendary, the frightening BABY FACE NELSON, in whose presence all men trembled and all women got, even if they never admitted it, the tingle. Because everybody admired the fellow who took things and didn't just sit there hoping someone would hand him something gratis.

He thought it through again. This time, the best way would be to avoid the bridge, wade across the river—but it looked pretty damned deep—and lay up just under the lip of the incline where the riverbank rose to meet the flats. That way, if the State cops netted Helen and J.P., he could move on them if he had to, as they'd be occupied, and it could still work out. And maybe he wouldn't even have to pop the cops, could just disarm them, toss their *pistolas* in the Red, shoot out their tires, and go on. See, people got all agitated if you killed a cop, to say nothing about how angry the cops themselves got.

But even as he was sorting this out, he wasn't moving. And doubts soon arrived that suggested the plan was a mess waiting to happen next. Maybe he couldn't wade the river, got swept away, drowned. What a way to go! What if he's down there and Helen and J.P. come by, don't see him, figure he caught a ride into the next town, and rented a tourist camp cabin and—

No matter which way he figured it, it came to catastrophe. So he just sat there, torn between doom and desolation, grief and anguish, thinking this whole thing was a goddamned stupid idea and he was screwed for certain.

"NOW, YOU PEOPLE," said J.P., "you had it easy, except for that clunk on the head of the president there. Don't make us mad. No screaming, no yelling, no alarms, no nothing, you just hang cool as lemonade for three minutes till we clear town. You'll have stories to tell your children for years. You'll never pay for a drink in this town again!"

Nobody seemed inclined to disagree with him, though the three elderly women kept that prim, holier-than-thou look on their pinched and dried-out faces.

"Sister," said Helen, "don't see why you're looking so put-out, nobody took a thing from you."

"Well, Miss Parker, 'tain't that. It's that I have mah-jongg at four and this'll make me so late."

"Well, you apologize to the girls for me. Now, hold steady, everybody."

She and J.P. backed out together, one looking forward, the other back. At the doorway, she pulled him close.

"That damned sheriff is sitting over there, big as life."

"DAMN!" cursed J.P. "I'll mosey over and try and get a shot into him through the windshield. You start the car and—"

"No, and the whole county'll be out here with shotguns and rope in two seconds. YOU start the car, Mr. Barrow."

Since she had conviction, and J.P. only experience, he yielded to her, put his head down, the gun low in one hand, the bag of swag pressed into his thigh, and beelined for the car. Meanwhile, Helen tucked her big .45 behind her purse and smilingly approached the man with the badge lounging sleepily behind the wheel of his big car.

He looked up.

"Oh, Sheriff," she said, "sorry, but I've got to do some, you know, business, is there a public facility in this town?"

The sheriff blushed as if he'd just been shown a French postcard displaying unlikely anatomical positions, then got his wits about him and started to offer the use of the restroom in the jail to her, but by that time she'd laid the barrel of the big Colt revolver on the sill of the window, pointed straight into his vitals.

"Your gun, sir. Left hand, upside down, nothing fancy, as I would have no pause in doing what I must do. Be a dear, won't you please?"

To emphasize her argument, she thumbed back the hammer of the revolver until it clicked locked. The sheriff, in his sixties, with many a mile on him, blinked, and his outsize Adam's apple became spastically active as he swallowed hard and got nothing down but a gallon of dry air.

The firearm, an actual cowboy gun in silver with engraving, came over to her backwards.

"What a nice revolver," she said. "I won't even take it. I know you treasure it."

She stepped back from the car, still smiling, turned and lobbed the gun up onto the porch roof of the ice-cream shop. Then she walked smartly around the car, stopped at first the left, then the right, front tire and fired a bullet square into each, the sound raising dust, chicken squawks, feathers, startlement, and confusion all along Main Street. She stepped across the street and climbed into the backseat of the Hudson, which J.P. had obligingly backed out of its space.

"Helen, I believe you have a gift for this kind of work," said J.P. as they sped away.

LES WAS RAISED CATHOLIC, and still considered himself a believer, but he didn't like to waste the man upstairs's time on minor matters. But he broke his own rule this time.

Dear Lord, he prayed, please, please, please let Helen be all right. Sir, I couldn't get along without her, and she's the best mom any kids ever had, plus my own mother loves her to death, and she only stepped off the path this one time to help us out of a jam, so please, sir, this is Lester from the West Side, please, sir, let her be all right.

It didn't seem to have much effect on reality, as nothing happened or changed. Before prayer, after prayer, he was the same, just a fellow in too fancy a suit sitting on a picnic table in a glade of trees right across the Red River Bridge into Texas from Arkansas. Maybe a cloud shielded the sun, maybe the breeze kicked up, but neither of these could be taken as a message from God, so he decided that God must be busy elsewhere, with much to do that day, and just didn't have room for Lester from the West Side. He didn't take it personally. Though his temper had gotten him in trouble his whole life—had invented his whole life, as a matter of fact—he knew it was absurd to be angry with the same God who had guided so many bullets fired his way to miss, and so he didn't feel at all ill-used by God.

He felt ill-used, he decided, by John Paul Chase. That was how his brain worked: he always had to have a target, a grudge, something to fuel the processing of his mind and thereby provide him with energy, passion, and courage. He had wanted to kill Homer, and if a chance had come, he would have. But now that seemed laughable, since Homer had gotten clipped in the head by a bullet and wasn't himself—all this after saving everybody's bacon in South Bend. He was the sort of man who said "I'd like to kill you" about people all the time and it didn't mean anything—that is, unless he actually killed you.

So he focused on John Paul. Like many men with close friends, he didn't really trust his close friends. He was too complicated for that. They got along so well, Les the boss, J.P. the servant, and as helpful as that was, it sort of sickened Les that J.P. took so much abuse, was so obedient. What was the problem with him? Les thought maybe he wasn't too bright.

And he could see J.P. making a stupid decision, just like that idiot farm boy Charlie Floyd had at South Bend, because he didn't really trust J.P. to do the right thing. So he could see J.P. panicking and plugging a cop, and he and Helen getting pinched when J.P. turned the wrong way down a dead-end street, and Helen goes up for accessory to murder one and is given fifteen-to-thirty, and he never, ever sees her again. That was a possibility, and it was so immense and destructive, it made him shaky.

Pretty soon he'd convinced himself not only that it could happen but that it did happen, and he decided, if so, he'd get himself arrested in

Arkansas, he'd go to the same prison just so that he could kill J.P. to pay him back for what he'd done to Helen, then somehow he'd bust out. He felt righteous rage steaming through his insides, building up a pressure so intense, he thought he'd burst, and the more he thought about it, not only the madder he got but the more tragic it seemed, until he couldn't tell whether he was in a killing rage or a sobbing tantrum. He knew one thing and one thing alone: he felt miserable.

"Honey?"

He looked up. Helen had a big smile on her face, and J.P. was smoking a cigar. Les hadn't even seen them cross the bridge, he'd been so wrought up.

He raced to them.

"This gal of yours," said J.P., "she's the best!"

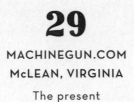

29

MACHINEGUN.COM

McLEAN, VIRGINIA

The present

ONE THING THE WORLD had no shortage of was machine guns.

A wonder of the late nineteenth century, the serial-firing, belt- or magazine-fed, recoil-operated weapon had been produced in bewildering variety since at least 1883 with the advent of the original, the Maxim gun. Every industrial culture tried its hand and the results were an infinity of ventilating holes, barrel jackets, cooling tanks, belt-linking designs, magazine curvatures, bolt protrusions, mounting iterations, stock or grip configurations, sight apparatuses, muzzle brakes or flash hiders (or both!), tri- or bipod support structures, carrying grips, to say nothing of the endless array of maintenance devices, ammo boxes, shipping crates, the detritus of the machine-made world, all in the service of chopping down men with industrial efficiency in battle. And of course each gun itself had then gone through model issues, dedication applications, prototypes, and experimental advancements, thus multiplying the base number by a staggering amount. There were thousands of the goddamned things, and the guns of '14 through '18 were particularly ornate, where the pressure of war had upped the pace of research and design and manufacture. The Great War guns lacked mobility—that would arrive in War 2—but were superb at their task, which is why the best of them, the Maxim, was often called the Devil's Paintbrush. It left landscapes of ruined flesh, which it had stroked on the world's scabrous battlefields, but there were dozens, perhaps hundreds, of imitations—Vickers, Browning, and so on—that attempted to duplicate the Paintbrush's effect on the world.

At a variety of websites, Bob wandered among these details at a computer station in the business center of his McLean motel. Next to the screen on the table, slightly illuminated in its moonlight glow, lay the mystery cylinder, that little bit of machined perfection that looked so similar to machine-gun muzzles from the world over, and generations of machine guns past, but never quite exactly.

Maxim?

No.

Browning?

Uh-uh.

MG-42?

Nein.

Degaratov?

Nyet.

Thompson?

Almost, goddammit. But not quite.

Type 92?

Bren?

Breda?

Chauchat?

Nix to all.

He knew the damned things. He'd carried, fired, maintained, deployed, taken down, improvised with them his whole life in the military. It was a key part of the infantry trade. It was warcraft at its most demanding, and whoever kept his own guns running hot, well-fed, and positioned creatively usually won the fight to fight again.

But even with all that time behind the hammering, and all the surgery on the gun's guts under fire or sweltering in tropic heat, struggling to keep track of pins and springs or any of the thousand tiny parts that made the thing go *bangbangbang* instead of *click*, all the miles draped in M60 belts slogging uphill or over dikes, the creature itself banging hard against his back on an improvised strap, all of that machine-gun time, machine-gun culture, machine-gun savvy, did not aid him in placing the cylinder in the machine-gun world.

He almost got a hit on a strange French heavy beast called the Hotchkiss Model 1922. This one looked as if it had been designed in a bar in Montmartre after a long day of whores and absinthe shots, being a crazy jigsaw of angles and latches and bolts. The version of it he found even had a thumbhole stock, which otherwise was shaped like a violin trying to act tough. But the Frenchies had happily affixed a big chunk of metal to its muzzle to keep the strings of 7.9s it fired from rambling all over the landscape. It looked to Bob as if he'd struck, if not pay dirt, at least dirt, though no Net picture got close enough to tell if it had twelve slots or not. If he couldn't get a close-up, he could at least get his eyes up close.

From a distance of six inches, alas, the French gun revealed its fraudulence. The rear of the piece, just where it reduced itself in circumference to mate with the barrel proper, didn't have the same graceful convex of angle as the thing on the desktop.

He looked at it anew and, anew, was struck by the artistry of the thing, the superiority of the metalwork. Guns being pieces of machined metal fitted together, he'd examined those pieces and the way they fit his whole life, and whoever was on the lathe for this one was a master machinist, one of those boys who over a lifetime gets so sublime at his skill, it almost beggars belief. Damn, the boy was good.

He checked his watch. Getting close to dawn in Northern Virginia. He'd gotten nowhere, learned nothing. Where was the big break, the eureka moment?

Like the thing on the desk, it was unknowable.

30

COMISKEY PARK
CHICAGO

July 24, 1934

CHARLES HAD A BAD ONE THAT NIGHT. The war, the usual stuff, the limitless landscape of mud and wire, the faces of slaughtered boys gone away for nothing that ever made any sense, the paleness of their bodies in the ever-falling rain, the delicacy of their faces, if the faces had refrained from being blown off, the hell where youth and laughter go, the silliness of the trinkets of tin and ribbon he'd come home with. He woke, all lathered up in sweat, hungry with rogue impulses about which he could not even think, consumed with self-loathing and a sense of so much Duty undone, so many obligations still owed, the infinite pain of his two sons, the sense of a universe without hope.

At 9 he rose, showered, put on his slacks and a short-sleeved shirt, but left his coat, tie, automatic, and shoulder holster locked in the suitcase under his bed and to his bed. He went downstairs to the diner—he'd forgotten to eat that whole lost Monday—and picked up the *Tribune* and the *Herald-Examiner* and ordered some eggs and bacon while he read, at last, what the world was making of the death of John Dillinger.

It bore no resemblance to any world Charles remembered. In this world, the heroic G-Man Melvin Purvis had tracked down and slain the monster almost on his own. Charles had to laugh because it was so extravagantly wrong and yet there it was, the product of the immutable logic of the odd politics of the Chicago Field Office.

Yes, Sam was boss; yes, Hugh Clegg was second in command. But, yes, at the same time, Melvin Purvis was sort of there, and him being extremely handsome, dapper, affable, and pleasant, the press congregated around him, and Charles could only assume that the longer he went on, the more the story became about him and the less it was about the Division of Investigation. If you knew the truth, it wasn't hard to sniff the myth, but, at the same time, it was hard to hate Melvin Purvis. He wasn't claiming to be a hero, really, and making immoderate boasts, it's just that he was there, the reporters knew and liked him, and the easiest way for them to do the job was to put some kind of Melvin shine on everything. It would have taken a man far stronger than Melvin Purvis to turn down the temptation of self-glorification.

Charles almost laughed. He knew the old bastard "bachelor" Director, off in Washington, was in need of a triple bicarbonate of soda this morning. The fellow must be apoplectic. It was exactly what he didn't want, but at the same time exactly what he couldn't prevent. What could he do now, fire his "hero"?

"The Man Who Got Dillinger" one paper had headlined under a fine file photo of the dapper Purvis, looking all serious, and the story began, "It came down to a duel of two men, the Man From Crime and the Man From Justice, and, fortunately for all of us, the Man From Justice won."

Charles had a good time pushing through the nonsense, amazed at just how wrong wrong could be, but at a certain point ran out of newspaper. He needed something to do, something to get his mind off all the politics of the office and the government man-killing trade. He thought of a movie, but that idea wasn't appealing because of its association with Johnny's end in Gable's shadow. Then he remembered that Sam had mentioned a ball game and that appealed to him. He checked the paper, saw that the Cubs, the nineteenth floor's unofficial mascot team, were on the road, and so he looked and indeed saw there was an American League game at Comiskey Park on the South Side. He knew nothing about the Sox, but that wasn't the point: losing yourself in the spectacle, the ceremony, the anonymous camaraderie of the stands, erasing the mind and numbing the spirit, that was the point.

Thus, he mounted the El station, which was like climbing into a gigantic iron-girdered monster—maybe an old dreadnought tied up at the dock, with its constellations of iron rivets and stout timbers everywhere, and the smell of the tar with which they sealed off the wood from the elements— caught the southbound train, rocketed through the Loop, and then plunged into loud darkness for twenty minutes as whatever lay between the Loop and Comiskey fled by unseen on the surface.

He emerged in what by lore was called Bronzeville, and the ballpark customers were obvious strangers in this all-Negro world. The two civilizations regarded each other across their great gulf as the fans passed among the residents down 35th Street, approaching the thing ahead, where the ball game would be played. But it was all in good cheer, for the sun was bright, the folks happy, the prospects enticing. The streets were full of hum and buzz, not quite thronged, but still heaped with people, while the park—a castle of brick? a cathedral?—dominated the area, as from all directions citizens approached. All sorts of bright hustle assaulted the newcomers, hot dog stands, fellows selling programs, cotton candy, Cracker Jacks and popcorn, souvenir pennants, little Sox caps, the works. If it was affiliated with baseball and could be sold on the streets approaching Comiskey, it was.

He bought a general grandstand ticket, entered the half-full arena, and got a jolt of pleasure from the green of the field, which dominated the structure, against the red brick of the walls and the quasi-Medieval stylings of the towers and ramparts of the stadium. At half throng, the place was still impressive, as fifteen thousand people of basically one mind and common interest made their presence felt. Charles drifted until he found a nice vantage point of the field, about thirty rows up from the demarcation between box seats and general admissions, a little this side of third base. Really, there wasn't a bad seat in the place, unless you were stationed behind one of the frequent steel girders that kept it upright, and Charles could see the young men on the field below him, full of life and speed and grace and strength. He made sure not to order a beer, though the whole stadium was generally a giant, circular beer barrel, and everywhere fans were overacting with the elaborate exacerbation of the nearly inebriated. Meanwhile, it was a festival of advertising, as the great American enterprises such as Coca-Cola, Standard Oil, Hamm's Beer from the Land of Sky Blue Waters, and the *Chicago Tribune* purchased space on the walls to sell their goods. Pennants and flags spanked the air, the smoke of ten thousand cigarettes and two thousand cigars rose to form a kind of gloriously hazing blur atop it all. It was like a volcano getting ready to blow. Everybody was loud, everybody was happy, everybody wanted to be no other place on earth that particular day, that particular time.

Not much of a game. The enemy team hailed from D.C.—perhaps the Director was a fan—and the Sox, themselves no prize edition this year, handled them pretty easily. The Sox scored in the first inning and never trailed. Swanson, in right, got a couple of hits to lead the team to four runs, and other guys with hits included Appling, Conlon, Simmons, Bonura, and Dykes, for a total of six. A fellow named Les Tietje pitched, lasted until the eighth, and got the win. It all went as it was supposed to go, and Charles took most pleasure from the green of the grass, the white of the uniforms and ball, and the long dramas of interception when someone skied one and it floated through its arc high in the hot, bright sky, then lost energy and began its descent to where it was nabbed in the glove of this or that young fellow, who then uncorked a long trajectory throw that rose a bit, fell a bit, and landed exactly where it had been aimed and was then tossed this way or that at speed, depending on the game situation. There was something soothing in watching the grace of these transactions, and the game, while lacking suspense, also lacked drama or intensity, both of which Charles was glad to leave behind him for a time.

In the seventh, someone said to him, "How about a Cracker Jack, Sheriff?" putting the box in front of him, and Charles looked up and saw that the Italian called Uncle Phil had taken the seat next to his. He wore a creamy-white linen suit, a red tie, white shoes, black, circular glasses, and a Panama shading his handsome face.

"Thanks but no thanks, friend," said Charles. "Say, are you guys watching me? How'd you know I was here? This can't be coincidence."

"Same way we knew where Johnny would be. We're everywhere. Not all the time, but enough so we can keep our eyes on things. Don't take it personally. We're just paying attention. Knowledge is power is wealth is a long, happy life."

"I don't like it."

"Nobody does, but you'll get used to it. Anyway, I'm hearing that despite all the yakkity-yak about Purvis, it was the sheriff who handled Johnny. And did a fine job on it too."

"I just did what my badge required," said Charles. "It wasn't nothing special. Any detective in this town could have handled it."

"Knowing a few of them, I'd have to disagree," said Uncle Phil. "They'd have ended up with dead citizens everywhere. Must tick you off to read the papers and see it's the *Melvin Purvis G-Man Heroic Hour*. He didn't do nothing but light a cigar, never went up against Johnny and his little Colt."

"I don't care about that. It's beyond me. I don't like nobody in my business anyhow, so if nobody pays no attention, that's fine by me."

"Give it to you, Sheriff, no need for stroking, like so many, and that stroking gets so many killed or crushed. It's an admirable trait."

"I don't put on airs. No percentage in it. I don't like them that do. What's this about anyway? I don't see you as no South Side ball fan."

"It's a good game, lots of fun. You would not believe the money that moves on it every day. It seems so straightforward here in the sun, with all the pops and kids and hot dogs, but every time one of those Apollos throws a ball, twenty million moves one way or the other."

"I don't know nothing about that," said Charles. "I'm not good at numbers. I leave that to the others. Now, do you have some dope for me?"

"The latest is that Homer's somewhere up in St. Paul but laying low while the bump in his head goes down. Baby Face cleared town but fast when you put Johnny in the morgue. He sees the writing on the wall. Pretty

Boy's too dumb to come in out of the rain, but that makes him hard to predict because he just bounces around with no plan. I think we'll have hard info on Homer next. Pretty Boy will fall victim to his own bad luck. Baby Face will come back. He's a Chicago boy, he knows which way the streets run and the shortcuts. But you already knew that. Here's why I'm here: I wanted to hand this over."

He laid an envelope on Charles's lap. Charles looked at it.

"Just a little extra. You're doing your job, you're impressing people, and we like to show our gratitude."

"I won't take that," said Charles. "It makes me a bounty hunter, not a cop."

"It ain't a payment, it's a gift from citizens who appreciate it."

"If I take it, I get used to it. You give me some more and I enjoy it. I buy stuff, I'm a hero to my wife, and I'm looking for more, which comes along soon enough. Then you've got me hooked. You own me. So let's get this straight right now. Nobody owns Charles Swagger. He pays his own way, he walks his own path, all of it for his own reasons, explained to nobody. I won't never meet with you again, you understand that, pal?"

"You throw 'em hard and tight, don't you, Sheriff? Like Wyatt Earp or some other old gunman. Dodge, Silver City, Laredo, other dirt-water shit-holes not worth dying for. Okay, you want to play it like that, that's the way we play it."

He smiled, picked up the envelope, and then rose and walked away.

Charles went back to watching the boys play their ball game.

31

MAVIS, ARKANSAS

The present

Not much remained of Mavis. It was one of those towns that had been passed by on the Interstate rush to throw concrete ribbons around America, and, far from any six-lanes, it languished. It didn't even have a Walmart or any fast-food joints.

Where the bank had been, a Dollar Store now sold cheap Chinese goods. There was a 7-Eleven, a one-story town hall/police station/public works department, clearly a relic of the '70s. A café sold coffee and pastry, but if you wanted food, you had to go out by the Interstate and feed at a TGIF's or a McDonald's or something off a gas station candy rack. No library, no Historical Society, not much of anything except people, all of whom seemed to be on welfare. Or minimum-subsistence jobs. Or crystal meth.

Nobody could answer any of his questions, as they seemed mostly to be in their twenties, the men living thirty or more miles from factory jobs in the last Arkansas town or the next Texas town. But the bank had to stand at the corner of Main and Western, and, looking at the structure, he felt it was probably the same building, though now occupied by Mr. and Mrs. Ling and their emporium of plastic goods from Szechuan Province. He doubted the Lings would know a thing about Bonnie and Clyde's visit eighty-five years ago, three months after they were killed in Arcadia, Louisiana.

He sat outside the coffee shop, sipping a cup, wondering what this trip proved.

What it proved was: yes, I am being followed.

He knew it. You get certain feelings, and if you're a field operator like him, those feelings are honed and developed over the years. Call it ESP or spidey sense or whatever, you can feel the weight of certain eyes on you, even through binoculars. This vividness of sensation had saved his life a thousand times, and it was never wrong, unless, all of a sudden, it was.

Am I that old? Has the little gizmo gone crazy? Is the mechanism not working? Am I losing it? Is this whole thing sort of an old man's vanity, a ridiculous concoction built on a lifetime's sniper paranoia and having been shot at way too much for anyone's psychological health? Do I need to be the object of some dark conspiracy, of forces that hide in shadows and pull strings? Does it make me feel . . . alive?

But he understood and obeyed the fundamentals of the game—the game being Man Hunting 5.0—that is, at the highest level. And that game was: if you are under observation, do not acknowledge it. Thus, you possess a microscopic advantage, which a clever operator might leverage into a victory when or if the guns came out. So, though his brain screamed at him to turn and look, to apply his still-great vision to the shadows and the horizon and the trees all the way out, he probed in another direction, along lines of staying loose-limbed, goofy, sort of pokey and old. If whoever was out there really was out there and they realized they'd been discovered, he—or they—would change their whole plan of attack, method of operation, and he might never find them until they decided it was time for the kill. To survive, he had to know they were going to kill before they did.

Keeping his eyesight determinedly local, he looked up and down the street in Mavis and noted a few of its oblivious citizens in the street, old pickups, a few automobiles of unidentifiable vintage, and not one thing out of place, different, new to the eye. No traffic had passed in ten minutes, except for a mom with a mini SUV full of squealers on the way to the Costco in the next town down the line, a State policeman of about thirteen, on patrol, and an old boy on a tractor. No sign of the Mafia, Soviet airborne, jihadhis, Japanese marines, rogue Agency cowboys, the sons, brothers, wives, daughters of men he'd killed, whatever or whoever else could be interested in him. Just daylight America, small, dying-town variety, edging quietly toward tomorrow without much in the way of drama or excitement.

But why was he being tracked? Because it's always and only about money. It's never vengeance, justice, irony, curiosity, envy, romantic competitiveness, any human motive, except the oldest of them all: greed. Cain probably whacked Abel out of greed. He figured he'd get an extra quart of goat's milk from the old man if his brother wasn't there. Somewhere, there had to be a money angle in all this, but, damn, if he could find it.

He drove to the Dallas Airport for tomorrow's flight back to Boise and his upcoming speech, and that night, in the hotel, he did what he'd done twice already. He inspected every single item with him, feeling, probing, shaking, sniffing, and if licking was suggested, he'd have licked. But nothing from sock to jock to razor to toothpaste, to the stuff you wore underneath, to the stuff you wore on top, to the thing you carried it all in, suggested a dual purpose, an intelligence usage. It was just bland, dreary stuff, like anybody's stuff. No bugs, no microprocessors, GPSs, new spy toys, James Bond buzzers or decoder rings, just . . . nothing.

Then he rose early and spent an extra hour before breakfast looking at the car, even though it was a rental selected randomly from a row of rentals. No way anybody could have anticipated in Little Rock which car he was going to choose of ten available. He didn't even know; he just picked the first one, and, he supposed, maybe he always picked the first one, so that's how they knew. But that was ridiculous, because there was no possible motive for such a thing, and the expense to penetrate a car agency and plant a bug to listen to a lone man who didn't talk to himself would be out of scale with any possible gain.

You are losing it, you old bastard, he thought, as he drove to the airport to fly back.

32

LITTLE ROCK, ARKANSAS
Two months earlier

LEON KAYE WAS the most respected rare-coin dealer in Little Rock, and his high-end retail outlet, The Coin, was swank, plush, serene, and soothing. There, he found and sold and bought and traded the most unusual specimens of the world's four-thousand-year history of money, with a mid-South clientele of many well-off collectors. If it was money, or looked like it, he was interested. He was represented as well on the Internet, which meant globally, and was an active traveler who would view and bid on spectacular items as they periodically came up. He dressed as one might expect, in sedate J.Press blazers and charcoal suits; shirts, blazing white, from Brooks Brothers; ties so trustworthy, they put you to sleep; and of course Alden wingtips, jet-black, and narrow in the British fashion. Manicured, buffed, coiffed, polished, shined, and blow-dried, he looked like a wealthy priss who'd been to Yale.

But there was another Leon Kaye whose eccentricities might have surprised, perhaps even dismayed, his many respectable clients. They never realized that he was also Mr. K of Little Rock's nine Mr. K's Pawn & Gun Shops, whose proud claim, on billboards all through the black, Hispanic, and poor-white neighborhoods of the Queen City, was *I Buy Gold. I Buy Silver. I Buy Diamonds. I Buy Guns! Hell, I Buy ANYTHING*. He did too. Then he sold it for more.

All his shops prospered, as a pawn license, extracted only via great criminal or political leverage from the Arkansas state licensing bureaucracy, was an excuse to xerox money. He also owned a few car washes, three strip malls, a laundromat, and the larger interest in a chain of Sonic Drive-Ins throughout the area. And a restaurant or two. And a porn shop or two. And a bar or seven, including three of the strip variety. He owned a Jeep agency, a country club, of which he was president and head of the greens committee, and a private airplane.

No one ever said of Leon that he lacked a nose for opportunity, and when opportunity came, he was shrewd in manipulating his way toward it. This is why he sat in the back room of The T&T & A$$ Club—his, naturally— in Little Rock's seedy little tenderloin, talking intently to two large men.

They were Braxton and Rawley Grumley. By profession, they were skip tracers, a sort of modern-day bounty hunter, by which effort they man-tracked those who'd skipped out on the money owed bail bondsmen—and bail bondsmen aren't the sort of fellows who can let such a thing happen. They take even the smallest sums quite seriously, and there is no humor or irony in their business. In all states, the law is vague on what skip tracers are allowed to do to recover the missing man, but some states allow more leni-ency than others. Arkansas allows a lot of leniency, which is why Braxton and Rawley had a ninety-seven percent recovery rate. They were extremely good at finding people, and though they looked like Country-Western sing-ers channeling '50s professional-wrestling-style types, they were technically adept, cunning, cruel, and relentless—all career prerequisites. It was also said they could be influenced to do certain other things for the right clients, and for the right fee, and nothing would ever be said about it.

They were large men, and one tended to notice them. They liked red or purple (or both) cowboy boots and belts, polyester jackets, paisley scarves, gold chains, tattoos of the figurative, heroic variety, and polished white teeth. Each had a blond pompadour and wore a selection of gaudy but ex-pensive rings on hefty fingers. If you looked at the fingers, you noticed the hands, and if you noticed the hands, you noticed the knuckles, and if you noticed the knuckles, you noticed the scars. They looked like their hobby was beating up radiators.

"All right," said Braxton, the more loquacious of the two, "we are here,

Mr. Kaye. You have our attention, and I assume you will soon be making us a pitch."

"Boys," said Mr. Kaye, who for this meeting had forsaken the Ivy trad look and was in jeans and a jean jacket—the so-called Arkansas Tuxedo— over a Carhartt work shirt, and who had driven to work not in his black Benz S but in his white Cadillac Escalade, with its vanity license plate I PAY CASH, "I want you to think back with me to the year 1934. Maybe you saw the movie *Public Enemies*? John Dillinger, Tommy guns, bank robberies, and, boys, think on this: cash. Lots and lots of cash. In thirteen months the Dillinger Gang stole over three hundred thousand dollars, and most of it was never recovered."

Mr. Kaye let that sink in, but Baxter and Rawley were not the type to be impressed by old-time crime stories.

"Sir, we are Grumley," said Braxton. "We have been working our side for one hundred and fifty years, against revenue agents, sheriffs, constables, federals, even congressional investigating committees. Millions done passed through the Grumley hands. That amount of swag, and supposed big shots like John Dillinger do not impress us, no more than a Moon Pie without a Dr Pepper to wash it down, so to speak, if you get my drift."

"I do, I do. However, three hundred thousand in cash is nothing to scoff at, but suppose—think about this—that cash were uncirculated 1934 bills, valued far more than for its face value. Depending on the bills, it could be worth twenty times as much, dispensed carefully and discreetly to collectors, of whom there are many. Three hundred thousand times twenty comes to six million dollars, and think how nice that would be, especially when the only thing you have to do is follow a seventy-year-old man who has a line on where it's buried. He has a map, he just ain't figured out what it's to."

"Is he dumb?"

"He's not. He'll figure it out. He's known for figuring it out. He always figures it out. He's working on it now. His father was good at figuring out before him, and his father's father before him. All of them, more or less, of the law. All of them, more or less, having conked many a head with the Grumley label. And that's the second part of this pleasure for you. It has a personal angle which you will oh so enjoy. So what I have for you is an odd confluence of opportunity. Cash money, unaccounted for and long forgotten, very rare, thus immensely valuable, untraceable in ways that many large sums might not be. Maybe other relics of extreme value. All of it being searched for by a fellow named Swagger, of the Polk County Swaggers. You know the family?"

"I know the family," said Braxton. Rawley cracked a pistachio between his large white molars, spit a spray of shell grit into the air, and ate the meat.

"There's Grumley sleeping eternally underground, and four or so yet in prison because this Swagger fellow got involved in preventing a certain Grumley enterprise at the Bristol Speedway," said Braxton.

"I know that."

"What else do you know?"

"His daddy, Earl, was involved in the so-called Veterans' Revolt of 1946, which was far bloodier than history tells us. Grumley deaths occurred in a plethora of Hot Springs shoot-outs, and in the end the town's spirit was broken, and instead of becoming Las Vegas, it became another decaying Southern town that the Interstate passes by. Earl was also, for a time, the bodyguard of the famous Congressman Uckley, a power in Washington in the 'forties and 'fifties, which made him untouchable, though in the end he got touched. The father's father was Polk County sheriff, way back in the 'twenties and 'thirties. He worked close with Judge Tyne's machine, and whenever the machine had to enforce its will on the unruly Grumley, Grumley head got busted, Grumley tail went to prison, and Charles Swagger did the busting and imprisoning. Does all this sound familiar?"

"We are well versed in our own family history," said Braxton. "Grumley have long memories."

"I thought Grumley might. So listen hard, fellows . . . More pistachios, Braxton?"

"*I'm* Braxton," said Braxton. "I don't eat pistachios. That's Rawley, with the pistachios. I talk for both, but don't think he ain't listening because he is, very carefully. He's the smart one. I just got the gift of gab."

Mr. Kaye nodded, and proceeded with his story. A short time ago, he had been approached by a fine Little Rock law firm to advise them on an old piece of money. Imagine his amazement when it turned out to be an AC 1934-A thousand-dollar bill of a very rare variety. It was a Friedberg 2212-G, graded as 66EPQ by PMG. Rated "Gem Uncirculated." Pretty close to perfect. It was easily worth ten thousand dollars on its own, and with a pack of uncirculated siblings still linked by Mint seal, its value went up astronomically. So Mr. Kaye advised the young associate who had sought the appointment and arrived with the bill, sensibly sealed in plastic. The young man was not discreet, as so many of them aren't, and soon revealed to Mr. Kaye that it had been recovered from a strongbox in the foundation of a house being torn down. And the strongbox included some other items, including a .45 automatic, an FBI badge, an odd metal contrivance that could have been a machine-gun part, and a map of some sort that pointed to yet more buried treasure, but was oriented to the wall of a structure that was only known to the creator of the map.

"Not hard to do some inferring, now is it?" asked Mr. Kaye. "Nineteen thirty-four was the year of the big bank robberies, the Dillinger–Baby Face Nelson–Pretty Boy Floyd combine. As I say, three hundred thousand dollars in all vanished, never to be recovered. The badge and pistol suggest that the grandfather may have been, for some time at least, an agent, as any history of the Bureau will tell you that in 1934 Mr. Hoover took in a batch of Western and Southern gunfighters to go bullet to bullet against the Dillingers. Charles Swagger of Blue Eye, victor in the famous Blue Eye First National shoot-out of 1923, and First World War hero, in two armies, might certainly have been one, and they would have been well served by him. There was indeed lots of killing. Gunfights all over the Midwest, agents down, gangsters down. But, as I say, no big-money stash ever turned up.

"Now we have a direct link to those days, direct evidence of purloined money taken in robbery but also not returned to authorities, as perhaps Charles Swagger, accustomed to the Arkansas way of doing things, might have allowed himself. I have made discreet inquiries and I have learned that the grandson, Bob Lee Swagger, seventy years old but spry, also a war hero, as well as a rancher, father, businessman, and a man bent on weird quests for his own private satisfaction, is now researching his grandfather and trying to find out what happened. A necessary part of that search will be placing the map against its palimpsest—"

"Its say what, Jack?"

"Ah, its objective correlative."

Rawley spit a large gunk of pistachio off into space. It landed on Mr. Kaye's desk.

"Its thing, whatever it is that is the basis of the diagram. As described to me—I have not seen it—it's a crude penciled rendering of the wall of some kind of building, with a diagonal, broken line radiating from a given point to the northwest, delineating about ten steps, orienting to and just passing a circle that must denote a tree trunk. There, X marks the spot, and I'm guessing the X might be something that Charles Swagger made off with in 1934 when his FBI career came to an end. Whatever this is will certainly be of value, perhaps great value. Would it not be a shame if, at that moment, Mr. Swagger were interrupted, his family legacy taken from him and put to other, more profitable uses. Imagine how disappointed he'd be."

"Hmm," said Braxton.

"You have the means to make this happen?"

"Sir, we track men for a living. This is easily doable by us, discreetly and with sophistication. So what remains is the deal."

"Seventy/thirty?"

"Seventy for us, thirty for you."

"Now, boys, let's not get greedy. Standard recovery in your business is fifteen percent. I give you twice that to show good faith. You have to show good faith too. And I believe I qualify for a Grumley family discount, since Grumley accounts will be settled."

"Perhaps. Sixty-forty, but you pick up expenses."

"Sixty-five /thirty-five. Yes to expenses, but only with receipts. No 'Miscellaneous: $68,925.32,' or anything like that."

"And," said Braxton, "the haircut fee."

"The haircut fee?"

33

624 NOYES
CHICAGO
August 1934

CHARLES WORKED FOURTEEN STRAIGHT DAYS, after his two days off, and didn't have another day to himself until halfway through the month. On that day, he ate the usual diner breakfast, while he read more fairy tales in the *Trib* and *Herald-Examiner*, checked yesterday's ball scores and saw Tietje had taken another loss for the Sox, making his fine showing at the game Charles saw even more of an oddity. It was probably too late for them to make much of a move anyway, and it was equally clear the North Siders weren't going to do anything memorable either. In a few weeks, college football would begin, but Charles had no feeling for Illinois teams and doubted the papers would pay much attention to the Arkansas Razorbacks. Maybe all this crap would be wrapped up before then and he'd get back in time to follow the season. But he doubted it, as Baby Face sightings were random and refused to fit into any pattern, and he'd heard nothing from Uncle Phil. And the same was true of others on the Public Enemies list, like Pretty Boy, Homer, the Barkers, and Alvin Karpis. Lots of work left to do.

He had two jobs to do today. First, he had to buy a car. He was tired of all this public transportation, or signing out, then signing in, a Bureau Ford or Hudson, which every hood in Chicago recognized as Division cars anyhow. The buy took an hour and a half, the transaction facilitated by him paying in cash from the squirrel fund he'd brought north with him. There was a place up Halsted, a garage run by a Mulligan, who was an ex-cop and gave the boys in blue and State Troopers, as well as G- and T-Men, good deals. Charles paid three hundred fifty dollars for a 1933 dark green

four-door Pontiac, a flat-8, said to be in good shape. He was more drawn to
a Plymouth coupe, but he saw that the Pontiac would do better for hauling
agents around, if it ever came to that, and wife and child, if he ever got back
to that.

That set him up for his second job, the dinner he would have at Sam's
place that night in Evanston. In the big new car, the drive was easily handled, pleasant. No traffic on the Outer Drive. The city fathers were glamor-
ously developing the lakefront, and new hotels, including a pink thing called
the Edgewater Beach, were rising, turning the zone into a kind of Miami.

At Belmont, the drive turned into the traffic-light-stunted Sheridan
Road, and Charles poked through the edge of the North Side until he
reached a cemetery, said to be a holding spot for gangsters waiting to get
into hell, that marked the passage between Chicago and the pleasant city
of Evanston. Evanston had elms, lots of them, and old, big houses, lots of
them, and colleges, lots of them, and traffic, not so much of it. Within a few
minutes, he found the intersection of Sheridan and Noyes, turned left, and
halfway down the block came to 624, a vast place roughly thrown together
of brown timber and sandstone boulders. It had porches everywhere and a
roof line as complicated as Texas history, with gables and mansards and
crests somehow forming a whole, which seemed to indicate an interior rich
in passageways, secret rooms, unexpected stairways, closets everywhere,
odd-shaped bedrooms, as if sort of invented on the spot, not drawn from
any plan. The house sat under trees, between Sheridan and the next main
stem, an Orrington Avenue, on a large chunk of land, guarded by a front
porch that looked like the entrance to a castle of some sort. The whole thing
in fact was a castle or fortress in mentality, presumably unassailable by anything short of Big Bertha or some other piece of Krupp hellaciousness.

He parked, went up the stairs, knocked, and Sam opened, immaculate in
three-piece and tie, and brought him in. Charles was glad he'd worn his
own suit, though he didn't ever *not* wear it.

If the atmosphere outside was Medieval, the atmosphere inside was childish. Children lived here, lots of them, and their smell, clutter, noise, and busi-

ness were everywhere. Sam led him through a foyer to a grand living room that ran half the length of the house, uttering pleasantries.

"Thanks so much for coming up, Charles. I hope it wasn't difficult."

"No problem, a nice night for a drive."

"Pardon the mess, but having six children is like having six horses under the same roof. You never get it cleaned up, you just get the mess under control, temporarily. Here, meet the brood and the heroic brood mare. KIDS!" he yelled.

They seemed to come out of holes in the walls, from under the furniture, through windows, down chutes and up ladders, more or less assembling themselves into a skittish mass of constrained energy and temporary attention. He was introduced one by one to towheaded boys and girls cut from the same perfect mold, running from fourteen years down to fourteen months, all more or less clean, more or less civil, but minds clearly set on adventures and mischief, not the tall, stolid figure before them.

Then the Mrs. Her name was Betty, still a beauty, tawny, blond, and sturdy. She'd been cooking but disengaged easily enough and greeted Charles graciously, making him feel her whole purpose in life was to ease his way. She was like one of those good officers' wives he'd met in the war stateside, a campaigner, game, tough, worked like a dog without a complaint, and always there for everybody who needed her.

It wasn't lost on Charles that this was a life worth aspiring to: respect, progeny, the best in shelter, prosperity, the best that America had to offer a man from nowhere, as he was, as Sam was.

"I'll spare you the tour," Sam said. "Unless you like socks, dirty underwear, unmade beds, broken toys, dolls missing heads, single shoes, and the odor of a monkey den."

Charles laughed.

"Sounds like a few barracks I've been in," he said. "Don't think it would faze me much."

"Actually, now that we've got a little time, I'd like to talk to you. Away from the office, so that no one will worry about it and spread rumors and

Hugh Clegg won't panic and wire the Director and Mel won't figure it's about him and call a news conference."

"Sure," said Charles.

"I could use a drink. I'm Mormon, but since I'm also an Elder, I grant myself one day's dispensation. Not sure you're a drinker."

"I had a bad spell with the hooch when I got back from the war. But I got myself straightened out. I don't drink the hard, but I can handle a beer or two."

"Sounds good. Honey, can you open a couple Schlitzes? We'll be on the patio."

"Be right out," Betty called, cheerily, from the kitchen.

Sam led him out a rear door, where they found a patio raised above ground level, a little redoubt from which a lord could survey his fief. The backyard seemed immense and it opened all the way around the side of the house. But as usual, trees everywhere, shrubs, the whole range of chlorophyll-kingdom enterprises, lurking, climbing, blossoming. Through the foliage, other equally prosperous houses were visible.

"Very nice here," said Charles.

"I didn't want the kids in the city. Evanston turned out to be perfect. They have a six-block walk to school, up Orrington Avenue. It's a great school, I'm told, equal to anything in the East."

"Beautiful place," said Charles.

"The traffic isn't bad if I drive, but mostly I just take a two-block walk to the El. Straight up Noyes. Gets me downtown in forty minutes."

"That's why you keep such long hours, I guess," Charles said.

"I hope you like steak, Charles. Betty's got three of the best rib eyes out there I've ever seen. She'll get the kids down—we won't put you through our mess-hall family-dinner ordeal, nobody deserves that."

"It sounds great, Sam. Thanks so much for having me. I was getting tired of diner cooking."

Betty came out and served the two beers in tall glasses, frosty up top, glistening with dew, yearning to be consumed. Charles lifted his, clanked a toast with Sam, who said, "To the end of the journey," and each took a draught.

It was good, as Charles knew it would be, and it opened longings that he felt but knew he was strong enough to withstand. Now, what was this going to be? Had someone seen him with the known Italian Uncle Phil? Was he in trouble? Had Hugh Clegg brought off some coup to have him exiled, which was the same as having him fired, since he wouldn't stay in the Division without Sam? Had some rumor, a suspicion, about a favor he may or may not have done for someone in Hot Springs in 1926 emerged? What the hell would this be?

"Charles, first off, between us, I just wanted to thank you for what you've brought to the office. I can't begin to tell you how grateful I am."

"Sam, I'm just doing my duty. Nothing special—"

"No, no, hear me out. You see, one of the things I have to know about is weakness. And I know my own as well as I know Clegg's scheming bitterness and Mel's vanity and Ed Hollis's lack of a first-class brain. Here's mine, Charles: I don't like the violence. To be honest, it scares me. Maybe I've got too much to lose, unlike some of the others—"

"Sam, nobody likes the violence."

"Well, I really don't like it. So it was important to me that I find somebody who knew it, could lead the boys through it and bring most of them home, who was as brave as he was honorable, who would be the me I could never be. I couldn't have done better. My first choice, Frank Hamer, with his big ways and hunger for glory, would have been a disaster, I see that now. Charles Swagger has been my finest triumph."

"We'll get you trained on the guns, and when you know how to shoot, the ugly stuff won't be a problem. The guns will get you through it."

"Well, perhaps. But there is one other thing I wanted to say, do you mind?"

"Not at all."

"I've been meaning to have this conversation with you ever since you stood wide open on that hill and fired at Baby Face. But when I learned you told the boys—no, they didn't tell me, they told a pal who told a pal who told a pal who finally was overheard by someone who was not a pal—that you went straight into Johnny's gunhand because you knew if he got a shot off it would be into you and nobody else—I realized I had to act. That accounts for this overly engineered little tête-à-tête."

"Yes sir?" said Charles.

"Charles . . . do you know what a 'death wish' is?"

34

SAN ANTONIO, TEXAS

August 1934

COURTESY OF HELEN AND J.P.'S ADVENTURING, they stayed at the Aurora Hotel, one of the city's nicest, a couple blocks from the old fort where the Texans had stood off the Mexicans for so long, setting a standard for bravery in the face of treachery and force for all, including bank robbers, to admire. And these bank robbers did.

But history's charms ran out quickly enough, and soon enough they turned to nourishment, which the old city offered in abundance. They ate well, in the Aurora's elegant dining room or the superb Mexican restaurants the town boasted. It was a streetcar city, and the amble of the big cars down the thoroughfares under wires that popped sparks at every junction was its own special pleasure, a kind of ongoing spectacle out-of-towners never tired of. But it was also a pastel-and-ocher city, in the colors of the desert, and it had the warm-climate casualness that outsiders find so appealing, and the availability of a smiling peasant class to facilitate all transactions. It was a city that wore its pride and grandeur well, like a beautiful gown.

They had plenty of money, at least for now, even if the unexpected triumph of five crisp, new thousand-dollar bills couldn't be touched.

"That stuff is so hot we'd end up in the stir before nightfall if we tried to pass it," Les said.

"Maybe I should have left it there. Who knew it'd be so much trouble?" said J.P. They sat on the balcony of Les and Helen's room, which overlooked the gently Hispanic city.

"Nah," said Les, "you were right to grab it. We'll hang on to it. It'll cool off, and somewhere along the line we can pass it off at a good rate, maybe in Reno. Right now, we wouldn't get one-for-five, but by this time next year it'll go easily for four-on-the-fiver. That's close to standard, can't bitch about that."

"Good idea, Les," said J.P., as if ever in his life he could have said, "Bad idea, Les." His submission was as complete as it was weirdly satisfying to him. It completed him.

"Tell you what," said Les. "We'll peel one of 'em off and put it in the getaway bag, with a few guns and some ammo, some license plates, something to grab if the Division starts to blast us. On the run, we can spend it, because we're moving so fast, and by the time they track it back to where it was passed, we'll be long gone. One way or the other."

"That's good," said J.P.

Both men had their feet up and were relaxed, coats off, ties loosened. Helen had gone to Frost's, the great San Antonio department store, to buy a few new frocks, as she was sick to death of the ones in her suitcase that she washed out every night after wearing. She'd earned a few new dresses, Les thought.

"So, tomorrow Lebman. I called him, he's expecting us at eleven and is very eager for the business."

Hyman Lebman was a great mystery to many of his gangster clients. No doubt, he was a talented gunsmith, and could modify a good gun into a perfect gun, almost too clever to use on the job yet too lethal not to use—but what did he know about his customers and the uses to which they put his brilliance? He pretended to know nothing.

If he was faking it, he was faking it brilliantly. He could be with Les and Johnny, showing them some work of genius—like his adaptation of the Colt Government Model automatic into a machine pistol, complete with compensator, twenty-two-round magazine, and Thompson grip, which Les had used to great effect on Carter Baum the night of the escape from Little Bohemia—and at the same time be completely oblivious to their identities. He just thought, or pretended he just thought, they were new-money oil millionaires giving their adolescent selves a fun binge, with a love of guns so intense, it had taken them beyond the normal range of hunting and target-shooting firearms. Their hobbies seemed to be acquiring the still-legal fully automatics and retiring to an obscure corner of the ranch for a few hours' and a few thousand rounds' worth of shooting holes at anything in front of them, amid a clatter of noise, a storm of dust, and a spray of debris. It seemed to suggest a sort of polo-with-machine-guns kind of life.

If anything else was involved, it never occurred to Mr. Lebman, who either made no connection between his clients and the massacres and bullet blizzards of the Midwest or, again, did a fine job of impersonating someone who made no connection.

That was fine all around. The guns were perfectly legal, no laws were broken—well, the National Firearms Act had just been passed in June, but it seemed nobody was much interested in enforcing it for now—and it freed Mr. Lebman to his own pleasures, mainly leatherwork, as he was also extremely skilled at that craft and his saddles and bridles were prized among the high-swell class of Texan.

So the next day, at 11, just outside the Flores Street shop in downtown San Antonio, a block from city hall and the police department, across the street from the sheriff's department, Les and J.P. pulled in. Both were smartly turned out after the fashion of the big-money gun aficionado, and they entered the store. It had the rich smell of leather to it, and was decorated with the owner's more flamboyant enterprises—saddles with elaborate scrollwork carved into them, bridles and reins, cuffs and chaps, which displayed the same kind of bas-relief tapestry.

"Is the boss around?" Les asked a clerk behind the counter, who was showing a silver buckle to a richly appointed cowboy millionaire.

"Sir, he's in back waiting for you."

"Great," said Les. He and J.P. went back, opened the door, and passed into another universe. Now they were in the world of ordnance.

No leather smell back here. Instead, the fragrance of Hoppe's No. 9, the ubiquitous bore solvent to the shooting fraternity, mingled with odors of petroleum lubricants of various densities, for one wouldn't oil a machine-gun bolt with the same delicate vintage one used on a tiny Colt .25 automatic pistol.

It was like a library of guns down here. The walls were lined with fine hunting rifles, many of foreign manufacture, as Lebman considered the European gunmakers far ahead of the American when it came to hunting rifles. A Mauser, a Mannlicher, or a Westley Richards far outshone their cruder American counterparts from Winchester and Remington and Marlin. Now, pistols were a different story. No one had surpassed the genius of Mr. Browning when it came to the automatic pistol, and Mr. Smith and Mr. Wesson had shown the world how to build a revolver, though the Colt revolver was a treasure, particularly its Officers Model that rode in so many police holsters, or its sawed-off cousin, the Detective Special, which many a plainclothesman carried tucked away. An ample supply of all these variants, plus dozens more, lay in shelves on either side of the place.

"Mr. Lebman, sir, how are you?" Les called, all charm and willed charisma. He could be a gentleman to you if he had decided not to kill you. Besides, he loved guns, he loved Mr. Lebman, he loved this place. He felt at home, happy, safe, which might be why he kept coming back.

"Mr. Smith," said Lebman, looking up from a bench where he'd been filing tiny checks into the grip of a Government Model with his strong, greasy hands, watching his progress through a jeweler's loupe. He rose, pushed the loupe up, stopping to wipe his hands, and then put one hand out. "Back in town, eh? So good to see you!"

"You know my associate, Mr. Davis?"

"Howdy," said J.P., and Lebman nodded.

"Still having great fun with the machine pistol," said Les. "I do think I like the .38 Super better than the .45. You need more weight in the gun to compensate for a .45's recoil, but the .38 doesn't move off its target at all."

"But was it designed to be a bull's-eye gun?"

"Hell, no. I like to get up close with it and just press the trigger. It's empty in a second, and whatever I'm shooting at looks like it lost a fight with a hand grenade."

Everybody laughed.

"Now, I heard you might have a little something I'd be interested in adding to my collection. That's why I'm here," said Les.

"I bet I know what it is," said Mr. Lebman.

"Folks do talk to folks, and you hear things. So I heard you had this particular piece. Hard to come by, I'm told."

"And you know, Mr. Smith, 'hard to come by' means 'hard to pay for.'"

"I do indeed," said Les. "Fortunately, we hit a new gusher on some property across the river, so I just have so much money coming in, I don't know what to do with it. I'd give it to the poor, but that would be communistic. So I'll just spend it, thinking that Texas has been mighty nice to me."

"Okay," said Lebman. "And you know the law has changed on us, so there's a new level of discretion advised. You understand that?"

"Jimmie 'Discretion' Smith, that's me. Fair price for the merchandise, lips sealed at no extra cost."

"Well, maybe we can do some business," said Mr. Lebman. "But not out here, where anyone might walk in. Hoping you'll come back at closing time, and when the doors are locked and the lights out, we'll see what we can come up with."

"Sounds square to me," said Les.

35

I T WAS BOILERPLATE, but it was good boilerplate, and he knew it well. He'd eked it out several years ago. Jen had helped him, when it got too tangled and the tenses threatened to go atomic, and he'd tested it enough times to know it worked. It's what came of a bit of fame in a little pond in the boondocks. But he took some pride in doing it well, an old guy with buzz haircut, a face that looked like raw leather beaten with a crowbar, a weird gait to his walk, and a wardrobe perfect—just perfect—for 1957.

"Now, I know we have a new president," he concluded, "and it's too early to tell which direction we'll be going, how wise, how just, how reasonable, how reluctant to use force, but also how willing to use force, hard and fierce, when it's called for. But I do know this, from hard-earned experience: if and when the time comes, the president—and you and I—can count on the United States Marine Corps, thank you very much."

Standard, but given meaning and dignity by the history he carried with him, having acquired it in rough zones. The applause was exuberant and he smiled, though tightly—he did everything tightly—and returned to his seat on the dais.

The banquet room of the Boise Hilton had been turned into a Temple to the United States Marine. Iconographic images dominated the walls, and the tables were full of prominent men, many former marines, many well into what passed for "establishment" in Idaho, who wished to share the marine feeling, express their belief and honor in country and service, and of course make business contacts and hand out cards. The chicken had been fine, the green beans not so fine, the bread awful, and he'd been speaking during dessert, so he'd missed the sheet cake with whipped cream and a pineapple chunk. Now, at the end of the evening, coffee was being served, and people were beginning to trail out.

"Nice job, Bob," said Dr. Bill Tillotson, the vet and friend who'd asked him to do this gig as a favor, and, being involved in business with Bill, Bob had been unable to say no. It was okay. A few others leaned over, offering nice words, while on the dais the president of the Idaho chapter of the league was wrapping up routine business before signaling the end of the evening.

Bob just sat there, slightly exhausted. It takes it out of you, and it took it out of him more than others because of his seemingly genetic recessiveness. He'd never thought, and couldn't have predicted, his business would be such a success, but things just took off, and he dealt with it as well as he could. Some cross to bear! he sometimes joked to himself.

But now the slight buzz of anxiety gone, he was free to relax and let his eyes find occupation in the photographs of marine history around the room. Of course he couldn't see the most famous, which was mounted directly behind him, and showed the flag raising on Suribachi, caught in a freak moment of exquisitely designed perfection that seemed to sum up the marine experience in the war: filthy, exhausted men, sublime grace.

His eyes passed to others, and other wars, until he came to his real favorite, because it seemed to sum up his father's war, though it was taken on an island his father never set foot on. It lacked the Iwo symmetry, and caught more of the awkwardness of combat, how men just did the best they could, and were almost always completely un-self-conscious as to how they looked or appeared, though the marines in the shot certainly looked solid enough. It had been taken on Wana Ridge, in the last great battle and slaughter of the war, Okinawa, in May of 1945, where the Japanese were determined to teach the Americans what an invasion of the home islands would cost them. Swagger had gotten interested in it once, and knew that the marine with the Thompson was named Davis T. Hargraves, and the BAR gunner, Gabriel Chavarria, and that they were from F Company, 2nd Battalion, 1st

Regiment, 1st Marine Division. Both survived the war; both even revisited this spot fifty years later.

Hargraves stood upright on a slope of ruin, almost in perfect profile, against a landscape of shattered and leafless brush, and leaned into his Thompson. Somehow, he achieved a shooting position that was range-perfect, braced into the gun formally, locking it against his shoulder by the strong backwards pressure of his right-hand clutch on the pistol grip, his left arm also locked, pulling hard against the forearm piece and drawing it back into the shoulder for as much muscle as could be brought to bear on ten pounds of sheer weight and highly volatile recoil energy. His head perfectly aligned, so that his right eye precisely indexed both rear and front sights, he was in the act of firing—carefully, in light of the mandates of marksmanship—a burst at a Japanese sniper fifty or so yards away. Given his position, he probably didn't miss. Just beyond him, Chavarria is pivoting to action with his BAR, rising from a crouch and following his comrade's fire to the target so that he might fire too.

But the photo always had its little mysteries, primarily the magazine in Hargrave's weapon. It was a twenty-rounder, a short, stubby thing. Why? Why, in an environment rich in both danger and targets, would you carry the smaller, twenty-round magazine instead of the longer, thirty-round magazine? An extra ten .45s could have saved somebody's, including the gunner's, life. Swagger could never look at the picture and not wonder.

Well, a couple possibilities suggested themselves. The thirty-rounders weren't designed until 1942, and didn't reach general distribution until 1943, so, in the meantime, plenty of twenty-rounders were in use. When the thirties came, no one bothered to collect the twenties. So they were equally accessible throughout the war. Maybe Davis Hargraves, who clearly would have begun the assault on Wana that morning with as much ammunition as he could carry, had used all his thirties and was now working his way through his few twenties. Or—this game was always fun!—possibly he thought General Thompson's trench broom balanced better with the weight of the twenties, was more maneuverable in the busy, vegetation-clotted, and cratered surface of Wana on that May day. It could be either of those. Or a host of others.

Swagger smiled. He wished he was still a drinking man. Here's to you, young Hargraves, and your buddy Chavarria, at the point of the spear, doing what had to be done, not because you loved it, but because it was a thing called Duty, and your generation—his father's as well—had a war dumped in their laps and didn't whine, complain, explain, they just went out and won the fucking thing, and Davis, standing stoic and stark against the Wana sky, was an emblem of just that.

"You okay?" said Bill.

"Ah! Yeah, fine. That picture, the guy with the Thompson. I always tighten up a little. Reminds me of my father."

"God bless him," said Bill.

"And all who went ashore with him. They were the best."

At that point, his eyes drifted. The photo, blown up so big, revealed itself in ways its publication in books or on the Net never did.

"You always notice something new," he said to Dr. Tillotson.

"What do you mean?" said the vet.

"I must have looked at that image five thousand times in my life. Yet not to this day did I notice something strange about the BAR that Chavarria is holding. Do you see?"

For those not of the gun, Swagger's ruminations may have seemed insane. But Dr. Tillotson had hunted on six continents and had the biggest trophy hall in Idaho, except for some oil people. He knew what a BAR was.

"I don't see anything," he said.

"Look at the muzzle. He's removed the compensator. It's just got a blunt muzzle. He must have been a strong guy, he didn't need any help holding the thing on target, though a .30 Government kicks like hell, especially in full auto. But—and I'm only guessing here—he must not have liked the upward flash signature the slots in the compensator created. The flash might have blocked his sight. He wanted to see what he was shooting at. I can't think of anything else that"—that's when it hit him, hit him so hard, finally, that it knocked him out of the moment, and he had to somehow get back into it enough to finish the sentence—"uh, would explain it."

He saw in his mind the standard BAR compensator as he remembered it from his own infantry days in the early '60s. From there, it was a small step to the realization that the odd, twelve-slotted cylinder he had been unable to identify was exactly the same length and, by measurement, also .30 caliber. It wouldn't have been included in any machinegun.com website or books because it wasn't technically a machine gun; it was, by definition or sheer whimsy of the Ordnance Department, an "automatic rifle." So it followed that perhaps at some point, in some forgotten iteration, some godforsaken experiment, or something, someone might have tried to increase the propulsive power of the compensator by enlarging the vault in which the expanding gases were trapped before they spit out of the twelve slots that dissected the roof of the cylinder to hold the muzzle down to counteract the principle of action/reaction. He could recall no such thing in his experience, but, then again, neither he nor anybody knew all the guns in the world.

It made some kind of sense if there had been such a BAR variation.

The hours elasticized into decades, then generations, before he got back to the computer in his house in Cascade.

"How did it go?" Jen called.

"Swell, fine," he yelled in a tone that meant "I'm obsessed."

He got on, googled Browning Automatic Rifle.

And that's when he discovered the Monitor.

It was another second before he realized that that's what Baby Face was doing in Mavis, Arkansas, in the week after the shooting of Johnny D. He was traveling to San Antonio, Texas, and the shop of Hyman Lebman, the gangster gunsmith and merchant. Lebman would be exactly the sort of man to sell him a Monitor.

Now, what the hell did he need a Monitor for?

Swagger realized: he had to go to San Antonio and visit what was left of Hyman Lebman, what was left of Baby Face Nelson, and, possibly, what was left of Charles Swagger.

36

THE PATIO
624 NOYES
CHICAGO
August 1934

"Have you ever heard that term, Charles? Death wish?"

They sat on the patio of the big house.

"No, can't say I have."

"Do you have any idea what it could mean?"

This was not Charles's game. He liked the real, the practical, the hard-edged world. Thinking deeply about things that couldn't be seen or touched held no appeal for him.

"Well, in the war," he groped, as the twilight came on and the lightning bugs began their illuminated pulses, "sometimes there'd be men who just couldn't take it. It was tough, you know, the shelling, the snipers, the raids and counterraids, the mud and filth, the pressure of seeing buddies killed, and, after a while, it was hard to believe in anything, especially the future. It was said—I never saw it in the American army but I heard about it in the Canadian, where we were involved in what they called trench warfare; you know, living in mud, just waiting to get hit, for months and months—it was said that some men just gave up and walked into the German guns. Would that be a death wish?"

"Very good, Charles. That would be a death wish at the most practical level, an immediate response to an immediate and overwhelming stimulus, with no end, no relief, in sight, and all social pressure demanding that you stick it out while everything inside you screamed to run away. Yes, that would be a death wish."

"But that's not what you meant. I can tell by your tone. You meant something else, and I haven't figured it out. I guess in your sense of the term, no, I ain't never heard of a death wish."

Where is this going? he wondered. He also knew he did not like not knowing where it was going. He hated not knowing what to do or say, being on the spot like this. What did it prove? How did it help?

"There's some new theories of how the mind works, Charles. Recent findings in medicine and thought processes. Some folks believe that your mind is divided into two parts. One part, where you live, operate, talk, love, fornicate, work, shoot—whatever—that part is called the conscious. It's everything you know, feel, or remember. It's everything you think or believe."

"Yes sir."

"But, as I said, some folks believe there's a second, hidden part to your mind. It's called the subconscious and it lurks beneath. It never forgets; it harbors urges, secret pains, angers, grudges, even the impulse to resort to violence. And in some ways, at some times, it reaches out and influences what you do. And you don't even know it. You're confronted with choice A or B, and clearly A is the best choice but somehow you are compelled to choose B. That's your subconscious working, influencing you to act, in some respects, against your best interests and to do things that otherwise make no sense at all. Do you see?"

Not really.

"Well, I suppose it's possible."

"Look, say, at these two men, John Dillinger and Baby Face Nelson. Johnny, who's from a conventional and quite decent farm family, is sent to prison early after doing something stupid. In prison, the kings are the bank robbers; he falls in with them, learns from them, and gets his whole education and orientation from them. He, quite logically, wants to please them—they're his real fathers—and sets out to become the biggest and best bank robber ever. See how it fits together?"

"Sure."

"But then there's Nelson. There's no criminal in his family. But there's a drunken father who beats his mother in front of him and he feels weak and worthless because he can't stand up for her. He hates himself. As he grows up, that hatred transfers into a generalized hatred of society. There's no influence on him, no bank robbers educating him and setting an example for him. It's all in his mind, and somehow he sees the banks specifically, and society generally, as his father, and now that he's brave and strong, he has this need to strike at his father. He does so by becoming a bank robber and, unlike Johnny, he's especially vicious, he likes to kill. He hates law enforcement and takes pleasure in killing symbols of authority, like Carter Baum. That's his subconscious working on him, making him do things that he doesn't fully understand but can't stop doing."

"He sounds nuts to me," said Charles.

"He is, in a way. That doesn't make him innocent, it just makes sense out of him."

"So you're saying this subconscious thing can help us catch him."

"Well, yes, but there is more to it than that . . . Here, let's have another beer."

Charles didn't want another beer. He wanted to get out of there. This whole line of talk was giving him the heebie-jeebies. It was so far above his head.

"Betty, another couple Schlitzes, please," Sam called, and in seconds she was there with two bottles.

"You two are *so* serious," she said. "Now, no more. I'm going to put the steaks on. Charles, how do you like yours?"

Normalcy! How do you like your meat? Another beer? Gravy for the potatoes or not? This was stuff he understood. But then she turned away and he was again alone on the patio, with the humming of insects and the squawking of birds. And Sam.

"See, he may have a death wish in there too," said Sam. "He hates himself for being so helpless where his mother was concerned. So he thinks he should be punished. So he takes insane risks. A part of him secretly wants the punishment of the bullet, has sought out a dangerous occupation and for that reason is unafraid in battle, because he welcomes the finishing shot. From the outside, it makes no sense. But it could from the inside."

"Well, when you put it like that, I suppose it could make some sense."

"I'm going this way not because I'm interested in them but because I'm interested in, and care for, you," Sam continued. "I want to see you get back to Arkansas, get your youngest boy some high-quality help, make peace with the older boy so that he can understand what a brave and honorable man his father is. He deserves that. *You* deserve that."

"I hope it works out like that, sure."

"But do you really hope it does, Charles? Does your subconscious hope it does? You see, when I look at your heroism, I see something in there too. A crazy recklessness, a willingness to die for the cause, for any cause, for no cause, just to die. That's why you put yourself way out front at both these shooting events you've been through, and I bet that happened in all your other gunfights, going back to raids in the war. It wasn't just heroism; it was also a subconscious need for death. It was pure death wish."

"Sam, I don't feel nothing like that."

"You can't feel it. I mention it to get it out in the open, to get you thinking about it. If you get killed, I want it to be because it was Duty, not because you took wild, crazy-heroic, reckless, completely unnecessary chance number two hundred forty-five and you finally cashed out."

"See," said Charles, "in a fight you have to be aggressive and reckless. That's how you win. Get close, shoot straight, keep moving. It's common sense, not something underneath."

It was such an odd conversation to have on the patio of a suburban mansion, amid the beauty and serenity of the well-achieved life, surrounded by comfort, ease, the succor of mild weather, the glow of a setting sun. Who could believe such a conversation would take place in such a place?

"Just hear me out," said Sam. "I think it's working like this. Somewhere in you is a secret. You've buried it way down deep, so deep you've trained yourself never to think about it. It's something you know is wrong, whatever it is, something you did, something you are, that I don't know, that I can't imagine. I know you hate it. It shames you. It tarnishes your ideal of your-self, it makes the man you want to be unattainable. You would do anything to make it go away, but you have no tools. It's an enemy that can't be shot or arrested; it never goes away and comes out at the worst times. At some level, you believe you should be punished for holding it."

"Wish my damned life were that interesting. I'm a country boy with a knack for the pistol, that's all there is."

"You're too brave and honorable to ever commit suicide, so the pain just lingers. So you are attracted to behaviors where you could easily get killed. You want God to kill you. You want him to punish you, so you give him chance after chance after chance, starting with the war. Put me out of my misery, you're saying to him. All those bullets that missed, you just want one of them to hit and end the whole thing."

"Never heard such stuff," said Charles. "Honest to god, Mr. Cowley, I don't have no idea what you're talking about."

"Nor would you. That's the point, Charles. This stuff is far below the surface."

"Well, I suppose I'll keep my eye on it, then," Charles said.

"I see other things too, Charles. Your style is solitude. Most of the other men marry and live with their families, or, if they're bachelors, they share apartments to save on expenses. They're always around other folks, they're part of a community. Charles lives alone in a small apartment. He doesn't hang out with any pals, he doesn't have any close office friends, he never goes drinking with the boys or bowling or to ball games. He's pure loner. He's separated himself from society. Maybe to keep himself pure, maybe because he's never relaxed around other people, maybe because he's afraid his secret will come out. It's not natural."

"Sir, I'm just trying to do the job y'all gave me best I can. All this other stuff, I don't know enough to even answer."

"Charles, you know I was a missionary, and for two years I lived in Ha-waii. Those people are different. They have no repressions, they hold noth-ing back, they just are what they are. Sometimes I think that must be the better way. We hold, hide, bury, smother, pound, deny our feelings, and the result is, we make them worse, not better. The Hawaiians, who act on every impulse and hold nothing back, are far healthier and happier. The only thing our civilization is doing is teaching them to be unhappy like us."

"Yes sir."

"So all I am saying, Charles, is this. You can talk to me anytime, and you need have no fear of holding anything back. Nothing can shock me, not after two years in the tropics. And if you uncover a secret, you will find that sharing it with someone who cares is the best medicine in the world. It's penicillin for the mind."

"Yes sir."

"I will be so disappointed, Charles, if you die racing into fire not because you have to but because your subconscious wants you to. What a waste that would be of the many gifts you bring to us. What a loss to your boys, the community, the Division. Charles, together we can work this thing out, I swear."

"Boys, it's dinnertime!" yelled Betty.

37

L EBMAN EMERGED WITH his trophy in both hands, shoulders bent to demonstrate the weight they carried.

"That's what we came fifteen hundred miles for," Les muttered to John Paul.

"Almost impossible to find," said Mr. Lebman, "as Colt only made one hundred and twenty-five, and most were sold to police departments, the Justice Department, and industry security squads. But now and then one comes on the market, and I was in the right place at the right time."

Les looked at it. The Monitor was John M. Browning's famous Browning Automatic Rifle for infantry warfare, principally trench sweeping, as reimagined by Colt for law enforcement use. It had a whole list of modifications for lawmen to make it handier, lighter, easier to control, easier to conceal, more portable, and probably more fun. The Colt engineers had shortened both the barrel and the stock, they'd added a stubby pistol grip to accommodate upright shooting (the military BAR being shot primarily prone), the bipod had been jettisoned and a newly designed, expanded compensator had been added, to harness the hot gases of a burst of .30 caliber fire. Colt had not been mindful of what it was truly building, but it was the ideal bank robber's gun, in that it was powerful enough to penetrate both the bulletproof vests and the car doors and hoods of the typical police department vehicle. It also outgunned most police departments, who couldn't afford such a high-end product. But with all that power, it was handy to handle in the confines of a car, where, unlike its longer parent rifle, it was unlikely to snag or catch on or get caught in the upholstery. That was its chief value to Les, who saw that cars figured in all future plans.

"Oh, boy," said Les. "I have to shoot that!"

"This way, boys."

Lebman led them to a cellar door engineered for airtightness, down the wooden steps to a chamber heaped at one end with broken lumber, stacks of newspapers, old mattresses, busted furniture, and various expendable bric-a-brac, the wall behind lined with sandbags. It smelled of gunpowder and brass, which emitted the unmistakable odor from the piles of casings that had been swept against the brick walls. Other odors generated an atmosphere as rich as it was unhealthy, much amplified by the total lack of ventilation: carbon, the stench of splattered, splintered lead, the more acrid tang of shattered copper, and the styphnate of fired primers.

"Smells good down here," said Les. "Man, I love this place."

It was no formal shooting range, but it let potential customers run a few rounds through whatever pleased them. He took the weapon from Mr. Lebman, reacting first to its weight—sixteen pounds, unloaded—and then experiencing its easy heft when tucked under his arm and braced against his body, the comfort of its pistol grip, the fluidity of its design that seemed to encourage firing from the hip.

"This is the aces," he cried in delight. "Man, it feels like a million bucks. Wait'll you try it, J.P."

"That'll be a toot," said J.P.

Mr. Lebman handed over another pound of twenty-round magazine, fully loaded with .30 caliber Government, and, knowingly, Les inserted it into the mag well. Then he reached up, caught the bolt handle, and slid it back to apogee, released it, and felt it slam home with a satisfying chunk as it stripped a cartridge from the mag and locked it in the chamber.

"Here we go," said Les. "Cover your ears."

Les squeezed off a five-round burst and the gun cracked hard and fast, leaping, spitting, filling the air with its exhaust and the explosiveness of its muzzle blast. It flashed so incandescently, it almost obliterated reality, since the barrel was shortened and only a portion of each cartridge's charge burned inside, the rest left to alchemize to golden radiance just beyond the muzzle. Twenty-five feet away, the chaos that had been junk furniture and other detritus seemed to detonate and fill the air with shards and splinters and pellets.

"WOW!" said Les. "Oh, boy, is that a blast! Here I go again!"

This time, confident of his control of the weapon, he hammered out the last fifteen in the mag, ripping the barricade up, down, sideways, left and right, driving yet more carbon stench, paper flecks, and hot gas, jet-spraying frags and bits into the atmosphere, sending a steady stream of brass from the blur of the bolt operation that landed with audible clinks on the pavement floor.

"HOLY COW!" screamed Les again. "That is the wildest thing I ever saw! Man, I can't wait"—and he almost blurted a fiction-destroying wish—"to hose down a State Police car and turn the coppers inside to hamburger"—but caught himself and instead said, "to get this on the ranch and shoot up some hay bales!"

"It *is* a superb piece of work," said Mr. Lebman.

"How much, Mr. Lebman?"

"Now, we have to be careful, fellas," said Mr. Lebman. "There is this new federal law, though I do so much business with Texas law enforcement, I think I'm okay. But, at the same time, just to be safe, I'd like some discretion. No walking out with the gun over your shoulder, then going to the nearest field for an afternoon's shooting."

"Of course not," said Les.

"Maybe pick it up on your way out of town. I'll break it down, clean it, lubricate it, make sure there's no cracks, though I've never seen a Colt product crack, and have it secured in a case for an after-dark pickup."

"No problem," said Les. "Extra mags, plenty of ammo, what's it come to?"

"Ten magazines, five hundred rounds of .30 Government, the gun itself, the secure packing, I'm thinking, fair profit for me, economical for you, five thousand seems right."

That was the standard underworld fee for the gun.

"Hmm," said Les. "Man, I love this piece, but five, I don't know. What about four, cash, right now?"

"Four?" said Mr. Lebman.

"Who knows, maybe the cops come by tomorrow and confiscate all the full-autos because of that new law. The longer you hang on to it, the more awkward it could become. The four is instant, right now, this second."

"Hmm," said Lebman.

"Four crisp thousand-dollar bills, you won't go wild with 'em? You'll sort of wait, or maybe spend them in Mexico or on a foreign buying trip, and just like we'd never tell anyone where we got the Monitor, you'd never tell anyone where you got the cash?"

"I think you've got a deal," said Lebman.

"J.P., want to burn a mag?"

"No, that's okay. I'm fine."

They headed upstairs, and Mr. Lebman took the gun to the back of his shop. Les got out his wad, peeled off the four big ones, and laid them out for Mr. Lebman. When the gunsmith came back, he took the money without counting and slipped it into his own pocket. No accounting was necessary; they'd done enough business before.

"Now, you call me when you want to pick it up."

"Absolutely," said Les. "I think we'll be in town another week. All that good Mexican food, man, I have five more restaurants at least I want to try."

38

"AH," said Mr. Leon Kaye, "haircut fee?"

He didn't like where this one was heading. It was going to cost him money and he didn't like spending money on something of little calculable value.

"Now, look here, Mr. Kaye," said Braxton. He put his hand on his hair. It was thick, luxuriant, golden, a pure Viking mane from the seventh century A.D. It cost Braxton about three hundred dollars a month to maintain it.

"This hair, see, I been growing it for twenty years. It's what's called my brand. Rawley and I are known for our hair in the way a country singer or a rock star might be known."

"Braxton, it's your choice how to grow your hair. It's nothing I'd be expecting to pay a fee for."

"It took me best part of three years to grow it out like this. It takes one of Little Rock's best beauty shops on healthy retainer for a visit twice weekly to keep it such a brilliant blond. Same for Rawley."

Rawley nodded. His mane, if anything, may have been a little more luxuriant, a little more blond, a little more Viking than his brother's. It was quite a head of hair. And, taken together, the two of them looked like Siegfried and Roy on HGH from Samoa.

"See, that's where you're misunderstanding the situation, sir," said Braxton. "What you ain't getting is that in the Negro community, where we do most of our work, and as well in the low-white community, mostly of

Appalachian heritage, found in trailer parks and government housing the mid-South over, this hair ain't only a certain look—a trademark, you might say—it's a communication, and it speaks in a certain tone to them that has to be spoken to. First off, it gets their attention fast. They ain't the most alert folks, you see, and getting them to pay attention is part of the battle right there."

Glumly, Mr. Kaye nodded. His pawnshops also served roughly the same demographic and he had to admit there was some wisdom in Braxton's assertion, not that under any other circumstances, and things being what they were, he would have acknowledged it.

"And here's the message it carries. It says to them: We wouldn't look so ridiculous if we couldn't kick your asses all the way to Tuesday. It says: We do this for a living. We done a lot of it. Best now you cooperate with us, you save yourself a lot of hurt that way. It says: See, we ain't no white person all teared up and gulpy over the horrible things our kind did to your kind. We the *other* kind of white people. We the kind that did them horrible things. We do 'em again, twice as hard, twice as mean, if you don't cooperate. That's a language our Negro clients understand, clear as a bell, and, like as not, they cooperate. Nobody done gets smacked about, arms broke, teeth swallowed, faces swelled like a grapefruit, right, Rawley? They have to know we represent the principle that it can all go away fast."

Rawley could speak. It was just that he didn't very often. At this point, he elected to say something quite strange.

"Sick. Transit. Gloria Monday."

Mr. Kaye swallowed. What the hell? Tongues? Gibberish? A lunatic's blubbering?

"Now, see if you can't follow where I'm going," said Braxton. "In order to follow the hero Swagger over the next few weeks, we will have to go in mufti, so to speak. Nothing showy, nothing with style and sparkle and ritz to it. No Viking tribal chief bouffant. No, it's hair close-cropped, dull-black Men's Wearhouse suits. No Lucchese boots, black inset with purple and red with silver skull points. It's Rockport walkers instead."

"I own a Men's Wearhouse," said Mr. Kaye. "I can get you a good price . . ."

But Braxton hadn't heard him.

"To get to that point, we got to stop at the barber and sit still while he shaves us near clean, as we are blond to the root. All that investment in time and care and money to attain a certain thing, all that will be gone. It'll be gone good and far away. And when our job is done and you have your serial 1934 bills and are counting all that money they brings you, we got months of downtime, waiting for our hair to grow out. We can't do our real jobs without no hair. Without our hair, we just two old, fat, bald white guys, and nobody is more invisible in our world today than old, fat, bald white guys. So it's only fair we be compensated for our sacrifice."

"Fellows," said Mr. Kaye, "I'm known as a bargainer. As a negotiator par excellence, good with money, quick with the numbers, able to see now versus then in any exchange, and patient enough to wait for the long-haul payoff. So I did my investigating. And I know you aren't really in a position financially—certain gambling debts, a lawsuit by the family of that boy you misidentified for that other boy—to walk away from the very generous amount of my initial offer. So I'm afraid it'll have to stand."

Braxton squealed with delight.

"He done 'vestigated us, Rawley," he said. "He ain't no fool, that Mr. Kaye! He didn't make a fortune in the gold business by being no fool, no sir!"

He smiled, his caps glowing like the Chiclets of Death.

"Now, because we are big, you're thinking, 'They's dumb.' But, sir, here's my news for you: we ain't dumb. You think we could run sophisticated software-intercept programs that get us in the most amazing places and be dumb? No sir. We smart enough, most important, to know what we know, and what we don't know. And if we don't know a thing, we get help. Are you following me, Mr. Kaye?"

"Of course," said Kaye, "but my position is firm."

"So, being Grumley, we ask another Grumley for help. Grumley always help Grumley. Like the Masons, only without the goofy hats. Who needs goofy hats when you got blood working on your side?"

"Braxton, I'm a busy man. I don't mean to be rude, but I need you to get to the point, if you have one."

"The point is, you invested heavily in property and development of a new Vegas to be called Razorback City, in Fayetteville. You done that to get in on the ground floor when gambling becomes legal in certain areas of our state. When that happens, you will make billions, owning the prime land in Razorback City. You can develop your own casinos; you can sell land to other interests, make a ton there. The sky's the limit, and the money just pours in. You're in the money, you're in the money."

How the fuck did they know?

"He looks surprised, don't he, Rawley?"

Rawley nodded.

"Yep, a Grumley can find anything out if he sets his mind to it. They found out that secret. And they found out the other secret too."

Fuck! thought Mr. Kaye.

"And that is, an interest payment came due for a certain party a few weeks ago and you just didn't have the cash, because even if you're pawn-shop and strip joint and Men's Wearhouse rich, you're cash poor, and so you borrowed from some nasty boys with Russian DNA now in Vegas. You expected a big surge of dough when the Recession got fixed under the new president, only it didn't. The economy just stayed where it was, flat like a 'tater pancake."

Mr. Kaye swallowed. Their intelligence was so good! These two . . . professional wrestlers!

"So this here game ain't some little minor con you got going 'cause you like old thousand-dollar bills, it's life or death because you need cash fast or the Russians will bring the big pain on you. They are not the sort to be persuaded to patience, no sir. You deliver to them when you say you will or you go for a swim with a slot machine chained to your thumbs. Sir, you are mortgaged so tight and in debt so far, you are breathing through a little tiny whisper of nostril left above the water. If you don't come through in a very short time, you going to be permanently in the big wet glub-glub."

Mr. Kaye said nothing. His eyes crinkled into a reptilian life-form's and seemed to see nothing, while, behind them, images of his own lungs filling with unstoppable cold Arkansas lake water took over his brain.

"So here's the deal. Haircut fee, five thousand dollars per man, now, in cash, from a fund not even your accountant/mistress—the Korean gal, she manages a pawn for you in Roberts, and, by the way, she's also fucking the guy that owns the Burger King across the street, and I sort of think she likes what he brings to the table more than what you bring, but I won't bother with the pictures for now—not even Miss Lilly Park knows about. Then, as agreed previously, a sixty-five/thirty-five split. Plenty of swag for both, gits you out of the deep lake water. And we will be with you every single step of the way so that we can follow the bookkeeping down to the penny. To the penny, sir. Miss Lilly Park will check the math."

39

THE TRIP TO Texas proved anticlimactic.

"More circumstantial stuff," said Bob. "Nothing hard, empirical, subject to other analysis, irrefutable, useful."

"Circumstantial is admissible," said Nick. "Sometimes it's all we have."

Swagger threw back another swig of Diet, again looked longingly at the highball in Nick's hand. They sat in the basement workroom, unofficial headquarters of Operation Charles Fitzgerald Swagger.

"So let's hear it."

"First, to Waco. Texas Ranger Museum. They have a Monitor there, only one I could find fast. Went to museum, looked at it—they say it was Frank Hamer's—and compared my little nozzle with the comp on the Monitor, through the glass case."

"And?"

"Yep, the same. That's why it was such a fine piece of machinework. Colt had the best machinists in the trade in those days, their standard product of the finest quality. Mine was actually a little bit better than theirs, but it's been sitting in a box since 1934. The Rangers probably haul theirs out to the range every six months for the fun of it and run a couple hundred rounds just to watch the dirt fly and the soda cans pop."

"Sounds like fun to me."

"With that, I headed to San Antonio to look into Mr. Lebman. After the passage of the National Firearms Act in June of 1934, he kept very careful records. He knew the federal hammer could drop at any second and that in the end his contacts with San Antonio law enforcement might not do him any good."

"He could feel their breaths on his neck."

"Exactly. So Bill Lebman, his grandson, let me look through the records. He guided me and we found it. In mid-August 1934, it's in the book as 'Colt Rifle IA-83-25433, sold to Jimmie Smith, Midland, Texas.'"

"Is that a Monitor number?"

"It is. I have a guy big in collecting circles with a contact at Colt. Called him, he made the call, called me back. It was a Monitor, one of a run of a hundred and twenty-five made in 1931, sold to Dallas Mercantile and Security in February of 1932. No further information."

"And Jimmie is Nelson."

"Yeah, because he's down as buying a .38 Super Colt machine pistol from Mr. Lebman in mid-1932, and that gun was found in a Dillinger arms cache in St. Paul in '34. Testimony from gang associates puts it as a gift from Nelson to his hero, Johnny."

"Solid," said Nick.

"But we can't prove the comp in Charles's strongbox was the comp on the Monitor sold to Baby Face. It's not a serial-numbered part. Still, it strongly suggests that Charles had an interaction with Baby Face in 1934 and somehow came into possession of the comp, maybe the whole gun. As I said, circumstantial, provocative—it certainly would follow that Charles could have that interaction only as a member of the Bureau. But . . . it don't prove nothing."

"And now for the bad news," said Nick.

"Wait, I missed the good news," said Bob.

"You ID'd the muzzle brake. You made it to Baby Face, then to Charles. It's getting tighter and tighter. Tight enough for public consumption. Well, I came up with something too. Or, rather, our senior historian came up with it and sent it on to me."

"Bad news?"

"Probably not. But you should know, it should be in the air, and it's something we should look to disprove."

"You've got me all tangled up."

"Come over here."

Nick led him to his computer, where he opened email, selected a message topic-lined "Recording," from the official Bureau address, and opened it.

"He came across a cardboard box marked 'Arkansas.' Went through it, nothing of note but an old reel of magnetic-tape recording. He played it. Nothing on it but a recording someone had made in early December of 1934 of the *Walter Winchell Show*. Know him?"

"Some big news guy?"

"Gossip, more like. Claimed to have the inside scoop. New York columnist, syndicated all over the place, got a network radio show when network radio was the TV of America. He was pals with lots of big shots, including a certain Director of the FBI, which wasn't even the 'FBI' until six months later."

"Okay. It has to do with Arkansas? So what?"

"Let me play it for you. If the voice is familiar, it's because you're old enough to have watched *The Untouchables* as a kid, and Winchell was the narrator on that show."

Nick moved the cursor to an icon in the text of the message, hit "Enter," and a voice emerged from eighty-odd years ago over the speakers, stentorian, witless, full of rectitude and certainty.

"Now, I'll never criticize Mr. J. Edgar," said Winchell into a radio mic the size of a hubcap in a studio in Manhattan on that cold December night, and Nick and Bob listened to it through technology Winchell couldn't have imagined eighty-three years later, "and the job he and his boys are doing against vermin like John Dillinger, Pretty Boy Floyd, and Baby Face Nelson, Public Enemies Number One, who are now Public Enemies Number Dead. But even J. Edgar makes mistakes. It seems one of the boys wasn't up to the task of going gun to gun against the Tommy-toting gangsters and he cut and ran—all the way to Hicktown, Arkansas, where he came from. Quitters never win and winners never quit. What that shows is two things: first, Mr. Hoover is capable of making a mistake. He's human too, after all, and admits it. Second, there's no room for yellow among the red, white, and blue."

"Can't be Charles Swagger," said Bob. "That old bastard didn't have any run in him."

"I'm not saying it is," said Nick. "But it could be aimed at Charles. It meant to destroy him. Someone in high places used Winchell to smear the only man in Arkansas who'd been in the Division. Really, to crush him. It's like erasing. I don't know what he did, but he managed to get folks real angered."

"A coward? No," said Bob, but, even so, he didn't like the feel, the sound, the direction. He shuddered. "A bastard. A crook, maybe. A drunk, absolutely. But a coward? No way."

40

A NOTHER STAKEOUT. This one was off a Purvis tip, so Purvis ran it. It was pure theater. Charles knew that he'd hear about Baby Face from Uncle Phil alone, and any other source was almost certainly bogus. But protocols had to be observed and so he and a team of young fellows set up in cars on the North Side, around a joint called The Yellow Parrot, once a favorite of Big Al's, and said, for tonight at least, to be a spot where Baby Face might make his presence known. In the cars was enough heavy artillery to make him regret the decision.

Charles, a Thompson with a fifty-round drum in his lap pressing heavily against his legs, sat breathing through a tailor-made in Division car number 13, a big Hudson, with Ed Hollis behind the wheel, his Browning rifle in the backseat for a fast grab if it happened, which it wouldn't. They smoked, they felt their wristwatches ticking the night away, they watched the occasional drunk stagger this way or that from one North Side gin joint to another, they tried to stay alert and ready.

"It's not going to happen, is it, Sheriff?" asked Ed.

"Probably not."

"I thought Baby Face was a homebody. He'd be screwing Helen, not prowling jazz cribs on the North Side."

"That's what they say. But maybe it's a professional meet, a job-planning session. That might get him out on the town."

"Wouldn't you see other faces on the wall in there by now?"

"You would. Inspector Purvis said he got this from a State Police informant inside a downstate car-theft ring, who's known to sell heaps to the bank gangs. It could be legit. It ain't, but it could be."

Both men sighed, smiled, and settled back. These things were usually called off around 2 a.m. And that was an hour away, so there was nothing to do but squirm after comfort, stretch cramping neck muscles, keep the hands loose and flexible, and eat up time diddling with the makings of yet another tailor-made.

Suddenly a phantom swept before Charles on the right. It was Purvis. Charles rolled down the window.

"Charles, can you do me a favor?"

"Sure thing," said Charles. "Name it."

"I owe a reporter a favor. I also owe myself a favor because everyone thinks I'm just out promoting myself. So this guy from the *Herald-Examiner* got wind of tonight's operation, and he's showed up. Can you chat with him a few minutes? He's pretty solid, can be trusted, okay?"

"Sure," said Charles, "but I don't know what I could tell him."

"Tell him Dillinger's last words. It's something we haven't released yet. He'll appreciate it. It's Page One for him. Then tell him you'll return his phone calls. But of course never return his phone calls."

"I never do," said Charles.

He set the Thompson down, after pushing the SAFE lever into position, and slipped out of the Hudson. His legs issued distress as they unfolded and found themselves required to perform labor again. He twisted, stretched his back, and followed Purvis down the dark street and into an alley, where a man awaited.

Purvis handled the intros, and the fellow was a Dave Jessup, *Chicago Herald-Examiner*, one of the more respectable rags, and immediately impressed Charles as someone never to play poker with. Feral, over-alert, a little nervous. City rat, knew the angles, the deals, where the bodies rotted. Oh, and of course wise-guy. Smart aleck. Fast lip. Wanted to write movies and hang out with stars.

"So, I guess that you're him?"

"Him?" asked Charles.

"You know, the cowboy gunfighter who plugged Johnny. Your outfit wants Mel to be the face of it, but I figure it had to be someone more cowboy than Mel, who's a little uptown for that kind of work."

"Sir, the policy is not to release details. I was there, I did my job as it came up, and that's all I can say."

"They wouldn't have put you there unless you'd been there a lot of times. It's the kind of game where experience counts, right? A lot of time behind a pistol. See it, hit it, bury it?"

He had an eager aggression that almost caused his face to shine.

"It's okay if you tell me," he said. "Off the record means off the record."

"Until it don't," said Charles.

"No, no, when I say it, I mean it. Ask around, you'll see that I keep my word. We're not the *Trib*, or the *Sun* or the *Times*. We run a class outfit and shoot square all the way."

"Well, I'm not the type that talks things up. I just did what was required by circumstance, and that's all I'd be comfortable saying, record or no."

"Okay. But I have heard you got to him first when he went down. You heard what he said."

"I did. Truth is, it didn't make much sense."

"Can you tell me?"

"Something about the way he was dressed."

"I guess he thought he was a dude. You remember the exact words? Something I can put in the paper?"

"I'm thinking it was"—what was it?—"something about wanting to be 'dressed right for people.'"

"Was it a joke?"

"He had a hole the size of a tomato in his face. His brains were on the sidewalk. I don't think he was trying to be funny."

"You know it, I know it, but the rubes don't know it. Say, pal, you're okay. I'm thinking something like, But I ain't dressed for church. Or, I'm not even wearing a tie!"

"He was wearing a tie. No jacket, though."

"Then, I'm not dressed for this."

"It might have been something like that, I suppose. But there was another element. I'm not dressed for folks, maybe. Or, I'm not dressed for company."

"So if I say his last words are 'I'm not dressed for company,' you're not going to call me a liar?"

"I'm not going to call you anything. I'm not going to call you."

"That's all I want. You just got me a bonus. 'I'm not dressed for company'—swell, the rubes think Hollywood writes everything, they want a snappy end line. Here, let me give you my card, it's got my number at the *Examiner*, and if there's anything I can do for the real hero of the day, you let me know. See, I know stuff, I know folks, I do favors and find things out. I always know the real story behind the story I print and I know the story I print is basically bullshit. Maybe I can do you a favor someday."

"Sure, and some day pigs will star in movies."

"Good one," said Jessup.

Charles slipped the card into his pocket and watched the fellow slip away, happy with his little fake prize.

CHARLES HAD ANOTHER NIGHTMARE that night, a particularly bad one. The war; men jostling and climbing to meet the bristling fire; gray, muttering faces, masked with fear—Jesus, when will it stop?—and, in the aftermath, the men who'd died, the paleness of their bodies against the mud, the reaching white limbs, the results of ballistics against the tenderness of flesh, the smell of shit that occluded the Western Front from start to finish. He woke, blinking and sweaty, glad at least he hadn't screamed. He was okay. But it was mid-morning and there was no point in trying to get back to sleep. He rose, showered, dressed, slipped the .45 in the shoulder holster, and left. Not much business at the diner, and he had a nice breakfast of eggs, bacon, coffee, juice. That would keep him going until a late dinner.

He got in about 11:30 and noticed it right away. It was a note from Elaine: "Call your Uncle Phil as soon as possible."

41

"O KAY," said Bob, "you got me all excited."

"This one is big. I think you'll be pleased."

They were in the study, sometime before dinner, and Bob had just arrived after a hasty call from Nick.

"I got another call from History itself," Nick explained.

Swagger knew that was the senior historian, who could find anything in the vast array of frayed papers stuffed into filing cabinets and cardboard boxes that occupied the entire floor of the Hoover subbasement, as he had with the Winchell recording.

"He was on another project, but he came across this and saw immediately how it might fit in for us."

Bob took the document, and looked at it closely. Unusually, it wasn't a photocopy but the real thing, typed on four pieces of real paper, each secured in a plastic sleeve to protect it from the elements, human touch especially.

"I was running late; he was running early," Nick explained. "He had a speech to give. Photocopying was backed up. He said, just take this one, but have it back on Monday. And be careful. Otherwise, no significance. We just can't make a paper airplane out of it."

It was a closely typed report of some sort, whose typeface, nomenclature, official seal, and catalog number all accorded with Bureau paperwork protocols as Swagger had encountered them. The title read

RECOMMENDATIONS FOR HANDGUN POLICY REVISION

Below that, it said "Submitted, June 18, 1934, by REDACTED."

Scanning the brief accumulation of pages, he saw also that at the bottom right of each page it bore the notation "REDACTED/EPD."

"EPD typed it," said Nick, "we know her. That's our favorite gal, Elaine Donovan, the hardest-working gal in showbiz. She also typed the thing from South Bend, or at least the original pages."

Bob began reading.

It was, clearly, in a voice of a man knowledgeable in handgun fighting, physics, mechanics, maintenance, and training; clearly, a man who had won more than a few gunfights. His suggestions also seemed radical for the time. He didn't believe in the concept of the static range, where agents stood still in rigid target positions and fired one-handed at silhouette targets twenty-five yards away. Instead, he recommended a "dynamic action" course of fire, in which agents would draw from concealment, move, engage sculptural targets from concealed positions at unusual angles, sometimes firing down, sometimes firing up, sometimes firing at movers, sometimes at chargers. They would be encouraged to fire two-handed, instead of the conventional one, to always use their sights, and to load under time pressures. It was just like the latest SEAL or SWAT doctrine. He encouraged high-hip carry, cocked-and-locked .45 automatics or Smith & Wesson Heavy Duty .38s on .44 frames, with much practice on draw and first-shot placement, fol-lowed by rapid movement toward cover or, if cover wasn't available, to evade return fire. For raid or arrest teams, he urged special training in maneuver-ing off a base of fire, based on army raiding techniques; use of short-barreled fully automatic weapons, such as Thompsons, with the stocks removed, or .351 Winchesters or .35 Remington semi-autos, tweaked to go full rat-a-tat-tat. He believed in a sniper component as part of deployment, and took it further by recommending establishing a sniper school, for he felt that the precise long-range shot was a useful tool in the law enforcement repertoire. He recommended the heavy-caliber bullet for both automatic or revolver, in the year before the .357 Magnum was developed and adopted.

"It sounds Swagger, doesn't it?" said Nick. "There may have been other fellows around who had the experience and had thought rigorously about the issue as well, but I don't think any of them worked for the FBI at the time."

"Someone fixed the grammar and spelling, for sure, but that's him. And he knew what he was talking about," said Bob.

"In that time period, only a few did, but they didn't have the Bureau's ear. I'm thinking of Elmer Keith, Ed McGivern, maybe some others. The other handgun-and-tactics writers and thinkers didn't come along until after the war."

Bob nodded.

"It really seems to cement the case," said Nick.

"Well," said Bob, "still in the goddamned 'circumstantial' zone. But maybe there's something else here."

"I missed something?"

"Not at all. But this paragraph, page 4, bottom, and on to page 5, top, is interesting."

Nick read:

"'It is also suggested that the Division field offices hire or place under part-time contracts professional gunsmiths, as opposed to the current practice of appointing an armorer from among the agent pool. Gunsmithing is a fine art, and a man who has mastered the intricacies and nuance of firearms can contribute a great deal more than simple maintenance, cleaning, minor repair, and cataloging, which is the limit of the armorer's abilities. A gunsmith, for example, can transform a stock automatic into a far more useful fighting tool that will give our agents the advantage, particularly in close-range public arrest situations that are so likely to occur. A Government Model Colt .45 ACP, for example, can be improved for reliability by judicious filing of the joinery between frame and barrel; its tiny sights, almost worthless in any kind of shooting event, can be replaced with larger sights, which are easier to pick up in the blur of action. The sights can also be painted red or white, again for faster visual acquisition. The grip safety, which all too frequently prevents a quickly drawn pistol from coming off safe if the agent misplaces his hands, can be neutralized, either temporarily by a rawhide tie-down or more permanently by the usage of a tapped screw. The safety lever on the frame can be enlarged, so that the thumb naturally falls upon it and depresses it with one hundred percent reliability in emergency situations. Finally, the trigger can be rendered, by polishing certain interior surfaces, much smoother, so that the gun is not apt to betray its shooter with a pulled shot when the uneven or gritty trigger pull torques the muzzle off target.'"

"I *did* see that," said Nick. "As I recall, the pistol you recovered from the strongbox in the foundation had been worked on in exactly that way."

"It had. I shot it, I think I told you, and it was a solid piece of work."

"But you think it has other significance?"

"Hmm, maybe. Maybe he did it right away, when he was issued it. But he was very busy, he was trying to impress people, first-day-on-new-job bullshit, he wanted to hit the ground running, maybe he didn't have the time. Maybe also he wanted to wait a bit until he'd built a reputation and was respected by management before he took a file to a piece of government-issue equipment. Some might have considered such an enterprise vandalism of government property. He'd want cover before he did it."

"Unprovable, but it makes sense via the universal workplace rules that apply everywhere, from the Third Reich to the building of the Pyramids and back, on up to NASA: the star gets to do what he wants. But I'm still not sure where this is going."

"Given that, what would impel him to take the file to the metal?"

"An upcoming arrest," said Nick. "Potential for action. He had to get the gun up to his standards if he knew he was going to a shoot-out."

"That's it."

"I get it. You think he was on the Dillinger team. He shot John Dillinger."

"It was his kind of party. It was what they brought him in to handle."

Nick chewed it over. The identity of the agent who shot Dillinger had never been released, as per the Director's mandate that no individual got the glory, the outfit did. Most people assumed it was Melvin Purvis because he was the "face" of the Division in those days, though Purvis himself had never made such a claim.

"I wonder if there's any way of proving it?"

"The serial number was recorded, even if his name was redacted. It was one of ten pistols received from the Postal Department, C-variants shipped to the Chicago Field Office. That particular one was marked 'Duty Loss,' but the other nine remained in service until they were retired, whenever. If we know that the agents they were issued to weren't present during the Dillinger shooting—those being the only issued .45s in Chicago—then that lost pistol had to be the one. That seems pretty airtight."

"I think you're on to something."

"But here's where I'm going with this. Remember how I said I couldn't figure out a money angle? There was no treasure. Why was I being followed? You told me it's always about money. I'm just following your advice."

"Sometimes I'm so brilliant, it amazes even me," said Nick.

"That gun—the verified pistol that shot John Dillinger dead in Chicago, July twenty-second, 1934, at the Biograph Theater—that gun might be worth . . . I don't know . . . thousands . . . hundreds of thousands . . ."

"It should go to the Bureau."

"It should. But if somebody who knew the rare-gun trade, who had contacts, who had connections in the black market, and knew a lot of wealthy collectors—let's take it another step—maybe then there are other guns from that era that my grandfather somehow ended up with—that trove of guns, all of them verifiable by serial number—Jesus Christ, now I see it—maybe even Baby Face's Monitor, we could be talking millions."

Then he sighed.

"Now all we have to do is solve the map and prove that Charles was in fact in the Bureau."

"Details, details," said Nick.

PART IV

42

ST. PAUL, MINNESOTA
August 23, 1934

"THERE HE IS," said the St. Paul detective, Sergeant Brown. "He's walking a little gimpy, but they say he's been loopy since he got shot in the head."

Charles and the three St. Paul officers, including the chief and the ex-chief, watched from their unmarked Ford as the man dipped across the broad, busy expanse of University Avenue at Marion Street, a perfectly unremarkable crossroads in a perfectly unremarkable section of a perfectly unremarkable city.

It was indeed Homer Van Meter, as Charles had stared at the photos for hours, committing the man's surprisingly pleasant features to memory: the thick hair, parted on the left, combed right; the lanky frame; the prominent nose and strong chin; the dark eyes. He had a gangling roll to his stride, looked confident, solid, like a taxpayer with no worries in his head, if just a bit shabby. Hard to believe—but, then, it always was, that was the mystery of these fellows—that, inside, he was a cool-handed killer.

This one was tricky. It was Sam's suggestion, after Uncle Phil had given Charles a solid where-when on Van Meter, that the Division take a low-profile approach on this one, unlike, say, the Dillinger arrest, where they'd flooded the street with agents.

"If the Division came crashing into town, there'd be squawks, tiffs, turf wars, lots of bitter squealing, lots of feathers sent flying," Sam had said. "Not good. Leaks would spring, and Homer'd take off for Kansas City. Moreover, rancor and contempt between the Division and the St. Paul cops

could get the Division a size-18 reputation in law enforcement circles, something the Director is keen to avoid.

"So, Charles, I want you to handle this as quietly as possible. I'd make it
abundantly clear to our St. Paul friends that the Division has no interest in
Homer on the subject of Minnesota corruption. We could care less. Our
task is to take down the big interstate bank gangs, member by member.
That's all we want. What we do with Homer once we get him singing is
something yet to be determined."

"I got an idea they'd prefer him dead to singing. Those detectives don't
want nobody messing with their business. They may see this as a way to
erase someone who knows a little too much about them. One squirt of the
Thompson and a whole lot of trouble goes away."

"That's the issue you'll have to deal with, Charles. You know what our
goal is: Homer in custody, a long, long talk with him until he sees his best
interests are served—maybe avoiding the fryer for that cop he killed at South
Bend—if he gives us Baby Face or Pretty Boy."

"Well, gents, let's get this done and go have a drink," said Chief Cullen,
who was with Brown in the front seat. That Cullen was the chief and Brown
the ex-chief showed how much juice the arrest warranted. They weren't
leaving this one to the rookies.

"You sure you need that subgun, Brown?" asked Charles, all amiable-
like. The bone of contention was the Thompson gun with full-up fifty-
round drum Brown carried. Charles had argued against it, since the arrest
would be on public boulevards amid civilians and a wrong-way burst with a
Thompson could have disastrous repercussions. But then, as now, the St.
Paul officers weren't to be denied.

"Mr. Justice Department, Homer's fast to pistol and fast to fire. We need
all the help we can get," said Chief Cullen, as he drew a Winchester '94
from between the seats, ran the lever to check and make sure a .30-30 was
set to chamber, then slammed the lever home. At the same time, Brown
hoisted his twelve-pound weapon from the floor, slid back and notched the
bolt atop the gun, keeping his finger far from trigger, as a touch could let

fly a maelstrom, and secured it tight to body for movement. Meanwhile, the fourth detective threw the pump on his Winchester riot gun.

The four emerged just as Homer made it across, moving away from them, and though bent low to support their guns and hold them close to the shoulder, they increased their pace to overtake him. It was like running to ground a fox who didn't know he was being hunted. They closed swiftly as Homer lollygagged along, enjoying the relatively cool air, the sense of freedom, whatever a normal man enjoys not knowing that his executioners approach.

As for Charles, it was clear he was hopeless to prevent what the St. Paul boys were determined to make happen, and he felt a twinge for having been a part of the setup, which was looking more and more like a Capone-style rubout than an arrest. He separated ever so slightly from the three and moved his hand closer to the .45 under his left arm, though with so much firepower on scene, he knew it was doubtful he'd need to shoot.

When the range had closed to within twenty-five feet, it was Chief Cullen who, lifting rifle to shoulder, shouted, "HOMER!" Homer turned, and Charles saw the flash of panic overtake his face, but just as fast the recognition of the guns bearing down on him. He went the hard way, thrusting his hand inside the jacket he wore for his own iron and, instantly, scuttling sideways for cover in an alley.

The Thompson settled the issue. Brown had time enough to come to shoulder, put weight against the gun to fight recoil, aim cleverly, and unleash. The hammer of the burst shattered the benign Midwestern air, and banished all other noise, as the fire stream roared into Homer and ripped him up bad. Brown was a good gunner, with lots of work on the Thompson, so it wasn't a broad sweep of bullets, kicking up a commotion over a large area, with Homer in the middle; the bullets instead went to and stayed on him, all the way through the fall, only a few puffing the dust. He went down, his jacket smoking and torn from the fusillade that had ruptured him. Maybe the chief fired too, and maybe the detective with the riot gun, for shots of another declension sounded, but the noise was lost as Sergeant

Brown fired multiple coups de grâce into the fallen man, causing his body to twitch and shudder. Then, silence.

The usual: the cops approached stealthily, as if a man could survive such a blast, while the chief raised his arm and began to shout, "Police action! Stand clear, folks, stand clear. Police action!" but the citizens became a circus around the torn figure at the center of it all.

Brown and the shotgunner knelt by the body, and Charles approached to note that among the wounds inflicted on the man, a string of slugs had evidently struck his right hand, which was so mutilated, it hardly seemed human anymore, the thumb removed as if by surgery, the fingers twisted in ways they were not meant to twist, the whole glistening with fresh blood.

"That's the way we handle it in St. Paul, G-Man," said Brown, evidently proud of his role in the drama. "He ain't going nowhere, that's for sure."

"Yeah," said Charles, holstering his automatic, "but you'll be up all night reloading that drum."

Homer did go somewhere, eventually—that is, to the morgue, after the morgue truck arrived, following on several patrol cars, whose inhabitants set up a perimeter that kept the public from scuffing up the crime scene. It was the usual police theater: photos, reporters with notebooks, from somewhere a city attorney, a few other sub-chiefs, white-coated morgue guys with the gurney—familiar in form, if not content, from the Dillinger business, though not quite as electrically charged as that, for Homer hadn't been as electrically charged as Johnny.

43

McLEAN, VIRGINIA

The present

NOT MUCH FOR TODAY. Just go over it, go over it, go over it. Maybe something would happen. Or maybe a break: one of the emails or interviews he'd sent out would bear surprising fruit. It hadn't happened yet, but maybe today would be the day.

Swagger had finished his shower and was dressed. The next step was coffee and a muffin in the hotel coffee shop while he diddled with his iPhone to check emails, and then someone knocked at his door. Too early for housekeeping; they knew he usually didn't leave for his coffee until 8:30.

It was Nick. Surprising, because Nick always called or emailed when he had something and their meets took place in Nick's big workroom.

"What's up?" Swagger asked.

"Something came to me. It was shortest here, no need to go all the way back."

"Okay."

Nick went to the desk in the suite, which was clear, and set down a sack from CVS pharmacy. He removed a freshly packed small file, a couple of No. 2 Eagle pencils, an unopened bag of plastic gloves, a ream of 8½ × 11 paper, and a $5.95 magnifying glass.

"Is that a junior-detective kit?" asked Bob.

"Nope, you have to be at least a GS-22 to get one of these."

"I love to watch a professional at work," said Swagger.

Nick picked up his briefcase.

"I was returning the handgun policy memo downtown," Nick said. "But something about it was turning in my mind. Don't know why, something seemed provocative about it."

"Maybe that it's an original, not a photocopy," said Bob.

"No, some feature beyond that. Some feature that takes off from that."

Bob tried to list features.

"It's thin, it's dry, it's fragile, it's old, Donovan was such a powerful typist that her periods blew clean through and opened little holes—is that what you mean?"

"Okay," said Nick, "let's see if I'm as brilliant as I think I am. Or even more brilliant."

He put on his reading glasses, snatched up the hotel-issue coffee mug and turned it over, setting it on its rim, presenting its clean, slightly concave bottom to the world. He took up one of the pencils, opened his pocketknife, and whittled a point of exposed lead into the flat end. He opened up the file package . . . Oof, why did they pack these things in superstrength, human-finger-indestructible Kevlar?

"You need the file to open the package," he said, "but the fucking file is *in* the package."

He got the file free and delicately applied it to the exposed lead of the pencil. A small dust of lead particles began to accumulate in the cup's concave bottom.

"I hope you're not in a rush," he said. "This may take some time."

"I'm Available Jones today," Bob said.

In five minutes or so, he'd accumulated a little heap of powdered lead in the cup surface.

"Okay, here's where it gets dicey," he said.

He ripped open the ream of paper, took out a sheet, and laid it on the desk.

Next, he opened the bag of gloves and, like a surgeon, pulled one onto each hand.

"Don't tell me to bend over," said Bob.

"Ha!" Nick laughed. He opened the briefcase, reached in, and removed one of the ancient handgun memo's pages, holding it by the corners only and as gently as possible.

Holding it up to the light, he located the blot of ink where, eighty-three years ago, some administrator had applied waterproof ink to the capitalized letters signifying authorship, the imprimatur of office standard practices. He held it up to the light.

"Can't see a thing," he said. "I'd hoped the initials of the author would stand out."

"They knew what they were doing," said Bob.

"But the one thing they didn't count on was the speed, power, and accuracy of Elaine P. Donovan, the best typist in Western Civilization. She typed so hard, and the paper was so thin, her keystrokes carried through to the other side of the paper. This was especially true of letter arrangements her fingers were familiar with."

He laid the memo facedown, next to the white sheet. The paper was so thin and crackly, the offending blot showed through it.

"Okay, Dr. Watson, watch this."

Taking the cup to the memo, tilting it a bit, he used his pocketknife blade to skim off some lead particulate onto the obverse side of the blot. Then, with the blade, he tidied the pile so that it was evenly applied over the blot.

"Here we go," he said.

Taking the memo up again, he neatly flipped it and laid it across the white, pristine sheet of paper. Then with his knife blade's dull edge he gently rubbed back and forth, applying enough pressure for his task, but not so much as to shred or damage the paper.

"See, they blotted out the top side. They didn't realize her powerful typing inscribed the letters through the paper. So now I've coated it with a light dusting of lead and pressed it against a sheet of paper. It's like Gutenberg's Bible; the raised surface of the letters should leave an impression."

And they did:

CFS/epd

Author: Charles F. Swagger / typist: Elaine P. Donovan.

"Welcome back to the Federal Bureau of Investigation, Special Agent Swagger," said Nick.

44

SAN ANTONIO, TEXAS

Late August 1934

HELEN AND J.P. were stunned by the weight of Les's grief. The news floored him, and he—uncharacteristically, without a tie, shoeless, sockless—just sat, face slack, eyes empty, locked in depression. He stared at nothing, and out of respect for his agony, they treated him like an infant, tiptoeing around him, speaking in whispers and mutters.

"Honey, you haven't eaten all day. Do you want me to fix you a sandwich and a Coca-Cola?"

He didn't respond. He just sat on the sofa with the newspaper in front of him.

GANGSTER VAN METER SLAIN, it said in a bold, eight-column headline, and underneath, in smaller type, COPS MACHINE-GUN DILLINGER PAL ON STREET.

There was a gaudy picture of Homer on the slab in the morgue, his head held alert by some sort of armature so that the wide-open eyes, the gauntness of his frame, the abrasions where he'd gone to earth, stood out starkly. He'd had better days. It was a grisly specimen of how unremarkable newspapers and citizens held death in the midst of both a crime and a heat wave, and a dead mobster on a slab, all his holes displayed against the alabaster of his skin in black-and-white photography, sold a lot of papers, as the national indoor sport had become keeping track while the law shot down the surviving Dillinger boys.

"It don't look like the Division had a hand in this one," said J.P. later in the afternoon to his silent best friend. "It sounds like the St. Paul boys decided they didn't want him hanging around town, they didn't want him bringing in the Division and having them looking too closely at things, so they just decided to deal with the situation themselves. I mean, they had to know he was there; they could have done this kind of thing anytime, they just happened to decide to do it yesterday."

Les didn't answer. He didn't make eye contact. He sat still in his coma, oblivious. Finally, lethargically, he called into the bedroom, "Honey, can you bring me a Coca-Cola, please?" Then he turned to J.P.

"You got it exactly. Why now? Why all of a sudden? Where does it come from, this sudden need to kill Homer? Something's not right here."

"Les, the guy's the object of a manhunt. He ain't as smart as you. He goes back to St. Paul where everybody knows him, he's easy to find."

"He thinks he's safe there. And he is safe, until something changes. What changed? That's what I'm asking."

"I don't know," said J.P.

"The deal is, they leave us alone if we don't do jobs in St. Paul. That's why St. Paul is safe. And far as I know, he was too daffy to work after he took that pill to the head. Remember, the night before they got Johnny he was supposed to go to that meet with us in Glenview and the guy never showed. That shows he was cuckoo in the clock tower. Not clear, not whole, not thinking."

J.P. knew it wasn't time to remind Les that he, Les, had been enraged with Homer for letting him down and that previously he'd even told a number of people he meant to kill Homer for his idiocy in not putting together the South Bend job well, for his endless spew of bad jokes, and for hanging around with that Mickey Conforti, who had entertained legions of admirers in her time, a liaison that Les felt profaned his own, richer love for Helen.

"Poor guy," said Les, taking a Coca-Cola on ice from Helen, then suddenly going all dramatic on them. It just poured out of him.

"I did four jobs with Homer. He was a professional. He was a guy who knew what he was doing. But what I remember best is that long run down the street to the car in South Bend. Cops everywhere, all of them shooting at Les, plus Les's got twenty-five pounds of bulletproof jacket on, twelve pounds of machino, and four or five twenty-round mags of .45s, plus one used-up drum, so Les's not exactly Red Grange. He's a slow boat to China, and all the cops have to do is take one second to aim and Les's head is splattered all over Indiana. Meanwhile, Les's pals are ducking into the car and they're happy as hell to have the cops shooting at Les and not them. But who saves Les? It's Homer. Homer doesn't run for the car. Homer stands there, a man's man, a soldier's soldier, a hero's hero, straight out in the open, and very carefully lays down .351s everywhere he sees a cop settling in for the finisher on Les. That's Homer: he doesn't give a damn about himself, he just gives everything up for a buddy, for a guy he don't even like, for a guy that's teased him about his girlfriend, for a guy that never laughs at his jokes and wants to wring his neck more often than not. Homer just stands there and saves all of Les's bacon, and when Les, with more crap on him than a doughboy going over the top, makes it back to the car, he's unhit and good for more action, only then—then and only then—does Homer himself head to the car to get the hell out of town.

"Stop and think about it. Would you do that for me, J.P.? Maybe. I sure hope so. But neither of us will know until the time comes. And maybe I'd do it for you, and I hope I would, but there's no telling. What I do know is, Homer did it for me: he risked everything he had for me. He was willing to die or spend the rest of his life in the Indiana state pen, all for me. That's the bravest thing, I think: not to be brave for yourself but for a buddy when it gets you nothing and costs you everything."

"Homer would be happy that you spoke so well of him," said J.P.

"It's the only epitaph someone in our business gets."

They went quiet for a bit, as Les worked on the Coca-Cola. But Les wasn't quite done.

"Here's the other thing. Homer leaps into the car, he's the getaway driver, and he catches something in the head and it knocks him out cold. Johnny pulls him over and climbs behind the wheel, and he's the one who saves everybody's bacon. In less than two months, both are gone. These guys weren't fools. They didn't make mistakes. Nothing random was going to get them. They weren't going to be shot by the kid in the gas station or even get picked up on a drunk-driving charge. So if they go down, they go down because somebody squealed them out. And who would know where they were—in two different cities, no less. Who? Helen, can you answer that? J.P.? Come on, you're smart, you've been around. Who?"

"It doesn't make any sense, Les. Why would the Italians turn on us? As long as we're getting the headlines, nobody notices them taking over the wires, the unions, the pictures, the banks even. They need us. That's why they let us stay at their safe houses, armor up from their weapons rooms, sleep with—excuse me, Helen—a Mob trixie. And I don't mean Les, Helen, he's as true as a cowboy."

"I know that, J.P. That's why I love him so much." She reached out and put her hand on her husband's wrist. He patted it but was not done with his riff.

"I don't know why they're doing this. I don't know who's doing it. But one guy is making this happen. I will find him. I will pay him back."

LES'S DEPRESSION DIDN'T CLEAR, even if he had returned to talkativeness. But inside, where the little wheels were, those wheels were whirring and buzzing and rattling like crazy, so that even if he was joking with Helen, or fucking her, even if he was out on the prairie working on his shooting skills—say, he was damned good, getting better!—he had that issue somewhere in his brain. He knew he couldn't move until he figured it out.

One day, he took a fiver to the bank, asked for quarters, walked through San Antonio until he found a phone booth in an out-of-the-way spot, and dipped in.

"Number, please."

"I'd like to put through a call to Reno, Nevada. Enterprise 5487."

"Yes sir. That'll be two dollars and twenty-five cents for the first three minutes."

"Got it."

He fed in nine quarters and waited.

"Yeah?"

"Long Distance. I have a call for this number from a . . . What is your name, sir?"

"Les Smith."

"Les—"

"It ain't collect?"

"No sir."

"Fine, I'll take it . . . Les?"

"Skabootch? Is that you?"

"No, Les, it's Doc Bone. How are you, kid?"

"I'm fine, Doc. This line clean?"

"Yeah, the heat's off for now. It comes, it goes—who knows why? Listen, you want Skabootch?"

"It doesn't matter, Doc. I need a favor, nothing big, just some help."

"Sure, kid. Ask, it's yours."

"You heard about Homer going down?"

"Yeah, a shame. Good man. I heard they chopped him bad."

"Bastards. Anyhow, here's what I need to know. You must have friends who have friends who have connections with St. Paul Homicide."

"If I don't, Skabootch does. He don't, Soap would."

"Well, whoever."

"What's up, kid?"

"I have to know how it happened. It's the Division that's got the itch for us, and Homer thought he was home free in St. Paul. No Division there. But he gets burned by coppers with choppers. So I have to know if there was anything going on? Any new players, any decisions made on high, just what the hell happened that guys he's palled around with suddenly park a drum on him. It doesn't make any sense."

"Maybe it was just bad luck, kid."

"Nobody's luck is that bad. Ask around for me, will you, Doc?"

"Sure, kid. You call me back tomorrow, this time, this number, maybe I'll have something for you by then."

"You're the best, Doc. I knew I could count on you."

So that buoyed Les up for a night, and he took Helen dancing in one of her new dresses, and then to a picture, and then took her back to the room and fucked her good. He awoke in good spirits too, and at the appointed hour, in a different booth, he put the call through to Doc Bone. But this time he got Skabootch.

"Yeah, Les, I know what you're after. Kid, some advice. You got friends out here, you're loved for your talent and guts, maybe you ought to give up on Chicago for a while. It ain't healthy. We could put you to work."

"In a few months when I get this stuff straightened out, maybe then. I could see it, Helen and me, J.P. too, we'd like it out there permanent."

"You always got a place here."

"Anyway—"

"Well, here's what I found out. It was three St. Paul detectives, plus some other guy. It must have been important, because one of the shooters was the chief himself, Cullen, and another was Brown, who'd been the chief, but is in all kinds of soup for taking bribes, and maybe even going on out-of-state jobs with certain individuals."

"The other guy? The fourth guy?"

"There's your million-dollar mystery. It was some tall guy, always wore a fedora, always looked buttoned-up and official. Hard eyes—man-killer eyes—the three treated him like a guy who had to be respected. Wasn't introduced to other cops by Cullen, so nobody knows. Disappeared right after the shooting, no mention of him to press or even to other coppers. The three on the job kept it to themselves, and nobody's got the balls to ask 'em. Nobody knows."

But Les knew in a second. It was the Western gunfighter who'd stood tall and straight on the hill off Wolf Road, while Les's slugs tore up the earth around him, and fired a handgun from a hundred yards that missed Les's head by an inch.

"Okay, Skabootch, thanks. Yeah, now I see. Now I know what I got to do."

45

"**S**O THE DOCUMENT is back in the archives?" Bob asked.

"Yes, but retrievable when we need it," said Nick.

Rawley was the smart one on tech, and he had the StingRay cell site simulator, which impersonated a cell tower. It gets the call attempt, analyzes it, and passes it along to a real cell tower. It's a highly advanced Gen 7 femtocell, small and portable, able to decrypt both sides of a cell call using NSA intercept software. It was about the size of a shoe box, had thirteen numbered LED displays, with up-and-down switches next to each, labeled "Target Phone," and another thirteen digits underneath, labeled "Connected Phone." The thirteenth made it feasible for deployment against foreign units. "On/Off" switch, self-contained speaker with volume control. Jack for headphone. He could tune into radio station WBOB anytime he was within two miles.

He sat in the back of the rented Chevy SUV parked in a McLean strip mall and had his program locked in, the device on his lap. It wasn't your garden-variety, Amazon-bought toy, and where the two-hundred-dollar Amazon job would have said SAMSUNG, this $119,000-per-unit said PROP OF US GOVT and AUTHORIZED USERS ONLY. It was a state-of-the-art, military-grade penetration device, top secret, and carried by serial number in the inventory of the 465th Security Battalion of the 3rd Brigade, Military Police Detachment, Pine Bluff Arsenal, which was responsible for making sure none of the army's stores of white-phosphorus munitions ended up in terrorist hands. Pine Bluff Arsenal was about sixty-five miles southwest of Little

Rock, and it was on Rawley's lap, courtesy of the battalion's commanding officer, who had been discovered in a compromising situation on one of Rawley and Braxton's recent adventures, something about a dancer in one of Mr. Kaye's strip joints in West Little Rock while the wife was out of town.

The genius of the system was that the phone didn't even have to be on for them to listen in. It was as if Bob was broadcasting, from wherever he went. But there were limits, if only to their own patience. They listened in whenever Bob was with anyone. Of course it made no sense to listen to Bob when he was by himself, as he didn't talk to himself, or God, or an imaginary girlfriend, or a large white rabbit. So they stayed far away, over the horizon in those situations, and listened only when he made phone calls and whatnot. But the sessions with Nick were pure gold because that's when he unloaded all his fears, his doubts, his frustrations.

"Okay . . . the way . . . you want to play . . . I'd get moving . . . form recognition . . . how bur . . . can be."

"I have to figure out the best route through all this, how to use the new confirmation. What do I owe Charles? What do I owe the Bureau? What do I owe history?"

"When you see it . . . you'll know it."

Rawley and Braxton found this whole thing very interesting. It was the primitive power of narrative. Everybody loves a story and wants to know how it comes out. The saga of the strange Arkansas gunman in Chicago in the middle of the gangster war provoked them.

But there was so much to learn. Why had Charles been eliminated from FBI records? Why had he returned home in seeming shame from Chicago? Why had his life then gone into a downward spiral until he was a drunk, bitter, isolated, indifferent to his wife and son? And why had he died the way he did? All that mystery was unpenetrated. And was liable to remain unpenetrated.

"It's impossible," said Bob, "since no one is left alive from those days except that old lady, and she didn't know much except that he had the smell of whiskey on him and a bandage on his ear. The kind of stuff he did, there were no records, no documents, no photos, no witness accounts, nothing. No place to go at all."

Braxton was by this time an expert on dialogue between Nick and Bob, its nuances, its leitmotifs, its subtexts, its Mametian elisions, and he said to Rawley, "He wasn't much on his game today. They've had better conversations. What was the point of going through it all over again? What even was the point of the meeting?"

They both knew Bob had called the meeting and had rushed to get there. But, for what? For this? Made no sense.

"Maybe he's losing it. He got a big breakthrough this morning and it's got him all mixed up. He's supposed to be so smart. I have to laugh. He's a dumber hillbilly than we are, Rawley. He still don't get who we are. He only has a suspicion he's been targeted, and he ain't making no progress at all. Mr. Kaye's going to be disappointed. He backed the wrong horse, and the Russians are going to send him for a deep dive in an Arkansas lake."

Rawley smiled once for seven-tenths a second. That was his way of saying he thought that was pretty funny. It also might have communicated the message that he knew something Swagger didn't.

"SO THE DOCUMENT is back in the archives?" Bob said, and slid a handwritten note to Nick.

Nick read the note, and then said, "Yes, but retrievable when we need it."

The note said "Can you check with technical people on iPhone-penetration technologies. Could mine be compromised? It's never been out of my possession and yet I get the being-followed vibe every time I'm with somebody—like now, for example. Then, when I'm alone, I get nothing. So somehow they KNOW when there'll be chatter and when there won't. And when there won't, they minimize the chance of discovery by disappearing."

"Okay, if that's the way you want to play it. I'd get moving on the recognition issue, though. You know how bureaucracies can be," said Nick, and wrote a response.

"I'll call Jeff Neill. I'm not up on this stuff, but I know it's a big item in security circles."

Bob continued with the chatter. "I have to figure out the best route through all this, how to use the new confirmation. What do I owe Charles? What do I owe the Bureau? What do I owe history?"

When Bob was done, Nick said, "But someone believes you're going to solve the mystery and find a treasure in guns or bills worth millions. Else why would they be following you?" During that time, Bob wrote, "Thanks. It has to be the phone. Nothing else capable of receiving and sending information is on me—no cards with chips, no GPS, my watch is fifteen years old, nothing."

46

EAST LIVERPOOL, OHIO

October 22, 1934

IT HAPPENED FAST. The day before, Charles got the message from Uncle Phil to call him and four minutes later the mystery gangster told him that something had just broken. Someone at a pool hall near East Liverpool swore that Pretty Boy Floyd and his pal Adam Richetti had just shown up, looking like hobos, and asked the owner, Joy, for some food and a place to rest. Joy obliged but gave the nod, as the word was out that certain people were very interested in Pretty Boy. So the news reached Charles, Charles was telling Sam, and at that moment the Director called Sam, said that in Cincinnati Purvis had gotten a call from the sheriff of Columbiana County, Ohio, that they were closing in on Pretty Boy Floyd somewhere outside of the selfsame East Liverpool. It was all coming together on Pretty Boy.

The news was that Pretty Boy, Richetti, and two frails, the Baird sisters, were traveling from somewhere out East back to the Midwest. They were probably going to lay over in East Liverpool, since it was an area Pretty Boy had worked when he was just the hillbilly Charlie Floyd from the Cookson Hills, in Oklahoma. It was years before he became, as he had on Dillinger's death, Public Enemy No. 1, and a priority for a Division that wanted him to pay the bill for the Kansas City Massacre, where two of its agents were gunned down. That had been a great Career Move for Charlie, putting him on the map in a way his somewhat obtuse mind would not have permitted, the irony being that while it made him famous, he actually hadn't been there. He'd killed over ten men, was as bold as they came, if that dumb too, a superb shot and cunning gunfighter, and liked the fame, even if he had to

explain to everybody that he would never turn the Thompson loose on anybody, even cops and Division men sitting in a car.

Anyhow, just outside of East Liverpool, a wide-open town on the Ohio
side of the big river forty miles west of Pittsburgh, Charlie had managed to
crack up in a ditch. Stupid is as stupid does. None of the other big bank guys
ever made such a dumb-ass move and ended up like these two, wandering
the countryside, waiting for the two girls (who'd walked into town) to pick
up some transportation and come fetch them. Another irony was that as
satisfying as it was for Charlie to be number one on the Director's list, it also
meant he was movie-star famous and couldn't flash his mug just anywhere,
as in the old days.

Once it became known that Public Enemy No. 1 was in play, things
pretty much turned into a carnival, East Ohio river town–style. The sheriff
and a couple deputies ran into Charlie and Adam, had a nice little gunfight with them, the result being that Adam was captured, and Charlie
dropped his Tommy gun, but, slippery as ever, somehow ran into the Appalachian woods and got away. He wandered a bit, caught a ride, almost got
nailed at a roadblock, skipped out again, and spent the night shivering in
the forest.

By today, the Division had flooded the place with agents from Pittsburgh, Cleveland, Cincinnati, and Chicago, under the nominal control of
Purvis, up by plane from Cincy, who was a little unsure how to handle the
situation. He ended up with five cars full of agents more or less roaming the
countryside, while two hundred local cops and State policemen set up roadblocks or did their own roaming. Cops were everywhere, and it was just a
matter of time before the bedraggled Charlie ran into them or they ran
into him.

Swagger ended up with twelve pounds of drummed-up Thompson gun
on his lap in the backseat of a Dodge as it prowled and pawed up and down
the dirt roads of Columbiana County, just north of East Liverpool, through
a melee of autumn coloration, the season wearing its full glory. Ahead of
him, wearing overcoats, scarves, fedoras, sat Purvis and Ed Hollis. Hollis

was behind the wheel, while Sam McKee, out of the Cleveland Office, sat next to Charles. He had a Winchester pump riot gun, a dangerous piece of equipment, but unlike so many of the kids, he was a disciplined former police officer and wouldn't accidentally shoot his or anybody else's foot off. Behind them, another sedan carried four somewhat disgruntled and perhaps untrustworthy East Liverpool cops, including that department's chief.

"Should we have gotten dogs, Charles?" Mel asked.

"You need something for them to read scent," said Charles. "They can't work without a scent. And since we ain't got nothing off of Floyd but reports, they'll just bark and shit and cause trouble."

"Good, good, I knew I made the right decision."

Everybody laughed. Mel, as always, was the charmer.

"I love it when I make the right decision," he added, to more laughter.

Outside, where all eyes were trained intensely, East Ohio farmland rolled by, but in this part of the state, just off the big river, almost in Pennsylvania and the real East, it wasn't the endlessly flat farmland of legend but instead hillier, full of clumps of gaudy orange-red trees, shadowy glades, small valleys, bare knobs, crosscut by streams, dotted with ponds, land that glaciers had torn all to hell a couple hundred thousand years ago, pushing boulders up here, squishing them down there, almost as if the ice sheets were designing a landscape in which desperadoes could hide efficiently. Wasn't much to grow on land so scrambled, so it was mostly small dairy or sheep or cattle spreads owned by hard workers who worshipped as hard as they worked and were as hospitable to outsiders as hard as they worshipped.

"If these people weren't so damned decent," said Ed Hollis, "we wouldn't have any trouble at all. In Iowa they'd call the cops the first sign of a stranger. Here, they invite 'em in, give 'em dinner, and a free night's lodging, a new suit of clothes, and loan 'em the car and the daughter."

Everybody laughed again.

"I take it they're more careful with their daughters in Iowa, eh, Ed?" asked Mel.

"Damn, look at one of those gals and you end up in jail! It was easier to get into law school than to get a date with my wife. I had to submit more forms, some in triplicate!"

Everybody laughed. Hollis *could* be funny.

Despite the heavy weapons they carried and the prospect of killing at any moment, the four were in a good mood, maybe happy to be out of the Chicago Office pressure cooker, and Mel, freed from the awkwardness of his situation, was especially relaxed, as he probably saw this as a way to get back in the Director's good graces. At the same time, he had no problem deferring the tactical issues to Charles.

"Where is that damned boy?" wondered Mel. "You'd think he'd have sense to know the jig was up by now, get tired of sleeping in mud and begging for sandwiches from farmers' wives, and turn himself in, if only for the hot food."

"He's not what you call blessed in the brain department," said Ed. "But, about now, he's probably figured out it's over."

"That ain't how their minds work," said Charles, looking intently out the window as trees and small hills covered in pasture grass rolled by. "They always think they can get away with it. They just don't believe in no odds, and they don't learn no lessons. They're just as stubborn as they are stupid."

"Farm ahead," noted McKee. "Maybe he's on lunch break again."

"He sure does like to eat, doesn't he?" said Mel. "I never met a hungrier bank— Hey!"

They all saw it. The farmhouse was on the right, behind a mailbox with the name CONKLE painted on it, and the farm's standard features included auxiliary structures—a barn, sheds, silo, and corncrib—and a car had just lurched to a rough halt on its journey out, then jerked backwards, in a rush, behind the corncrib, which, loaded to the brim with cobs, offered concealment from the road.

"Oh, boy," said Mel, "another brilliant move by Pretty Boy. Don't keep driving, as if it's a normal trip. No, halt and pull back. Make sure we notice."

Hollis stopped the car, and the four agents peeled out, as Purvis gave a hands-up halt signal to the trailing vehicle and indicated with the same crude gesture that the four East Liverpool officers should move in on the oblique rather than going straight up the gut as he and his agents were about to do. The four men in blue got out, all with lever-actions or pump guns, and began their circle around toward the back of the farmhouse.

On the crouch, the other three agents began to close in on the vehicle behind the corncrib. The next sound was pumps gliding back, then being slammed forward, primed for firing. Charles went alone on the right. He didn't need help because he held the Thompson locked against his shoulder, but downward at a forty-five-degree angle. The thing was a beast, especially with the flair of the drum guaranteeing extreme awkwardness, but it was otherwise so brilliantly designed that all the weight seemed to pull it toward the target, and you couldn't heft it without feeling that near-gravitational force yank it toward the act of shooting. He'd checked the bolt—back—and with his thumb felt that the safety was off and the fire selector set on full automatic.

It was a sunny afternoon, twilight just coming on, the air crisp and biting, a brisk north wind pushing down from the higher latitudes, chilling all in its path, yet aside from the rush as it poured across the land, not a sound could be heard anywhere. It was a good day for killing, as fall seems to stir the blood for the hunt.

When Ed and Sam seemed to have almost completed the circumference of the corncrib but hadn't quite come into the open to face the car, they looked to Mel, a little behind, who nodded and then yelled, "Floyd, Justice Department! Give yourself up. We're heavily armed and we will shoot!"

Another moment of silence, and Charles, on the right, eased forward just a bit, edging around the wire cage jammed with the corncobs, drying out to make winter feed for the Conkle cattle. The old car eased into view, and he could see two men in it. The door opened, one of them, in overcoat and hat, spilled out, a heavyset guy in his thirties, with a square face with a look of bitter determination on it. It was clearly Pretty Boy, but Charles held fire, as it was still possible his hands might fly up. And even if they didn't, there was that fellow still in the car a little too close for comfort.

Floyd appeared to study the issue for about a tenth of a second, then dipped, spun, and took off. He raced across the front yard, through an orchard of apple trees, and Charles's companions opened up with shotgun and automatic pistol, blowing the hell out of the low-hanging branches, so that they disintegrated into a spray of twigs, sprigs, dry russet leaves, and chunks of fruit, a sudden blizzard accompanied by the roar of the guns. Yet Floyd scampered through this inclement element without missing a step, as he in fact found a surge of power in himself, knowing that he could easily outrun the range of the shotgun or the pistol, and he ran like hell.

He took off at a diagonal into the field behind the farmhouse, his obvious goal another line of trees a hundred yards away. Head down, his strong legs attacking the turf like a running back's, his arms clawing in rhythm against the atmosphere, his shoulders bobbing and weaving to that same rhythm, he made astonishing headway, opening up the distance in seconds.

"Charles," yelled Purvis from the left, still invisible behind the crib, "bring him down!"

Without willing it, he drew the Thompson gun to shoulder and rotated it upward, and his two strong hands clamped its two swept-back grips hard against him, mooring the heavy thing solidly. Through his right eye, through the aperture in the rather too complex Lyman ladder-style rear sight, and at the point of the blade of the front, he tracked the running man, computing for deflection, velocity, and trajectory, rolling smoothly in pace with the runner's speed, and when all equations suggested to him they had been solved, his finger feathered against the trigger. With a hydraulic spasm, as if operating in an environment of thick jelly, the gun fired four times in less than a third of a second, with only the last shot seeming to miss the target, as the Cutts compensator on the muzzle compensated, as usual, nothing. Four spent shells tumbled to the right.

Over the top of the gun, and through the sudden screen of gun smoke, he saw a thin gray smear of blur, which seemed to appear from nowhere, as Floyd took his shipment of lead hard, and went down hard, as if his knees had been poleaxed, and he rolled in the high grass, squirmed, wriggled, tried to rise again.

"Give him another squirt!" screamed Mel.

Charles set about to comply, but at that instant two East Liverpool officers were on the fallen man, subduing and disarming him.

"Good shooting, Sheriff," said Mel.

"Nice work," said Ed. "Man, you're a terror."

Charles thumbed the safety, set the gun at a forty-five-degree angle upward toward the Ohio sky, tucking the butt into the well of his hip with the trigger untouched by his finger.

"Let's see what we have bagged," said Mel.

They set out to examine the downed man.

"Hope it ain't the postman," said Ed.

"Maybe it's the Widow Conkle's boyfriend," said McKee.

"He tried to outrun the Thompson," said Charles. "Only Pretty Boy Floyd could be so stupid."

It was indeed Pretty Boy. He lay in the grass, his coat twisted, his hair a mess, his face knitted in pain. He was punk tough even now, with a prize-fighter's aura of physical strength though clearly broken in bone and pierced in flesh by the bullets. But he didn't seem to be worried about his wounds or his fate. He was okay with it. The world wouldn't see Charlie Floyd go soft at the end. The two officers stood over him.

"He tried to get cute with these," one of them said, holding out a .45 automatic he'd stripped off the wounded man. The other officer had one too.

"What's your name, fella?" asked Purvis, kneeling.

"Murphy," said the man, as if he was hungry to get in a bar fight. Maybe they could kill him, but, goddammit, they couldn't pacify him.

"Sure looks like Charlie Floyd to me," said Ed Hollis. "Same square-headed hillbilly mug, same pig eyes, same Negro lips."

"Fuck you, G-Man," said the man.

"You're Floyd," said Purvis.

"Yeah, I'm Floyd," said the man, sneering. "I just made you famous!"

"How bad you hit?"

"Stretch there hit me three times in the brisket. I'm done for."

"I'm afraid you are," said Purvis. Then he turned, rose, and said, "Okay, I'm going to take the car and find a phone to call Washington. You ride with this guy to the hospital or the morgue, whichever, I'll catch up."

"Yes sir," said Charles.

"Nice work, fellas. The Director will be proud."

He turned, and as he jogged back to the car, they could see other police vehicles pulling up to the Conkle farm, perhaps drawn by the sound of the shots or the smell of the blood.

McKee leaned over Floyd, who was knitting in pain as he adjusted to his fate. Now the accumulation of blood seeping out from beneath him was beginning to show.

"Got anything to say, Oklahoma? Was that you at Kansas City?"

"I ain't telling you nothing, you sonovabitch," Floyd said.

"Okay, pal, if that's your choice, that's your choice."

"Fuck you," Floyd said. "I'm going."

47

"TONY!" yelled Les.

Tony Accardo turned, saw his old pal, and ran to him. They had a nice embrace, as both had grown up in the Patch, that tougher-than-tough square mile of West Chicago where so few made it out, but both of them had. Both were successes. Tony was a high-level manager in the organization, yet to be named but referred to colloquially as "The Italians," under a Mr. Nitto, known incorrectly to the press as a Mr. Nitti. Les was a true star, now Public Enemy No. 1.

"Good to see you, pal!"

"Good to see you!" said Les. They were outside the new Marshall Fields Department Store, on the main street of the little city just north of Chicago, with its own miles of beautiful lakefront. Evanston was, as well, a city of elms, and the smell of burning leaves choked the air, as every fall the good folks of the town burned the fallen leaves in the street. A clock overhead showed that it was exactly 1 p.m., as Les had planned.

"*Brrr!* Come on, it's cold, let's get inside somewhere."

Tony—"Joe Batters," to the trade—crossed the street, and Tony led Les down a brisk block, across Orrington Avenue, right at the library, turned past the Carlson Building, walked a few dozen feet farther, and then dipped into a restaurant called Cooley's Cupboard.

"Whoa! Hate the chills," said Tony. "The older I get, the thinner my skin gets!"

"Ain't it the truth!" agreed Les. "I'm just up from the South. Texas. I forgot how cold Chicago gets."

They found a booth in the place, which was done in hardwood after the fashion of something Medieval. It was a popular joint, now abuzz with lunchers, many from the big Carlson Building next door, Evanston's only skyscraper and leading professional building.

"You'll like this place. They do curly fries up real good. I can't get enough of 'em."

"Sounds great," said Les.

"And no booze. Evanston's still dry, but I know you're a teetotaler and don't like boozy slobs all over you."

"God bless the WCTU!"

They both laughed, as indeed Evanston was the national headquarters of the Woman's Christian Temperance Union, their building not a block away.

"So how's Helen?"

"Great. Love her so. Best gal in the world. How's Ginny?"

"Ah, she's fine. You know, they get touchy, kid two out, kid three on the way. I got something on the side downtown, so I still get my fun in, though not as much. You'd never do the deed with nobody but Helen, though?"

"That's right. I'm a one-woman guy, God help me. He made me a bank robber, but he also made me a guy who only fucked one gal in his whole life and considered himself lucky each and every time."

"Les . . . God, you haven't changed. Still stubborn, brave, one-track. Crazy, maybe, but honest crazy, no-bones-about-it crazy, crazy with guts, still going strong, even as they're bringing you guys down, one at a time."

"That's me."

It was an entrance into the subject Les had in mind, but he decided not to force it. Instead, he and Tony chatted about old times, remembered scrapes, near misses, bad cops, good cops, mentors, enemies, grudges, allegiances, who had gotten whacked and who still kicked around—this, that, and the other thing—and if you'd noted them in the back of Cooley's, eating chicken in gravy with curly fries and drinking Cokes, you'd have taken them for insurance men, each well turned out, in sleek suits, starched shirts, bright ties, shined shoes, nice hats, looking so bourgeois it would break your balls to find out what the deal really was.

"So anyway, Les," Tony finally got around to asking, "I love you, but you ain't here to hear that, you got something going on. What can I do for you? I owe you, buddy, and always will."

"Ah, that's old stuff, forget all that," said Les, knowing it was impossible to forget all that. In 1924, when both were sixteen, they'd boosted a haberdashery in Melrose Park, just west of the city beyond Oak Park, and when they came out, the beat cop was waiting. He grabbed, they squirmed, and Les got away clean, but Officer O'Doyle, or whatever his name was, laid eight inches of kibosh on Tony and, when he was down and out, cuffed him. Then he dragged him back to his feet, hauled him to the nearest call box, sat him on the curb, and started to call in the paddy wagon for the bad boy.

Since it would have been Tony's tenth or so infraction, he was looking at hard time. Since they'd clunked the haberdasher so hard, he never woke up, it would have been murder in the first degree. At sixteen, Tony wouldn't have gotten the sizzle seat, but he was looking at forty years in Joliet. No big place in River Forest, no Ginny, no two kids, number three on way, no downtown side action, no place in the Nitto organization, no prospects except getting drilled by jigaboos in the shower every day until 1974.

But before Officer O'Whatever could punch the phone, Les jumped him from the roof and laid him out with a brick and laid him out cold. Les hadn't run a step. He'd doubled around to set his pal free. You don't buy loyalty like that. It took a few minutes of rummaging, but they got the key off the slugged cop, popped the cuffs, and took off, laughing wildly in the night.

"I do need a favor," said Les. "I don't think I ever asked you for one, even when Capone's people told me to go blow."

"So shoot. I'll see what I can do, you know that."

"You mentioned the guys going down. Johnny, Homer, now Charlie.

You don't even know that I got jumped by a cowboy, who almost parted my hair permanently, just barely scrambled out of there with my head still in one piece."

"Well," said Tony, "I hear that Floyd got himself blown out because he ran into a tree."

"I did some jobs with him. Yeah, the guy was no genius. Dumb as a cockroach. But still—the other guys were all smart, careful, professional, the best. Seeing them notched, feeling myself almost done the same way, it's damned strange when nobody came close for eighteen months before. It just suddenly starts happening. See what I'm saying?"

"I'm listening."

Les laid it out, his fear that the only outfit that could collect and coordinate intelligence from all over the Midwest and put together a solid idea about when-where on the bank robber stars was the one run by the Italians, and that they had decided as policy, for some reason, to put all these Thompson gunners out of business.

"Well, I haven't heard anything like that," said Tony. "Honestly, it don't make no sense, because while the Division is so busy hunting you guys, we're just oozing into this and that. Jesus, Les, you have no idea where we are. Not just whorehouses and clubs and the book. No, in unions, in shops, in the movies, for god's sake, controlling the racing wires, radio. Man, we are everywhere!"

"It doesn't make sense to me either," confessed Les. "But I know they got long-term thinkers, and soldiers like you and me can't figure on their level."

Tony had to admit that was true.

"So you want me to look around, see what I can nose out?"

"Not quick enough. No, I want to plug this up now, fast, and get back to business."

"Don't go to war. These old Eye-ties can have a hundred guns on the street in an hour, all of 'em looking for you. They'd go hard, and full-time, on you. I'd hate to see that."

"Wouldn't think of it. But if there was one guy putting all this together and someone were to rub him out, who would know? Nobody would put it together. They'd think it was some old feud. You guys are famous for your feuds, and they get settled in every alley in Chicago six nights a week."

"It's true. Maybe it'll change, but it's true."

"So here's my plan. I'm guessing Mr. Nitto would give this to someone high up. Someone who could make phone calls and get answers. He'd have a rank or something. I know you got ranks, divisions, sort of like the army."

"It's all in Italian, so you wouldn't understand. But there are four 'under-bosses' that basically run each quarter of the city and report only to Mr. Nitto."

"That's what I figured. So I figure it's one of them. They're the only ones with the power to get the answers. He's snitching to the Division each time he's able to put two and two together from reports that a certain guy will be at a certain place, like Wolf Road, or the Biograph, or a street corner in St. Paul."

"How do you find the right guy?"

"Here's how. You go, one at a time, to each guy. You say to him, or to one of his guys, real casual-like, 'Say, Louie'—or whatever his name is—'Say, Louie, I got a call last night from my old pal Les—you know, Baby Face Nelson.' 'Yeah?' says Louie. 'Yeah,' you say. 'He's back in town, hanging out in Morton Grove at a motel called The Star. He's trying to put together a big job. Thought I ought to share with you.' 'Good man,' says Louie."

"Okay," said Tony.

"So, we go to The Star Motel in Morton Grove, or whatever. If the Division jumps us, we know it's Louie. If they doesn't, we know it's not."

"Les, I hate to say it, but that's a crazy plan. If the Division hits you, you're probably going to be dead."

"Nah. For two reasons. First, I've upped our firepower. I've got a Monitor, real handy in the backseat, plus it'll cut right through the Division cars. They only have one guy who can shoot, far as I can tell. He'll be there, but I know him, and if I put a pill through him, they'll break and run, and that's my plan. Plus, second, we're waiting for them. If we can, we'll cut and run, but, if not, we'll go to the Monitor and leave their heaps smoking in the road."

Tony regarded him with wide eyes and a gaping mouth. "Man, you got balls. I never heard of anyone with balls like that."

"I just want to nail the guy who got Johnny and Homer. And even dumb-bunny Charlie. If I get that Division gunslinger in the process, so much the better. This is the only way I can figure out how to do it."

But Tony couldn't get over it.

"You got the biggest set in the world. You make Capone look like a little purple nancy!"

48

H IS IPHONE RANG. It rarely did. He hated it, and seemed only to get bad news out of it, and kept trying to lose it, but people kept bringing it back to him. He almost never gave out the number, and those few to whom he did knew better than to call frivolously, if at all, unless absolutely necessary, by which he meant an announcement that the world was ending.

He looked at it, saw a Texas area code in the number box, followed by integers of a certain familiarity, and then recalled he had given the number to Bill Lebman, Hyman Lebman's very helpful dentist grandson in San Antonio.

"Swagger . . . Hello, Bill."

"Mr. Swagger."

"That's Bob, Bill."

"Thank you. Bob, your visit sort of haunted me, and I was sorry I couldn't do more. And you do remember that I said Grandpa was worried about Treasury agents because of the National Firearms Act and so he started keeping very careful records?"

"I do."

"Well, I didn't know the half of it. The way this happened, I remembered an old bookcase of Grandpa's and that we'd dumped all the books in it in a box, and I thought maybe . . . Well, I finally found the box."

Swagger was interested.

"Please, go on."

"At first, nothing. But one of the books, still in its dust jacket, was something called *The Postman Always Rings Twice*. Crime thing, about a cook and a wife who kill her husband and almost get away with it. Anyhow, it didn't seem like his kind of thing. He didn't read novels, especially murder novels, he was more into history and stuff. So I opened it and it wasn't the novel at all. He'd just wrapped the dust jacket around it as a security measure. It was his journal."

"Did you find anything?"

"I think so. It's too much to tell, let me fax you the relevant pages."

"Please do."

"I need a fax number."

Bob grabbed the hotel guidebook, found the number.

"It'll be a few minutes," said Bill.

"You're the best, Bill. Really, above and beyond."

"My pleasure," said Bill. "Hope this helps."

December 22, 1934: A Curious Encounter

He came in late. Mackinaw jacket (it was in the 40s outside), fedora, work pants, and boots. Tall, thin, gaunt. Odd thing, he had a bandage on his right ear, or on the top half of it. Hard eyes, sunken cheeks, wary, cautious. I know the type, man hunters, I've seen enough of them. Not cops, but the kind of cops that specialize in hunting men.

He waited for the last customer to slip out, then moseyed over.

"Sir," he said, "have you got a few minutes to entertain a proposition?"

"I do," I said. "But times are hard, and I'm not buying much."

He reached into his coat and pulled out what I recognized to be the compensator of a Colt Monitor, just like the one, maybe *the* one, I'd sold a couple months earlier to Jimmie Smith.

"You should recognize this," he said.

"May I ask where you got it? Last I saw, it was attached to a rifle I sold to a young gentleman from West Texas."

"It's legit, at least in that no one else claims ownership. I came by it in ways I'd prefer to keep to myself, if it's all the same to you."

"I'm known as a fellow who can keep his mouth shut."

"That's what I've heard. I just use it to establish bona fides. It so happens, again by ways I'd prefer to keep to myself, I have access to a rather unusual cache of weapons. Some are full-automatic—"

"See, right there, that's trouble. Before June, no problem. But there's this new law on the books, and right now it's against the law to even possess such a gun without a federal tax stamp. Do you have the tax stamp?"

"No sir."

"I was you, I'd take these guns to a bridge over a big, deep river at midnight or later and one by one dump 'em in, and think no more of it. That's the safe way."

"I can't do that. Good men fought bad men with these guns, and death was involved on both sides. Can't just toss 'em. It wouldn't be right. I know you have connections with law enforcement people here in Texas. I'm sure there's plenty of small departments who'd like a weapons upgrade for these dangerous times but can't afford it. It seems to me you could see these guns channeled, one at a time, to such departments. I'd like to know that they could save a law agent's life sometime down the road."

"It's a tall order," I said. "The new law is federal, and headquarters people don't care much for the locals and for local ways of doing things. If they stick their nose under the tent, it's hell to pay to drive them out."

"You'd make money; it's not charity I'm after. You'd do swell, I guarantee it. I'm not on the far side of the law, by the way, I've broken no laws. These came to me via an honorable means, and at present nobody's looking for them or has even thought of them. So they're pretty clean."

I wanted to help him. His intentions certainly seemed good, and he wasn't out to make the big money. But the new law was unsettling. No one had yet figured if it was going to be the start of a crusade or one of those things nobody bothered to pay attention to. Or, worse, first one, then the other. And I didn't want to end up in Alcatraz.

"You'll have to tell me what they are, sir. I can't do anything more to it without that knowledge. I also have to convince myself you're not a Treasury officer yourself, and this isn't a way of bringing Mr. Lebman down. I know those boys are interested in me. I have friends in law enforcement and they have told me."

"Believe me, I am not connected in any way with the federal government."

"*Were* you?"

"Again, it would be my business. I don't think you'll find any record of me or files anywhere. I'm not on any wanted list, as I said. To them, it's as if I don't exist. And, at least right now, they're not looking for these guns. They've got other fish to fry and probably won't settle down and pay attention to them for some years, if at all."

He wasn't exactly drunk, but I could smell the rye on his breath, and his overly precise diction was that of a fellow concentrating hard on avoiding slurring.

"Well, tell me, then, what exactly are you talking about?"

"It would be two Thompson guns, drums, mags. There's a Super .38 and a couple .45 autos. One of the .45 autos is a newer C model, and has been worked on, so that it's ready for fast fire out of the holster. It's a fine gun and served its owner well. Then, there's a Remington riot gun, their Model 11, semi. Finally—and I guess this is the one that'd turn heads—there's the Colt Monitor."

It was news I didn't want. I'm pretty sure who Jimmie Smith was and unsure how to feel about the fact that I'd sold him so many weapons over the years. I knew it was a big vulnerability and could bring me down, and my family as well. It was an extremely awkward piece of business that I did not want anywhere near my life.

"I suppose, then, I can guess where you got them, if I've read the newspapers in the last month."

"Sir, I just want these guns passed on AND placed where they'll do some good. I also don't want to get nabbed with them myself. It would complicate things a bit. I'm not in this for the money. In fact, I have a crisp, new thousand-dollar bill right here I'll happily give you. Let it be an advance on any expenses you yourself incur in trying to place the guns well. When that's done, you figure out how you want to handle it financially and that'll be fine by me."

Of course then I knew exactly where the guns had come from. The thousand he offered me was part of the same stack of bills that now rested in my account across the border, with which Jimmie Smith had paid for his Monitor.

"You make it hard to say no, but I have no choice in the matter. You deserve credit for trying to do the right thing, but who knows how the federals would act if they got whiff of such a thing. Do you see?"

He nodded.

"My best advice, now that I understand that destroying them would be a sacrilege: wrap them carefully—I'll give you the makings of a very long-lasting Cosmoline solution—and bury them. Disguise the site well so that nobody bumbles onto them. In that condition, they can last almost indefinitely. And then . . . wait. That's all. Let the years pass, pay attention to the situation. Maybe a decade or so down the road, times will be different. Maybe there'll be an amnesty on these National Firearms weapons, maybe your own disposition vis-à-vis your employers will be adjusted and whatever happened to drive you away will be forgotten and their return can be effected. In the meantime, nobody's using them on banks, small-town cops, strikers, postal carriers, what have you."

"I suppose that's my only recourse."

"Here, I'll assemble a package for you. No charge. My pleasure to help keep the guns now and saved for sometime in the future when they and the men who fought with them can be properly acknowledged."

"Thank you, sir."

So I hustled downstairs, quickly grabbed the Cosmoline components, gathered them in a cardboard box, and returned. I gave him some instructions about preparation and he seemed fine with it. And though he was shabby, by the gravity of his carriage and the maturity of his remarks, I believed him to be a capable man, rye on the breath or no rye.

"Thank you again," he said, and shook my hand.

"I wish you luck," I said.

"I guess I'll stick 'em in the ground near my hunting shack. Ain't nobody going to find them out there," he said.

49

THE THOMPSON RESTED heavily on Charles's lap, an awkward fit because the curve of the drum pitched it at an angle so that sight wings and bolt dug in his legs. Ahead of him, he saw dark streets, an El station that looked like a fortification against the invading Hun, a lot of blinking Schlitz and Hamm's signs in white, red, and blue from the windows of the still-open bars along Grand Street. This one wasn't The Yellow Parrot; it was The Red Bird, avian monikers being fashionable among the Windy City's barkeeps.

Baby Face, or so the rumor now went, was said to hang out there. Thus, Sam and Charles, as well as at least twenty Division agents in other cars, all with heavy weapons, sat along the street in anticipation. But, so far, no one had entered or left the place who looked remotely like the gunman, and the two agents inside at the bar hadn't moseyed out to signal his arrival by means other than the street. It was nearly 4.

"I doubt he'd come this late," said Sam. "He's probably all snuggled up to Helen's bosom about now."

"When he ain't killing folks, he's a real homebody, ain't he?" said Charles.

"You never thought he'd show, did you, Charles?"

No, Charles did not. The tip hadn't come from Uncle Phil, so it seemed unlikely to be true. But that was the sort of objection that could not be raised, and so the whole parade was organized, rehearsed, and eventually lumbered into place, for what Charles knew would be a feckless evening.

"I guess I didn't," he said.

"Your mysterious 'cop' friend from Arkansas, he didn't confirm, right?"

"It ain't set up so I can call him. He calls me when he has something. It's awkward, but it's for his safety."

"Charles, as your friend, I'm here to tell you there are many in the office and in Washington who don't believe your story of the cop in the Chicago Gang Squad giving you info that the squad isn't going to act on, for various reasons. First off, they aren't that good. Second of all, we did check, and no one on that squad has an Arkansas background."

"I may have blurred a few details," said Charles, "to protect both him and us. I thought it was my call. The info's been good so far."

"Good? It's been great!"

"You want me to stop?"

"God, no. We're addicted to it. But can you brief me, just so I know where we stand. Off the record, which is why I chose now to bring it up."

"Sure," said Charles. He told it quickly: how the judge reached out to him, saying how he knew the boys sometimes needed to place certain info; how that had led to Uncle Phil: how Phil called him when he had hard information.

"Okay," said Sam, "I think maybe you should write all that down, give it to me in a sealed envelope. I'll sign it, have it notarized, and put it in my office safe. I don't think anything will come of it, but I just don't know how it's going to play out. That is, unless Baby Face Nelson walks out of The Red Bird this second with his hands up."

"Helen would never let him do that," said Charles.

"You're probably right," said Sam.

"Now, since we're talking man up, out of the office, and this subject is here, there's something I'd like to ask you."

"I'll try to answer. Man up."

"See, to me it seems like it's foolish of the Italians to rat out the bank boys. The bank boys are getting all the attention, nobody's doing much to the Italians. It seems like they'd encourage them, especially since they're not stealing from the Italians. Baby Face is too smart for that."

"Here's my thought. They do see long-term, that's their strength. Not next month, next year, even next decade. They know they'll be here for keeps. So here's what they're doing. Their real target is us. The Division. They're fighting us, not the bank robbers. They're only using the bank robbers to get at us."

Charles said, "I don't get it. The bank robbers ain't bringing us down. They're making us better."

"That's it right there. Look at it from their point of view. The Director, who is a political genius, among his many remarkable attributes, is using the 'crisis' of the bank robbers to nurture the Division. Look at how we've changed in the past eighteen months: we've gone from a gaggle of career idiots, like Clegg, and inexperienced kids, like Ed Hollis, to a solid organization. We've acquired a reputation; we've acquired hundreds of snitches; we've learned tactics, techniques, skills, tricks. We've gotten powerful weapons like the Thompson in your lap. We've found a cadre of brave men who can shoot it out with anybody on the planet and win. Our scientific apparatus is the world's best, and getting better. We've captured the public imagination and now they're making movies about us, radio shows, and writing books and magazine stories. Boys used to want to be John Dillinger, now they want to be you, though they don't know who you are so they want to be Mel Purvis. They want to be G-Men."

"So why are the Italians helping us?"

"Because they know war makes us better and stronger. The longer the war, the better and stronger we get. Just like the army in the Great War. But what happened to the army after the Great War? It got smaller, weaker, less efficient. The good people got bored because there were no interesting fights, budgets were cut, promotions frozen. So they left, looking for more money and a sense of purpose. The army turned into a nest for the hacks, dilettantes, and timeservers, for those with shallow talent but deep ambition. For the Hugh Cleggs of the world. That's what the Italians want: they want us to be a pathetic little group of hacks and dilettantes, men of shallow talent and deep ambition. They want the Division full of Cleggs, not Swaggers. They want to defeat us in the big war by helping us win the little war."

50

R AWLEY STUCK HIS THUMB in Braxton's ribs, bringing his brother jerkily out of a wonderful dream that consisted of Dallas Cowgirl cheerleaders (all of them), white snakeskin Lucchese boots, many quality folks who called him sir, and an Escalade in gold, with gold hubcaps, grille, and aerial.

"Wha! Wha! Wha!" he said, his hands naturally clenching into hammer-like fists, for a poke in the ribs usually meant a fight was oncoming and he always wanted to get the first lick in.

But Rawley just handed him a pair of earphones that ran from the Sting-Ray to which he himself was connected and whose LEDs displayed Bob's cell number, and immediately, as Braxton pulled the phones on, he heard Swagger's voice, and a new one.

"A Monitor, you say?" asked the new voice.

"That's right."

"Baby Face Nelson's Monitor?"

"That's right."

"Verifiably?"

"I believe elsewhere in the notes it is admitted that Lebman sold Jimmie Smith, a well-known Nelson fake name, a Monitor for four thousand dollars. My grandfather, whose employment in the FBI we can now verify, never claims that it's Baby Face's, but the other guns in the cache would almost certainly further verify it. Two Thompsons, a Remington riot gun, a .38 Super, and, not in this cache but from the same source, a .45 automatic that can be verified as the gun that killed Dillinger. Maybe some other as-sorted Baby Face Nelson handguns that can be verified."

"All of it untouched since nineteen-when?"

"Nineteen thirty-four, when all this was the news."

"Well," said the voice, "on the open market, it might be problematical to move the automatic weapons. The NFA act of course means that all guns had to be registered by 1984, and new ones couldn't be added. But—"

"But what? Come on, tell me, dammit, Marty."

"Well . . ." This Marty seemed suddenly reticent.

"Did he say where this shit was?" asked Braxton, during the pause, and Rawley nodded, scribbled a note, and handed it over.

"He said he figured the map out. The building is a hunting cabin his grandfather owned, his father owned, and he guesses he now owns, in the Ouachita Mountains."

Braxton nodded.

"Look, without my testimony, you're in prison," Swagger said, "and your little scam is the talk of the industry. You're professionally dead. Plus, you're getting fucked every night by the Pagan Animals M.C. So I'm thinking, you owe me."

"All right, all right, Swagger. Well, the thing most people brokering this discovery would do is try and find a museum that would take them so they could be appreciated for their historical significance. It would be a magnifi-cent gesture, earning endless goodwill, and also, assuming the paperwork was carefully handled, a legal one. I'm not sure of the tax ramifications, but I believe a clever accountant could take a substantial deduction for the effort."

"But that's small-time and you know it. An operator like you wouldn't never let a chance to make big bucks go to waste."

"You're so critical of me," said Marty. "You're so judgmental."

"Get on with it."

"Well, there are offshore collectors. Some in South America, some in the

Middle East, some in Russia. Men of great wealth and greed with very little interest in trivial legalities."

"So if you had the guns and the verification, you could do a deal with somebody somewhere—an oil billionaire, a cartel boss, a Russian mobster. How much?"

"I am confident those guns as described, verifiable, untouched since 1934, would be worth in toto no less than three million dollars. The Monitor is the queen of the collection. It would be an amazing addition to anyone's collection. Three million, cash on the barrelhead. Fast, clean, no records. They're very liquid. The problem would only be laundering the money, but an astute financial operator could handle it easily. The man in charge would need a rare combination of attributes—contacts, and a reputation in the fine-gun world, where the prices are getting astronomical, plus financial acumen: experience in moving sums around to disguise their origin and at the same time avoid the tax bite. I could name some people if you gave me a few days."

"Yeah, Marty, get busy on that, will you?"

"I will. Thanks, by the way, for testifying on my behalf."

"You'd steal the gold from your mother's teeth on her deathbed, but I never thought for a second you'd be capable of taking part in a murder plot."

"So harsh," said Marty. "So harsh."

With that Swagger broke contact, then called Memphis. It was a short call, just an announcement of his triumph and his plans to recover the treasure, would Nick care to come along?

"You just want me along to do the digging," said Nick.

"Damned right," said Swagger. "You got a back that still works."

"Only on Tuesdays."

"I can do Tuesday."

"Hmm, Tuesday, November third, 2038?"

"I'll write it down," said Swagger.

"Maybe you ought to contact Treasury first," said Nick.

"I'll call my lawyer for advice, I guess. If he says we can put them in a bonded warehouse, or I can get Arkansas State Police to take temporary custodianship, that might work. But I don't know if they're there, I want to get that out of the way, and then we'll see where we are."

"Good, good."

"I got to get up there, I figure Jake Vincent and his kids or one of the other Vincents can help me. I got to get a three-wheeler. I can find the place. It ain't far from Hard Bargain Valley."

"I *do* remember Hard Bargain Valley," said Nick.

"I'll bet you do. Anyway, this'll take a little time. I'm aiming for, say, a week from now to get it all set up, the three-wheeler bought, borrowed, or rented, some picks and shovels, maybe a wagon to load the shit on behind the three-wheeler."

"That would be the fifth," said Nick.

"Yeah, that's it. The fifth, write it down. Just for the security, I'll go and dig the stuff up after dark. Can you go ahead and start talks with the historian? See if the Bureau is interested?"

"Of course."

"Okay, talk to you later. Got some calls still to make."

"Congratulations. Maybe the guns will tell us the story of how it all turned out."

"If it's worth telling."

Braxton and Rawley waited, but Swagger evidently decided to put off calling his lawyer until the morning. When the eavesdropping phone relayed the sound of the even breathing of sleep, they disconnected.

"We got it," said Braxton.

Rawley nodded. They shook hands, and hugged, and then a wolfish smile came across Braxton's face. He got his own iPhone out and fingered a number.

"I just figured how to smoke a few more bucks out of our fat cat," he said.

A few rings and the phone was answered.

"Yes? Oh, Christ, it's late. You woke me up," said Leon Kaye, from his bedroom in Little Rock.

"You're about to be very glad I called," said Braxton.

"Give me a second . . . Uh, oh, okay, let me get out of the bedroom . . . Okay, now I'm okay . . . You have some news?"

"Have I ever!" said Braxton, who then laid out what he had just learned.

At the end of it, Kaye said, "Marion 'Marty' Adams, he's the dealer Swagger called. He plays his game very close to the edge. I don't know how they know each other, but Adams is exactly the right person. I'm impressed. But, no matter. You know what has to be done?"

"I know what has to be done. Do you know what has to be done?"

"Uh, Braxton, I'm not sure I like your tone."

"This next step has to be addressed. If we take the guns, but leave Swagger alive, he will hunt us down and hunt you down. That's what he's good at. That's what he does."

"Hmm," said Kaye. "I don't like discussing this."

"It has to be discussed."

"What are you proposing?"

"The hole that has the guns, it has to have Swagger in it when we close it up. That costs more. Get it?"

Nothing for a few seconds.

"I'm not sure I . . ."

"The alternative is a deep swim in an Ozark lake wearing a charm bracelet with a color television on it while the Russians play vodka pissing games in the boat two hundred feet above your head."

"Do what has to be done."

"You pay off the Russians, we take everything else. Got it? No profit for you, just survival. Got it?"

"You drive a hard bargain."

"We are hard men. We do hard things. That's where the money is."

"So be it."

"All right, now you get somebody to get to the deed registration or tax records or plat index, or whatever it is, and you find the precise location of that property in the Ouachita near the National Forest. We have to be there before Swagger. No way in hell a couple triple cheeseburgers like us going to be able to follow him through the woods without him picking up on it."

"Got it."

"We have to be there, hunkered down, quiet as mice when he arrives."

"You're a little big for a mouse," said Kaye. "You're even a little big for triple cheeseburgers."

51

MELROSE PARK, ILLINOIS

Mid-November 1934

"I CAN HARDLY WALK," said J.P.

"You don't have to walk. You just have to shoot," said Les.

"I can't bend, I can't twist. I don't even think I can get my head down to the sights."

"You can do all those things if you practice. That's why you have to practice now. So when you use it, it won't be new, you won't make mistakes and get yourself killed."

"I have a better idea. Let's go to Reno and work for Skabootch, Doc Bone, and the guys. Let's live to be ninety. We're going to die for sure, under your plan."

Helen said, "Les, J.P. has a point. This is insane. Honey, you could get killed so easy. And then—"

"You two, what is this, some sort of plan you cooked up? You're both against me."

His voice rose, even if he didn't mean it to.

They sat in the small, stuffy living room of a tourist cabin off the highway in Melrose Park. It was no swank Aurora Hotel, but it was a good place to go to ground.

Les hit his fist against his chest. The sound produced was a sort of bonk.

"It'll stop anything up to a .30 caliber, and the Division hardly ever uses its .30s," he said. "They'll come at us with Thompsons, .45 autos, .38s, buckshot, and Super .38s. The steel stops 'em all."

"I can hardly drive in it," said J.P.

"Helen can drive. You *can* drive, can't you, Helen?"

Les's wife scrunched up her cute little face, communicating, yet hardly expressing, disagreement, but she yielded to the force of his urgency. "I suppose," she said.

"Are you putting her in steel?" asked J.P.

"Nobody's shooting at her."

"No, but they're shooting at the car. She's in the car."

"Helen will be fine. Nobody shoots women. This stuff saved my life at South Bend," said Les. "Stopped a pistol shot cold. Otherwise, I'm now drinking with Johnny and Homer in hell's hottest nightclub."

The steel armor had been welded together by someone Tony Accardo knew. It was solid, tough, heavy, though less clumsy than the Knights of the Round Table stuff the cops bought from the police ordnance trade, which Les had worn at South Bend. It was like a sandwich board but cut slimmer, a more reasonable silhouette. The front plate had been fabricated off an actual human shape and thus had a bulge in it so that it didn't bang against the stomach but cupped it instead. But, for comfort, that was the only feature. Each plate weighed fifteen pounds, and they were strapped together by heavy leather. They only extended to the waist, so that pants could be worn beneath, belted tight, while a shirt, tie, and jacket could be worn over. Thirty extra pounds, and if you were upright too long, the straps cut hard into your shoulders, and the whole rig took the energy out of you fast, so that once you survived the fight and your adrenaline was depleted, you were almost flattened by exhaustion. But it was the best rig that could be had, even if it left legs, pelvis, testicles, sides, and head open to incoming fire. The federals were trained to shoot midchest, and in battles they reverted to training, which meant they'd try to put their rounds into Les's and J.P.'s chests.

"Okay on the vests," said J.P., finally collapsing to the sofa in the tourist cabin. "The vests aren't really the problem. The vests make sense, if we do the plan. It's the plan that doesn't make sense."

Les sighed. He loved them both. But they did not see it. They could not grasp it. It was so clear to him. It was what had to be done.

"It's one thing to go against the Italians," said J.P. "But to go against the Italians, we first have to go through the Division. Now, I'm not good at counting—ha-ha—but even I can count to two, and that's all of us, plus Helen, who drives but won't shoot. Gee, forty Division agents with Thompson guns, maybe three hundred Italians also with Thompson guns: the odds don't seem much in our favor."

"Honey, honey, honey, listen to J.P. This is crazy. It's suicide!"

"We have been betrayed," said Les. "One of four guys collected dope from all over the region, put it together, and then ratted us out to the Justice Department. He has to be paid back. He murdered men we all loved. That can't be forgotten, forgiven, postponed. The point has to be made, even to the Italians, that there are certain men who can't be betrayed."

"You're crazy with honor. Are you some kind of knight or something? Where does all this pride and screwball guts come from? I thought you were a bank robber, Les, but you're some kind of Avenging Angel of the bank robbery religion."

"Look," said Les, "the whole point of driving twelve hundred miles and fronting four grand was to get a Monitor. The Monitor is God. We see the Division boys before they see us. If they see us, we put a squirt of .30 into their engine blocks, and they're out of the fight. That's the power of the Monitor, but also the fact that it's easy to handle and easy to manipulate, with that pistol grip and big compensator. We vanish without the car taking a hit. Then we know who it is. Carmine DePalma, North Side. Phil D'Abruzzio, West Side. Alberto Mappa, South Side. Antonio Bastianelli, the Loop. Tony has told us where each guy lives. We wait outside his house, he gets out of his car—or maybe he don't even get out—we pull up, and I hose him down with the Monitor. That .30 caliber goes through any car like a home run through a window. We turn him to chop suey in five seconds. Then we're gone. Reno, here we come. They never know who hit 'em until the word reaches them: you fucked with the man they call Baby Face

Nelson, and Baby Face Nelson—that is, me, Lester Gillis—I fuck back, twice as hard. But by that time we're under the auspices and protection of Doc Bone and Skabootch, and there's nothing they can do about it. And, who knows, maybe thinking at least it's over, Mr. Nitto gets sloppy. We come back and turn the Monitor on him. The Monitor doesn't care how big he is, it just cares if he's alive, because if he's alive, the Monitor will make him dead."

"Okay, Les," said J.P., with a sigh. "I love you—you know that—I'll go along. Helen loves you too. But at least I don't have to fuck you like she does."

52

A JOINT
CHICAGO
Mid-November 1934

COLD DAY. The hawk snapped through Chicago's harsh streets, lifting a screen of dust, dead leaves, debris, crumpled classified ads, whatever it could move. Grit and sting filled the swift air. Men cowered against the wind's bite, shivering in thin coats, gathered around garbage cans with flames pouring from them, prayed for spring but knew spring was a long time coming.

Charles looked up and down the street, made sure nobody afoot or in a car had followed him. Nope, clear. He pulled his overcoat tight against the wind and slipped into the place.

It wasn't much. A Windy City bar and grill, largely empty at this hour, its government-green walls awash with heatless sunlight, a few thigh-and-garter calendars on the walls, a beefy thumper of a bartender. This one was called The Paragon, a little west of the Cubs' now empty ballpark called Wrigley Field. He looked around, saw a face nodding his way from one of the dark booths in the rear, nodded in return, and headed over.

"Okay," said Dave Jessup of the *Chicago Herald-Examiner*, "pigs do star in movies. You did me a favor, now I do you a favor."

"We'll see how you handle the Irish boyos that run this town, and particularly those that wear blue. I know how the Irish mind works. The cops, especially the big shots, they're loud, and they brag and shove and throw a punch, and they have big bellies, red noses, and a fondness for the pint, but that's all bluster. Inside, they're clever and cunning, and they pay attention. That's why they run all the cities in America and three-quarters of the towns."

"I hear you," said Jessup.

"What that means is that somewhere in that big new building at State and Eleventh, they have what they probably call The Italian File. Or maybe they call it The Wop File. Everything they know about the Italians—how they work, who they know, what they make, what their plans are, how much they pay, who they kill, and, most of all, who they are—all that's in there. But it's not open for anybody but the top people, and access is guarded. They sure won't share it with Justice, or, if they will, they'll very carefully pick out what they give, and they'll never give the full story."

"You want in? Why not use the badge, go all official-like?"

"See, if I go to my boss, and he goes to Commissioner Allman, and he goes to his cardinals, and they talk about it, play it, test it, consider it, finally, eventually, some kind of tit for tat is arranged, and six months from now I'll get a peep at a small part of it. But every Italian in the city will know a Justice man is looking at them, they'll know who he is, they'll know all about him, and they'll start paying attention to him, as they try to figure out whether or not to squish him."

"Probably an accurate summary."

"But then there's Dave Jessup, *Chicago Herald-Examiner*, smart-ass, big mouth, wiseguy. He knows the system, he's studied it hard, knows where the skeletons are: who's smart, who's dumb, who's strong, who's weak, who drinks, who don't, who can be touched and for how much. He knows how to operate, to pull in favors, to flatter the strong, to scare the weak, to rub on the magic lantern until out pops what I want."

"I might know a little something."

"I bet. Here's how I want you to use it. I want somebody to go through The Italian File. It's too big to move, and I could never get into the room anyway."

"You want him to take it out? It must be gigantic!"

"No, of course not. But I want him to pull the file on everyone named Phil. It's a common name among the Italians. There's probably at least a dozen, but I don't think there's so many, it would take a crate to get them out. Pull them and get them to me. Maybe I'm in a car across the street. Give me an hour with them, that's all I need. I'm only interested in one Phil. He knows me; it's time I should know him. A photo of him attached to a bill of particulars would do the trick. Do you get it?"

"I do."

"Can you make this happen?"

"It's doable. The head of Gang Intelligence has a very nice summer cottage with six bedrooms in Petoskey, Michigan. Everybody knows. The story is, he bought it with money inherited from his wife's father, one Seamus O'Sullivan. However, what I know that nobody else knows is that Seamus O'Sullivan was a drunken firefighter in Peoria, Illinois, who died when his future wife was thirteen. Believe me, he doesn't want anybody else to know that."

"You play hardball. I like that."

"I do. And if all this should put those files in your hands for a bit, what would be the benefit for reporter Jessup?"

"When I kill Baby Face, you'll be the first to know."

53

WAUKEGAN, ILLINOIS
Mid-November 1934

LES CHECKED HIS WATCH. It was 4:30, getting dark. A cold wind blew in from the lake, but that was nothing new. His topcoat was tight, his scarf tight, his hat tight, his gloves tight—but he still felt the clammy chill of late Midwest fall.

"They ain't coming," said J.P. from the front seat. "They wouldn't come this late, they don't want to do it at night, and the sun is almost gone."

"Les," said Helen, behind the wheel, "he's right. This is not the time, this is not the place."

Les didn't say a thing. He had the Colt Monitor across his lap, and, as usual, proximity to such an interesting, powerful weapon had him slightly jazzed. He didn't want to give up on this place, he wanted to shoot, send a few Division cars into the gutter, trailing flame and smoke. He was also encased in his steel girdle, and though the seat supported the weight, the tightness of it and its coldness was discomfiting.

But it was indeed getting dark fast. Shadows lengthened across Route 42 on the northern outskirts of the small industrial city just beyond Chicago-commuting range, and the parking lot to the A&P was practically deserted, as most of Waukegan's homemakers had gotten their supplies for hubby's dinner and long since bolted for home. Across the street, a cheap motor hotel called the Acme had turned on its flashing-white-star road sign but had attracted no business yet.

He had to face it.

"Okay," he said. "Helen, rev it up. Let's get the hell out of here."

"Okay if I put the Thompson down?" said J.P. "The goddamned thing is heavy and it's squashing my balls . . . Excuse me, Helen."

"Don't talk dirty in front of Helen," said Les.

"It's all right, baby," said Helen, as she eased the car into traffic. "J.P. was just being funny."

"Ha-ha—I forgot to laugh. No, hold on to it. You don't know, maybe they're laying a few blocks off and want to jump us unawares . . . Hell, this thing is twice as heavy as that one."

"Yeah, but you like it. Holding it makes you happy. It does, doesn't it, Helen?"

"He does sort of like it," said Helen.

The crew was getting rebellious. It was no fun sitting in a car in a parking lot on a frosty fall day in a crummy noplace like Waukegan waiting for Division gunmen to roll in. The steel was cold against their flesh; the heavy guns dented their muscles, giving off odors of lubricant, not a problem in short spells but hard to take after eight hours; and the thermos had run dry at 3, meaning they'd been without hot coffee just as the weather was turning bitter. And being this close to the lake meant the wind was windier and the cold was colder.

"All right," he said, "we cross DePalma off the list. Tony told his number one guy that he'd heard from me, I was hanging out in Waukegan at the Acme, casing a job in Lake Bluff. If DePalma was our spy, he'd have ratted us out to the Division and we'd have gotten a batch of them today, and him tonight, and be on our way to Reno."

"No to DePalma: I hear you. I want this done so I don't have to wear this armor stuff ever again, but somehow I wasn't in a machine-gun-battle-to-the-death mood today."

"I'm always in a machine-gun-battle-to-the-death mood," said Les.

They coursed down 42, finally reaching the civilized sectors of the North Shore, whose stylizations put humble Waukegan to shame. Now the road was called by the classier name of Sheridan, and it took them past big houses along the lakefront where the millionaires lived—Lake Forest, Highland

Park, Winnetka, Kenilworth—all before reaching modest but pleasant Wilmette. There was even a casino in a little unincorporated area between Kenilworth and Wilmette called No-Man's-Land, but its temptations were lost on the task-focused Les.

"Helen, turn your lights on. Yeah, J.P., put the gun down, keep your finger off the trigger, and don't blow any holes in anything."

"Agh," said J.P., sliding the Thompson delicately to the floor of the automobile. He managed to do it without sending fifty hardballs into the door.

"That doesn't mean go to sleep," said Les. "Keep your eyes open, keep on the scan. Helen, watch that speed, we don't want to be pulled over by some small-town clown cop. He'd see the guns and we'd have to dump him."

"Yes, yes, yes, Your Majesty," said Helen.

Traffic was thin, and so was conversation.

Pulling into Evanston, Helen suddenly found a topic.

"Say, honey," she said. "You know, suppose the Division had showed. *Bang, bang, bang*—lots of bullets winging. The ones they fire at us—"

"They aren't going to fire at us. We jump 'em first and put 'em out of the fight. That's the plan."

"But plans never work. So the bullets they fire at us, they go on into that A&P—housewives, kids, old people—is that a good idea? It gets the newspapers all twisted against us. And it gets some little children killed."

"Helen, *this* is what we do. You know this is what we do."

"She has a point," said J.P.

"Another country heard from," said Les.

"You're sort of loved, like Johnny. Especially now that you're number one and you've got such a cool name. You're a hero for a lot of bitter folks—that is, until you machine-gun a baby in a carriage."

The prospect of a dead baby didn't engage Les a bit; instead, he turned to an old slight, and he heated up fast. "I should have been number one before Charlie Floyd. I don't know why they . . . Anyway, what's the point?"

"All he's saying," said Helen, "is that getting civilians killed doesn't do us any good. You have to risk it for a bank, because the banks are where they are, downtown or on Main Street. But if we get to pick the spot, let's pick a spot where Mr. and Mrs. America aren't buying their Ann Page biscuits for Sunday dinner."

Les grumped up, locked his eyes off in the distance, and turned to stone. He said nothing, as they reached Dempster in South Evanston for their western turn, then left—southwest—on Niles Center Road, angling toward Melrose Park. America rolled numbly by, the other America, not theirs, as they'd gone outlaw, gone for flash, spurts of pure adrenaline, fast profit, lots of cash, pix in the rags, but death always looking over their shoulders. It was okay, except when they rolled by a cemetery on the right and that got Les to feeling mortal instead of immortal (it happened occasionally) and he said, "Hey, look at that."

"I hear they have dead people in there," said J.P.

"All of 'em," said Helen.

"When it's time, drop me there," said Les, squinting at the sign as the headlights scanned them. "St. Peter's, a Catholic place, would make Ma happy."

"Nobody's killing you," said J.P.

"When you get that in writing, let me know," said Les.

But both Helen and J.P. knew that if he suddenly jumped off topic, Les had reached a decision.

Finally, he said, "We'll do the Como Inn, Lake Geneva, next. That's off by itself in the woods. No babies die because Mommy had to have Ann Page biscuits!"

54

ARKANSAS 88: it was the road of his life, same as it ever was. Well, almost; he passed the old place where he'd been raised, where he'd waved good-bye to his father for the last time on the last day of 1955, neither of them knowing it, and saw the familiar land now going through some process called development where new houses rose like ghosts against the fields he'd once roamed with a .22 hunting rabbits. He felt nothing but the cash in his pocket the place had finally deposited.

Beyond that came a nowhere village called Ink, still just a spot in the road, with a convenience store now run by hardworking Koreans, and beyond that to another nowhere place called Nokana, neither place figuring much in a childhood that was drawn west to the county seat, called Blue Eye, where Sam Vincent, in a sort of way, had become his father after 1955; and he'd gone to high school, been an athlete of note, if still enduring the stares that said "Poor Bob Lee, he's Earl's boy. You know, Earl got killed in 1955" until he could stand it no more and left, on the first day of the rest of his life, for Parris Island on his sixteenth birthday in 1962. So this flat stretch of road to Mount Ida, and then Hot Springs, meant nothing until he reached a certain turnoff and headed north, into the green bulk of the mountains in front of him.

He rose, he rose, he rose against the incline, past the trees, in Jake Vincent's SUV, towing a rented Honda Recon, a four-wheel all-terrain vehicle that resembled a Harley after ten years' worth of six-hundred-pound dead lifts and squats. At a certain point, the road quit. He parked, unhitched the

Honda, opened the rear of the SUV, and removed a shovel, a pick, a crowbar, and a backpack containing a heavy flashlight newly primed with lith-
ium batteries, six protein bars, four bottles of water, and a hunting knife,
and secured all to the Recon cargo space by bungee cord.

He checked his watch. The sun was low in the west, pitching bright
beams vertically in the west, the glow turning the edges of the ruffled clouds
fiery. He took his iPhone out of his jacket—though still summer, it grew
cold in the night the higher you went—and called Nick.

"I'm at road's end, just about to head into the woods."

"What do you figure?" asked Nick.

"An hour. But most of it's uphill. I'll be all right."

"Call in every hour. I'll alert the State cops if you miss two in a row."

"Old lady! There ain't another human within a hundred square miles."

"That's what they all say."

He climbed aboard the Honda, turned the key, and it roared to life.

BRAXTON LISTENED.

They heard the phone go off, even if the microphone didn't. Put in a
pocket, all its information was muffled. Then, softer, the crank of the Recon engine could be heard, the change in pitch as it went into gear, and the
thumpa-thumpa of the man negotiating the mechanical billy goat over
trails meant for bipeds. That was all.

"Okay," said Braxton. "An hour. All we got to do is wait."

Rawley nodded.

"Let's go to the masks. I don't want to be putting them on when he's here."

The two balaclavas came out; each man pulled his over his head, until
his face was but a black blank with eye slots.

"Now the kit."

"The kit" was a hypodermic needle, loaded with 50ccs of sodium
pentothal—truth serum. The point wasn't the truth. The point was to in-
ject Bob fast and put him under. He'd be asleep for forty-eight hours, wake

up with a hangover, fuzzy memories, inchoate fury, and no idea what had happened. They'd be long gone, the guns long gone, maybe in Mexico by that time, and they'd be three million dollars richer, in cash, and it would be another week or so before clown-ass Leon Kaye figured out they hadn't killed him, just knocked him out chemically, even if Leon had paid for the full hit.

"I ain't killing that guy," Braxton had said to Rawley, who nodded in agreement. "He's a hero. I don't kill heroes. Bad for the reputation. It would be like killing LeBron."

Still, if they had to, they could: Braxton had a Serbu shorty, a Remington 870 cut down to a total of eighteen inches, with a pistol grip fore at the pump and aft behind the trigger guard, with a SureFire WeaponLight aboard, laser-equipped to put a bright red dot on any area that was about to get carpet-bombed by double-aught buckshot. At close range, it would blow a hole in a whale. Then there was Rawley with his Smith & Wesson .500 revolver. It was a giant framed wheel gun with a magic half-inch bore width that launched Double Tap 350-grain XPD buffalo stoppers at about 3,032 pounds muzzle energy. What it hit invariably returned to its pure atomic state. It too was guided toward accuracy by electronic application, another fine item from the SureFire inventory, a laser unit that projected the same red dot of destruction on anything it was aimed at. In both cases, the red dots were enough to end any argument without difficulty.

They had been helicoptered in on the other side of the mountain, moved by compass through the night with surprising grace and stealth for such big men, and set up, Imodium-prepped and diapered for urination issues, by dawn. They had not moved an inch all day and rarely said anything, as Rawley monitored the StingRay cell site simulator in his backpack for progress reports and read a well-thumbed paperback of Borges's *Labyrinths*. Braxton dreamed of the Dallas Cowgirl cheerleaders and a solid-gold Escalade, squished ants, ate energy bars, pissed in his diapers, and kept saying, over and over, "Three million dollars."

HE TRIED NOT TO HAVE a memory-wallow when he pulled in. The foundations still stood, as they were stone. But the timber, unmaintained, had yielded in large part to rot. One wall remained erect, though it looked creaky, and part of another wall, though angled toward collapse and buttressed only by rotting slats. The interior was gutted, most of the floorboards broken, and tendrils had begun to insinuate their way through cracks, gaps, fissures, and collapse. It had the stink of the old and disused. Dust and spiderwebs and dead leaves and vegetative debris lay everywhere.

Against his will, he remembered otherwise: when the cabin was whole, when it was painted green, when his father and Sam Vincent and various other men had hunted there every fall. Rustic, never chic, it never leaked, held the warm in, the cold out. It had once had a porch where the men would sit after the day's hunting, drinking bourbon, smoking cigars, telling stories, enjoying everything, but most of all enjoying being men. Much laughter while the boys were off in the yard, cleaning the deer, learning the responsibilities of the hunt that *Field & Stream* never wrote about. Then, when they were done, the boys might sit together in the lee of the porch, listening to the men talk, about politics, baseball, Razorback football, sometimes the war, though Earl never said a word on that subject and was never asked, as all respected the harshness of his five-island ordeal against the Japanese.

Now ruin and decay, the past. Dust and dead leaves of a distant cosmos. Untouched by human hands in decades. Again, he was good at repressing, the essential sniper talent, and so he finally tossed those memories down a hole somewhere in his brain.

He reverted to task. Consulting the map, he immediately found the ragged wall of foundation that corresponded to the diagram, found next the window well, which was the starting spot. He'd measured, found the degrees of northwest direction from the corner of the window well to be 43, and, using a compass, established that as his line of march. The dashes on the map had to be steps, and as there were fourteen of them, he walked fourteen and, just as the map indicated, came to the trunk of an elm. The elm was still there, still magnificent, and would outlast him, as it had outlasted Earl and, before him, Charles. It was stately, magnificent, calm, unperturbable, still leafy and healthy.

Now he stepped around it, tracked five more steps outward on the same line, and stood where X marked the spot.

Digging is never any fun, unless you're clinically insane or have an IQ of about 34. Neither of those conditions applied to Swagger. But it gets even worse if you're seventy-one and have been shot thirteen times, cut badly once, waterboarded, and are currently working your way through artificial hip number two. Still, he did what he had to do, and the light went away, the forest grew still.

He found a rhythm for the pick, with which he scrambled the hard topsoil and scruff vegetation and weeds to clods and lumps and grit, all of it easily movable by shovel. The shoveling also demanded not only rhythm but more back, and though the work never quite achieved the threshold of sheer torture, it was never less than profoundly unpleasant. The hip was okay, being relatively new to his body, but his lower back sang an aria of hurt on each downstroke, and his chest issued squeaks of distress. The pile beside the hole grew, as did the hole itself, and as usual it seemed to violate all the rules of physics, including relativity, that such a vast heap should be drawn from such a tiny penetration.

The sun disappeared totally, and though it was not strictly necessary, he set up his big light to illuminate the task that remained. He'd always been a worker and allowed himself no lollygagging, took five off in sixty and one sip of bottled water, and kept at it till it seemed he ought to be done, unless the old bastard had gotten all the way to China and stashed it there.

In the next moment, he felt the thud of striking something hard and vibratory, surely wood. Bingo!

But still another two hours remained, even if being on the downslope of the task filled him with energy, dulled his hurting, cooled his brow, dried his sweat. On and on and on it went until at last he'd excavated what the light revealed to be a coffin.

God, I hope there ain't no body in it.

It seemed unnecessary to actually remove the dirt that packed the bottom half of the box. Instead, he went hard at it with the pick, chopping, loosening, reducing its adhesion, and more or less freed the base of the structure from the earth that had claimed it all these years. The next issue was pulling it upward and out, and once he got it over the eighteen-inch lip of the trench, it was all right. It took all he had left in chest and arms but, in the end, wasn't as formidable as a body might have been, since, as he totaled it, it had to be less than fifty pounds' worth of weight.

And, finally, it was there, in the bright blaze of the light's spot. A coffin, wooden, crusted, and stained, but evidently still intact, having yielded to no incursion over the years. The old man must have shellacked it, or slathered the Cosmoline on, or whatever, amplifying the Georgia pine's toughness and resistance to the encroachment of moisture.

He got the crowbar, worked it under the nailed lid, and pushed. The wood yielded an inch, so he repeated this process around the edge of the box, and finally the lid raised a bit, loosened on its nails. He drove the bar in deeper, applied full strength, and with the creak of wood relinquishing its grip on nails the lid lifted a few degrees more. He repeated the same drill up and down the box. Finally, a mighty yank, and the thing stood opened.

He snatched the light to examine the treasure. Hmm, it was a batch of tightly wrapped bundles in oilcloth, each secured by an enthusiastic abundance of woven cord. He selected one that seemed the most promising by shape and weight, cut through the cord with his knife, unrolled the bundle and laid it bare to see before him Baby Face Nelson's Monitor.

There it was, though glutinous, almost luminescent, in the freaky light, with gobs of Cosmoline, that miracle grease that protects metal against all comers for years and years and centuries, oozing off it, out of its openings, dribbling and melting. Bob couldn't believe it. He pulled it out. By god, it was indeed the thing itself.

The familiar contours of the base Browning Automatic Rifle, though lighter at sixteen pounds than the familiar Marine Corps twenty, the incredible density of the piece, all evident, even if the magazine well was empty. He checked the geegaws that made it a Monitor instead of a BAR, and sixteen pounds instead of twenty: the shorter barrel, the shorter buttstock, and, most peculiar of all, the pistol grip descending from the trigger guard on the underside of the receiver. Only the Space Cadet compensator was missing, and that was in his pocket.

At that moment the world flashed to red, as a laser dot hit him in his eye, knocking his night vision to crazyworld. He blinked to clear away the dazzle, and when he got some focus back, he saw the dot nesting on his chest. He tracked the beam back forty yards to a scruff of brush. Then another light blinked to vivid and nailed him in the chest, holding solid and still.

"You're busted, sniper," came the call. "Freeze! Hands on head, knees on ground. All the slack's out of my trigger. I don't want to kill you, but you're about six ounces and a twitch from it, so don't move a whisper."

A black shape behind one of the beams detached itself from the earth and came at him. He felt a hand quickly slip inside his coat, and the 157345C, cocked and locked on hardball, came out and was set aside. The gunman moved away, keeping the red dot plastered on the side of Swagger's head.

The other shape came over, setting himself up close enough not to miss, but too far to be taken down by a fast move. These boys were professionals. Two large men, but not fatties, more like pro-football players of the linebacker variety, their faces hidden by balaclavas.

"Thanks for digging the guns up for us," said one of them. "Now, you take it easy, you get out of this alive. We know you'se a tricky motherfucker, full of surprises, but don't you be doing no fancy work on us or you will die regretting it. We are pros." They sat him down on the edge of the hole he had dug, and one of them pulled a smallish leather case out of his jacket.

"We just gonna zip you full of sodium p and take the treasure out of here. When you wake up two days from now—"

But then he froze. There was a red dot on his chest.

"Drop the guns, fat boys. I got M4 rock and roll on you. And I'm eager to shoot."

It was Nick Memphis, emerging from the rubble of the cabin with his carbine tight to shoulder.

The two fat things abandoned their weapons, which fell like ingots to the earth. Their hands came up.

"Joke's on you, chubbo," said Swagger, picking up his grandfather's pistol. "You thought you were hunting me. All the time, I was hunting you."

55

CHARLES HAD A BRIEFCASE full of pistols and revolvers, plus ammunition. He had a Colt .45 Government Model, a Colt Super .38 Government Model, a Smith & Wesson .38 Special Military & Police, a .38/44 Heavy Duty Smith & Wesson, a Colt Official Police .38 Special, and, finally, a Colt Detective Special .32.

He thought Sam, who had finally agreed to a shooting session, would end up with the Super .38, if he could just get the loading and cocking down. It was the easiest to shoot, had the least recoil, was more powerful than all except the .45. Many of the younger men—Ed Hollis, for one—carried them. He thought the safety, absent on the revolvers, would improve Sam's confidence. He just had to commit to the cocked-and-locked carry mode and condition himself to the easy-as-pie downstroke on the safety lever as a part of the draw. He was worried Sam would opt for the dick special in the banker's caliber, .32, because it was light, smallish, and had even less recoil than the Super. Unfortunately, it had less power, and small guns with small sights are notoriously hard to shoot well. They're for men who carry much but shoot little.

Sam was testy that morning, evasive and unsettled. Charles had never seen him so restless or irritable. On the six-block walk from the Bankers Building to the Chicago Police Headquarters Building at State and 11th, where Charles had reserved a booth at the shooting range, he said nothing, just grimly poked his way through the fall crowds that thronged the Loop, his topcoat tight, his scarf tight, his hat pressed down to his ears. He seemed like a grumpy insurance salesman.

Finally, they reached the big cop building, and Sam turned to Charles before they crossed the last street.

"Look, we have to have a talk, okay? Come on, let's get a drink. Mormon exception granted by the nearest Elder, who happens to be me. Come on."

They crossed the street and halfway down the block found a darkened place called Skip's. They went to a deserted booth and took a seat. Skip himself ambled over in time, agreed to fetch two drafts, and did. They were the only customers.

Sam took a good big swallow.

"Are you all right, Sam?" asked Charles.

"Not really," said Sam.

"Can I help or anything?"

"Not really," said Sam, taking another swig.

"Look," he finally said, "I'm going to be honest with you. Nobody's really figured it out, but I seem to be out of wiggle room."

"What are you talking about?"

"The guns."

"The guns?"

"They scare the hell out of me. I don't even like to be around them. You never see me in the arms room. If you notice, I sort of wander away when the discussion turns to shooting. I've been ducking you on this one for months now. I just don't think I can do it."

"Sam, they're just tools. They don't have brains, blood, feelings, souls. They don't wear a certain size shoe or favor red ties over blue, are Catholic instead of Protestant."

"Yes, yes, it's silly. And silly as it is, it's still not even the truth. Excuse me for unburdening myself. The guns are only the first part of it. It's a bigger problem: I'm a coward."

"Nobody's a coward," said Charles. "You just have to find something to fight for, that's all."

"No, I'm the real thing. I'm your first coward."

"Sam, I—"

"Poor Charles. You can't even imagine such a thing, can you? This must be so baffling to a man of your natural courage."

"I get scared every time," he said, even if it wasn't true.

"Not like I do. I get physically sick, my hands shake, I can't breathe right, and I hear a voice screaming, 'Run! Run! Get the hell out of here!' I backed down from at least ten fights as a kid."

"As a kid, you were too smart to fight for the bullshit kids fight for: reputation, a gal, to get back at Jack for what he said. Damned few things worth fighting for, you saw that. I was in a whole war that wasn't worth fighting. But some things are, and if that day comes, you'll be fine."

"I'm only here because I liked the 'scientific' part of the Division. I had a talent for organization and administration. I like making the calls, moving the parts around, solving the puzzle. It's endlessly fascinating. But the joke's on me: I ended up in the middle of a battlefield! The last place I wanted to be!"

"The battle's almost over," said Charles. "And if you don't mind me pointing it out, I think you won it."

"Charles, you're trying to put it in such a good light. I opted out of every possible violent episode over the past five months. I wasn't at Little Bohemia. I was across the street and down the block at the Biograph. You went to St. Paul, not me. You went to East Liverpool, not me. I am so glad I found you. I knew I'd chicken out, and the best thing I did was find a surrogate with guts."

"I don't know any such thing. I ain't heard nobody say such a thing, and if he did, he'd have me to meet in the alley. You shoot a bit, you'll see the guns ain't dramatic. They ain't. A bit. You get used to them. After a few hundred rounds, they're just things. I see that all the time. These young guys, they get such a charge the first time, they think they're Billy the Kid, and the second time they notice guns are heavy, greasy, dirty, they rip your clothes, and, if you don't watch it, make your ears ring for the rest of your life."

"Charles, you are so forgiving. But I think I need a psychiatrist, not a man killer."

"What I really am is a range officer, and I can talk you through it. That's all you need, is a good range officer. To hell with the witch doctors. I will say this with pride: I am the best range officer in the world, and have taught many a man the drill, and when he does the drill, the drill gets him through the fight. Saw it happen a hundred times in the war, saw it happen here, and, by god, I will get you over this."

IT WORKED OUT. Sam didn't set any records, but, guided by Charles's gravity and precision and confidence, he found himself more or less comfortable, and, as Charles predicted, took easiest to the Colt Super, and while he'd never whack out the center of a bull's-eye target, in a hundred fifty rounds he'd learned to keep the holes pretty much in the center of the silhouette at fifty feet. It was the same for him as anyone, not magic but an orderly process: front sight, press, recover, front sight, press.

"Well, maybe there's some hope for me yet," said Sam, weirdly relieved after the session, as they headed back. "I think I could even do it again."

"Next week, same time, same place," said Charles. "In a couple months we'll have you blazing away with a Thompson gun."

"That's graduate school. I'm years from that. Look, I feel good now. Let me buy you a drink. A *real* drink. We have something to celebrate. I insist."

"I try not to drink the hard stuff."

"Make an exception this one time, that's an order. What harm can it do?"

THREE SHOTS IN, Sam got a little carried away.

"Don't you see? When we get the Baby Face thing settled, I'll be returned to Washington. The Director will be in my corner. My hope would be to get you seconded to training, and eventually put in charge of our firearms unit. Charles, you could implement your ideas. You could make our boys the best shooters in the world and our reputation so sterling that nobody would fight us. The better our reputation, the fewer men we have to kill."

Charles didn't agree. If his knowledge of the world held water, there'd always be men who needed killing and men who had to kill them. But he said nothing, just sat there, as bottled up as if a cork were plugging his mouth.

"Charles, you go to the East, you have a big, secure job, a big, secure house, you contribute to society, you save lives, you get attention for your second boy, your wife isn't so sullen and withdrawn, you give your first boy something extraordinary to return to from the banana wars—my god, Charles, what a life you will have had! Few men have had such a life!"

"It sounds pretty good," said Charles, the booze reaching him too.

"Charles, why are you so glum? I can tell, you don't believe a word I'm saying, and you think I'm a fool for saying it."

"It ain't you, Sam. I do appreciate your faith in me. I want so bad to get help for that boy. But what you predict, it ain't gonna happen. I just know it."

"Charles, why do you say that? Why are you so pessimistic, so down on yourself?"

"There's things about me you don't know. Nobody knows. But they hold me back. God is punishing me for my failings. He's warning me to know my place and to stay in it."

Why was he so loose of tongue? Was it the booze, Sam's unfettered admiration, a particularly bad line of nightmares, anxiety over Baby Face, worried about how deep he was now in with Uncle Phil?

"Why, Charles, I've never heard such nonsense."

"You yourself called it a death wish."

"Yes, but you can make it go away. You have made extraordinary progress. You are out of your shell, a success in the big city, an object of respect for the whole community. What on earth could assail you?"

He paused. Then he just said it.

"I dream of lying with men," he said.

Sam sure hadn't seen that one coming. He looked like he'd been hit in the mouth with a tuna. He sat back, his expression reflecting his shock, his emptiness of word or emotion, his inability to respond.

Charles looked at him, appalled though he was at spilling his deepest secret. He'd never said it before, out loud. He'd never even put it into words. It just happened in his dreams, or in those blurry moments before he fell into sleep and his subconscious momentarily took over his conscious.

"I don't—" said Sam, then stopped.

The rest came out, the whole thing.

"I ain't never done it," said Charles. "I don't know why I want it so. But, goddammit, it's there, and God is punishing me for it. He took my son's mind as a warning. He made me good at killing so I'd always be apart. He made me sick and ashamed of myself and what goes on in my mind. So that's my secret, and that's why all that fine-sounding stuff you say ain't ever coming true, Sam. Sorry, if you now disrespect me, but I have to keep you from backing the wrong horse."

"Oh, Lord," said Sam.

"It's even worse now. I heard there's a place in Hot Springs that could take care of me for more money than it ought to be worth. Ain't been there, but, damn, I want to go. Got it all figured out. Thought and thought and come up with the idea to tell my wife I was going to the Caddo Gap Baptist Prayer Camp to pray to God to help me with my drinking, so I'd be gone overnight. My wife don't know no Baptists, so she'd never say, 'Oh, how's Charles doing?' and get 'Who's Charles?' as a response. Don't think nobody would recognize me, but I do realize I'd be risking everything. But, goddammit, I can't help wanting what I want."

Sam thought a while. Then, finally, he said, "I don't disrespect you at all, Charles. In fact, now I respect you more. The weight you carry, the dignity with which you carry it. Charles, listen to me, I can help you, I will help you. This doesn't have to be permanent. I just have to show you the way and it's the sort of thing I can do. I had a case like it in Hawaii and I helped that man, and I can help you. It just takes trust on your part, and commitment. Charles, you have to know: there is hope. There is hope."

Charles finished his fourth shot.

Sam said again: "There is hope, Charles. I can help you. It'll be our bargain with each other. You help me with the guns and make me coura-geous, I'll help you with your secret pain. I'll be better, you'll be better. You've already taken the hardest step, which is acknowledgment and unbur-dening. Now at last you're ready to progress, and I'm here to help you."

No one had ever made such an offer to him before, and Charles smiled tightly.

"Well," he said, "if you can show me the way, it would mean a hell of a lot. It would mean everything. Been lost in the goddamned forest too long."

WHEN THEY GOT BACK to the office, it was deserted except for the hard-working Ed Hollis, cleaning guns, and a few guys spread throughout the squad room in pools of light, working through phone lists. Troutmouth Clegg had long since gone home, Purvis was on an inspection tour to keep his yap as far from the newspapermen as possible, and most of the others had gone home to wife, kids, girlfriends, dormitory, or movies.

Sam left soon, and Charles helped Ed clean the guns he and Sam had fired. They had a good time chumming around until finally, the guns logged in, Ed departed.

Charles went into his own office, just to make a last check. He was hun-gry to get home because he had a very solid feeling he'd sleep without night-mares tonight.

He picked up the phone.

He heard the operator putting the call through, heard the connection up and down the line, then the phone ringing—was she there?—and finally she answered and told the operator she'd take the call.

"Charles? Is something the matter?"

"No, things are fine," he said. "I just wanted to check in, that's all. Is there any news?"

"None of it good. He's taken to burning himself with cigarettes. I think I got them away from him, but it's getting harder and harder. This child is really disturbed. It breaks my heart."

"I hope I have good news," he said. "You just have to hold out a little longer. I got a fellow here who believes in me, he can help me—us—in all sorts of ways. I'm seeing a move to a big house in Washington, D.C., a job doing what I'm good at and for a good purpose, I see help for Bobbie Lee, Eastern help, the best doctors, and maybe a good place where they'll work with him and he won't feel like a monster."

"Oh, Charles, if only—"

"Make Earl proud, maybe my success would help him in the Marine Corps, if that's what he wants to do."

"Charles, how can such a thing happen?"

"It's my boss, Sam Cowley. You never met a finer man. I can't wait for you to meet him. Sweetie, I think this thing is almost done up here and then we can move on. I promise you, I will take care of things and be the man you thought you were marrying."

"Oh, Charles."

"You will see, honey. I will make this happen."

He hung up, feeling a weight gone at last from his shoulders. But then it all changed. A memo was lying on his desk. He picked it up, recognizing Elaine's handwriting.

"Uncle Phil called. He says don't bother to call him back, but the word is in: Lake Como Inn, Lake Geneva, Wisconsin, later this week."

56

S WAGGER GOT THE FLEX-CUFFS tight on each of the big boys, did a
quick body search, coming up with several knives and, in each left boot,
a small backup sidearm, a Kimber Solo 9mm, and an S&W Bodyguard, all of
which he tossed away. Then he turned them around and sat them down where
they had sat him, on the lip of the trench he had excavated to free the guns.

Nick came over, having retrieved the main hardware, the Serbu shorty
and the Smith .500.

"Wow," he said, "big-time ordnance. These goobers must have been
hunting buffalo and just bumbled into you. I bet that's their story too."

"Okay," Swagger said, "let's see who these mystery gents are."

He snatched the two balaclavas off to reveal broad, heavy-boned faces of
no particular distinction under a frost of stubbly hair. They looked tough,
that's all, one with a broken nose that spread across his face, the other with
a filigree of stitch scars running from the corner of his mouth to his ear.
Both had gray eyes, not surprised, not frightened, not engaged. They just
regarded him sullenly.

"So," said Nick, *Thuggis Americanus*—what, two hundred forty
apiece?—look at those mugs, like both these guys were hit in the face by
gorillas with trailer hitches and neither of them particularly noticed. They
did go to the doctor . . . two weeks later."

Swagger opened the wallets.

"Grumley, no less. The foot soldiers of the criminal South. Law's been fighting them two hundred years, including my grandfather, my father, and me. You too. Remember Bristol. That was all Grumley."

"Were those your brothers or cousins or kids? Or can you tell 'em apart?"

The two big guys exchanged glances, rolled their eyes, and settled back into their obdurate silence.

"They're skip tracers," said Bob, examining the credential. "Bonded-by-the-state, legally armed man hunters. Tough game. Takes a hard man. Lots of physical stuff. Guy doesn't want to come along, they have to convince him."

"Okay," said Nick. "Let's see. Start with conspiracy to felony, armed robbery itself, unlawful use of firearms in the commission of a crime—I'm figuring at least fifteen, maybe twenty. Plus, I'm guessing that all over the state there are cops and prosecutors with particular grudges, waiting to pile on with this and that. So they'll do hard time, and find themselves among many of the guys they sent up and whose skulls they busted. They're tough, no doubt about it, but I think their years in prison will prove highly stimulating."

He leaned close, shined a light in each set of sullen eyes.

"Anything to say, gents?"

They just looked at him.

"All right," he said. "I'm calling the State Police. Once I do that and troopers are dispatched, it's legal, it's on the record, and there's no turning back. The system takes over and it does with you what it wants."

One of them laughed. Then the other.

Nick shook his head sadly, as if this were the greatest tragedy since Agamemnon or New Coke.

He punched seven of the eight keys.

"All right," said one of them.

"Well, well, well," said Swagger, "they speak English."

"Now, Mr. Swagger," said the speaker, "I hate to squish your big moment here, having bested two Grumley and enjoying the damned hell out of it, down to victory laps, high fives, and fireworks, but do you really think we'd move against a tricky bastard like you and this federal man without no Plan B?"

"Oh, boy," said Nick, "I'll bet this Plan B is something. This one'll be good."

"I think you'll cotton to it," said the talky one. "In fact, here's my prediction: I bet that, inside of a half an hour, not only have you let us go but you'll have given us the Colt Monitor there so we can complete our business successfully. It ain't yours, after all, it's Baby Face's; you've no particular right to it except the right of salvage. You can have the FBI shit for the museum, if you want it. Not only will you wave us bye-bye but you'll both be thinkin', Damn, I'm glad we run into Grumley. Damn, that was the luckiest thing ever."

"He's got a pair," said Nick, "I'll say that."

"What have you got that I want?" said Swagger, leaning forward.

"We know what happened to your grandfather," said the Grumley, smiling.

PART V

57

COMO INN
LAKE GENEVA, WISCONSIN

November 27, 1934

I T COULD HAVE BEEN the road to nowhere. Trees—dense Wisconsin pines—deep on both sides, nothing ahead, nothing behind, no noise, just a sense of being removed from the real world. This time of year, there wasn't much activity in the woods, and most of the ground vegetation had turned to thatching. A gray chill clarified the air, and breath turned to vapor.

"It's spooky," said Helen.

"It's Wisconsin," said Les. "Come on, you've been here before. Fish, deer, stuff like that. Farmers who talk funny—"

"Cheese," said J.P.

"Last time, they put me in jail. Anyhow, the farmers are all inside by their fireplaces," said Helen.

Les drove the newly stolen black V-8 Ford down this ribbon of dirt. He was all steeled up, as was J.P., and the Monitor and Thompson were cocked and locked, out of sight in the backseat well but could be up and in play in seconds, yet nothing was set to happen today. They had told Tony Accardo they wouldn't be there for another few days and wanted to take the time to examine the layout, figure out routes in and out, switchbacks, other cars to steal in an emergency.

"I want to know which side road dumps me in Chicago and which one dumps me in Lake Geneva," Les said.

In time, the nondescript road through the forest approached the lakeshore of the body of water that sustained a playground for Chicago vacationers, with plenty of room to speedboat, water-ski, and fish, under the blue sky amid the perfume of the pines. Before them lay the Lake Como Inn, a rambling, white-clapboard joint with country-house aspirations, including a long porch under a roof supported by three Doric columns, and out back were docks and a lakeside lawn, and cabins. Fifty yards farther down the shoreline, a two-story house stood, where the owner and well-known Mob pal, Hobart Hermanson, lived. In late November, however, the whole place had the look of abandonment, as all the vacationers were absent, the water was gray and choppy, and no speedboats flashed across its surface. A few Adirondack chairs shed paint in the chill, and the grass looked like Shredded Wheat.

"Boy, will Hobe be surprised to see us," said J.P.

Hermanson was, among other enterprises, the Slots King of Wentworth County, who'd opened the place to the gangster trade. Most of the boys, going on back to Big Al, had logged vacation time there, including Les and J.P. Hobart had big-city aspirations in a small town, and had a speakeasy in the basement during Prohibition, serviced by none other than Jimmy Murray. Hobart always had a welcome for the profession; he enjoyed the excitement of hanging around with the big-time rollers.

As they pulled in, a guy in a suit came out onto the porch of Hobart's house and watched them approach. They waved, the guy on the porch waved back, and Les looked at the man and, rolling down the window, asked, all friendly-like, "Hey, is Eddie around?" meaning Hobart's gofer, Eddie Duffy, and the guy's face locked up hard.

Then Les saw that he looked straight at the man who'd tried to kill him off Wolf Road and whom he'd tried to kill off Wolf Road.

Angular face, eyes hidden under a low fedora, a grim jot of mouth, in a dark suit like a funeral director's. He had FEDERAL written all over him in letters two feet tall. The two faced each other for a second that lasted a decade, as each tried to wrap a brain around what was going on.

"You sonovabitch!" screamed Les, reaching for his .45.

AFTER UNCLE PHIL'S MESSAGE, things again happened fast. The next day, Sam, Charles, and several other agents took two cars to the Lake Como Inn. They reconned the place, made drawings, calculated fields of fire, places for cover, methods of locking off the complex once the prey was in the trap.

Two days later, Hobart Hermanson himself showed up at headquarters in Chicago. He figured which way the wind was blowing and he didn't want to be on the wrong side in the Baby Face drama upcoming. He volunteered what he knew, told the agents he'd clear his people out so there'd be no civilians to worry about in the field of fire—Little Bohemia, anyone? Cowley made another trek up as the week progressed to see how preparations were going. He left Charles and two other men as early preparation, though Nelson wasn't expected for another two days.

The agents took over Hermanson's house, and kept a steady lookout, but on the third day, the twenty-seventh, they were running out of food, so the other agents, Metcalf and MacRae, went out to get supplies. They took Charles's car, which he'd driven up in with Sam. Meanwhile, the Division car was parked around back, but, as it turned out, Metcalf had taken the keys with him on the shopping trip.

Charles sat in the front room, his pistol in his shoulder holster, but all the heavy weapons—two Thompsons and a BAR—were stored upstairs out of sight in case visitors dropped by. There was nothing particular to do except worry and hope, and he was doing both when he heard a car drive in. Had to be Metcalf and MacRae coming back from the grocery store. He thought he ought to help with the provisions, as he'd always hated the kind of officer who ran things but never pitched in.

He got up and pulled on his hat and ambled out.

It was about 2 p.m., the temperature about 45, a wan sun pushing half its light through high clouds, no blue anywhere in sight. No wind, as the pines were still and the empty elms and maples didn't rattle in a breeze.

He smiled, noting immediately it wasn't his Pontiac but a V-8 Ford, shiny black, as if just off the lot, and he wondered if someone had tipped the local cops, who'd come by for a look-see or a pitch-in, or maybe even some tourist or a friend of Hermanson's. Through the windows of the car, he noticed the fellow on the passenger side waving, and he waved back, trying to put a smile on his face, though such an enterprise was always difficult for him, and as the car pulled to a halt, he watched the window roll down and the fellow, square-faced, youngish rather than oldish, oddly familiar, with hat low at his brow—a homberg, no less!—said, "Hey, is Eddie around?"

That was the instant Charles recognized him as Baby Face Nelson and the instant Baby Face recognized him as federal.

"You sonovabitch!" screamed Nelson, twisting as he went for his shoulder holster.

Charles beat him cold and had a mere six ounces left of trigger before his pistol fired, but Nelson had vanished.

Whoever was driving was quicker than either of them and punched the accelerator, and the V-8 took off like an Indy racer, throwing up a screeen of raw dirt that furled and flapped about Charles, and by the time he'd dropped to a kneeling position for a solid long shot, the car was too far away, and, not being an amateur, he had no call to waste hardball on phantoms. Instead, he fixed his eyes on the plate and read it: Illinois 639578.

It vanished in the next second.

Charles shook his head clear, turned to run to the Division car parked behind Hermanson's, remembered that Metcalf had the keys, and realized he was frozen in place and time. And history.

Goddammit!

The rage and frustration broke like a falling wall in a six-alarm blaze, engulfing him, and he felt his whole body jack with fury and regret. If he'd made the recognition a half a second earlier, Baby Face might be gone, but he'd be wearing a hardball where his left eye used to be. A half a dozen other scenarios unreeled before Charles's eyes in which, by this or that fraction or twitch or fate or zephyr of whimsy, Baby Face was in his gunsight one second earlier.

But it hadn't happened. Baby Face was gone, and Charles could do nothing but watch the dust settle in the air from his roaring getaway.

Where were Metcalf and MacRae? Time seemed to coagulate in an ugly wound and would not advance. The world stood atomically still, with nothing moving anywhere except the last layers of dust that finally floated to its reunion with the road, and Charles put his full force of will into getting Metcalf and MacRae back—suppose they'd stopped for coffee?—so he could get on with the chase. But time, to say nothing of Metcalf and MacRae, refused to cooperate, and he was trapped there in a nightmare of frozen-solid paralysis.

"GODDAMMIT!" howled Les. "I had him. I had the edge on that G-Man! I was going to put a slug into the sonovabitch."

"Les, sure. But maybe there were ten more guys with Thompsons and Brownings in there, and you pop that guy and they hose us down like Bonnie and Clyde," said J.P., hunched over the wheel, having roared down the road to U.S. 14 and cranked left to take them through the town of Lake Geneva.

"J.P.'s right, honey," said Helen from the backseat. "You don't know what was in there. It could have been curtains for us."

That they were right—that J.P. had probably saved his life, that his plan was working, that the future as he had forecast lay perfectly ahead—did nothing to mollify Les. He wasn't constructed that way, though he managed to get it through the vortex of red screaming rage that filled his brain that he should not yell at his wife and his closest friend.

Instead, he sat there and sunk into himself. He took on himself all the rage and frustration he felt, somehow distilled it into pure bravado, feeling it leak through his bones and his organs to his gut and, there, alchemize into something monstrous. It was the urge to destroy as pure as he'd ever felt it, to reach out and, in the infantile core of his mind, simply crush any and all in front of him until his ego was the only structure left in the world. He would, if he could, destroy the world, and if he went along with it, as it perished in cinders and grit, that didn't particularly upset him. He felt Nietzsche's pure happiness of the knife.

They got beyond Lake Geneva and in twenty minutes were into Illinois, on the straightaway that was Northwest Highway to Chicago.

"Now what?" J.P. finally asked.

Les slid out of his craziness slightly.

"Just keep going. Straight on, into Chicago."

"Les—"

"Just do it," screamed Les, who didn't feel up to explaining.

More silence, and finally Les said, "Okay, okay, we have to get to Chicago, we know where. We have to be there when Phil D'Abruzzio gets back from downtown in his limo with his bodyguards. Okay, we know it's him, he ratted us to the feds, we're going to light him and his boys up like a Christmas tree, and then we're done. Next stop, Reno. Next stop, peace and quiet. Next stop, retirement. This one last thing."

More silence.

"Les," J.P. finally said, "let's think this through."

"Nothing to think through," said Les.

"Les, listen to J.P., will you please. As a favor to me."

Les sighed.

"Okay, we know who to hit. But we also know the Division is on us. Nobody's behind us, but you can bet they called ahead and they're sending guys out from Chicago. Meanwhile, they're on our tails, running hard, especially the guy who shoots so good. Nothing's going to stop him short of a full Tommy mag. So we can be jumped at any time. Now, what about I take a hard right, head us west, and we'll bunk tonight in Iowa? Right now, we've got a free run to make a getaway, nobody's on us. Nobody's behind us, nobody's intercepted us. Okay, we do some soft time in Iowa, then, a week or so down the line, we come on back, do the D'Abruzzio thing, we pick up Helen, pick up the kids, and it's on to Reno. So much less risk, so much fairer to Helen."

"He's got a point," said Helen. "We don't have to finish this thing today. We're being chased we—"

"No," said Les. "If they think about it, maybe they figure it out. The Division has connections with D'Abruzzio, maybe they alert him of the possibility. Maybe D'Abruzzio goes underground, or moves, or beefs up his security, and we did all this for nothing. He will be most vulnerable tonight. We have to do him tonight."

"Les," said Helen, "it's—"

"Helen, please, this is how it has to be. This guy did us all, all us road bandits, Johnny, Homer, dumbbell Pretty Boy, and now me, I'm the last. It can't stand. There's got to be payment on those accounts. We owe it. Now, Helen—you too, J.P., if you want—I'll drop you off at a motel and go on alone. With the Monitor and a Thompson, I can do it. Then I come back tonight and pick you up and off we go. If I don't make it, Helen, I love you so, but J.P.'s a good man and he'll take care of you, and I'll die knowing you're in good hands and that makes me happy. But this has to be done— don't you get it?—it has to be done!"

They were silent. Who could speak out against such conviction?

"Okay," said Les. "J.P., pull over. Let me drive now. You saved our bacon once, let me pilot us to the hit. You get some shut-eye so you can drive through the night."

AFTER THE LONGEST twenty-two minutes in history, Charles's Pontiac straight-8 came up the road. Metcalf and MacRae, good men, if young, saw right away from his tension on the porch that something had happened.

"Sheriff, what's going on?" Metcalf asked, getting out.

"He was here. Nelson, a little while ago, drove up big as life."

"Jesus Christ!"

"He took off like a shot."

"What's he doing here so early?"

"I have no idea, Okay, you guys, out of the car, get the heavy weapons loaded, and come along as soon as possible in the Division vehicle. I'm going after them now."

"Charles, you'll never—"

"I ain't sitting here. I also have to stop and call Sam. I have the plate number and the car make. Mark this: shiny black 1934 Ford V-8, Illinois 639578. I'm going after it now, you come along with the automatic stuff."

"You don't know where he's going!"

"I'd guess back into Chicago. If not, then we lost him. But I have to assume it's Chicago. I'll tell Sam to send people the other direction, out Northwest Highway, with the car description. If he's going to Chicago, we may still nab him."

"He can't be that stupid."

"He can. Now, get out and start loading."

They dashed into the house to unlimber the BARs and Thompsons, plus the ammunition that still had to be loaded into spare magazines. Meanwhile, Charles jumped behind the wheel of the Pontiac, turned the key, backed up, oriented down the dirt road, and accelerated out of the lodge property. It wasn't five minutes before he was in Lake Geneva, and he pulled into a filling station, had the attendant fuel him up while he ran to a phone booth.

He looked at his watch; it was 2:30.

He got the operator.

"Law enforcement emergency, Justice Department, Chicago, Randolph 6226."

In a few seconds, Elaine Donovan answered.

"Elaine, this is Swagger. Get me Sam—fast."

Another second.

"Charles?"

"We had him. He just showed up and saw me and took off."

"Oh, Christ," said Sam.

"Sam, he's in a 1934 shiny black Ford V-8, with two or three others, the license plate is Illinois 639578. He may be heading straight down North-west Highway to Chicago."

"I don't have anyone. Lord, Charles, I've got the boys all over the place and no way of reaching them."

"Well, if anyone—"

"No, Ed's here, that's right. Okay, we'll load up and head out Northwest."

"Sam, be careful. This guy's crazy. He wants to go all the way. If you get him in your sights"—the thought of Sam in a gunfight with Baby Face Nelson filled Charles with horror—"fire. Don't mess around with arrest orders or anything like that. He's too dangerous. Put him down like a rabid dog and go home to your kids. Let Ed work the Thompson, he's real good with it. Ed can take him, Sam. Please, don't you try."

"I hear you, Charles."

58

"**W**E KNOW WHAT happened on that last day," said the one that talked, Braxton, according to the ID.

"And goobers can fly," said Nick. "They can even carry passengers."

"You don't want to hear? Fine, we'll do our time. We got some pals too, and it won't be so hard on us as you think—ha-ha. And the sniper there, he's got to spend the rest of his life wondering, What did them boys know? How'd they know it? And since we been living in his iPhone for six weeks, we know he's as serious about this as anything on earth, except the welfare of his kids. Sniper, you want to just wonder? You'd pay that price to put two only sort of bad bad guys away for a few years?"

Swagger said, "Keep talking."

"Look at him, Rawley," said Braxton. "He's all cur256361ed up. He's got to know."

He laughed.

"You know, Rawley," he said, "I think we should have just come in with Plan B in the first place. So much easier. Saves us all this stomping around in the woods. I wouldn't have had to put on no diapers, though I have grown fond of the Depends lifestyle." He laughed again, and even Rawley, who resembled an Olmec stone head settling into its second thousand years under the vines, cracked a smile.

"We'll hear the pitch," said Bob.

"You only get pitch. You don't get no info. The pitch is enough."

"We'll see," said Bob.

"Here's the bargain. We tell you what happened. I prove to you it's legit and can be backed up at any time. I also tell you where you went wrong and where Rawley went right. You are a hundred percent pleased with the info, and you believe it. You snip these cuffs, present us with the Monitor, and wave bye-bye. We're over the hill in ten minutes. Oh, we get our guns back."

"I'll drop the guns at some place in Little Rock, if that's the way the decision goes," said Bob.

"You figure he's on the level, Rawley?" Braxton asked.

Rawley nodded imperceptibly.

"That one doesn't talk much, does he?" asked Nick.

"I speak when I have something to say," said Rawley. "I save a lot of time that way. Okay, Sniper Swagger, you think you're so smart, but I figured out your next move in the investigation, where the genius FBI agent here couldn't, and I went ahead with it, so I have the document in question. That's why I have the answers and you never will."

"He can talk," said Nick.

"He's a goddamned genius," said Braxton.

"Your initial problem was conceptual," said Rawley. "As I followed the investigation, I have to say that you were certainly doing a professional job, and a few of the discoveries were impressive. Tracking Baby Face back to Lebman by means of the compensator, that's very solid. But it's also clear to me that you have reached the limits of your known world and it's unlikely that you'll get any further. What that represents is a failure not of logic but imagination. Your brains are limited by boundaries. You can't see beyond them, have no concept of what's beyond them, and, lacking that, no process for navigating them."

"Don't he talk purty?" said Braxton.

"No points for style and grammar," said Bob, "only content."

"Oh, it's about to get interesting. Go on, brother, the floor's all yours. Oh, Mr. FBI Man, sir, maybe you could change my diapers, as they're beginning to chafe."

Braxton enjoyed his own joke immensely, and Rawley did him the courtesy of letting him finish his laugh.

"You scoured the overworld," he finally said, "that is, the bourgeois matrix of propriety, rule, order, documentation, memory, index, memoir, rumor, myth, and Google. You were thorough, precise, and diligent. But you never got close to the truth. The truth isn't in the overworld. It's in the underworld."

He let that sink in.

"We Grumley, and all like us, we like what we do. And so we talk and remember and pass along. We know it's historically important and explains so much. We know it tells us things you could never understand, many of the whys and hows of history. The fact that it's ours, and not yours, is fabulously enjoyable."

"Get on with it," said Swagger.

"I looked at the same data you did, but I saw possibilities extending into our world. One of the things I noticed was that the single witness to that last day lived until 1974."

"We read the Bureau interrogations of John Paul Chase," said Nick. "He seemed to say a lot, but he really didn't say much. He didn't even call it a Monitor, just a machine gun."

"He was a professional criminal and, as you will see, he had a mandate to lie. So he told the story that your people wanted to hear, and they were so pleased to hear it, they bought it. It became the narrative. But it's far from the truth."

"And you learned the truth?"

"Let's not get ahead of ourselves. First, I had to find what remained of his presence on earth. Not easy. You could not have done it. But I saw he spent his time at Alcatraz, and I asked older Grumley to come up with names of other Alcatraz veterans. It took some time, but, one by one, I got in contact with these old salts and found one who remembered Chase as quite a mild fellow who, when paroled, went to live with a relative in Sausalito, his hometown. The birth records of Sausalito led me to the tax records, which led me to Chase's great-granddaughter, and, through a lawyer, I approached, feeling my two hundred forty pounds and KILL and MAIM tattooed on my knuckles might scare her off. Through the lawyer, I put out a gentle tender. You could never have done that, Swagger, because the crucial connect with the ex-Alcatrazer is denied you. You could never have found him. And if you had, he wouldn't have spoken to you, overworlder. He sang to me. This is why it's so much fun being a criminal."

Swagger said nothing. Dammit, he was impressed. Maybe he could have—but maybe not. Anyhow, Rawley was back on his pulpit.

"So here's the John Paul Chase story. He was paroled in 1968. An old man but spunky. He went to live with a great-granddaughter and spent the next six years in pleasant circumstances in his hometown, painting bad landscapes. To Grumley, that's a happy ending: comfort, memories, the sense of singularity and accomplishment the professional criminal feels, because no matter how you punish him, you've only punished him for a fraction of his crimes. He has the last laugh. And, believe me, John Paul had plenty to laugh about."

"Where is this going?" said Nick.

"To the heart of the heart of the matter. Now, would you mind shutting up so I can finish?"

Even Nick's irritation was tamed by curiosity. Was this it? Could this unlikely creature with his giant guns, tattoos, skull fractures, and overbrightened teeth actually know something?

"Initially, Chase was silent. He enjoyed it too much to share it. He never talked about the old days because that was his treasure and he enjoyed hoarding it. His great-granddaughter begged him to write it all down, but he wouldn't because he said nobody cared and spilling it all for nothing would be disrespectful."

"But he talked in his sleep?" asked Nick.

"No, the environment changed radically in 1972. Can you guess why?"

"You're ahead of us on everything," said Swagger, "I guess you're ahead of us on 1972."

"I guess so. The great American movie *The Godfather* is released, from the Mario Puzo bestseller. It's the rare hit that deserves its fame and fortune, but it ignites a fire in popular culture regarding organized crime. Mobster, mobster, mobster, twenty-four/seven, and for the next two years three out of every four movies, and six out of every ten books, are about the gangster world. Can you imagine the impact this had on the old man living in the basement in Sausalito who knew things? It was like he was holding stock in a gold mine or Haloid before it became Xerox. So finally, he sat down and wrote it, the true tale of the end of FBI war on the motorized bandits, in a public park in Barrington, Illinois—oh, yes, and elsewhere—on November twenty-seventh, 1934. He wrote it down. I've read it. Several times. Would you like to, fellows?"

Silence.

"You know the price? Snip the flex-cuffs, hand over the Monitor and our artillery, and be quit of us, just as we will be quit of you."

"You have the thing?"

"Not only do I have it, I have it not far from here. You'll laugh at this, Swagger. Not only were we not going to kill you, we were going to leave it with you, so that when the sodium pentothal wore off, you'd know that you hadn't been robbed, you'd been given fair value: your goods for ours. So you'd have no need to come looking for us. We don't want you dogging us, any more than you'd want us dogging you. Call it professional courtesy."

"How can I verify it? I mean, even if it's authentic and you put it in front of me, how can I know it's authentic?"

"Well, first of all, does it seem likely that Brax and I had a three-hundred-page handwritten manuscript in several 'thirties-era notebooks fabricated against the possibility of this occurrence? We're smart, but nobody's *that* smart. I'd guess you could have the rag content of the paper, the age of the ink, the fading of the cover pages, any number of forensic factors, analyzed."

"That would only take six weeks. Do you want to sit in that hole in flex-cuffs for six weeks while we check? It's okay by me."

"I'm simply noting probability, not actuality. As for the actuality, he notarized his thumbprint on it. He knew that if he were going to have it published, instant authentication was part of the sale. So it's got his notarized 1974 thumbprint and his Chicago 1934 fingerprint card. You can compare the prints. Even with the naked eye, you'll see they're the same."

"Why didn't his family publish it?"

"As you will see, they realized it tells a different story. Maybe they thought that the different story would do more harm than good. Maybe that's an issue you'll have to contend with as well. Wasn't there a movie where some newspaperman says, 'When the truth conflicts with the legend, print the legend'?"

"*Liberty Valance,*" said Nick, who knew of such things. "Starring John Wayne, the Charles Swagger of the movies."

"Tell me where this manuscript is."

"*Snip, snip,*" said Braxton.

59

Sam gave Elaine instructions to relay the Baby Face information and car ID and plate number to any agents who called in and then he went swiftly to the arms room.

"Okay, Ed," he said, "Charles just called. I'll explain later, but we've got to move fast. Nelson may be coming down Northwest Highway to Chicago. I have his make and plate. Maybe we can intercept him."

Ed jumped.

"Sam, are you sure you don't want to wait until we get some more fellows in? You and me against Baby Face, that's a tall order."

"The others will join us as they can. Charles is in pursuit from Lake Geneva. Come on, we've got to get cracking. What's loaded?"

Ed keyed open the gun vault, revealing empty racks, but for one Thompson and one Remington riot gun.

"All the other stuff is out with the boys," he said. "I just loaded up a drum for the Tommy."

"Good, you take that, I'll take the shotgun. I've fired a shotgun before, at least." It was a short-barreled Remington Model 11, a semi-auto with a capacity of four rounds. It had come over from the Department of the Army, where it had been acquired for trench warfare.

The elevator doors opened and he and Ed stepped in.

They rode down the shaft to the government garage, headed to the Division section and toward a blue Hudson, Chicago Division car number 13. Ed jumped behind the wheel, Sam in the passenger seat; they laid the two weapons in the space beneath the dashboard and leaning upward to rest on the seat next to Sam. Ed turned the engine over, backed out of the space, and headed out of the garage. A bolt of gray sky hit them as they climbed the ramp to Adams Street.

"Go north to Touhy," said Sam, looking at the map he'd taken out of the glove compartment. "That's our fastest route to U.S. 14. Then we'll head out that, with our eyes open for a shiny black V-8."

"What if we run into him?" said Ed. "Are we going to follow?"

"We'll just see how he wants to play it," said Sam. "Maybe the Thompson will convince him to give up."

"Anyone else," said Ed, "but not this guy."

"CAN'T YOU GO A LITTLE FASTER?" J.P. said. "They might be getting close."

"We don't want some country cop pulling us over for speeding," said Les.

"Yeah, yeah," said J.P., his mouth dry, no spit, his breathing hard and ragged.

The land changed after the Wisconsin border, the pines giving way to Illinois prairie, towns of no particular distinction, farm structures spread here and there in the little stands of trees.

Les looked back to Helen in the rear seat, where her seatmates were a Colt Monitor and a Thompson with a drum, plus assorted magazines and automatic pistols.

"Are you okay, honey?"

"I'm swell," she said.

"See, no problem," he said. "We're way ahead of the game. That fed's probably still trying to get his mind around it, he has no idea where we went to, he's probably just going to file a report and call it a day. As I say, we hit D'Abruzzio without a hitch and then we're home free. Next stop: Reno. J.P., you can get your girl Sally over from Sausalito and we can rent a house together. Helen, you'll like Sally. You gals can go shopping, and J.P. and I'll play golf or something. We'll get the kids out pretty soon. It'll be great."

Why did none of them believe it?

Beyond Crystal Lake, the road turned due east for a while. It was flat country, though dotted with brush and clusters of trees. Two lanes, separated by a median strip, ran unerringly toward Lake Michigan, still thirty miles or so ahead. Traffic was sparse, no police cruisers were seen, and Les kept scanning his rearview mirror for evidence of a Division fleet, but nothing came over the horizon that wasn't another civilian car dawdling through errands or sales calls. He began to relax. He could almost believe himself. Yeah, they were going to get away with it, and it would all be just fine, exactly as he had said. He cranked around and smiled at Helen.

"How're you doing, sweetie?"

She smiled back.

"Just fine," she said. "I hope none of these damned things go off, though."

"They're fine," he said. "Just don't get curious and start poking at them. You could blow fifty holes in the roof."

The road turned again, though not so severely, adopting a forty-five-degree angle to the southeast. In time, they passed a wide spot in the road called Fox River Grove, of no consequence except as the locale for a well-known Mob watering hole called Louis's and the bridge over the Fox River.

"Next stop," said Les, who knew the road, "Barrington. Then we're practically there."

CHARLES DROVE. Since it was his own private car and not a Division vehicle, he had to stay just above the legal speed limit for fear of losing even more time being stopped for speeding by a local. His automatic weighed heavily under his left shoulder, though as a precaution against fast, sudden action he'd unsnapped the strap.

He ran into traffic, had to pull over for an ambulance, got caught behind an at-grade train crossing, each little incident putting him farther behind than where, ideally, he could have been. He ground his teeth, scanning the band of road ahead of him for the shiny black Ford V-8, but it never came up.

It seemed there were 8s all over the place, however, and each demanded a close examination, but none was the 1934 model year, or particularly shiny. Each one, as well, cost him some time.

He was driven by an image of Sam in a fight and the prospect ate a hole in his guts. He found himself secretly hoping that Nelson had been smart, had gotten off Northwest Highway as soon as he got into Illinois, and had chosen a less direct route into Chicago. He tried to put his mind inside that of the man he was hunting. It made sense. Knowing he'd been made by Justice, Nelson would default from the straight, clear, obvious highway into the big town and either worm his way in via the jiggly little roads of the North Shore or go wide around the city on a western arc and come into it from another direction. He might even have gone north from the Lake Como Inn and would now be headed deep into Wisconsin or would have turned again and be coursing west to Minnesota.

Why would he shoot like an arrow into Chicago? It made no sense at all.

THE TRAFFIC OUT TOUHY was not heavy, as it was still mid-afternoon, and they hit Northwest Highway by 3:15 p.m. Turning right, they began the angle out toward Wisconsin, still sixty miles distant, which would take them through small towns just at the edge of bedroom-community distance from Chicago, like Park Ridge, Des Plaines, and Arlington Heights.

Sam placed his hand on the two heavy weapons to secure them, to hold them still, to keep them from bouncing. He tried to think of something to say but came up with nothing. Though technically in command, he was well aware that Ed Hollis had been blooded at Little Bohemia and was Charles's co-shooter on the Dillinger kill.

He looked over, took some pleasure in the young man's calm visage and straight-ahead concentration on the driving issues before him. Ed betrayed no symptoms of fear; he didn't appear to be breathing hard, he wasn't abnormally blanched of color, he wasn't licking conspicuously dry lips.

Fine, being paired with a solid guy like Hollis was a great break for Sam, whose insides trembled at the thought of what could lie ahead. He tried to order his heart to beat more slowly, his breathing to lose its rawness, his mouth to moisten. The body would not listen to his mind.

Think of the guns, he thought. Think of what Charles said. You concentrate on the gun, the shooting, that clears your mind of fear and you are able to operate. He tried to imagine looking over the flat receiver of the Remington and pulling the trigger, feeling the hard bark of the gun against his shoulder, and seeing the man of his many nightmares stagger backwards and drop. But the image disappeared and was replaced by another, of himself pulling the same trigger and nothing happening and him struggling, banging it, pushing levers and pulling cranks, trying to get it to work, while Baby Face Nelson, laughing, walked closer and closer . . .

"There," said Hollis.

Sam looked at what was indeed a shiny black V-8 in the other lane, across the median, and his eyes locked on the license as his hand clenched the barrel of one of the guns.

Illinois 556091.

He breathed an involuntary sigh of relief.

"Close, but no luck," said Hollis.

Sam said nothing. He wanted it to be Baby Face; he didn't want it to be Baby Face. He wanted it to be now; he wanted it to be never. He wanted it to be finished; he wanted it to never start.

He laughed. Manhunts were such a trite, pulp thing, and yet here in life, as in pulp, the ending was the same. The head man hunter faced the quarry, gun to gun, face-to-face. It never happened that way except in pulp! In life, the boss was usually far away in an office or a thousand miles away in a capital city! Yet somehow this boss had ended up in this car with this riot gun.

They ran into some traffic as they hit a jog in the road just outside of Barrington; that little bedroom village contributed more than its share of cars to the traffic stream, and the two agents eyeballed each one, their car going the opposite direction, feeling both frustration and relief as each passing car turned out to be innocent.

Beyond Barrington, the traffic again thinned, and a sign announced that FOX RIVER GROVE would be next, six miles farther down. The land was flat, gone to thatch, the trees skeletal in late fall, the weather gray and chilly, at 40 degrees just cold enough to produce vapor from breathing to smear the windshield. Ahead, a single car came toward them. Yes, it was black. Yes, it was shiny. Yes—

"It's them," Hollis said.

Sam caught the first three numbers of the plate before the angle of passage took the view away: 639—

The cars passed, Sam turned, craning to verify the plate, and saw the last three: —578.

With a calm that surprised even himself, he said, "Okay, Ed, get us across the median and we'll close on him."

Without thinking, he took up the Thompson.

"OKAY," said Les, eyeing his rearview, "I got a guy coming around on us."

He watched in the mirror as a heavy, dark vehicle raised dust as it bounced across the median, and, in profile, the car he made out was a dark Hudson. It hit the pavement, rammed its way through a hard left, and began to come after them.

"He's Division," Les said. "That's what they drive."

"Oh, hell," said J.P.

"I wonder how he got on us?" said Les.

"Les, I'm scared," said Helen.

"Honey, it's nothing," said Les. "We'll let him get close, then J.P. will give him a squirt with the Colt rifle in the hood and blow out his engine and he'll be dumped way out here with no way to call headquarters. We'll get off this big road and zip into Evanston and lay up. Tomorrow, we'll get a new set of wheels and go on with the plan. It's nothing. J.P., you get that thing ready. Honey, get down on the floor, just to stay out of the way."

His voice was falsely chipper, and he watched as whoever was behind the wheel of the Division car leaned on the pedal, and it seemed to go from very far away to damned close in a single second.

Beside him, J.P. leaned over the seat and pulled the Colt Monitor over the obstacle of the seat back and oriented it toward the back window, nesting it against his shoulder, his forearm on the seat back, lowering his eye to the sights, exactly when Helen slithered to the floor.

He could feel J.P. squirming, adjusting, fiddling with the heavy rifle, cocking it, checking the mag, trying to get comfortable in what was admittedly a tough position from which to shoot well off his knees on the seat, against the sway and jiggle and roar of the car. Still, J.P.'s clumsiness with the task deeply annoyed Les and he wished he'd been on the gun, J.P. driving, because he was such a better shot and so much more effective in action.

"Have you got him yet?"

"This car's bouncing, that car's bouncing, the gun's bouncing, I'm bouncing, the whole world is bouncing. Maybe if you slowed down a little bit."

"He'll be by us if I slow down, and he'll have shots into us and we won't have a thing to throw back. Goddammit, hit him. Hit him!"

J.P. fired a short burst, insanely loud in the confines of the car, the smell of burning powder and the spew of flecks and debris, driven by the fury of gas bleed-off, as well as the hot-as-hell spent shells pitching into the Ford's cabin, one scorching shell hitting Les in the bare neck and making him flinch.

He saw the Hudson evade left, out of the line of fire, through the galaxies of crack and puncture of the back window.

"Did I hit him? I had him good!"

"He's still coming, he's around on us, trying to get into the blind spot. I'm gunning it. Get ready to fire again."

Les punched it hard, felt the small car buck ahead and put a few feet of distance between his vehicle and the government men's, which brought the Hudson back into J.P.'s field, and he squeezed off another short burst, repeating the drama of the heavy weapon firing in the confines of the small cabin.

"Goddammit, I thought I had him."

"He's still there. The guy's got a machino!"

Les punched again, spurting ahead, just as the rip of the Thompson announced that a squad of hardball had been launched. One or two of the five or six seemed to hit the Ford, announcing their arrival with a smack of rending metal upon penetration, and a shiver of vibration, but most of the rounds blazed off in the direction of Barrington.

"Go for the windshield," Les screamed. "Kill these bastards!"

IT WAS SO HARD. The gun was moving, the car was moving, dust filled the air, and Sam tried to hold the wedge of the front sight on the wavering image of the Ford a few dozen feet ahead, also roaring along at seventy-five miles per, but it was a total universe of swerve and jounce and tremble and shudder, the blur of the world, and even as he fired, he knew a rogue lurch had taken the sight off the target and, by the time he'd stopped shooting, he was staring at empty space above the Ford's roof.

"Dammit!" he screamed to nobody.

The gun was so heavy, and he was resting the drum on the sill, trying to pivot with the wanderings of the two cars in the hot, blurry world of seventy-five miles per hour, but it was all but impossible. He pulled both grips tight against him, drawing the weapon hard to his shoulder, even as his back was in a strange twist in defiance of anatomical regularity, driving a pain into him, but as the car seemed to go calm for just a second. He had it, he was there, at about forty-five degrees to it, and he fired three and knew that two of them had blown blisters in the hood. Then the fragile relationship of car to car shattered in the random swerves of the chase and the Ford spurted ahead again, out of position for him to pivot the muzzle on it.

He looked in horror as the gunner in the Nelson car yanked his gun off the seat back, where it had rested for aiming through the window, cranked hard toward them, and just at that moment Ed hit the brakes, the Hudson fishtailing out of contention and the opponent's field of fire, and the heavy sounds of the Colt were only sound and fury, signifying nothing.

The Hudson slid, wavering left, its tires grabbing for traction but finding none, and suddenly it was perpendicular to the direction of the road. Ed fought the wheel, finally got control of the car, but both saw that the gangster Ford had blown the chase open and was opening distance at a relentless pace. Ed cranked the wheel, stood on the accelerator, and rocketed ahead.

"He may have too much on me now, goddammit!" he screamed.

"Go, go, we can catch him!" Sam heard himself yelling, feeling magnificently without fear, his blood hot and angry, his instincts in a place they'd never been before, demanding that they close the gap, get into muzzle-burn range, and kill the gangsters.

"He's slowing," yelled Ed.

It was true. For unknown reasons, the Ford was decelerating, careening right, off the road to the shoulder, and then fishtailed down a dirt road, which had suddenly presented itself, where it came to a sloppy, dusty stop maybe fifty yards off Northwest Highway.

They roared by as Sam got the Thompson set again and dispatched a long burst, hoping to rake the car and send all its occupants to the morgue, but his shots started high, and went higher as they passed, while Ed pumped the brakes for control and brought the Hudson to a halt fifty yards or so beyond the turnoff.

"We've got him now," yelled Sam, spilling from the car to get behind it, find cover, and resume firing.

"BASTARD PUT ONE INTO THE ENGINE!" screamed Les. "I got no speed or acceleration."

"Pull over!" screamed J.P.

Helen just screamed.

Les fought the dying car through a rocking right-hand turn, and as he transitioned from the pavement to the raw dirt of the smaller road, the windshield went red with dust, which typhooned through the open windows, blanketing everything in choking grit.

Then it was over, as the car came to a halt and its engine finally died.

At that moment the federal car flew by, trailing its own column of rup-tured earth, even as one of the G-Men fired a Thompson burst as he passed them. It was bum shooting, and neither Les nor J.P. had time to react, or really any need to, the bullets spending themselves fecklessly far beyond their target.

"We take these guys, we grab their car, we detour into Evanston, it's fine, it's no problem," Les directed.

Helen, crumpled in the rear seat well, screamed again.

"It's okay," Les said. "Sweetie, jump out and take a powder. Nobody's going to shoot the woman. We'll pick you up in a few minutes."

Helen popped the door, rolled out.

"I love you, baby," she yelled.

"I love you too, baby girl."

She scampered away, as Les, outside on his side of the car, reached across the backseat for the Thompson gun, fetched it by its front grip, and brought it to the shoulder. Behind him, J.P., with the Monitor, squirmed out, slipped down the car body to the front tire, and came over the hood, bracing the heavy weapon on it.

"Try not to hit the car," Les yelled. "We need it in one piece, and we need to do this goddamned thing fast."

He brought his own gun up, oriented down the receiver, Lyman aperture to front sight, and confronted the blue Hudson, about a hundred fifty feet out, on the shoulder. It faced due south, while the Ford had died facing due west. Between them, the contested ground was a triangular chunk of grassy Barrington parkland unmarked by trees or bushes, just open ground, its yellow-brown grass alive in the chilly breeze, while, all around, skeletal trees stood in twisted postures, as if arranging themselves for the best view of the fun in front of them. Les squinched his eyes and could make out behind the Hudson the shapes of the two agents as they secured their weapons and set themselves for the fight of their lives.

Les raked a long burst across the rear of the Hudson, kicking yet more dust in the air. He heard the more convulsive blasts of the Monitor, as J.P. squirted a short welcome in the same direction; his bullets being faster and more powerful, they didn't so much kick the dirt up as detonate it, blowing huge gouts of loam skyward, driving the guy who'd risen over the hood back.

The G-Man with the Thompson fired a long burst that pecked its way down the length of the Ford's exposed side, blowing out windows, making the thing bounce and shudder as the bullets riddled the metal. Les answered with a mag dump, again aiming his shots into the ground just to the rear of the Hudson, again filling the air with a screen of grit, driving the Tommy gunner back. He wondered where G-Man number two was. No action from the other end of the car yet. Les came over to hunt for him, having just a little angle onto the car's grille, but the fellow was too canny to make a dumb mistake like that, so Les's burst was just an exercise in suppressive fire.

He dropped the mag, skittered back to the rear seat, and reached in to grab two more just as a burst of hardball blew through the door, shredding it, letting gray sky in through the new crown of twisted steel.

That was too close for comfort.

He rushed through the mag change, exposed himself briefly, and jacked out a short burst.

"WE JUST GOTTA HOLD 'EM!" yelled Sam from his position behind the rear of the Hudson, his Thompson trained on the Ford a hundred fifty feet away, as he scanned for targets. "There'll be cops and State boys and even Charles here in minutes, maybe seconds. Just hold 'em."

"He's too far for the shotgun," Ed yelled back from his crouch behind the wheel at the car's other end, just below the crest of the hood. "Goddamn, I need a rifle!"

"I have 'em pinned," yelled Sam. He ducked up, squeezed a small dose of lead off, then dropped down.

Ed had his Super .38 out. He rose over the hood, and though it was a long shot, he knew his chances improved with stability, so he placed the gun in both hands against the flat of the hood, held high, eyes pinned on the front sight, and fired three times at the hunched figure behind the hood whose automatic rifle was sending hellacious strikes toward them. He slipped down immediately after the third shot, hoping that one of these too-long attempts had connected but suspecting they hadn't. He squirmed farther down and emerged around the grille of the Hudson and this time fired left-handed at the figure with the Thompson, again holding high, again doing everything right except hitting.

"Goddamn," he screamed as the slide locked back, and he dipped back just as the earth next to him broke into spurts of dirt and grit, sending a sting of debris toward him. He reached into his suit pocket, yanked a Super .38 mag free, and slammed it into the shaft of the pistol grip, came back over again.

He saw Baby Face.

He saw him coming right at them.

"He's coming, Sam. Hit him, hit him, hit him! He's coming!"

LES FIRED, the gun quit on its own, and he looked to see a stovepipe jam at the breach, the shell trapped between the bolt and the breach opening at a weird angle. He pulled hard on the bolt, to no effect, felt a scalding column of steam rise from it.

This has to be over, he thought.

Every second we are stuck here, we are closer to going down.

I have to end this thing now.

He stood, slipped over to J.P., crouched at the other end of the Ford, and slid the Thompson to him.

"Fix this goddamned thing! Here, give me the big one."

They exchanged weapons, J.P. taking the Thompson, looking at it, realizing the magazine follower had jammed the shell up too quickly. His quick fix was to hit the mag button and drop the defective mag, even as Les gave him a new twenty-round magazine. He locked it in, found the bolt free, drew it back.

Les grabbed two more Monitor mags out of the back, dumped the half-full one, and pushed a new one into the well.

"I'm going to finish these bastards," he shouted. "Cover me, goddammit."

He rose, the Monitor locked under his right arm, his right hand crushing the pistol grip, his left guiding the muzzle from the fore end, and began to walk toward the Hudson, squeezing out short bursts. He walked in a fury of hatred and fear, everything he was, or had dreamed of, expressed in the insane trudge into the guns of the Division, daring them to bring him down, not caring if they did, his mind crazy-bent on one goal, which was to kill. He walked, he walked, he felt three thumps as three hardballs hit him hard in the belly and chest but did not penetrate the steel that shielded his body from them. He walked, he walked, he fired, he walked, the shells flipped from the breach, the heavy bullets tore huge detonations of dirt and shredded grass skyward. He felt his legs light up in pure sting. He walked, he walked, he walked.

"He's coming, Sam! Hit him, hit him, hit him! He's coming!"

Sam slipped around the body of the car and saw the killer stomping furiously toward him, hat low, face red, bent over his automatic rifle in some kind of desperate concentration, and Sam got to him first. He put the wedge sight square in the middle of the chest and squeezed off a burst and knew that he'd hit with three dead-solid, perfect killing shots to the center of mass, but still the man came on, unperturbed by the death that had just eviscerated him.

Sam got back on target, this time leaning harder into the car for more support, clenching the gun to shoulder, and all his muscles tight against it, looking through the Lyman aperture at the front sight's triangle, and squeezed off another burst, but at two rounds the gun went quiet.

What the hell?

He brought it down and realized he had no idea what to do. He banged hard at it with one hand, then pulled back on the bolt and it slid, perfectly and smoothly, locking back, and he looked into the breach that his move had opened and saw only emptiness where a cartridge should have been and realized, with horror, that the gun was empty and that he had no pistol and that—

It felt like he was kicked hard in the stomach twice, and a wave of dizziness crashed across him. The gun slipped from his grip, he tried to compensate for the spinning but he lurched forward, nose down, smelling the dirt and grass of Barrington.

Somehow, he found the strength to look up and saw the gunman twenty feet away, but having turned, now addressing Ed.

"Ed, Ed!" he called, not so much voice but heart, for he wanted nothing more than to protect the young man, but then it all went away and he blacked out.

LES SAW THE LAWMAN go down, as by the application of a sudden bolt of energy his body moved by the velocity of what had struck him, not by anything he himself had done. He alchemized in a microsecond from alive and vital to sheer weight falling in obedience to gravity and hit ground, twitching. Les knew the man had taken two solid through the gut. He knew such hits had permanent results. He knew you didn't come back from two Government .30s.

Another rage of bees tore at his legs, sending tendrils of angry pain through him. He turned and saw the other agent a few yards away, in midrush, as, having just abandoned his shotgun for empty, the man yanked on his pistol to bring it to bear.

But Les's instincts had oriented the Monitor, and his instincts had motivated his trigger finger, and without willing or thinking, he felt the hydraulic spasms as the rifle fired four times in less than half a second, and one of the rounds smacked into the agent's forehead, its force blowing his hat off as it cratered his face, which began to foam with blood. The man went down, hard and flat, stirred, rolled over, and then just lay still.

Suddenly it was quiet.

Suddenly it was over.

Les's legs were on fire. The anesthetic of pure combat rage had abruptly quit and he felt the pain where he'd taken lead. He felt a dozen wounds, he felt the rush of blood, he felt steel clamps of hurt pinching hard, he felt the bones themselves crying to yield, to sag to earth, but he turned and yelled to J.P., then scanned for the approach of new enemies. Far off he could see people hidden behind stopped cars or peering around telephone poles, but no one wanted to enter the battlefield.

He limped to the Hudson, walked around it, and climbed in, dumping the heavy Colt Automatic Rifle in the passenger seat. The car was still running, as the driver had leapt from it at such a speed running for cover that he hadn't switched off the ignition. Les dropped it into gear, legs still burning, and cranked the wheel, delivering the car in seconds to the Ford, which had been almost thoroughly eviscerated by the fight. It looked like it had been jackhammered by a crew of laborers. He pulled up next to it, stumbled out his own door, opened the rear door, and rolled in.

J.P. was on him in seconds.

"Load the guns and get us out of here."

"How bad?"

"He had a shotgun. He put some buck in my legs, they hurt like hell, but I don't think I'm bleeding out, and I couldn't walk if he'd broken any bones."

It took J.P. thirty seconds to toss the Thompson in, then he was behind the wheel and the car was in motion.

"Do you see Helen?" Les moaned from the backseat.

"No, I— Oh, wait. Jesus Christ, yes, here she is."

Helen ran toward them as J.P. halted. She jumped in, screaming, "Oh god, baby, are you all right?" and J.P. punched it, the tires spinning on the grass, bucked to the pavement, and took off down Northwest Highway.

"Christ, it hurts," Les was saying.

"It's all right, baby," said Helen.

60

THERE WAS NO DOUBT about authenticity. The handwritten manuscript was spread over several stocks of old, old paper, dry as bone, delicate to the touch, a total of one hundred and fifty-one pages, all in the same hand, a big, looping, semi-literate cursive. None of it was written in ballpoint. You could track as the pencils, some blue, some red, some plain lead, wore to nub against the pressure of an eighty-year-old man's rush of memories. It bore the title, handwritten in clumsy capitals, "THEY CALLED HIM BABY FACE!"

J.P. was no writer. His prose was barely serviceable, riddled with cliches and other forms of staleness, tripe, and banality. He frequently misspelled, had much trouble with tenses, and that American bugaboo: the mysterious apostrophe. But he wrote with energy, directness, and without any literary attributes, such as irony, sarcasm, archness, coyness. He just was racing death to get it all down. He almost made it.

But when they read the account, something almost magical occurred. In spite of its crudity, each man saw it as J.P. saw it—as if when the narrative intensified, J.P. became more of a writer, and pure memory elevated his prose—and by their need to know.

Nick put down the last page of his account of the battle. They sat at a dilapidated picnic table not far from the ruins of the cottage. It was sunny and quiet in the high woods, under a blue sky, where the mayhem just de-scribed was a million miles and eighty-three years away. Rawley had fetched the first chunk, stashed a few hundred meters away, while Braxton, still flex-cuffed but patient and obliging, played the hostage.

"Good reading, huh, boys?" he called, noting the completion.

They ignored him.

"No doubt those two guys were brave," said Nick, "but they were so over-matched."

"I'd hate to think of the rage Charles must have felt," Bob said. "He could have handled Nelson and Chase, but he wasn't there. Christ, the anger he must have felt."

"This belongs to the Bureau," said Nick. "It's a perfect example of what not to do in a gunfight. It's Dade County all over again. Or, rather, Dade County was Barrington all over again."

He was alluding to an infamous Bureau gunfight where an anti-bank-robbery team had jumped a duo of heavily armed hard cases who wanted to go all the way. Who had to go all the way. Who, like their predecessor and icon, Lester "Baby Face Nelson" Gillis, had been dreaming of such an Armageddon in a very small space his whole life, and when it happened, he was ready for it, all gunned up, crazy-brave as any SS lunatic on the Eastern Front, and you could only beat him with courage, a mind as tough as his, experience, and bigger, faster bullets. That's how Michael Platt killed two agents and wounded four more in three minutes of gunwork in August of 1987.

"Ballistics," said Bob. "If you have ballistics on your side, you have God on your side."

"Baby Face had the big gun, no doubt about it," said Nick.

"That .30-06 on full auto must have been a terrifying thing. I'm just thinking that even as it hit the earth, even as it missed, it blew out such a chunk of planet, it had to drive the agents back, taken their aggression from them. In 'Nam, first tour, some of the RVNs were armed with old War Two stuff, and the BAR and the Browning Thirty did a job on any structure, any man, any vehicle, any anything they hit. There's poor Sam, with a Thompson he'd never fired before, sending three-quarters of his shots into the sky or the dirt. There's Hollis, a good man in a fight but stuck with a shotgun with a range of fifteen good yards before the shot pattern breaks apart. He goes to pistol, but he's shooting a moving, advancing killer, while another one is suppressing him with full automatic."

They were silent.

Then Bob said, "Charles Swagger would have shot Nelson in the knee, blown it out, and when he was down and still, shot him in the head, all from a hundred feet out. Then he would have set the car tank afire with Thompson tracer, and when Chase ran out in flames, screaming, he would have tracked him and blown his head off. And we wouldn't be sitting here reading this."

More silence.

Rawley emerged from the woods line, as before, his hands up.

"Last chunk," he said, bringing the package over.

"This one's got some surprises."

Swagger took it, flipped through it, took a deep breath.

"You sure you want to read it now, sniper man? You may learn something you don't want to," said Braxton.

"Shut up," said Nick.

"Fair warning," said Rawley. "I've read it. He hasn't."

Rawley was right. Whatever Charles did or didn't do, whatever he became, why his spiral was downward toward dissolution and death, it was here in this little nest of pages.

61

Just inside Barrington's limits, the traffic backed up. Charles opened his door, and stood to see it was stopped by the presence of two police cruisers by the side of the road a hundred yards ahead. He got out his badge, got back in, and rolled down the window. Honking, he got enough room to maneuver to the shoulder, and progressed to the scene, where an officer halted him until Charles showed his badge.

The cop said, "Okay, sir, go on. They're your people, all right."

Charles felt his stomach drop out when the cop spoke. Never in a fight had he had such a feeling, but this one was straight off the cliff, all the way down, faster and faster, until he hit and was smashed to pieces.

He took a deep breath, moved ahead a few more yards to the police cruiser, and got out.

He could see Sam on the ground, blood everywhere on his lower trunk, the Thompson ahead of him in the grass, chinks of brass littering the site, a cop kneeling over, not doing much since there wasn't much to do. Even from where he was, Charles could see the wound. He'd seen it before, in the war, and a fight or two along the way. The gut, straight through, blowing chunks and tubing out, opening a dozen unstoppable bloodstreams, pulverizing the mysterious organs that kept you alive. It was fatal.

He looked and a hundred fifty feet away saw the Ford, not so shiny now. Windows all shot out, one tire flattened, so the thing perched at a broken angle, dust and bullet holes all across it. From the site, he could pretty much read the story of the fight, and the tracks of the missing Hudson, heavy in the grass, told him the rest of the story.

He went to Sam.

The man had the death pallor, a rim of blood around his lips, his eyes sliding toward glassiness as he contemplated sky and nothing else. Flecks of blood dotted his skin. His Brooks Brothers striped shirt was seeped in magenta and flecked by kernels of black dried blood. His breathing was hardly there. But as Charles knelt, Sam managed to turn his eyes. Charles put his hand on the man's shoulder, for there wasn't enough energy left in him for him to lift a hand.

"Charles, he wouldn't go down. I hit him over and over. I put that front sight on him, I fired short bursts. I know I hit him, but he kept on coming."

"I'm sure you hit him bad, Sam. I'm sure he's dead and they've dumped him in a hole somewhere. We'll find him soon."

"Oh god, Charles, I tried so hard. Tell my boys how hard I tried."

"You can tell 'em yourself, Sam. They'll sew you up and you'll be back in no time."

"How's Ed, Charles? I haven't heard anything, I haven't seen him. I . . ." He trailed off.

Charles looked at the cop on the other side of Sam and the cop gave him the bad news with a quick shake of the head and Charles knew Ed was gone.

"They're working on him now, Sam," said Charles. "Like you, he's going to pull through."

"I know you're lying, Charles. It's okay. I was brave, wasn't I? I did the job, the Duty. No one can say—"

"What they'll say is that Division agent Sam Cowley stood up and shot it out with the most dangerous man in America. They'll say that, because it's the truth. You're the best, Sam."

"Charles, go now. Get him. He went south on the highway only a few minutes ago. He'll stay under the speed limit. It's the number nineteen car, blue Hudson, plate G45511."

Charles nodded. He pressed Sam's hand, and rose.

"The ambulance will be here in seconds," he said.

The cop said to him, "Sir, you'd better take the guns along. This place is going to be hopping in minutes and there aren't enough of us to keep control of the scene."

"Good idea, Officer," said Charles. He bent, picked up Sam's Thompson, noting from the weight that it was empty. He walked to Ed—the blister of the entry wound was right above the eye—and picked up the Remington 11, also empty, and Ed's Super .38. He walked back to his Pontiac and dumped them in the trunk, locking it. Then he had a second thought. He picked up the Thompson, hit the thumb latch, and slid the empty drum off the gun. In his trunk was a bag of assorted training items and he reached into it now, withdrew another fully loaded drum, fitted it to the rails on the receiver, and slid it home. He didn't notice a *T* for "Training" painted crudely on its dark frontal surface. It locked solid. He pulled back the bolt, feeling the slide through resistance as the spring recoiled, until it too locked. Then he thumbed the safety prong to up—this is "On"—and put the weapon on the offside front seat. He thought he had time and returned to Sam.

"I'm going now."

"Get him, Charles. I know you can."

"You keep fighting and we'll laugh about this on the patio one night."

But he knew it wouldn't be so, just as he knew what hope Sam had given him was lost now, bleeding out in the grass of a town nobody ever heard of, as the only man who could have saved him lay dying. He knew he had been killed too.

He went back to the car, turned the ignition, and accelerated, finding no traffic at all, as the crime scene had dammed the road. He drove less than a mile until he saw a phone booth outside a bar, cognizant, as he drove, of sirens as finally the ambulances pulled by.

He got the number out of his wallet, dropped in his nickel, the operator told him how much more it was, he dropped in another three dimes, and waited as she put the call through.

"Sorrento Social," someone answered.

"Put D'Abruzzio on," he said.

"Hey, who do you think you are, bud? Mr. D'Abruzzio is in—"

"I don't care where he is. He'll talk to me now. My name is Swagger. He knows who I am. Go get him."

It seemed to take forever, but finally Uncle Phil was there.

"How the hell did you get this number, Swagger? What is—"

"Shut up, meatball," said Charles. "Five minutes ago, Nelson shot and probably killed two Division agents in a town called Barrington, on Northwest Highway. He's probably hit. Where would the nearest safe house be from there? He has to lay up. Where would he go?"

"Okay, I'll find out. But later, you and I are going to have a talk about this phone number and what games you're playing."

D'Abruzzio put the phone down, and more hours, possibly even a month or two, dragged by. Finally, he was back.

"Okay, they say he'll turn east on Palatine Road, somewhere off of Northwest up around you, just south of Barrington. It goes by the big airfield, then jigs a little at a religious place called Techny, and then it turns into Willow Road, but basically it's a straight shot into Winnetka, which is next to Wilmette. Jimmy Murray has a house on Walnut Street, just off the downtown section: 447 Walnut. That's his best shot, his fastest shot. But he'll be pokey. He can't go over the speed limit or he'll get cops on him. If he's cool enough to mosey along, he'll be okay. Can you catch him?"

"Bet on it," said Charles.

It was time to hunt.

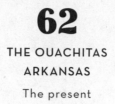

62

THE OUACHITAS
ARKANSAS
The present

"WAIT A MINUTE, SNIPER. Something you should know. Okay, sniper. Take it straight, deal with it."

Bob fixed him with a hard sniper's eye.

"What are you talking about?"

"This thing became just as big an obsession for me as for you," said Rawley. "I called around, I talked to guys who told me stories told to them by their dads or granddads, who were cellmates of this fellow or that fellow, and I know what was said about it all. On our side of the street, that is—not the shit you call history."

Bob waited.

"This story was big in the underworld in 'thirty-four, 'thirty-five, maybe even 'thirty-six. Somehow, it got forgotten as all the action moved to the East from the Midwest, where Dewey was going after the big New York people. Then the war came, and more stuff was lost, and so nobody remembered anything. But I found some memories."

"Go ahead," said Bob.

"You sure? You have an image of yourself and your kin, what kind of men you were, what you stood for. What's it going to do to you to see that challenged, threatened. As I say, can you deal with it?"

"This is bullshit," said Nick. "This creep is playing con games because he can't do anything straight out. It's not in the Grumley DNA."

"The Grumley DNA is criminal, yes indeed," said Rawley. "But inside of it, it's about hillbilly honor and guts. It's about standing straight and taking it, not ratting, not running, doing what's right by a Grumley standard, even if death is the price. And maybe that describes Baby Face too, the big villain of the piece, but he gave it all up in payback for Johnny and Homer, and, in the fight of his life, walked straight into the guns."

"That's what Swagger is too," said Nick. "With that minor detail, it does right by the standards of civilization, not by some backwoods clan of peckerwoods, chicken snatchers, cousin-fucking and sister-raping inbreds."

"This fellow needs anger management," said Rawley with a smirk. "His rapture over stereotype is quite disturbing. Antidepressants? Cymbalta? Zoloft? Anthrax? Okay, I am not shitting you, Swagger, it got around that somebody quit. One tin soldier ran away."

"We ran into this one too. It's crap."

"We'll see."

"Don't make me laugh," said Bob.

"No, they say one of the Division studs called in, said, 'Enough.' He'd seen his buds shot to bits on the playground. He couldn't take it no more. Too much blood, and he didn't want to end up full of lead under the swings. He went away, just when they needed him most, back to Passel O'Toads, Arkansas. No names, but all fingers would point toward Charles, the man who shot Dillinger from behind and Pretty Boy from a hundred yards away."

"Charles Swagger didn't have no run in him," said Bob.

"You don't have no run in you. Maybe he did have run in him. Maybe not. I ain't saying. I'll let John Paul Chase tell the story. That is, if you've got guts enough."

"He's pure guts, goober," said Nick.

Bob turned to page 152 of "THEY CALLED HIM BABY FACE!"

63

S HE HAD ROLLED HIS PANT LEGS UP, counted the holes—fifteen—and applied Mercurochrome to each one, painting orange over the red.

"How bad?"

"That stuff stings! But, generally, it's better now."

They had passed Curtiss Airport, taken a wide jog around some kind of religious place, and the road was now called Willow. It climbed a slope, crossed Waukegan Road, and they found farm-flatness on either side. Since it was chilly November, it was now dark, even at 6, and they rolled steadily on, through the sparse traffic of the sticks, with J.P. keeping a good lookout in the rearview as he held straight on.

"Anything?"

"Nah. Saw lights a few minutes ago, but they've gone now. He must have turned off. You okay?"

"He's doing fine," said Helen. "The bleeding's stopped, no bones broken, and the bruising hasn't started. Baby's going to be fine."

"Sure you don't want a belt of hooch, Les?"

"Never touch the stuff."

"Okay, we're crossing Sunset Ridge Road, which means we're coming into a nowheresville called Northfield, and just beyond it is Winnetka, and then a couple miles to Mr. Murray's place in Wilmette. It won't be long now."

"Great," said Les, snuggling his head against the warm and ample bosom of his wife, who held him close to her, her arms locked around his shoulders, her face next to his.

"I'm thinking clear now," Les said. "I was sort of dingy in the head after I got shot up, but everything is clear now. We'll go to Mr. Murray's, someone'll know a doc or a vet, they can dig these things out of my legs, and I'll be good as new. Then we'll visit our pal D'Abruzzio and be on our way."

"You know what, Les," said J.P. "I always thought it was a screwball plan, but you pulled it off. You made it happen. It turned on sheer guts, and you did it."

"Yeah, me and an inch of steel." Les laughed, and banged his fist against the sheet of metal under this shirt that shielded his vitals from the bullets of the law. *"Bonk, bonk, bonk!"* he said, "three times Mr. Federal nailed me in the boiler room with his machino and I didn't feel nothing. Joke's on him. He forgot to wear his. Bet he wears it everyplace in heaven!"

Les and J.P. laughed, though Helen felt a little squeamish laughing at the death of the federal officer, as she didn't share Les's rage at such men. If they had to die, they had to die, that was the bargain, but it was somehow wrong getting all sis-boom-bah about it.

"Les," she said, "let the poor man rest in peace."

"Come on, Helen," said Les, "I made him famous. And since he's a Justice Department guy, he should be glad he died for justice—my justice on Phil D'Abruzzio—instead of a lousy bank job or—"

Where did it come from? It was suddenly just there, beside them, angling in at their speed and clipping the fender hard. Les raised his head, as Helen screamed and J.P. fought the wheel for control, and saw a large dark car boring against theirs.

In the next second, the phantom had forced them off the road into a field, dark and immense, where J.P. hit the brakes to keep from spinning out of control, the car skidding as the locked wheels failed to bite into the loam, the car rocking, sliding, grinding, Les banging his head on the seat in front of him, Helen screaming again, the whole universe suddenly gone screwball, as nothing made any sense at all.

They came to rest a few dozen feet off of Willow Road, the intercepting vehicle angled ahead of them. At that point, its driver flicked on his own lights, so that his double beams cut into the Hudson's double beams, and the area suddenly came alive in the glow of the illumination.

"Are you all right?" J.P. said.

"Take the machino!" responded Les, sitting upright, lifting the Thompson from the floor with a single arm and trying to get it over the seat to J.P. But he hadn't the strength, even if it was the lightest of the two weapons available, and it fell back to the floor. His hand squirted to his .45 in the shoulder holster, as J.P. also went to pluck his pistol from concealment.

The door of the other car opened and a man stepped around it and into the light.

It was the G-Man. He had a Thompson.

64

"ALL RIGHT," said Bob, "he's there. I didn't see any run."

"Maybe it's in the next chapter," said Rawley.

Bob regarded him harshly, but such was Rawley's intense sense of Grumley self-adoration, it made not a dent in the man's smirk.

"I'm just trying to make you aware of what's in the air," he said. "I don't want you feeling bushwhacked and getting all disappointed. Maybe Swagger, disappointed, doesn't keep his word."

"I'll keep my word," said Bob.

"But maybe I won't keep mine," said Nick.

"That fellow," yelled Braxton from his seat on the edge of the hole, "bears watching. You keep your eye on him, brother."

"I will, brother," yelled Rawley back at him. Then, turning to Bob, he said, "So Charles has finally caught up with Baby Face. What happens next, do you suppose, sniper?"

"I'd say death in a hat comes to call on Mr. Lester J. Gillis," said Bob.

65

FULL MOON, but not yet risen off the horizon. Orange, maybe umber, throwing its thin hue across the known world. A cold and blustery evening. An empty field in a farm town in a Midwest as flat as the Atlantic when calm. Otherwise, not much information: no traffic, no lights, no sign of civilization. Wind rushing through the high, dry grass, the stalks rubbing and whispering against one another. A vault of stars across the sky, pinwheels and whirligigs and clouds of light a billion miles away. The intersecting beams of the headlamps of the two twisted cars throwing an odd lattice of brightness across the land, illuminating the still-settling dust.

They watched him come. Tall man, low fedora, open topcoat, white shirt, black tie. Gunman. Face grim, sunken, maybe cadaverous, but those eyes! Dark and mournful and without flutter or tremor: blinkless. He moved with panther grace, big hands loose and ready on the submachine gun. He stared hard at them, hard enough to melt the glass through which they saw him.

"We both draw and fire," said J.P. "Helen, you get down and—"

"No, my arm is pinned behind Helen and you aren't fast enough. Hold steady, hear him out."

The agent opened the passenger door.

"Hands on wheel, Chase," he said. "If I see them move, I'll part your haircut with hardball."

J.P. swallowed. It did not occur to him to defy.

"You," he said to Les. "Out here, little man. You and I have business."

"He can't walk, sir," said Helen. "His legs are shot up."

"Then I will kill him where he sits," said the agent.

"My legs are okay," said Les. "And I'm not afraid. If it's a gunfight you want, mister, you have knocked on the right door. I fear no man and back down from no man."

The agent stepped away, insolently turned his back, daring them to shoot. They would not—they could not—for they all believed that among his talents would be seeing behind himself.

"Still got the steel vest, Les?" asked J.P. in a whisper, having not moved his head, his hair, or his hands.

Bonk, came the answer, as Les slid over the Monitor, hooked the Thompson, and removed himself from the car. The first weight of his body and all that steel against his legs produced fifteen jets of pain that made him wince and cave, but he steadied himself on the car door, took a step, and then another, and found the pain at first bearable and then forgettable. He moved out twenty feet and faced his opponent.

"You cut that steel loose or I will put one between your eyes and turn your friends to Swiss cheese," said the agent.

Hell! How did he know?

Les set the gun down in the grass, reached into his jacket, and unbuckled the two supporting straps. As the second one went, the two pieces of steel fell to the ground and then toppled flat to earth.

"Les!" screamed Helen.

"Don't you worry, honey," said Les, eyes riveted on the G-man, "this boy wants to play with the machino. No man in this world can take me on the machino."

He picked the Thompson up, easily hefting it to his midline, where it rested in the familiarity of his two hands.

"You say we have business, sir?"

"I am Charles Swagger, Special Agent, Department of Justice," said the man. "I hearby place you under arrest for multiple outstanding felony warrants, including first-degree murder this afternoon, against federal agents in

Barrington, Illinois, those warrants forthcoming. I order you to surrender your weapon and raise your hands or prepare to face the consequences."

"I am Lester J. Gillis, wrongly called 'Baby Face' by the newpapers, and you will have to take me the hard way," said Les.

Two men, thirty feet apart. Each cranked a bit, quartering himself with respect to the other, with the Thompson gun on the diagonal across his body. They held still, each exploring the other's face and body, reading what data the smear of lights from moon and headlights permitted, reading the position of the hands, the set of the chin in the jaw, the narrowness of the eyes, the tension, or absence of same, in the muscles of the face. Another second passed as the face-off approached—first, anticlimax; then farce, or even parody; and then—

Moon, wind, chill.

Les was fast as a burning cat. In pure blur he leveraged the big gun up and his talented eyes read the line that extended from back sight to front sight to target, calculating angles and muscle energy, graceful as any skeet champion, matador, or épée artist, a man with a true gift for the gun, all reflexes and experience that no instrument yet devised could measure, and he felt his finger find and caress the trigger straight back so there'd be no torque and the gun would hold true to the intentions of its shooter but—

The rustle of dry grass, the hum of double-winged navy FF-1 vectoring low toward Curtiss, a reveler's far-off honk from a Model A.

Les had talent, more than most. Charles had genius, more than all. His speed had no place in time and his imagination saw the weapon as merely another pistol, and so he didn't bother with the guidance of the left hand on the front grip, much less sights or hold or breath, but merely by vice-like strength of those long fingers, that thick wrist, that articulated forearm, put the gun where whatever autistic worm that lived deep in the ancient part of his brain instructed, and his wasn't the first shot, it was the first six shots, and when Les's finger closed on the trigger, it could but jack three useless rounds off, one of which clipped off half an inch of Charles's ear, a wound Charles did not even notice.

Meanwhile, Charles's Thompson delivered its cargo in less than two-tenths of a second, six reports un-separated by pause or click, sending the 230-grain missives into the night in consecrations of radiance and spark and spinning flecks of flaming powder, which yielded to yet more pyrotechnics. The *T* for "Training" on the drum also meant *T* for "Tracer," designed to demonstrate to rookie agents the power of the Thompson. It now demonstrated that power to Les. Six red-tipped Frankford Arsenal M1 .45 slugs streaked across time and space as if such trivial human conceits didn't exist, each leaking a plumb-line contrail of sheer incandescence that bleached the black from the darkling plain as they reached and sank into and through the middle parts of Lester J. Gillis, then, still at killing velocity, vanished into the Illinois prairie at unpredictable angles.

Darkness returned to the planet a splinter of a second later, but the bullets had done their work, arriving in a three-inch cluster, blowing out viscera, vein, and artery, coil of intestines, bits of liver and spleen and spine, gobbets of muscle, ligament, and gristle, opening a hundred roaring Mississippis of blood that no force on earth could dam.

First shim of ice on the pond, the snap of dry leaves whirling in the air on a whisper of breeze.

Les stepped back, felt his weapon disappear from his grip, tried to compensate for his sudden blast of vertigo, lost his footing, and sat down hard in the grass. He touched the wound and was amazed at the blood flow, and how quickly wet his hand became.

He looked up to the lawman, who stood ready to fire again.

"You killed me," he said in disbelief.

"I believe I have," said Swagger.

66

"I DON'T GET IT," said Nick. "That's not the Baby Face story. Or, rather, it's the Baby Face story but with a new ending."

Swagger didn't say anything.

"Did he make this up to sell books, I wonder," said Nick. "It's more dramatic, it's more movie-like, it's better, certainly, as story."

Swagger and Memphis looked at Rawley Grumley, who returned their stares evenly. No tremble in that boy.

"Grumley, the standard story about Nelson is that—"

"I know what it is," said Rawley. "I read the history books."

"So why would he make this up? Or is this the truth and the official story is the fable? 'When the facts conflict with the legend, print the legend.'"

Nobody said a thing for a bit. Blue sky, the odd spectacle of three men sitting around a ruined picnic table, a fourth man, hands bound, sitting halfway in a hole, a coffin, a pile of gun-shaped objects shrouded in tightly wrapped canvas, and a Honda Recon sitting parked, all in the lee of the remains of a cottage.

"If it's true, Charles should be a hero. Every schoolboy should want to be Charles."

"How about you, sniper? You got anything to say. He's your blood."

"I don't know."

"Let me just check something," said Nick. He took out his iPhone. "Let's see if I can get anything out here or just— Well, well, hello, Internet. Okay, let's check on the moon. Easily done now, not so easily done in 1973 or '4 when Chase was writing at the age of eighty in his great-granddaughter's basement in Sausalito. Come on, Google, where are you, you bastard?"

Google arrived, and Nick carefully ordered it to look for "Condition of Moon, Central Time Zone, November 27, 1934."

One-point-eleven seconds passed, and Google loaded the iPhone's small screen with possibilities, and Nick, like every other Google user since the beginning of Google, chose the first entry, to find that some insane person with way too much time on his hands had indeed put together a moon phase website indexed to all the years of the calendar.

"Well?" said Swagger.

"Okay. The moon was full. It didn't reach apogee till eleven thirty-four, which means that at six, or whenever this action took place, it was indeed low. It would have been red, because its light was passing through more atmosphere."

"All right," said Swagger, "it seems real. But, like Nick, I don't know why this isn't the story we all know, why the papers weren't all over it, why it's hidden or something. I don't get it."

"Maybe the old man killer had something up his sleeve," said Rawley.

67

WILLOW ROAD
NORTHFIELD, ILLINOIS
November 27, 1934

CHARLES STOOD ABOVE the man he'd shot, who sat clumsily in the grass, his shirt rapidly loading with dark blood, whose face still showed disbelief and stupor, his open, slack fingers useless.

"Now I'm going to give you something you didn't give nobody. You sure didn't give it to Sam or Ed. They checked out alone."

The man looked at him. His brain still half worked, and Charles knew he was comprehending. He blinked, maybe tried to speak but only swallowed, then coughed some blood sputum.

"You get to die in the arms of your wife with your best friend standing by."

He turned to Helen and J.P., who were out of the car now and bearing witness to Les's death.

"Dump the guns and get him out of here. You can take him to the hospital, if you want, but it won't do no good. I've seen that wound before. All those holes. It's always fatal. He's got an hour or so left before he pumps dry."

"Thank you," said Helen. "You are a decent man."

She ran to Les.

"Oh, baby, baby," she said, holding him, unfazed by the copious blood that soaked his midsection, "we'll get you out of here, we'll take care of you. It'll be all right, you'll be fine."

He'll be fine in hell, Charles thought.

He stood by as Helen and J.P. lifted the bleeding man and took him to the car, out of which J.P. had already pulled the Monitor, a batch of magazines and cartridge boxes.

"And one more thing. Helen, you come here now."

Helen turned from her comforting and came to Charles. She was a pretty gal, no doubt about it. Why do they give themselves away on such trash? It was one of the great mysteries of life.

"You listen to me, now," he said. "This didn't happen. I never ran you off the road, there was no gunfight, it wasn't my bullets that hit him. Sam Cowley put six slugs into him in Barrington and he bled to death on account of that. There was no Swagger, nothing in a field, in a hick town, a hundred miles from anywhere, no moon, no wind, no grass blowing. That's the story you tell in exchange for giving him the sort of death he don't otherwise deserve. If I hear different from either of you, I will come visit and you won't like that a bit."

They looked at him, not comprehending.

"Just do what I say. You will be caught, you will be questioned, give 'em some cock-and-bull about safe houses in Wilmette. It don't matter, they won't care. Just set your mind to it. You're doing it for him, think of it that way."

"I don't understand," said Helen.

"You don't have to. Now, get out of here. Take Lester to the cemetery he so richly deserves."

"We'll put him in St. Peter's in Niles Center. He likes it."

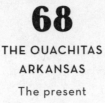

68

THE OUACHITAS

ARKANSAS

The present

"So WHERE DOES the story he chickened out come from?" asked Nick. "I don't see any—"

But then he halted.

Bob broke his silence.

"He couldn't save Sam. That would dog him the rest of his life. Maybe it destroyed him. But he was able to save Sam's reputation, his memory, his heroism, in the story that Sam killed Baby Face. Along with Ed Hollis. To do that, he had to take himself out of the story. He had to erase himself from history and from the FBI. We'll never know how he did it, but the 'running away' lie was part of it. He had to do what Baby Face couldn't do. He had to kill himself."

69

C HARLES WATCHED THE HUDSON pull out with its cargo of dying gangster. Where it went, what they did with the body, all that meant nothing at all to him. It would take care of itself.

He reached into his pocket and pulled out his handkerchief and applied it to the wound on his ear. The linen came away saturated with red. He went back to the wound, cleaned it as best he could, satisfied himself that he'd lost the top half inch, and that it would scab over for a month or so, but that it wouldn't kill him. He'd stop and get some disinfectant for it.

He went to the guns, which lay in the grass. The Monitor was heavy, but not so heavy that he couldn't also take up the Thompson by its front grip. He got the load to the Pontiac, opened the trunk, and laid the weapons next to Sam's Thompson and Ed's Model 11. He went back, picked up the various .45s and magazines that had spilled out of a getaway bag, the bag itself, and took it all to the trunk too. One item was an envelope, which held a crisp, new thousand-dollar bill. He threw that in the trunk too. Then, standing there, he peeled off his topcoat and his suit coat, unsnapped and unbuttoned his floral-carved shoulder rig with its automatic. He looked at it, a man who trusted a gun, and the gun protected him and did its duty for him. Can't ask more of a gun. You did good, bud, he thought, and laid it on the pile. He closed the lid, got his coats on fast—it was cold, the moon was higher now, full and bone white, the wind still whistled through the grass.

After his labor, he awarded himself a cigarette. One last thing remained.

He went to the car, started, backed, turned, cranked the wheel, and returned to Willow Road. He followed it, over a bridge, to an intersection with one Happ Road, a turn to the right, a turn to the left, a transit over some tracks, and he found himself in the tiny village of Northfield. A turn past the town hall took him to a gabled, shingled house that was called Happ's Liquors and Bar & Grill. It had a phone booth outside, near the entrance.

He went to it, dropped in his nickel.

"Number, please?"

He gave it, then fed in another dime for the downtown call.

"Jessup, *Herald-Examiner*."

"You recognize my voice?"

"Jesus Christ, where are you? You heard? Baby Face killed two—"

"Baby Face is dead," said Swagger. "Here's your scoop, as I promised. He was shot by Sam Cowley of the Justice Department, who put a .45 into his guts with a Tommy gun. He bled out. They dumped him at St. Peter's Cemetery, in Niles Center. You show up there tomorrow at nine a.m. and you'll find him somewhere, on the ground. Do you hear me?"

"Niles Center, St. Peter's."

"You call the Division, got that? And this has nothing to do with me."

"You killed Baby Face?"

"Sam Cowley killed Baby Face. That's the story you're telling, and you got it first. It ain't got nothing to do with me. You never heard of me, you never got this call."

"I—"

He hung up, pulled another nickel.

"Randolph 6226."

"That's another dime, please."

The dime tinkled as the phone swallowed it.

"Justice Department." It was Elaine, still on.

"Elaine, it's Swagger."

"Sheriff, thank God! They've been looking for you. They'll be so glad."

"Who's running things?"

"Inspector Clegg."

"Elaine, you're the best. You did so much for me, and, believe me, I do appreciate it."

"Sheriff, I—"

"Can you put Clegg on?"

"Just a second."

But it was four seconds.

"Clegg."

"It's Swagger."

"Jesus Christ, man, where are you? Do you know what's happened? Nelson jumped Sam and Ed Hollis in Barrington. He killed 'em both and stole their car. I've got all the men out looking for Baby Face. I need you, dammit, Swagger. The men need you. Get in here!"

"No sir," said Charles.

"What? Where are you?"

"I'm in a bar, drinking. And getting drunker."

"Swagger, what is—"

"I was at Barrington. I saw Sam's guts shot out, and Ed's head with a hole above the eye. No thank you. Not me. I come through enough already with the war, with the fights I been in. I ain't ending up in some field, bled out, while the small-town cops stand around clucking."

"Charles, you've been drinking. It's understandable. Go home, go to bed, sleep late, and come in ready to go tomorrow. We need you. The men need you. They look up to you for leadership and steadiness. They don't have to know about tonight."

"By tomorrow morning, I hope to be well south of St. Louis. You tell them what you want, a crack-up, a breakdown, a chicken dance, I don't care. I ain't gonna end up like Ed or Sam. That's for suckers. They're only dead because some fat Nancy J. Swish in Washington, who wanted to poke Purvis's pretty ass, wants to get more money in the budget. That ain't worth dying for, not a bit of it. I'm done. I'm headed out."

"Swagger, Jesus Christ, you cannot say . . . That is so . . . Swagger, if you do this, I will wipe the slate clean of you. You will be expunged from the record and nobody will mention your name again. You will be shunned, banned, despised. You will be cast into outer darkness. You will be—"

Charles hung up.

He climbed the steps, went to the counter, and bought a pint of Pikesville Rye.

The guy at the counter took his money, but said, "Say, bud, you okay? That ear needs tending."

"It's fine," said Charles. "It don't hurt a bit."

Then he went outside, got in his car, opened the bottle, took a swig, and pulled out for the long drive ahead.

70

AHMED'S TURKISH BATH
CHICAGO
November 29, 1934

THE STEAM WORKED ITS WAY in through his pores, seemed somehow to drain all the toxins and regrets from his soul and urged him to relax. He had much to contemplate with pleasure.

They were working meatpacking. Take over the union, threaten a strike, the big boys paid to keep the men on the line, and it was more incoming cash, bushels of it. Nobody could stop them, nobody could risk standing against the Italians. And this was happening everywhere! Right now, the thing against Swift, the biggest, was proceeding as planned. Swift had seen the others roll over and knew that resistance was pointless. Mr. Nitto would be pleased, as would the New York people.

He stretched his legs. Vapors occluded his vision, isolating him in a world of fiery fog. He breathed in, feeling the purifying rush of the superheated moisture as it rode the currents into his lungs. A man could fall asleep coddled by such total pleasure.

They had found Baby Face Nelson's body in some graveyard in Niles Center. He was the last of the big ones on the list, which meant that enterprise could be concluded. It was another triumph. The only loose end was the sheriff, who had gone chicken—who'd have thunk?—and disappeared, but sooner or later he'd turn up. That would have to be dealt with, but it wasn't a big thing. After all, the guy was a hick.

He felt like a Roman emperor. It was hard not to, given the wealth, the power, the prestige, the future that lay ahead. His towel was like a toga, and he best rode the world like a colossus. A long way from Palermo, that was for sure.

The door opened and D'Abruzzio saw the attendant through the vapors, bringing him a replacement for his iced tea. That was Jackie, good at his trade, knowing exactly what a big-time customer needed in terms of tending.

He mopped his brow with his towel and smiled at Jackie, who leaned toward him in the fog. Except it wasn't Jackie, it was a well-dressed man, sweating profusely, in a suit and tie.

The man smiled back at him, and D'Abruzzio was struck by how handsome he was—a matinee idol?—and how familiar. Had he seen him onscreen?

Then he realized he'd seen him in the papers. It was John Paul Chase, Nelson's gofer, who'd gotten away from Barrington unscathed.

Phil wondered if he wanted a touch but instead saw the muzzle of a .38 snub two inches from his nose.

"Baby Face Nelson says hello," said Chase, and shot him through the eye.

72

THE GRUMLEY HAD their prize rewrapped, their weapons retrieved, their StingRay gizmo stowed in backpack. They were headed back to skip tracing, strip bars, and hitting Negroes in the head and face—their life, in other words.

"You're not going to shoot up a Piggly Wiggly or a bowling alley with that old Colt rifle, are you?" Swagger asked.

"No sir," said Braxton, Rawley having retreated into silence again, "it goes on an outward-bound flight to some collector in Uzbekistan, or maybe Colombia, paid for in cash money, most of which will be in our wallets by six p.m. You understand, we can't disclose the name of our client."

"You don't have to," said Nick. "I made a phone call. If Mr. Kaye thinks he's out of the soup, he's got another think coming. I'd stay clear of him after you cash out because a whole lot of federal heat is about to light up his sorry little life. He's going to learn no Russian mobster can fuck him up as badly as a nasty virgin spinster GS-20 from the IRS."

"We're just the help," said Braxton. "Don't know nothing, didn't do nothing. It pays to be stupid sometimes."

"Don't it just?" said Bob. "And here's a little something to bring a smile to his face. It's the last time he'll smile in the next thirty years."

He reached into his jacket pocket, pulled out a compensator in a wadding of material, and tossed it to Rawley, who caught it deftly.

"You just screw it on, right at the muzzle. Completes the outfit," he said.

"Thankin' you kindly," said Braxton, and the two were off.

NOW BOB AND NICK drove in silence. The Ouachitas were soft green humps thirty miles distant in the rearview. Meanwhile, the remaining weapons were in the trunk and would be delivered to the FBI field office in Little Rock, there to be shipped to D.C. for the collection.

The tires hummed against the pavement, the radio was off, roadside retail slipped by on either side of the road, and it seemed a little numb. The manuscript lay in the backseat.

To nail it shut, Nick had called a friend at the Bureau, and an intern had run a check on Chicago unsolveds from 1934. Indeed, as Chase had claimed, on November 29, a Mob guy named Philip J. D'Abruzzio had been shot to death in a steam bath on the West Side. A Tony Accardo—"Joe Batters," by trade name—took his place, eventually becoming the head of the Chicago outfit in the 'fifties.

Helen served a year for harboring—really, for being Mrs. Baby Face Nelson—then lived out her life in Chicago, raising her kids. She never gave any interviews or wrote any accounts. She loved Les hard and full until the end. Purvis quit the Bureau in 1935. Clegg became an assistant director.

"But what about Charles?" asked Nick. "How did it end for him? I don't think you ever told me."

"In 1942, he was found behind a general store in Mount Ida, halfway between Hot Springs and Blue Eye, bled out from a small-caliber bullet," Bob explained. "They say he'd been at one of those prayer meetings at Caddo Gap. We never found out why he turned so religious."

"I hope it helped him," said Nick.

"I do too," said Bob. "Anyhow, they think he saw something, stopped to investigate, and caught a .32 in the chest."

"Such a shame."

"I don't buy that last one for a second. Rumors put him tight with Hot Springs people, particularly since the big train robbery in 1940. That was almost the same day his youngest son, Bobbie Lee, hung himself in the barn.

So Charles lost everyone he tried to save, Sam and Ed and his youngest son. He'd already lost his oldest son, my father, Earl. I think by '42, he had become so dissolute that he was unreliable, and the Mob had to get rid of him. If my father knew, he never said, and any knowledge died with him in 1955. But Charles was a drunk by 1942, so he made it easy on his killers."

"It's such a shame," said Nick. "And they went unpunished."

"Not sure on that one. My father Earl came back from the war in 1946 and somehow he got involved in an anti-Mob campaign in Hot Springs. It was a lot bloodier than the history books say. I have a feeling my father closed out some overdue accounts. He was that kind of man."

"Good for him. Are you going to write that book about Charles? He deserves it. Nobody braver, nobody tougher, nobody better. I don't know how you could sit on it. The man who shot Baby Face Nelson, he was the bravest of them all," said Nick. "It would get the old bastard his due. Finally."

"Charles Swagger never cared about 'due,'" said Bob. Then he added, "He was naturally reticent, as if he was hiding some deeper secret. So, no, I don't think so. In fact, I know exactly what I'm going to do."

He pulled over, into the lot of a convenience store. Grabbing up the manuscript, he went into the place and came out with a cheap butane lighter.

He walked to a barrel trash receptacle in the parking lot and dumped the pages in. Bending over, he put the lighter beneath the rim to shield it from the light wind. He flicked it to life and pulled some of the pages out, put the flame to them, and stepped back.

In a minute, the manuscript, dry and crackled like old skin, was consumed in a rampage of incandescence, a white, pure burn without tremor or waver. It looked like a welder's torch.

"He didn't want it known, and we'll leave it as he wished. The record will stand. Sam Cowley killed Baby Face Nelson at the cost of his own life. He was a hero, along with Ed Hollis. Charles Swagger never existed except as the drunken, corrupt sheriff of a no'count small town in West Arkansas."

"Talk about a death wish," said Nick.

"He had some problems. But when it counted, he stood there and did what had to be done and took the consequences. What did Grumley call it? Hillbilly honor."

The ashes rose, whirled about in the funnel of heat, and were gone on the wind.

ACKNOWLEDGMENTS

I have wanted to write a Baby Face book for decades, but, as usual, the impetus that turned ambition to labor was ire, a big motive for cranky old men. The object of my anger was Michael Mann's movie desecration of 1934 in his idiotic version of Bryan Burrough's majestic *Public Enemies*—and I'm not even talking about Depp as Dillinger! Why buy a nonfiction book if you're going to make it up and don't move the story one iota beyond John Milius's el cheapo *Dillinger* of 1973? What's annoying particularly is that the Mann disgrace will probably be the last big-budget 1934 re-creation.

So my ambition was to write a 1934 book in which Dillinger and Purvis were cameos and the real action centered on the far deadlier Les and the far more heroic Sam, a great, powerful, and tragic American story, ending in one of the most hellacious gunfights on record and the only time in history when the head man hunter and the man huntee end up facing each other over Tommy guns. Who but an idiot tells a story that ends at the Biograph instead of Barrington and tells the love story of Dillinger and one of his (many) hookers, not the one—twisted, unexplainable, but somehow, I hope, moving—between Les and Helen?

But it's a novel, so I get to fictionalize, even if I try my hardest to keep chronology, personality, action, weapons, technology, and geography as close to the real thing as possible. Obviously, my access to the year was via the completely fictional Charles F. Swagger, though those familiar with the Bureau's history will understand that he's a version of the great agent Charles

Winstead—who did bring down Dillinger. I added some psychological twists from my own father, Charles F. Hunter, to get them out of my system.

Otherwise, I've tried to discipline myself in my alterations to history. One factual alteration was to make a bigger deal of the Baby Face Monitor than should be made, while at the same time eliminating the semi-automatic, Lebman-doctored Winchester Model 1907 that Les probably did use that last day. The reason was simply taste, as the Monitor has to be the coolest full-auto in use in 1934! Then too I streamlined the Northwest Highway car chase, eliminating an earlier run-in between Les and two FBI agents.

I should also mention that much of the imagery of Charles's Great War nightmares is drawn from the poetry of Siegfried Sassoon.

On to thanks. Once again, old friend Lenne P. Miller was number one researcher and mastered the data and the sources in a way I never could. Besides Burrough, Lenne made great use of Steven Nickel and William J. Helmer's *Baby Face Nelson: Portrait of a Public Enemy*. They got Baby Face in a way nobody else has. (Still the best account of Barrington is probably my friend Massad Ayoob's article in the July/August 2007 *American Handgunner*.) Gary Goldberg, another great friend, helped on all manner of technical and electronic matters, like the Grumleys' StingRay. Alan Doelp pitched in when Gary was out of town. Thanks to good buddy Ed De Carlo, ex-Top and 'Nam vet, of On Target shooting range, for loaning me the use of his persona in Chapter 6. As well, I pretty much counted on the same inner circle of readers for thoughts as I progressed. Thanks to Mike Hill, Bill Smart, and Barrett Tillman, for suggestions and, perhaps more important, encouragement. The great Jim Grady pitched in with enthusiasm and introduced me to serial-murder expert Mark Olshaker. Dan Shea, editor of the *Small Arms Review* in Henderson, Nevada, helped me plumb the mysteries of the Monitor, as did old friend John Bainbridge. Dr. John Fox, senior historian at the FBI, and Rebecca Bronson, also with the Bureau, got me some material on the Chase interrogations and trial preparation that are the only source of information on Barrington. Phil Scheirer, of the NRA, gave me insights into the values of '30s gangster weapons. Bill

Vanderpool, retired from the FBI, got me to Larry Wack, another retired agent, who is an authority on early Bureau personnel, though I should say that my workup of Chicago Field Office culture and personality is completely out of my own head and probably has more to do with the *Baltimore Sunday Sun* in 1976 than anything else. My sister, Julie Hunter, and her husband, Keith Johnson, put up with me in Madison, Wisconsin, on my trip up to Little Bohemia. My mother-in-law, Erlinda Marbella, put up with me on my trip to the Biograph and other Chicago-area sites.

In the publishing world, my agent, Esther Newberg, supervised the transfer between publishers and reunited me with old friend David Rosenthal, who originally bought *Dirty White Boys* all those years back and is now the major figure at Blue Rider.

And of course my indefatigable wife, Jean Marbella, supplied the coffee that has more to do with this book being finished than any will of my own. She provided other comforts as well.

To all of them, my thanks. And of course all mistakes, willed or accidental, are fully my own responsibility.

ABOUT THE AUTHOR

Stephen Hunter is the author of twenty novels and the retired chief film critic of *The Washington Post*, where he won the 2003 Pulitzer Prize for Distinguished Criticism. His novels include *The Third Bullet, Sniper's Honor, I, Sniper, I, Ripper,* and *Point of Impact,* which was adapted for film and television as *Shooter*. Hunter lives in Baltimore, Maryland.